Bella Osborne has been jotti̶̶̶̶̶̶̶̶̶̶̶̶̶̶̶es as far back as she can remem̶̶̶̶̶̶̶̶̶̶̶̶̶̶̶̶̶̶ed that 2013 would be the year t̶̶̶̶̶̶̶̶̶̶̶̶̶̶̶̶ned a full-length novel.

In 2016, her debut novel, *It Started at Sunset Cottage*, was shortlisted for the Contemporary Romantic Novel of the Year and RNA Joan Hessayon New Writers Award.

Bella's stories are about friendship, love and coping with what life throws at you. She likes to find the humour in the darker moments of life and weaves these into her stories. Bella believes that writing your own story really is the best fun ever, closely followed by talking, eating chocolate, drinking fizz and planning holidays.

She lives in the Midlands, UK with her lovely husband and wonderful daughter, who thankfully both accept her as she is (with mad morning hair and a penchant for skipping).

Also by Bella Osborne:

It Started at Sunset Cottage
A Family Holiday
Escape to Willow Cottage
Coming Home to Ottercombe Bay
A Walk in Wildflower Park
Meet Me at Pebble Beach

One Family Christmas

BELLA OSBORNE

avon.

Published by AVON
A division of HarperCollins*Publishers* Ltd
1 London Bridge Street
London SE1 9GF

www.harpercollins.co.uk

HarperCollins*Publishers*
1st Floor, Watermarque Building, Ringsend Road
Dublin 4, Ireland

A Paperback Original 2020

4

First published in Great Britain by HarperCollins*Publishers* 2020

A catalogue copy of this book is available from the British Library.

ISBN: 978-0-00-833134-4

Typeset in Minion Pro by
Palimpsest Book Production Limited, Falkirk, Stirlingshire

Printed and Bound in the UK using 100% Renewable Electricity
at CPI Group (UK) Ltd

MIX
Paper from
responsible sources
FSC® C007454

This book is produced from independently certified FSC™ paper
to ensure responsible forest management.

For more information visit: www.harpercollins.co.uk/green

To Iylah and Hunter on your very first Christmas.

Prologue

Five weeks until Christmas

Lottie tripped over the cat and watched the bag of flour sail through the air. There was a moment's relief when she could see it was going to land on the kitchen table, but that soon disappeared as the bag exploded, sending a pure white mushroom cloud into the air. The radio merrily belted out 'Let It Snow' and as the flour settled, Lottie could see the ghostly figure of Nana Rose – white from top to toe.

There was a small splutter. 'It's a good job I've stocked up on ingredients,' said Nana, shaking her head and scattering more flour.

'I'm so sorry,' said Lottie, watching the white dust catch in the light from the window. It was quite pretty, really. It looked like it had snowed inside and made Lottie feel instantly Christmassy. 'I'll get the dustpan and brush while you have a shower.'

'No need for that,' said Nana, dusting herself down. 'We'll probably make more mess anyway. We'll have this cleared up in no time.' She gave her granddaughter an indulgent smile. 'Cheer up. It's not the end of the world.'

Nana Rose was old school and immensely practical, and Lottie loved her dearly. Being back at Henbourne Manor might have felt like a backwards step for Lottie had it not been for the love Nana Rose had wrapped her in the moment she had returned. It had made it feel like a smart decision to live with Nana at twenty-seven, rather than her only option.

But she wasn't going to think about the mess her life was in. Today was Stir-up Sunday: the day that, traditionally, up and down the country, everyone was busy making their Christmas puddings. Although Lottie was pretty sure Nana Rose was in a minority – these days most people bought theirs from the supermarket; but however much the labels professed to be 'luxury' or 'extra-special' they were never a patch on Nana Rose's pudding.

They soon had the kitchen cleaned down, and this time Nana was in charge of the flour. As far back as Lottie could remember, she had made the Christmas pudding with her Nana. As a small child she had been balanced on a chair, and then later she stood on the upturned metal mop bucket until she was big enough to see over the top of the mixing bowl without it. Lottie was aware that after so many years of helping to make the pudding, she should be able to make it herself, but there was one main issue.

'That should do it,' said Nana, tipping some flour into the large stoneware mixing bowl.

'Why don't you measure anything?' asked Lottie, passing Nana an assortment of dried fruit.

'Don't need to,' said Nana, a puzzled frown appearing for a moment before her usual smile chased it away. 'As long as I've got my trusty bowl, I'm fine.' She gave the bowl a reverent pat with her gnarled fingers. Some of her recipes were written down in her frayed cookbook but most of them, including the recipe for the Collins family Christmas pudding, were safely locked in Nana's memory. Lottie still felt privileged to be involved in making it, as countless relatives and friends had asked for the recipe and Nana would never reveal her secret ingredients.

'Now, while you grate that carrot, tell me what's bothering you.' Nana Rose fixed Lottie with her grey eyes. There was no escape from Nana's knowing look. Lottie fidgeted distractedly, adjusting her sparkly hair clip. Her hair didn't need clipping back, she just liked sparkly things. A little sparkle seemed to make even the darkest day better.

'It's Mum. She's driving me potty as usual.'

'Ah.' Nana gave an understanding nod. 'There's nothing you can tell me about our Angie that will surprise me. Remember I've known her a lot longer than you have.' She winked. 'What is it this time?'

'She's writing her memoirs,' said Lottie, rolling her eyes so hard she feared she may strain something.

Nana chuckled, not looking up from where she was deftly chopping pecans. 'Well, if anyone has plenty to write about it's my daughter.'

How did Nana always seem to see the positive in everything?

'Yes, but she keeps ringing me up and reading long passages out over the phone. And . . .' Lottie paused. 'It's terrible, Nana.'

Nana reached out and gripped Lottie's arm. 'Is it upsetting, hearing about your mother's life?'

'No, it's not that. It's the writing – it's truly dreadful,' said Lottie with a giggle. A relieved-looking Nana joined in. 'It's all lustful looks and heaving bosoms.'

Nana's eyebrows jumped. 'You know what I always say?'

Lottie shook her head. Nana had lots of sayings and wise words, so knowing which one she meant would be like trying to pick a book from a whole library. 'If it's not harming anyone else, then leave her be.'

'It's harming my ears,' said Lottie with a sigh. The mental images it was conjuring up were the stuff of nightmares. And worst of all, Angie had only got as far as her eighteenth birthday meaning there was a lot more to come. Lottie hung on to the hope that her mother would stay true to form, get bored and move on to something else.

Lottie added her carrot to the mixture. Nana sprinkled in some spices and added fresh breadcrumbs and some suet. Under instruction, Lottie added clementine zest and juice. Nana sloshed in some stout, followed by some brandy. 'Right, you had best give that a stir and make a wish,' said Nana, sitting down.

'You okay?' asked Lottie.

'I'm fine. Don't you worry about me. No use standing up when there's a good chair going begging.'

Lottie made a wish. It was the same thing she wished for every year – even though she knew it was pointless. She put the bowl on Nana's lap. 'You need to make a wish too.'

Nana's eyes sparkled. 'I wish for a big family Christmas,' she said with a chuckle.

'But we do that every year.'

'I know. So every year my wish comes true.' Christmas at Nana's was sacrosanct – or, more accurately, nobody was brave enough to go against the force that was Nana and disobey her orders to attend. Which meant every year without fail, Angie, her brother Daniel, their partners and offspring would descend on Henbourne Manor for the festive period. It was an annual pilgrimage to Nana's and Lottie loved it.

Once the mixture was safely decanted into the traditional pudding bowl, Nana showed Lottie how to cover it with parchment and wrap it in kitchen foil, her old fingers working quickly to tie it with string, knotting together a makeshift handle to lift the pudding in and out of the boiling water. When it was safely bubbling away, Lottie began tidying up.

'I can't wait for Christmas,' said Lottie, thinking out loud. Whatever had happened in her life, Christmas was a life raft of happiness she clung to every December.

'Nor me,' said Nana, with a yawn.

'Why don't you have a lie down, and I'll finish up here.'

Nana stood up and gave herself a little shake. 'Actually I've got things to do. I need to get my Christmas cards written.' She took off her flour-smeared apron.

'That's a bit early.'

'No time like the present,' said Nana. 'Now, do you think you'll remember the pudding recipe this time?'

'I think so,' said Lottie, although she was hoping Nana wouldn't test her on it.

'That's my girl,' said Nana, giving her a floury squeeze.

Chapter One

Two weeks until Christmas

Even the sight of Great Uncle Bernard running over a few toes in his mobility scooter didn't bring a smile to Lottie's face. She looked about her. People of all shapes and sizes were dressed in black – with the exception of her mother, who was wearing a dress that made it look like a rainbow had dribbled on her and heels most people would need a ladder to get into. The atmosphere seemed quite jolly, for a wake. The small village pub was rammed and, in contrast to the mourners, was decorated for Christmas: fairy lights were twinkling happily overhead and the tinsel shimmied with the heat from the open fire. The noise levels were high, and everyone was in good spirits. But it didn't seem right to Lottie. She'd just laid her beloved Nana to rest and she wasn't sure how long it would be before she'd smile again. The landlady added another log to the roaring fire. It spit its displeasure, as if in agreement with Lottie.

'Darling!' Lottie's mother almost danced up to her. She kissed Lottie's cheek fleetingly, but still managed to almost knock her own large designer sunglasses off her face.

'Hi, Mum. Are you okay?'

Angie pulled her head back slightly, adjusting her sunglasses. 'Why? Don't I look all right?' She stretched her neck out and looked about, as if searching for a mirror.

'You look fine, Mum. I wondered if perhaps you had the sunglasses to hide tears . . .' Angie was looking confused, 'because you've just buried your mum.'

'Oh.' Angie gave a cough. She held a manicured hand to her surgically enhanced chest. 'I'm hurting inside, but I'm a strong woman, Lottie, and I work hard to keep my emotions under control. And anyway, when I cry my eyes puff up like yours.' She pointed at both Lottie's eyes in turn. *Thanks for that*, thought Lottie.

She stared at her mother. There was something not quite right with her facial expressions; there weren't any. 'Have you had Botox again?' asked Lottie, her voice rising involuntarily.

'Shhh,' said her mother, totally expressionless.

'Really, Mum, I worry about you. I hope you didn't go to that cowboy outfit again.' It was always the same with her mother. She focused on how she looked and everything else, including common sense, went by the wayside.

Angie gave a pout, which Lottie was actually pleased to see because it meant one part of her face was, thankfully, free from the muscle-paralysing toxin. 'They're not cowboys. They're lovely at Pins and Needles.'

You'd have thought a name like that would be enough to put people off, thought Lottie. She took a deep breath and let it go; now was not the time to have an argument. 'Are you staying at the house tonight?' asked Lottie. Angie wasn't the most reliable or attentive of mothers, but she was all Lottie had, and she didn't fancy rattling around

8

the big house all evening on her own once Great Uncle Bernard went to bed (at nine o'clock precisely).

Angie gave a pretend wince. 'Darling, I would love to, but I have to get back to London for something important.'

'What's this one's name?'

'Don't be bitter, it doesn't suit you,' she scolded. There was a very brief pause. 'He's called Scott, and he has been "this one" for three months now.' Lottie was tempted to call Guinness World Records as this was most definitely a record for one of her mother's relationships. 'I'd love you to meet Scott. He's drop-dead gorgeous, has an arse like a pair of freshly pumped-up basketballs and worships the ground I walk on. Doesn't he sound perfect?'

Lottie held on tight to the judgemental sigh desperately trying to escape. She grimaced in a way that probably made it look like she was holding in wind. 'Just be careful, Mum.' She had been here many times before. When it came to men, Angie was the living embodiment of hope over experience.

'Oh, don't be all doom and gloom.'

'At a funeral? I wouldn't dream of it,' said Lottie, with a disbelieving shake of her head.

Her mother gave her a wilting look over the top of her sunglasses. 'We must catch up in the new year, once the house is sold.' She leaned in to kiss her cheek and Lottie jerked backwards.

'Sold?' Lottie knew the house would have to be put on the market, but she'd figured that wouldn't be any time soon as she and Great Uncle Bernard were still living in it. After three months, she had just been starting to feel settled.

'Lottie, please be realistic. The will splits everything between me and Daniel, with a chunk for Bernard, so it has to be sold. I wish there was another way. I really do.' Her mother held her hand briefly and Lottie assumed that, despite her absent frown, she was probably trying to look sincere.

'I guess,' said Lottie. Although that didn't make it any easier to accept.

'Daniel is rushing the estate agent along, so hopefully it'll be sold pretty quickly. Large house, huge potential. I don't get involved.' Although Lottie knew her mother would become very involved when the money appeared. 'Prime building land. Blah, blah, blah.'

'Building land? What? Knock down the manor house?' Nana would have been horrified, and so was Lottie, and she couldn't even imagine what the villagers would think. An image of an angry mob of old people wielding pitchforks and tartan wheelie trolleys ran through her mind.

'If someone buys it, they can do what they like. A dusty old village like Henbourne could do with some new style injecting into it. All those decaying properties. Rat-infested thatch . . .' Angie gave a shudder. She saw things very differently to Lottie. The village Lottie loved was dotted with quirky cottages and even quirkier locals, nestled in a sleepy corner of the Cotswolds and wrapped in a patchwork of fields. Angie was far better suited to the bright lights and superficial side of London, even if she could barely afford to hang on to the outer reaches of the city by her manicured fingernails.

'But I'll see you at Christmas?' Lottie tried to hide the plea in her words.

'I don't think so, sweetie. We're thinking of—' her mother's voice tailed off as she became distracted by her brother, heading for the exit without even a goodbye.

'Daniel!' she beckoned him over. His wife, Nicola, looked irritated but came with him.

Daniel appeared suitably embarrassed. 'We need to dash off I'm afraid.' He rattled his car keys.

'Will we see you at Christmas?' asked Lottie. She needed some things to stay the same, and for now she was clinging on to Christmas. This was all happening too fast. One moment she was being cosseted by Nana, licking her wounds after finding herself suddenly single; the next, Nana was gone. And now she was facing being homeless, and very alone in the world.

Daniel was pulling a face and checking his Rolex. Nicola piped up. 'Actually, now we've been released from Nana Rose's annual summons, we thought we'd jet off to Bermuda. Or possibly Aruba.' Lottie thought Nicola was looking more and more birdlike each time she saw her. Her beady eyes darted about, as if keen not to miss anything she could pounce on.

Lottie was starting to feel the tides of change slosh in her gut. 'That sounds lovely, but—'

'First I've heard of it. Sounds expensive,' said Daniel, his eyebrows knotting up.

Lottie thought of Nana's Christmas wish. 'But don't you think we should all have Christmas at the manor?' Her voice had taken on a desperate tone.

'It might be sold by then,' said her mother. 'Won't it, Daniel?'

'Sadly not that quick,' said Daniel. He turned back to Nicola. 'We went to Australia this summer. That was meant to be our *big* holiday.'

Nicola gave a tinny laugh. 'It's not like we can't afford it, Daniel.' She slapped him on the arm and laughed, and from the wince he gave, Lottie guessed she had used some force. Nicola pulled Daniel to one side and a hushed but animated discussion continued. Angie was checking her phone. Lottie felt like a kite caught in a tree; no longer anchored, but also not ready to fly freely.

Lottie's brother sidled over to her, looking his usual laid-back self. Zach had always been far more easy-going than her. He gave her a warm hug. 'Lovely service,' he said, his eyes full of sadness.

'Yes,' said Lottie, with a nod.

'Although,' he smirked, 'the bagpipe player was a bit of a surprise.'

'Agreed,' said Lottie. Uncle Bernard had assured her it was what Nana would have wanted, so she'd gone along with it. She'd had second thoughts when she'd heard what sounded like a hyena having a thistle rammed up its bum echoing through the church. It was certainly something they'd all remember for quite some time – the ringing sensation in their ears would see to that.

'It's my first funeral since . . .' His voice tailed off, and Lottie gave his arm a squeeze. She thought time was meant to heal, was meant to help you cope with the harshness of the past but in this case, she was pretty sure she felt a tiny bit worse each time she saw Zach. But then that was probably guilt, rather than anything else.

'You all right?' Zach asked, doing up his coat.

'Not really, no. What are you doing for Christmas?' Lottie pulled her brother to one side.

He pushed his bottom lip out. 'I guess it'll be just me and Jessie.' Lottie's niece, Jessie, was six years old and the apple of her Daddy's eye. Lottie thought the world of her too. She'd spent every Christmas with her since she'd been born, thanks to Nana's three-line whip. Another pang of loss gripped her.

'And will you be joined by . . . ?' She left a pause where Zach's girlfriend's name should be. It wasn't that Zach had lots of girlfriends, he was thankfully not like their mother, it was more that he rarely introduced them to the family, so they were just a name. '. . . Emma?' she ventured.

'Emily,' he corrected. 'She'll probably spend it with her folks.'

'Yes, and that's exactly what we should be doing.' *This is it*, thought Lottie, glancing past Zach. *This is the very last time all my family will be together until someone else dies or my mother gets remarried again. Unless I do something about it.*

What would Nana say? she wondered. The answer came to her almost instantly. *Be brave. Stand up for what you believe in.*

Lottie reached past Zach and picked up an empty glass and a fork which someone had abandoned next to some pork pie. Lottie held up the glass and tapped it firmly with the fork. The noise ebbed away as everyone turned to stare at her. Her heart beat a little faster and she swallowed hard.

'I just wanted to say . . . Um, thank you all for coming.' The expressions softened and some of the guests smiled at her. Great Uncle Bernard waved his glass, and Lottie was surprised to see he was still awake. 'I'm sure you'll agree that we've given Nana Rose a good send off, and one she would approve of. She would have been pleased to see all of you here and she would have been especially delighted at having all of her family together.' There were nods of agreement. 'So thanks again. Safe journeys home – and could I have all the family join me in the snug, please.'

'We really need to go,' said Nicola, looking irritated again, but Lottie ignored her.

'Well done, darling; you did quite well for someone who's not really a public speaker,' her mother chimed in. Lottie ignored the barbed comment and ushered her into the snug.

When everyone was assembled, she clapped her hands and took in a lungful of air. 'Nana has arranged Christmas at Henbourne Manor this year, like she does every year. Everything is planned, the food is ordered, the decorations are down from the loft, she's even got the Christmas tree. In a few weeks the home she treasured will likely be sold and that will be it.' Lottie found she was waving her hands about as she spoke. 'No more family Christmases to share and remember. I think we should have a big family Christmas at Henbourne Manor, one last time. For Nana – like she would have wanted. What do you all say?' There was a long pause. Lottie bit her lip while she waited.

'That's all very lovely, but I think we've had quite enough Christmases to remember, thank you,' said Nicola. 'We'll likely be in the Caribbean enjoying five-star all-inclusive,' she added, to nobody in particular.

'It's all paid for, and I'll cook,' said Lottie, trying hard not to sound as desperate as she felt. She searched their faces for an ally.

Uncle Daniel's head jolted up. 'Actually, I think Lottie has a good point. Mum was expecting us all to come, so I doubt any of us have made alternative arrangements. And who doesn't like a free Christmas?' Lottie had appealed to his thrifty side. Nicola was looking like she might be about to peck him to pieces as he turned his attention to her. 'All the best five-star resorts will already be booked up.' Nicola appeared to contemplate this information.

'I think that's a lovely idea,' said Zach. He'd always been supportive of his little sister. 'I'm in.' He turned to Angie.

'Mum, you'll join us and spend Christmas with your granddaughter?'

Angie's cheek twitched. 'As long as you both guarantee that I don't have to cook. And that nobody refers to me as a grandmother.'

'Absolutely,' said Lottie. She knew she was guilty of teasing her mother about being a grandparent. She could probably manage not to mention it for a few days if she really had to.

'I didn't think we'd be doing anything else, Button,' said Great Uncle Bernard, wheeling himself over, leaving a trail of people hopping in his wake.

'Thanks, Uncle Bernie,' said Lottie, giving him a wink. 'We're all agreed then?' Lottie asked, wanting to seal the deal. 'One last family Christmas at Henbourne Manor.'

Chapter Two

Christmas Eve

Christmas Eve dawned and Lottie pulled on her tatty old dressing gown and slid her feet into her battered *Star Wars* slippers, silently hoping Santa might bring her some replacements. She padded down to the kitchen, yawning as she went. She scanned the room for any signs of the Duchess, but all was quiet. The Duchess was Nana's aptly named cat. She was a seal-point Persian from a long pedigree line and seemed well aware of her heritage. She had been out of sorts since Nana died, which Lottie could relate to.

Lottie unbolted the back door. 'Duchess!' she yelled into the gardens, and quickly shut the door again as an icy draught whipped around her. The Duchess had her own door, as was befitting her status, but it was a cat flap via the garages and the utility room. This, it appeared, was not as the cat would have liked, so she was frequently to be heard pawing at the back door demanding a member of her staff promptly open it.

Lottie wrapped the dressing gown more tightly around her, rubbed at a chocolate smudge on the front and flicked the switch on the kettle. She slumped onto one of the many kitchen chairs and felt the cool wood touch her calves. The kitchen was vast, draughty and old, like the rest of the manor house, but it was home to Lottie.

It was the house her mother had returned to, with her and Zach in tow, every time she'd had another relationship slide spectacularly down the drain (as they so often did). Angie would pack up, often in the dead of night, throwing clothes into much-used suitcases and drag the children back to Henbourne on the Hill to seek solace and a place to lick her wounds. Nana always welcomed the children, but Lottie had slowly become aware of how Nana appeared to admonish her mother a little more strongly each time she returned.

When Zach went off to university at eighteen, and Angie was set on following her latest beau to France, Nana had suggested that Lottie move in with her to give her some stability while she studied for her exams. The next few years had firmly cemented Henbourne Manor as Lottie's home.

She hated the comparison, but like her mother she, too, had returned there each time a relationship had failed, the latest being a real low point in her life. Her relationship with Anthony had been crumbling for a while, but it had spectacularly imploded when she'd called into his office to surprise him with fish and chips and Prosecco when he was, yet again, working late. But it was Lottie who got the surprise when she found him in flagrante with some woman in full lawyer wig and gown. She had momentarily thought it was a strippagram before the harsh realisation had struck her and she'd dropped her chips.

Finding out that Anthony was a rat had hurt her, but

her trusting heart had been damaged far worse a long time ago and she really didn't have time for moping. It was Christmas Eve and she had too many other things to think about. She made herself a pot of tea using a scoop of loose tea – as Nana had always done – and settled herself down with the back of an old envelope to make a list. She felt like she'd been getting ready for Christmas for days, but there was still so much to do. Her hasty invitation at the wake was coming back to sink its teeth into her backside.

When the list covered both sides of the old envelope, she started to panic. There was just her, and she had – she checked the clock – five hours until they started arriving. A creak upstairs reminded her that she wasn't completely on her own; there was Great Uncle Bernard, her late grandfather's brother, but he relied on his wheelchair more often than not these days so she didn't hold out much hope of any assistance there. She wandered through to the utility room, feeling the temperature drop, and opened the washing machine. She'd hang this lot out, have a shower and then tackle the biggest task on the list – making up all the beds for the umpteen family members who would be descending.

Lottie slid her feet into Nana's old wellies. It wasn't the most fashionable of looks, but there weren't any neighbours for a mile so it was fine. She braved the bitterly cold weather, juggling the full laundry basket with the door whilst the wind whipped up the old dressing gown. It had been chucking it down with rain all night and the ground was soggy underfoot. It was a bit of a march round to the side garden where the washing line and prop were. She noticed the old gate at the bottom was swinging open and made a mental note to add it to her growing to-do list.

She hung up the washing as fast as she could; she wanted to spend as little time as possible with Great Uncle Bernard's smalls. A muffled yowl was carried on the wind and she paused to listen, a very large pair of Bernard's greying pants in her hands.

'Duchess?' she called, and was surprised to hear a bark in reply. The old gate banged back against the wall. She turned to see the Duchess come charging into the garden, closely followed by a small scruffy dog. Lottie had to think quickly. Either run and open the back door for the cat and risk falling over on the wet ground, or scoop her up in Great Uncle Bernard's pants – they were certainly big enough for the job. Lottie opened the pants wide and stepped into the cat's path. Duchess was taken unawares and was quickly wrapped in the pants as the small brown dog charged towards them. Lottie was expecting it to come to a halt, but it didn't. It took a leap and tried to join the Duchess in Lottie's arms.

'Whoa!' she yelled, as the dog effectively drop kicked her in the stomach, sending her toppling backwards to land with an audible squelch. She hung on to the cat, keen to protect her from the monstrous canine who was now jumping up and down on Lottie like she was a trampoline. 'Shoo!' she said as she writhed about in the mud. The Duchess began to yowl her protest at an ear-bleeding pitch.

'Are you all right?' asked a man's voice above her. For a second it reminded her of someone.

'Fine. Thanks,' she said automatically, although she blatantly wasn't – lying there covered in mud, with her Grumpy Cat pyjamas on display and an even grumpier cat hissing in her arms. She scrabbled onto an elbow to get a look at the intruder, but he had his hood up and

19

was already racing after the muddy little dog as it darted back down the garden.

'Sorry!' yelled the man, as he and the dog disappeared.

'Well really,' said Lottie, quite put out. The Duchess emitted a low growl of agreement.

After a hot shower, things looked a little better. She had even managed to bath the Duchess, who was used to the procedure – and unlike most cats, tolerated it – and who was now enjoying a light blow-dry on Lottie's bed. Lottie switched off the hair dryer and gave the fluffy cat a stroke. 'You'll do,' she said. 'And that's another thing I can tick off my list.' The cat glared at Lottie with her bright blue eyes. 'No, pamper time is over. I have work to do.' The Duchess swished her tail in reply. 'If you could avoid being chased by dirty little dogs that would be a help.'

Lottie went on to her next task. She popped a little blue cleaning block in the toilet and gave the bathroom a once-over. It looked fine; no sign of muddy cat anywhere.

Lottie spent the next hour making beds up as fast as was humanly possible. There was a shortage of duvets, but they had plenty of blankets – you had to in a draughty house like Henbourne Manor. It would be first come, first served on the bedroom front. Lottie had left Nana's room untouched – she couldn't bear to think of someone else sleeping in there just yet – but with five other bedrooms and a box room that wasn't an issue.

When she was happy with the upstairs, she headed to the kitchen. She pulled out Nana's cookbook and turned the pages reverently. This was the book that Nana always referred to. It was filled with handwritten notes and passed-down recipes, including one that Nana swore blind had been smuggled out of occupied France during the

First World War. Lottie ran her fingers over her grandmother's words and felt a tear trickle down her cheek. Nana was gone, and she was finding it hard; the silliest things could set her off. She straightened her shoulders and tried to pull herself together, thumbing through until she found Nana's trusted tomato soup recipe. It was one she'd made with Nana before, so it wasn't entirely new to her. And most importantly, Lottie knew it was easy to make.

Today's menu was soup, spaghetti Bolognese and cheese and biscuits. She was keen to keep it simple, given that everyone would be expecting the works tomorrow. Lottie tried hard not to think too much about it. She wasn't known for her domesticity and had never cooked on this scale before. She was up for the challenge and she wanted this to be as much like one of Nana's Christmases as it possibly could be, but that was going to be no mean feat.

She followed the soup recipe and was pleasantly surprised at the results. She put the large saucepan to one side. It would be easy to reheat later.

'Hello, Lottie?' came the accented voice of Great Uncle Bernard's carer. Dayea was a lovely Filipina lady who did far more for the old man than she was paid for. Lottie got the feeling she was quite fond of him.

'In the kitchen!' called back Lottie.

'I brought you lumpia,' she said, greeting Lottie with a warm hug and a large Tupperware box.

Lumpia sounded to Lottie like something you might catch abroad, but the spring-roll-like objects Dayea was pointing to in the box smelled divine.

'Thank you, Dayea, that is kind of you.' Lottie decided she might try a couple soon, as thanks to the falling-in-the-mud incident she'd skipped breakfast. Her stomach had been rumbling for a while.

They heard the stairlift start up and Dayea dashed off to help Bernard. Lottie finished mopping the kitchen floor and was hanging up the squeegee when she heard the Duchess scrabbling at the back door. She glanced up at the window: it was raining again; the cat would be soaked, as would the washing. Lottie eyed her just-washed floor. She tiptoed across it and opened the back door. In shot the Duchess, and she wasn't alone – the scruffy little brown dog was hot on her heels.

'Nooooo!' yelled Lottie as the cat dived from surface to surface like a Ninja Warrior contestant. The dog skidded on muddy paws, careering around the kitchen like a let-go balloon. She hung on to the door as the wind and rain buffeted it about. If she shut it, the dog had no escape route but, while she kept it open, she was getting soaked. 'Sod it,' she said, shutting the door and skidding after the dog. There followed a game of high-speed chase where Lottie shooed the dog from room to room, mentally calculating how much cleaning would be needed, until she finally had the thing cornered back in the kitchen.

She took a moment to get her breath back. 'Right, now don't bite me. Okay?'

The dog was panting after all the chasing about, his tongue lolling out of his mouth. He watched her with big brown eyes. As Lottie got closer, she could see he was literally covered in mud, apart from a white patch on his neck, which was splattered but not completely coated like the rest of him. 'Now, listen,' she said, in what she hoped was a calming voice. 'I'm going to pick you up. You're not going to bite me because I'm only going to put you outside. Got it?' She nodded and the dog tilted its head on one

22

side. Lottie reached out a hand for the dog to sniff and he began to lick her fingers. She smiled at the gesture. As she went to pick him up, the back door swung open and the howling gale brought in a man in a dark hooded coat.

'Argh!' yelled Lottie in fright, terrifying the dog, who clattered past her into the utility room. Lottie stood up straight. 'You can't just go letting yourself in,' she said as forcefully as she could, scanning the room for a makeshift weapon. 'You can take your filthy mutt and . . .'

The man pulled off his hood and shook his damp hair. Lottie would have fallen backwards if the kitchen table hadn't been there for her to slump against. 'Joe?' She gasped his name. She could barely believe her eyes. Here was the man she truly thought she would never see again. It was a sucker punch to her stomach.

'Hiya, Lottie,' said Joe. 'Sorry about this morning. Are you okay?' His voice wasn't how she remembered it – there was a hint of an accent. But his easy carefree tone was exactly the same, as though he'd last seen her yesterday rather than nine years ago.

Lottie's mouth opened and closed, but making actual sound was proving difficult. 'Joe?' she ventured again.

'Yeah. It's me.' He ran his hands through his hair. 'How's Rose?'

Lottie really needed her brain to find a gear it could operate in. She blinked and he was still there, meaning it wasn't her imagination playing tricks. She took a steadying breath. 'Nana died three weeks ago.'

'Oh Lottie, I'm so sorry to hear that.' She watched him in bewildered awe as he took off his muddy boots. He was back, and she had no idea how to process it. 'How are you?' he asked.

It was a fair question, but one that caused her issues.

23

How was she meant to feel when he had rocked up out of thin air? Joe, the boy she'd grown up with; the teenager she'd lost her heart to; the man she'd fallen in love with; the soulmate who had walked away from her without looking back.

But that wasn't what he was asking about. 'Um. I'm okay. Been better, you know?'

'I wondered why the house was up for sale. I've got such fond memories of this place.' He paused and looked around the kitchen. 'How's your mum?' That was the other question people always asked.

'She's fine. Upset, obviously, but fine.'

Joe was staring at her. The intensity made her look away. 'Wow; is that your natural hair colour?'

When Lottie was younger she'd dyed her hair at every opportunity. She'd been sent home from school countless times. She'd not dyed it for years. Not since . . .

'Yeah.' Lottie automatically smoothed her hair down. This was so odd.

'Looks great.'

'Thanks.'

They nodded at each other and Joe gave her that shy smile that was etched on her heart. It was like they'd been thrown back in time; here they were, chatting in Nana's kitchen like they'd always used to do. Lottie pulled out a chair and sat down before her legs gave way. It was a shock to see someone she'd spent the last nine years trying to forget because they had clearly forgotten about her.

Chapter Three

'It's good to see you, Lottie,' said Joe, pulling out a chair and joining her.

'Um. I, um . . .' She had no idea how to respond. She put her hands on her thighs and took a deep breath. Her initial bewilderment was ebbing away, and now a tsunami of new emotions was threatening to breach her carefully built defences.

'What have you been up to?' he asked. His casual attitude irritated her.

'Joe, whilst I'd love to chat,' *and ask you why you buggered off to America and deleted me from your life*, she added in her head, 'I have a house covered in muddy pawprints, and hordes of guests arriving in . . .' she checked the clock, 'holy crap! Three hours. And your ruddy dog is hiding behind a bucket in the utility room!'

'Not my dog,' said Joe, unzipping his coat. If he was expecting a cup of tea he could think again.

'What?'

'The dog.' Joe pointed at the muddy face peering at them from the shadows. 'He's not mine.'

'Then why the hell were you chasing after him?'

'He was reported as a stray so I was trying to catch

him.' Perhaps this made sense to Joe – only, to any sane person, it didn't.

Lottie rubbed her temples. Her brain actually hurt. 'Right. Shall we catch him now and you can take him to the rescue or wherever it was you were taking him?'

'He's staying with me.'

'Staying with you?' Joe lived in America.

'I've moved back. I'm the new vet. I'm renting Mr Bundy's old place in Dumbleford for now. There's only a shower there. Can we give the dog a bath here first? Then I'll give you a hand cleaning the floors.'

Too. Much. Information. Lottie realised she had been shaking her head. New vet? There was no vet in the village; they had to go to Stow-on-the-Wold for the nearest surgery. Mr Bundy had been dead about five years and his home had changed hands twice in that time, but she knew the little cottage Joe was referring to well. She had far too many questions and a million concerns, so instead she focused on the issues in hand – the dog and the floor. She really wished she had a better solution than Joe's, but her mind was overloaded. And as she looked at the floor, she knew she could do with some help.

'Okay, but you're cleaning the bath afterwards too.'

'Of course.' He gave a broad smile. 'It really is good to see you again, Lottie,' he said, pausing to study her. She wanted to say the same but she couldn't, hand on heart, say it with conviction. Was it good to see him? She didn't know. She was still in free fall waiting to hit the ground. There was much she wanted to ask, but it was all a muddle in her head. So instead she looked away and busied herself with trying to get the dog out of the utility.

* * *

After they managed to corner it, they quickly discovered the dog wasn't used to being bathed. It took both of them hanging on tight to keep him in the tub and wash him with the Duchess's pet shampoo and conditioner. It was surreal being in such a small space with Joe, who had been a world away for such a long time.

Lottie kept her focus on the little dog and was amazed to discover that, under all the mud, he was predominantly white, with a number of tan-coloured patches and a whiskery chin.

'He's a proper Heinz fifty-seven,' said Lottie, giving the dog a rub over with an old towel whilst Joe washed down the bath and the mud-splattered bathroom.

'Jack Russell cross. Probably a bit of bichon frise or poodle in the mix to explain the soft coat and longer legs.'

Lottie paused in her towel drying. 'Joe, why have you come back? Why now?'

The dog saw his chance to escape and scurried out of the towel and through the open bathroom door. Lottie let him go.

Joe turned and sat on the edge of the bath, his head bent down. His hair was still wayward, even though it was cut short – it had always been that way, and Lottie remembered that when they were children his mother had despaired at how it stuck up. He lifted his head and gave her a wonky smile. 'It just felt like the right time.'

'The right time for what?' Lottie tried hard not to frown.

'To come home.'

Lottie opened her mouth to speak but a great crash from the kitchen had the dog barking and them both hurtling downstairs. They passed Great Uncle Bernard, who was heading down on the stairlift wearing his standard-issue old man's burgundy cardigan with leather buttons.

'Is that Joe? By Lord!' bellowed Bernard.

'Hiya Mr Collins,' Joe called back up, jumping the last few steps and landing with a thud.

Lottie skidded into the kitchen, coming to an abrupt halt and surveying the devastation. It appeared that the cat had tried to jump onto the top of the kitchen cupboards where the old pots and pans were kept and, in her haste, had knocked them onto the worktop; they were now scattered about the kitchen. But the bigger issue was that the large saucepan that was cooling on the worktop had also been sent crashing to the floor. Tomato soup was now liberally splattered everywhere. It looked like a cheap horror movie set. The Duchess was standing in the middle of a sea of tomato. She yowled in protest and flicked a tomato-sodden paw in disgust. The little dog, who was streaked in red like a zombie hound, made a run for it. Joe scooped him up as he tried to dive through his legs.

'Oh Duchess!' said Lottie, paddling through the soup to retrieve the cat. Lottie pointed a finger back at Joe – 'I blame you for this!' – but he was holding up the scruffy dog and hiding his laughing face behind it. Something passed between them – whether it was the ridiculousness of the moment, or their shared history, she wasn't sure. Joe was laughing hard and it was a sound which took her back to happy times: football on the green; scrumping apples; catching minnows in the stream behind the pub.

The thought of her family arriving extinguished the happy thoughts. 'Bloody hell.' She was fast running out of time. The small dog started to bark; Duchess puffed up like someone had inserted a foot pump up her bum.

'I'll wash the cat, *again*,' said Lottie. 'I suggest you take that mutt back to Mr Bundy's.'

'Okay,' said Joe, holding the dog away from his clothes. Tomato soup dripped to the floor. What a bloody mess. She knew Joe was smiling at her as she left with the protesting tomato-soaked feline – she didn't need to look.

When Lottie came back downstairs, having left a slightly traumatised Duchess on her bed to recover, she found Joe mopping the kitchen. So much for him going back to the cottage.

Lottie checked her list. 'Sod it – I'm late for my shift!' She grabbed her coat and ran for the door.

'What?' asked Joe, his head turning in confusion.

There was no time to explain. 'You can leave all this. I've got to go. I'm late. Sorry!' She shouted behind her as she exited the kitchen and ran out of the house.

Emily was the happiest she could remember being. She'd been dating Zach for over a year, and at last she was going to meet his family. She'd been introduced to his daughter Jessie in the spring and, despite a few hiccups, she and the six-year-old had forged a relationship. Emily knew she would never replace Jessie's mother, but she desperately wanted them to get along – she was a delightful little girl, and besides, it was essential if she was to stay in a relationship with Zach, which she wanted more than anything. He'd been busy with work and family stuff, so she'd not seen much of him over the last few weeks. She reached out and put her hand over his as it rested on the gear knob. He smiled at the contact.

'You okay?' he asked.

'Bit apprehensive. I just hope your family like me.'

He gave a chuckle. 'They'll love you, Em.'

'I hope so. Are you okay? You seem preoccupied. Are you worried about me meeting them all?'

'Nope, they're all so bonkers they make me look like the best of the gene pool. Only thing on my mind is I'm sure I've forgotten to bring something. But I've checked all the presents twice, so it can't be that.'

'Any last-minute tips?' She wanted to make a good first impression. At work her reputation went before her, but this was a very different situation. She knew she'd be scrutinised and she wanted to win them over. She felt a lone butterfly flutter inside her, and it was a surprise. She was usually confident, but being accepted by Zach's family was a whole new experience. It meant more to her than she'd realised.

'Blimey, where to start? My mum is really into how she looks, so she'll take compliments all day long. Aunt Nicola, on the other hand, will be suspicious of any flattering comments. But she considers herself an authority on most things, so just ask her opinion on anything. It'll be Great Uncle Bernard's last Christmas—'

'Oh no. How awful. What's wrong with him?'

'Nothing. He's being saying it's his last Christmas for as long as I can remember, and he's still here. He can talk the hind legs off a herd of donkeys so he's always good value. And then there's my little sister Lottie.'

'Ah,' said Emily. 'I know what sisters are like. Mine drives me nuts. Always sniping, always putting down your achievements and bigging hers up?' Emily and her sister had been in fierce competition ever since Emily had exited the womb, which her sister had seemed to take as an open challenge. Everything since then had been a game of one-upmanship.

Zach chuckled. 'No, Lottie's not like that at all. She's the best of the bunch. She used to annoy the heck out of me when we were kids, but when . . .' Zach stretched his neck to look at his daughter in the rear-view mirror. She had headphones on and was concentrating hard on the latest Disney film, ' . . . when we lost Melissa, Lottie was the one that held my world together.' A tear formed at the corner of his eye and Emily squeezed his hand. She loved how open he was with his emotions. He was one of the few men she'd known who didn't apologise for crying or try to dismiss his feelings. Zach had always been honest about how much he'd loved his wife, and in an odd way it had been refreshing – though also mildly terrifying, because she feared being compared to Melissa and she had no way of knowing if she'd ever match up.

Zach's Adam's apple bobbed and he continued. 'I saw Lottie in a different light then, you know? Not just my kid sister but a smart woman who talked sense. It gave me the kick up the bum I needed when I was struggling.'

'Wow, she sounds amazing.' *And not a bit like my sister at all*, she thought.

'She is. But whatever you do, don't ask her advice, because she makes lousy decisions. Oh, and here's the really bad news: she can't make toast, and she's cooking Christmas dinner!'

'She can't be that bad.'

Zach shot her a look. 'Some people cook to relax. Lottie does it to test the fire alarm.'

Emily retrieved her hand and pondered everything he'd said. She really wanted to make a good first impression. She studied her outfit. She was aiming for smart but friendly, which had been tricky as her wardrobe was mainly suits and jeans. She'd changed her mind a few times over what to wear and had ended up settling for a wrap dress which she hoped didn't show too much cleavage because the shift dress she was going to wear had been too tight round the tummy. She'd been busy at work and missed her regular spin class, and it showed.

Zach clicked his fingers. 'The wine! That's what I've forgotten. We can grab a couple of bottles from the village stores. Okay?'

'Of course. We can't turn up empty-handed.'

A few miles later they left the A-roads behind them and followed some winding lanes before he turned in to an old-style petrol station. 'We're nearly in the village, but this is the last place for petrol,' Zach explained.

Emily was curious to see where Zach had grown up, and the lane into the village looked pretty. 'I'll get the wine,' she said, releasing her seat belt.

'Okay I'll pick you up when I'm done here. The village stores is along there on the corner before you reach the village green.'

Emily pulled on her woolly hat, grabbed her coat from the boot and set off down the lane. It had stopped raining and the crisp winter air was fresh against her cheeks; the kind of cold that makes your nose tingle. She adored winter because she liked the contrast of the chill outside with the warmth of the indoors, bringing with it the opportunity to curl up with a good book in front of the fire. Although those opportunities were becoming fewer as work commitments squeezed her personal time.

She turned a bend and saw the village in front of her. A sign welcomed her to Dumbleford. She crossed a trickle of a stream at the ford, caught a glimpse of the shop and post office and headed towards it.

A loud bell announced her arrival and Emily felt conspicuous in the empty shop. She found the wine section and, surprised by the good selection, chose two bottles of Saint-Émilion. Making for the till, she got distracted by some fig rolls. She hadn't had those for years and suddenly fancied one. Actually, she could have eaten the whole packet. She picked them up but then remembered how her tummy had looked and put them back.

Then another thought struck her: perhaps her period was due. That was probably what it was. It was just bloating. She reached for the fig rolls again. Exactly how long had it been since her last period? It had been a while. Her eyes widened at the thought. She threw the fig rolls back on the shelf, pulled out her phone and scrolled frantically through her diary. 'Shit!' She was five weeks late. How had she missed that?

'Hello?' came the voice of a woman who had clearly heard her swear.

'Oh, hi. Just these thanks,' said Emily, rushing to the counter and putting down the wine. She noticed some medical supplies behind the till and scanned them quickly.

The young woman serving followed her gaze. She had short, dark hair, delicate features and a warm smile. 'Was there something in particular you were after?' she asked.

'Mmm.' Emily's brain was working overtime. She couldn't be pregnant – they'd used protection. Although they did say they were only ninety-eight per cent effective . . . No, surely not.

The woman reached under the counter and pulled out a selection of packets of condoms. 'The older residents prefer us not to have everything on display in case it encourages promiscuity in the young.' She rolled her eyes as she spoke.

Emily slowly drew in a breath. 'I think it's a bit late for

that.' She met the woman's gaze and the understanding passed between them.

'Ah, then you need one of these.' She rummaged under the counter and produced a pregnancy testing kit.

Emily swallowed hard. 'I guess I do. Thanks.'

The woman gave a kindly smile from over the till. 'Exciting times ahead.'

'Thanks,' said Emily, thinking the opposite. She paid, and hastily put the tester kit in her handbag before scooping up the wine.

'Good luck,' said the woman. 'And a merry Christmas!'

Emily managed a weak smile. 'Thanks, you too.'

Chapter Four

Outside the shop, Emily paused on the pavement for a moment. Her eyes were drawn to a young family on the village green. A small boy and two adults were playing football with two very large dogs. Another boy – and yet another huge dog – came out of the nearby pub to join them. The woman in the group was laughing and managed to kick the ball whilst balancing a baby on her hip. The man ran over, kissed her and the baby before racing off after the boys. Was she looking at her own future?

Emily was just getting her head around having Jessie in her life; she wasn't ready to be a full-time mother and all that that entailed. She was a career girl, and far too busy trying to outdo her sister to start a family. The toot of a horn dragged her back to the present as Zach pulled up.

'Daddy, look at the cute dogs!' exclaimed Jessie from the back seat as Emily opened the door and got in.

'They're huge,' said Zach, watching the dogs-versus-boys football match on the village green.

'I love them. I wonder if that's the sort of dog Santa will bring me?' she asked, her breath steaming up the glass.

'Jessie, we've talked about this,' said her father. 'Santa doesn't bring animals as presents. You can't wrap a puppy.'

'What else is on your list?' asked Emily, aware that Zach was already shaking his head.

'Hmm,' said Jessie. 'I asked for a puppy, a unicorn, a real ice-cream van and boobs.'

'Boobs?' whispered Emily to Zach. He nodded.

'Yes, boobs, like yours,' said Jessie, very matter-of-factly. Her father went back to shaking his head. 'Amy Renton said that her daddy said that big boobs get you anything you want. But it's a puppy I want the most. Boobs are second.'

Zach indicated and pulled away. Jessie sighed dramatically and watched the dogs playing on the green until they were out of sight.

'You okay?' Zach glanced at Emily.

She nodded vigorously, clutching the wine bottles to her stomach whilst she checked and rechecked the dates in her mind. They headed up the hill to the next village and past a sign that read Henbourne on the Hill. This was it. This was where Zach's family lived. She realised she wasn't ready to face them yet; not while she had this giant question mark hanging over her. But she could hardly ask Zach to turn around. Emily spotted a farm, a few cute cottages and a church with a pretty lychgate, but within moments they were through the sleepy village and out the other side. She was confused: had Zach changed his mind? For a moment she felt relief.

'We're early, but I know a great little pub where we can get a good meal. It might be the last one we have for a couple of days,' said Zach, with a grin. Emily suddenly wasn't hungry any more.

* * *

Lottie ran through the back garden, clutching her coat to her, and came flying back into the manor in a similar style to how she had left – but the sight that greeted her was a pleasant surprise. The kitchen was tomato free. Joe put his head around the kitchen door from the hallway and gave her a timid wave. Why was he still here?

'Thanks, but you really didn't have to clean up,' she said, taking her coat off.

'Yeah, I think I did. I've bathed the dog and he's asleep in the cat basket. The cat's gone off in a huff.'

'Thank you.' She meant it. It was just such a struggle to look at him and not feel a torrent of emotions.

'I found the Christmas tree in the garage and figured you'd need a hand . . .' She followed him into the hall where the large real tree Nana had ordered was standing, majestic, if a little bare. The smell of fresh pine wafted over her – a wave of Christmas. They both stared at it for a moment, until Lottie noticed that Joe was now looking at her instead of the tree. 'Do you still decorate the tree on Christmas Eve?'

'Yep. Family tradition.'

'I used to love all your funny traditions,' said Joe, sounding like he was thinking out loud.

She adjusted her hair clip. 'Can you help me move it into the drawing room?'

'Sure,' he said, already taking up the position.

Lottie got the other side and they inelegantly waddled their way down the hall and into the drawing room. 'Any early arrivals?' she asked.

He shook his head. 'Nope.' They positioned and repositioned the Christmas tree until Lottie was happy with it. There was a moment where they both eyed each other at the same time and then looked away. This was a whole new level of awkward.

'I should probably make a move.' Joe pointed at the door. 'I'm picking up a car. It's an old Land Rover actually. Nothing special, but I'm collecting it in like . . .' He checked his watch. 'Nowish.' He seemed startled to see it was almost two o'clock.

'Of course.'

'I'll take the dog with me. Check if he's got a microchip. Hopefully I can reunite him with his owners in time for Christmas.'

'That's a nice thought,' said Lottie. Joe had always been thoughtful. *Apart from—* She banished the memory.

Joe paused in the doorway and turned slowly, making Lottie hold her breath. 'Perhaps after Christmas we could catch up properly?' he asked, his eyes barely meeting hers before they flitted away. Her mind buzzed with what he meant by that. 'You know. Catch up over a coffee,' he added.

'Let's get Christmas over first. Then, we'll see.' She couldn't commit to anything more than that right now. She felt like her space had been well and truly invaded. He gave the briefest of nods, picked up the dog and walked through to the kitchen. Lottie followed. 'Thanks for all your help today.'

'It's nothing.' He sounded dejected.

'Merry Christmas, Joe.' She couldn't hide the melancholy in her tone.

'You too, Lottie.' He gave a weak smile and ventured out into the blustery winter weather.

The pub had been lovely, but Emily's two trips to the toilet had been accompanied by Jessie waiting outside the cubicle, humming 'Baby Shark', so she'd not been able to do the pregnancy test. An hour later, they were back in Henbourne on the Hill and turning into a large gated drive. 'What the . . .?' Emily started to pay attention.

The sound of tyres on gravel, as if announcing their arrival, seemed to add to the grandeur of the setting. This was not what she'd been expecting. Her head was almost spinning as she tried to take it all in. There was a large turning circle with an ornate fountain in the middle, and beyond that a grand house. Emily was thrown. She'd never set foot inside a house like this before; she had only driven by them or seen them on the telly. Her standard-sized family had lived in a small terrace. She wished Zach had warned her. Thinking back, he'd said something about 'the estate'; but she'd automatically assumed he meant *council* estate not *country*.

'Wow,' said Emily, trying hard to stop her mouth falling open. 'It's beautiful.'

'Faded grandeur,' said Zach, switching off the engine. 'It needs a lot of updating. The new owners will have their work cut out.' He pointed at the 'For Sale' sign being buffeted by the wind.

'Has it been in your family for generations?' she asked, her eyes scanning the many windows and grand steps up to a huge arched front door.

'No, my grandfather bought it in the seventies. That was the last time it had a full makeover,' he said, with an affectionate chuckle. 'Come on.'

Emily checked her handbag was fully zipped up and tried not to think of the tester kit inside as she got out of the car. Time to make a good first impression.

* * *

Almost as soon as Joe had closed the back door, the sound of someone tugging the bell pull at the front door echoed through the house. Lottie took a deep breath. This was the start of what could be a very long Christmas.

She skidded into the hallway and wrenched open the heavy old door. Her brother strode in, giving her a perfunctory kiss on the cheek as he passed. 'Hiya, sis. Have you got the dinner on yet? Those sprouts need to be boiled for at least a week.'

'Ha, ha,' she said, looking past him for a glimpse of his girlfriend. This was something of a milestone, because she'd not met her yet, and Zach had made her promise in triplicate not to make a fuss. But this was the first girlfriend he'd brought home for Christmas since his wife had died; it felt like a big deal to Lottie. She put on her best smile and turned to greet her. 'Oh, hello,' said Lottie, wrong-footed by the sight of the blushing woman in front of her – it was the woman she had sold a pregnancy test to when she had been doing her shift at the village stores.

Lottie tried to hide her shock by greeting Emily with a kiss on each cheek, but both women were too rigid and kept turning in the same direction. A nervous laugh escaped from Emily.

'Nice to meet you. I'm Emily.' She offered Lottie the bottles of wine with shaking hands.

Lottie cleared her throat and tried to act nonchalant. 'Lovely to meet you too. Ooh, Saint-Émilion – thank you.' She knew it sounded like she was reading from a dodgy script, but that was how it felt. She couldn't stop her eyes darting to Emily's stomach and then back up to her wide eyes. She looked terrified, poor thing. Lottie gave her a smile. 'Come in and get yourself warmed up.'

'Auntie Lottie!' shouted Jessie, pushing past Emily and throwing herself into Lottie's arms, almost displacing the wine.

'Jessie!' She put down the bottles, picked the little girl up and swung her around, thankful for the distraction. 'You are getting taller – look at you.'

'I told Santa I would be here for Christmas so he knows where to deliver my puppy,' said Jessie, excitedly. Her father spun around and she made a quick amendment. 'Presents. I meant presents.' She gave a big cheesy grin.

'You are a smart cookie,' said Lottie, putting her niece down and avoiding eye contact with Emily.

'Nana Rose!' called Jessie and all the adults froze.

'I thought she knew,' whispered Lottie to her brother.

'She does,' replied Zach.

Zach crouched down in front of his daughter. 'Jessie.' His voice was tender. 'Do you remember what I said about Nana Rose going to be with the angels?'

Jessie frowned. 'I thought she wanted to be made into ash to help the garden?' Lottie was glad she wasn't the one having to answer the tricky questions.

'Yes, but your soul, the bit that makes you special, that goes to Heaven to be with the angels,' explained Zach.

'Or a star,' said Jessie. *The Lion King* was one of her favourite films.

'Yes, or a star,' agreed Zach.

Jessie appeared to be thinking hard. 'But can't she be a ghost and carry on living here?'

'I'm afraid not,' said Zach.

'Is that because there's already a ghost that lives here?' asked Jessie.

Emily made a noise somewhere between a croak and a gasp. 'Ghost?' she asked.

'You hear it moving things at night,' said Jessie. 'Where's the Duchess?'

'Not sure,' Lottie replied. 'She's a bit out of sorts at the moment, so she could be anywhere. Why don't you see if you can find her?'

Jessie didn't need asking twice and ran off.

'Duchess?' said Emily, her voice a little shaky. 'Your mum's a duchess?'

Zach and Lottie burst out laughing and took a few moments to get it under control.

'Not in the slightest,' said Zach.

'It's the cat's name,' said Lottie. She saw Emily's shoulders drop with relief.

Lottie eyed her brother. 'Gingerbread?' Zach didn't answer; he raced to the kitchen with Lottie hot on his heels. There was a brief fight over the cake tin until Zach pulled the lid off and stared at the contents with a puzzled expression.

He poked the deformed figures crouching at the bottom of the tin. 'What are these? Ginger dead men?'

'Oi! I made them yesterday. They took me hours.' Lottie grabbed the tin off him and ran to the other side of the table.

'Hello?' called Emily from the hallway. Zach rushed back to her.

'Sorry, Em. This house is a bit spread out. I'll give you the grand tour in a mo,' he said, beckoning her to the kitchen.

'Please treat the place as your own,' said Lottie, joining them and biting the leg off an already headless gingerbread man. 'Gingerbread?' She offered her the tin.

'Last year Nana made a treehouse out of gingerbread. It was incredible,' said Zach.

Emily took a gingerbread body part from the tin. 'I wanted to come last year but my mum had won a hamper and she wanted us all to go to hers.'

'Last year?' said Lottie, failing to hide her astonishment. She widened her eyes at Zach. She had no idea they'd been together that long. She spoke to her brother regularly and he'd first mentioned Emily a few months ago. He'd definitely been playing this low key for quite some time.

'You must have thought I was his imaginary girlfriend. It's taken so long for us to meet up, what with so many of your family being ill,' volunteered Emily, trying to bite into her gingerbread and having to have a second go at it.

Lottie opened her mouth to query Emily's statement but Zach was waving frantically from behind Emily's back. She'd challenge him on that one later. It was reassuring to know that Emily wasn't just a fling, but the fact Zach had kept her existence quiet for so long troubled Lottie a little.

'I've made up all the beds so take your pick,' said Lottie, wagging a finger at Zach out of Emily's eyeline as they all walked back to the hall.

'Blue room free?' he asked, picking up their bags and mouthing 'Thank you'.

'All yours. Camp bed and sleeping bag for Jessie are on the landing. And I've put the dolls in the box room.'

'Excellent,' said Zach, ushering Emily up the stairs.

'Dolls?' asked Emily.

'Nana collected them,' explained Lottie.

'They are the creepiest things you've ever seen,' said Zach. He took the stairs two at a time like he'd used to as a boy and it made Lottie smile. Lottie turned to head back to her to-do list in the kitchen as the front door opened and an icy wind blew in her mother.

'My God, this place is grim. I can't believe the cost of a taxi from Stow.' Angie wheeled in her case and slammed the door shut behind her. 'Hello, darling,' she said, eventually turning her attention to her daughter.

'Hi, Mum. Good journey?' They air-kissed over the briefest of hugs.

'Bearable. If I'd known Zach was already here I'd have got him to pick us up.'

'Us?' questioned Lottie, observing her mother, alone, taking off her expensive-looking coat.

As if answering the question, the old oak door burst open again and in strode a man whose age, Lottie guessed, was far nearer her own than her mother's. 'This is Scott,' said Angie, proudly pulling him to her side.

'Hiya,' said Scott, flicking his auburn hair out of his eyes. Lottie blinked rapidly. He was good-looking and had a warm smile.

'Hello,' said Lottie, aware that she was staring at the unexpected guest.

'Do close your mouth, Lottie. You don't want people to think you're simple,' said her mother, handing Lottie her coat. Angie kissed Scott in a way no child would ever want to observe of a parent. Lottie pulled her eyes away and busied herself with folding and refolding the coat.

Her mother finally stopped snogging Scott and scanned Lottie with a critical eye.

'What?' asked Lottie. She was wearing her favourite Darth Vader Christmas jumper and flashing Christmas tree earrings. She could sense the disapproval cascading over her in waves. 'It's Christmas so flashing earrings are acceptable. And I love this jumper.'

'Nothing, darling. Don't be defensive. It's very you, and I can see it's much-loved.'

'Here,' said Scott, pulling two large bottles of champagne out of a bag slung over his shoulder. ''Tis the season to drink Bolly, Fa la la la laa la la la laaa,' he trilled.

Distracted from Lottie's outfit, Angie giggled like a child. 'He's so much fun. Isn't he fun?'

'Oh, yes,' said Lottie, reaching to take the bottles and inwardly freaking out. This was one more person to feed at breakfast, lunch and dinner for the next two days – not to mention the fact that she didn't have a gift for him.

'Sorry, we'll need those,' said Angie, intercepting the bottles at lightning speed. 'I assume I'm in *my* room?' Angie was already heading upstairs.

'Actually, I'm afraid that's been my room for a while now, Mum.'

Angie stopped and turned, her face fixed; not from Botox, but from trying not to react in front of Scott. 'Blue room, then?' Her tone was strained.

'Um, sorry, Zach's in there.'

'Green room?' Angie was beginning to talk like a ventriloquist's dummy.

'It's got single beds. Perhaps you'd be happiest in the Roman room as it's next to the bathroom.' Angie shot her a warning look and Lottie frowned. She wasn't trying to be annoying, she was simply thinking of her mother's need to get up for a wee in the night. Lottie thought it had been quite considerate of her and the mattress was comfier in there as well.

'Fine. The Roman room it is then,' said Angie, continuing upstairs without a backwards glance.

'What, no colour scheme?' Scott asked Lottie, reaching for the luggage.

'Er, no, a previous owner believed that the Romans had a camp near here, so over the years Nana and Granddad collected prints and Roman-looking jugs and it's all in there.'

'Like *Gladiator*?' asked Scott, looking enthralled.

'Not really, more *Life of Brian*,' said Lottie, wondering why her mother hadn't warned her that she was bringing her latest boyfriend with her. *No need to panic*, she told herself. She could definitely cope with one extra; she'd bought food like she was expecting to be under siege for the festive season, so it would be fine. Scott gave a jolly shrug and headed upstairs, having a good look at the paintings on the wall as he passed. Lottie gave herself a mental pat on the back – she was over the first hurdle.

Chapter Five

Joe was checking his emails when someone banged hard and repeatedly on the door of his rented cottage. The dog sat up and he patted his head. So far Joe had discovered that the dog had no microchip and he'd not been reported missing to the local police, nor any vets or rescue centres. The continued banging made him hurry to answer it, being careful to shut the little dog in first. He opened the front door and found himself looking straight out across the wet street – there was nothing in his eyeline to obstruct his view. Looking down, his eyes met a small elderly woman and a tartan wheelie trolley, which she was already thrusting forwards towards his legs. He leaped out of the way with moments to spare.

'Um, can I help you?' he asked the lady, who was already heading into the cottage.

She took off her rain bonnet to reveal hair like a dandelion clock. She turned her head and her fluffy white hair bobbed about. 'You can, Joseph Broomfield,' she said, handing over the tartan trolley on wheels and giving him a thorough look up and down. 'Well, you've grown up a bit. How was America?'

'Shirley,' he said, recognising the old woman and marvelling that she was still alive – she'd been ancient even when he was a child. 'It's good to see you again.' He leaned over the trolley to give her a kiss on the cheek. 'America was a great adventure.'

'Are you stopping for good?' She scanned him with unblinking eyes.

'For now, yes.' He gave a cursory check outside before shutting the door.

'Excellent.' She seemed genuinely pleased. 'They tried to close down the village stores, you know, but the residents were having none of it. We protested,' said Shirley, proudly. 'Now a lovely lady called Beth runs it and there's a group of volunteers that all do an hour or two each to help out. I'll put you down for a shift.'

'Er, well, I'll be busy setting up the new veterinary practice and—' But it seemed Shirley wasn't really listening.

'Now, are you sure your fancy American veterinary qualification allows you to practise over here?' She narrowed her eyes at him.

'Yes, I've been accepted by the Royal College of Veterinary Surgeons, so I'm good to go once I get the practice up and running.' The nearest vet was in Stow-on-the-Wold in one direction and Cheltenham in the other since the local village offshoot had been closed some years ago. He'd spoken to both practices and, whilst they weren't over the moon about the competition, they both admitted there was more than enough business.

Shirley waved her hand as if swatting a fly only she could see. 'Excellent.' She popped her hand into the trolley, barely lifting the lid, and he thought for a moment she was going to produce a rabbit like a magician. Instead she pulled out a bottle. 'Sherry?' she offered.

This probably explained why she was so well preserved. 'No, thanks. What can I do for you, Shirley?'

'Ah, now, here's the rub.' She took a swig from the bottle and made an *ahhh* sound. 'What would you give someone with arthritis?' She patted the top of the trolley.

Joe wasn't sure if it was a trick question or not. 'Um, you know I'm not allowed to treat people. Right?'

This set Shirley off cackling, like a witch from *Macbeth* but jollier. 'It's okay, I'm not after a shot of ketamine.' She tilted her head as if considering something. 'Arthritis in animals – what would you recommend?' She fixed him with a disconcerting stare.

Joe was puzzled by the random question. It was as if she was checking he was fit to practise. He treated it like an exam. 'Well, it would depend on the animal, its age, medical history and the severity of the condition.'

'Cat. Sixteen. No other problems. Stiff as a board.'

Joe chuckled. He was warming to the game. 'Okay, assuming the stiffness isn't rigor mortis . . .' Shirley thumped him on the arm for his cheek, and as he laughed he marvelled at the force behind the tiny woman's swipe, 'then I would ask if the owner would like to try to help the condition with food supplements first. I'd recommend cod liver oil or green-lipped mussel extract. Then I would discuss options like acupuncture.' Shirley's eyebrows shot up. 'I know, makes a change from cats sticking their claws in us, but it has good results. Alternatively, I would prescribe Metacam drops and want to see them again in six weeks' time.' Shirley was nodding sagely. 'Did I pass?' asked Joe, trying to make eye contact as Shirley returned the sherry to the trolley and patted the lid.

'Hmm.' She looked up. 'I'll let you know,' she said slowly. 'Right, I'd best be off. I can't be hanging around here all day.' She scuttled for the door, trolley first. Joe stepped to the side.

'Okay. Nice to see you again, Shirley. Have a lovely Christmas.'

'Will you be joining us at the pub for Christmas dinner tomorrow?' Shirley asked.

'Don't you have to book?'

'Nah, they'll squeeze another one in. Especially if I say you're my date.' She nudged him with a bony elbow and gave another cackle.

'I'll think about it,' he said, touched at her offer. 'Take care going down the hill, Shirley.' He had visions of the trolley setting off with her flying behind it. He picked it up and set it down outside for her.

She held up a hand as she shuffled off. He'd nearly shut the door when he heard her call his name again. He opened it a fraction. 'In case I never said. I was very sorry to hear about your parents.' She gave a firm nod and then carried on down the hill.

Joe was going to respond but she'd caught him unawares. Instead he just stared after the retreating figure. Eventually he took a steadying breath, closed the door and went in search of a much-needed beer.

Emily observed that the blue room was large, and indeed, extremely blue: the walls, carpet, curtains, bed covers and even a throw across the end of the bed were all in various shades of the same colour. The only exception was a procession of large dark wood wardrobes and a matching dressing table, like an indoor wooden Stonehenge. Emily unpacked her things whilst Zach and Jessie set about putting up the camp bed where the little girl would be sleeping for the next couple of nights. Emily hadn't realised they'd be sharing a bedroom with Jessie – this obviously ruled out anything physical. Normally this would have put more than a dampener on her Christmas but, given the fix she might be in, sex was the furthest thing from her mind. Thoughts of the pregnancy test and Lottie in the village shop dominated her thoughts. She wasn't sure if it was a good thing or bad thing that Lottie hadn't outed her immediately. Initially she'd been relieved, but now she was waiting for it all to blow up. Her own sister would definitely not have kept quiet and, despite what Zach had said about his sister being a good egg, it was hard not to assume that Lottie would be the same.

Zach and his daughter seemed to be having fun pretending the sleeping bag was a tunnel, so she opened up Zach's case and started to take things out and hang them in the antique wardrobe.

'Hey!' said Zach, his tone uncharacteristically sharp. 'There's no need. I'll unpack later,' he added, in a much softer tone. 'Why don't you go and find Lottie? Have some one-to-one time. Get to know her before the rabble arrive?'

Emily really didn't want to spend any one-to-one time with his sister. In fact, she was intending to spend the whole of Christmas avoiding exactly that. The last thing she wanted was to be confronted about her pregnancy test. Worse still, what if his sister said something directly to him about it? Actually, it probably wasn't a 'what if'; more of a 'when'. She was bound to, wasn't she?

Emily was simply mortified that the woman from the shop had turned out to be Zach's sister. He'd never said that she worked there. But then Zach rarely said much about his family at all. She wished now she'd not been quite so keen to spend Christmas with them in a remote Cotswolds village.

'Emily?' Zach waved a hand in front of her face. 'Are you okay?'

'Sorry. Miles away,' she said, realising she hadn't responded. 'No, I'm sure Lottie's got enough to keep her busy. It's probably best if I keep out of the way.'

'Okay,' he said, with a shrug.

'Where's the loo?' she asked, picking up her handbag.

'Along the hall. Last door on the left.' And he went back to trying to capture Jessie in the sleeping bag while she giggled excitedly.

Emily left the room and tried to control her rampant thoughts. She needed to do the test and find out what she was dealing with. At least then she could work out what, or if, she needed to do anything. She scurried along the dark corridor, her heels making an echoey sound on the wooden boards as they creaked. When she got to the end, there was a door on each side. Which one was it again? She could hear voices. She leaned to the right and the door suddenly burst open, making her squeal in fright.

'Oh my, don't you look guilty?' said a tall, well-made-up woman.

Emily knew she must look like a rabbit in several head-lights. 'Er, I was looking for the toilet.' The woman cast a critical eye over Emily, making her straighten her shoulders and suck in her tummy.

'Or listening at the door?'

'Oh, no,' said Emily, somewhat relieved that that was the assumption this woman had jumped to because she, no doubt, looked guilty of something.

'I believe you,' said the woman, offering a thin hand to shake. 'I'm Angie.'

'Oh, hello. Lovely to meet you. I'm Emily.' Great, it was Zach's mother. She clutched her handbag a little tighter.

Angie's face was blank. 'Hello Emily. Are you a friend of Lottie's?'

Emily felt momentarily stunned. Was this woman trying to unsettle her? Because if she was, she was doing a very good job. 'No. I'm Zach's girlfriend.' *Surely he's mentioned me*, she thought.

'Then it's lovely to meet you too. Scotty, darling, come and meet my Zach's latest.'

Emily felt a little winded by the statement. She was in two minds whether to run back to Zach or lock herself in the bathroom. An auburn-haired man with a broad, friendly grin popped his head into the hallway. 'Sorry, just taken all my clothes off,' he said. Emily's face must have registered her alarm. His grin broadened further. 'I'm going for a shower.' He offered a hand to shake and Emily took it briefly, looking away in case the door opened too much.

Then silence fell. Angie and Scott were looking at Emily and she felt distinctly uncomfortable. 'Which one was the bathroom again?' she asked.

'Could you wait until Scott's had his shower? Or there's one downstairs?' asked Angie.

No! Emily wanted to shout. *No, I can't wait a minute longer, but I also probably won't be able to pee if I know you're all hovering outside waiting for me to finish*. She gave her sweetest smile. 'Of course. Take as long as you need.'

'I'm looking forward to getting to know you over the next few days,' said Angie, with a smile that would challenge Cruella De Vil for malevolence.

Emily nodded and tried to look happy about the prospect as she retreated along the corridor.

* * *

Lottie had been avoiding the difficult conversation of where Great Uncle Bernard was going to move to when the house was sold. She had tried a couple of times to go over it in her head, but each time it had seemed so harsh that at the age of seventy-two and in wobbly health he was being forced out of somewhere that had been his home for the last twenty-odd years. Lottie had decided that she would encourage her mother and her uncle to have that conversation with Bernard over Christmas. They would be far better at it than she would be, and hopefully they had already thought through some suitable options for the elderly man.

A whirring of the motorised wheelchair announced Bernard's arrival. 'Hi, Uncle Bernie. You okay?' said Lottie, without turning around.

'I'm grand, as always. How are you getting on?'

'I'm fine,' said Lottie, but the manic giggle that followed gave away that she wasn't. Despite her list, everything already felt out of control. That feeling hadn't been helped in the least by the shock return of Joe, who kept popping up in her mind like a cork bobbing to the surface.

'Have you cooked the ham?'

'I don't think it needs cooking. Does it?' Lottie had struggled to get the huge joint that had been part of the order Nana had arranged into the fridge.

'It does. Rose did it in the pressure cooker.'

Lottie knew her eyes had gone into cartoon mode. She hated the pressure cooker. It made a weird hissing noise like it was about to explode, and seeing as terrorists used them to make bombs they were obviously a dangerous piece of kit. 'I'm not using that thing. It's lethal.'

'Ah, don't be a wuss. I'll show you.' And Bernard powered off towards the utility room. Lottie added 'cook 'ham' to her lengthy to-do list and then swiftly ticked it off, which gave her a little buzz of satisfaction. Although looking at all the other things still to do, it was a tad misplaced.

Bernard came back in with the pressure cooker on his lap and the large vacuum-sealed ham balanced precariously on top. 'I don't want to be bothering you, Lottie, but you have defrosted the bird. Haven't you?'

'Bum,' said Lottie, dashing past him and wrenching open the giant chest freezer where the turkey almost sneered back at her. She managed to lug it out without falling in and plonked the heavy solid mass on the kitchen table with a thud. They both stared at the imposing frozen lump.

'Hot water,' said Bernard.

'Sorry, what?'

'Sit it in hot water to defrost overnight. It'll be fine.'

'It has to be, otherwise it's salmonella all round.' Lottie ran her fingers through her short hair. 'Or Marmite sandwiches.'

'Ew, I don't know which of those would be worse.' Bernard pulled a face and moved round to the cooker. How had she forgotten the turkey? And if she'd forgotten that what else had she missed off her list? 'It's okay if Dayea joins us for dinner tomorrow, isn't it?' he asked.

'Um . . .' Lottie was frantically scanning her list but not really taking any of it in.

'Because I've already invited her.'

'In which case it's absolutely fine,' said Lottie, giving the old man a pat on the shoulder. It was a very big turkey and, assuming it did defrost in time, then there would be enough to go around.

'Champion,' said Uncle Bernard. 'You know Rose would

be proud of you standing up to everyone over this.' He looked at her with sincere eyes and hugged the ham. 'You did the right thing, Lottie. Families should be together at Christmas, despite how much they think they shouldn't be.'

Lottie had a lump in her throat almost as big as the turkey, so she just gave him another pat on the shoulder.

Chapter Six

Lottie was busy making sausage rolls. She appeared to have more flour on herself than anywhere else. Nana's handwritten recipe had very few instructions. 'Knead pastry' was an example. No explanation of what type of pastry or for how long to knead it or exactly what kneading was for that matter. Lottie had thumped it about a bit and now, despite the abundance of flour, it was firmly attached to the worktop. Lottie huffed and a cloud of flour plumed in front of her. She decided she and flour were not a good combination. This was stupidly hard.

Footsteps coming down the stairs at high speed announced Jessie's arrival. 'Hiya,' said the little girl, running into the kitchen. 'Where's the Duchess? I couldn't find her before.'

'I don't know where she's got to. She had a bit of a fright earlier and she's had two baths today so I think she's hiding. Why don't you help me instead?' asked Lottie. Jessie nodded happily. 'Great. Please can you lay the table in the snug with the white tablecloth and the pretty mats? They're in the sideboard in the dining room.' She didn't get a reply because Jessie was already running off.

Lottie crossed 'lay table' off her list. She had another

look at the sausage roll recipe, and seeing Nana's neat handwriting afresh spiked at the sadness inside her. She took a moment to compose herself. It would be ridiculous to cry over a sausage roll recipe.

The clang of the bell pull sounded through the house. She pulled back her shoulders, grabbed a damp sponge and rubbed at her hands as she went to the front door.

'Auntie Nicola, hello – and happy Christmas,' said Lottie, greeting her aunt warmly at the door. Nicola dodged a doughy hug and stepped inside.

'I always think it should be merry Christmas – otherwise happy gets overused with Christmas and New Year. Don't you think?' said Nicola.

'Um, not really.' Lottie gave her hands another rub and watched her uncle struggling with a large case and a bag as the rain pelted down on him. He eventually lugged them inside to the background noise of Nicola's tutting.

'Uncle Daniel,' said Lottie, giving him a kiss and ignoring the large smudge of flour she left on his cheek. 'New hair cut?'

Daniel rubbed his hand over his newly shorn head self-consciously. 'Bald patch was expanding so it was time to bite the bullet. Happy Christmas, Lottie. Are you baking?'

'Sausage rolls,' she said, trying not to sound too pleased with herself. Uncle Daniel was nodding at her. 'My first time,' she added. He no longer looked so enthusiastic.

'Come on, Rhys,' yelled Aunt Nicola, through the open door. Their nineteen-year-old son was sitting in the back of their Range Rover with his head bent down. He didn't respond.

'He's got his headphones in, he'll never hear you,' said Uncle Daniel, rolling his eyes out of sight of his wife. 'Leave him. He'll come in when he's ready.'

Lottie pushed the door closed, thankful to shut out the wet and cold. It wasn't looking like it would be the white Christmas she'd hoped for. She was an incurable romantic, especially during the festive season. She didn't care that some people thought it was commercial; she loved every little bit of it, from the hustle and bustle of Christmas shopping to pulling crackers – it was all part of the fun to her. But the Christmases when it snowed always felt extra special.

'Are you both well?' asked Lottie.

'I'm very busy,' said Nicola.

'What with?' Daniel was scowling at his wife.

'My business. I'm swamped right now. I did wonder if we should consider dressing the manor for sale. My company could do it for a fee. We could take out all the outdated furnishings and show a buyer its potential.' Nicola eyed the antique dresser in the hallway, now heaped with coats.

'I don't know—' began Lottie.

'We're not spending money on this place,' Daniel interjected. 'Any buyer will need to see its potential with or without new cushions.'

'There's far more to interior design than cushions,' said Nicola, giving Daniel a frosty glare.

'Could have fooled me,' muttered Daniel.

'Shall we take the blue room?' asked Nicola, shooing her luggage-laden husband upstairs.

Lottie pressed her lips together. Here we go again. 'Actually Zach has taken that one. I thought—'

'Roman room it is then.' Nicola gave a tight smile.

'Ah, sorry. My mum has bagsied that one. She's brought her new boyfriend.' Nicola fixed Lottie with a hawk-like stare. 'Green room is all made up. And I'd assumed Rhys would be in the box room as usual. Well, not quite as usual, I've moved the rest of Nana's doll collection in there.' Lottie gave a jaunty shoulder shrug.

'What about Rose's—'

'Noooo,' said Daniel cutting over her. 'We'll be fine in the green room, Lottie, thank you.' She heard them bickering all the way up the stairs and along the corridor, until they finally shut the bedroom door behind them.

Lottie let out a sigh. That was it; everyone was here. Although, technically, Rhys was still in the car; but he was on Manor land so that counted. She could finally relax and start focusing on everyone enjoying Christmas – because ultimately that was the only thing that mattered.

Lottie made a cafetière of coffee, filled the large teapot and added a jug of squash for Jessie. She grabbed a can of Coke for Rhys and laid out a selection of biscuits – some from the cheap box and some from the posh one (like Nana used to do). 'They'll never know they're not all the pricey ones,' she'd say, and she was right. When everything was ready, she went in search of people. It seemed they had all squirrelled themselves away in their rooms since arriving, and Lottie intended to root them out. She headed upstairs, deciding she'd pop to the loo first. When she reached the toilet she heard someone behind her. Emily gave a weak smile, looked away and headed back to her room. *Odd*, thought Lottie.

Whilst in the bathroom, she checked there were enough towels and toilet rolls; she knew they'd go through lots over the next couple of days. Her mother, for one, didn't seem capable of reusing a towel – they went in the laundry after barely getting damp. Lottie went along the hallway tapping on the bedroom doors. 'It's the tea fairy! Tea, coffee and biscuits being served in the snug.'

Jessie was out first. 'Biscuits! Hooray!' She raced past Lottie and downstairs, closely followed by her father.

'Biscuits! Hooray!' he mimicked, giving Lottie a wink as he scooted past her. She chuckled at him. Despite what he'd been through over the last few years, he was still the big kid she remembered.

'Is it decaf?' asked her mother, joining her on the landing.

'Nope. It's fully leaded, just how Nana liked it.'

Her mother winced. 'Fine by me,' said Scott. 'I like strong coffee. I have two shots when we go to Starbucks,' he added, looking completely serious. Lottie refrained from the urge to congratulate him. He seemed nice enough, but she would be reserving judgement as her mother's men tended to start off okay but then would get rapidly bored with her mother's high-maintenance ways. Before long they were a mere speck on the horizon.

Lottie checked that Daniel, Nicola and Rhys were joining them and then followed the others downstairs to take up the role of hostess. It was strange without Nana. She had always done all of this. She had been a proper matriarch, and an excellent host, so it was more than daunting that that role should fall to Lottie this Christmas. Lottie wasn't sure she was up to it – she certainly wouldn't deliver to Nana's high standards – but she would do her best, and that was all she could do.

Jessie was already eating a biscuit and nursing a glass of squash when she entered the room. 'I hope you've saved me a chocolate one,' said Lottie.

'Oreos?' asked Scott, appearing behind her. She wouldn't have put him down as an Oreo person. People's biscuit choices fascinated Lottie. She doubted that you could tell a lot from it, but it interested her all the same. Personally, she was a big fan of the custard cream but loathed Bourbons. They promised so much – they looked like a chocolate biscuit – but they didn't taste of chocolate, so they let you down. Joe was a Bourbon biscuit.

She tried to banish thoughts of Joe and Bourbon biscuits from her mind. Zach was watching Scott, and Lottie watched them both. At last Zach spoke. 'Hi, I'm Zach,' he said, offering a hand. Scott juggled his biscuit and shook hands with Zach. 'Do I know you?' asked Zach, scrutinising Scott's face.

'I don't think so,' said Scott. 'Do you drink in the Bricklayer's Arms in West Norwood?'

'Er, no, can't say I've ever been to that part of London,' said Zach.

'Then I've probably got a double.' Scott gave Zach a manly slap on the shoulder, although Lottie thought she saw a glimmer of anxiety in his eyes as he did so. He went to snuggle up to Angie, which was about as far away from Zach as he could get.

'You okay?' Lottie asked Zach quietly.

'I know him from somewhere. I just can't place him, and it's bugging me.'

'It'll come to you when you least expect it,' she said, dunking a shortbread finger quickly in her tea. She watched Dayea fussing over Bernard, adjusting the rug over his knees and ferrying cups of tea and assorted biscuits to his side. She was a sweet lady and very attentive, especially given what she got paid. Even though her English was as good as any native speaker, she wasn't a chatty sort of person. Lottie often wondered how old she was. Her minimal wrinkles and dyed-black hair made it tricky, but she guessed she was in her early sixties. She caught Lottie staring and gave her a sweet smile before sipping her tea.

'Who's coming to the carol service in Henbourne this evening?' asked Lottie. It was one of their many family traditions. There was a set agenda that a Collins family Christmas ran to, and this was a key Christmas Eve event.

'No thanks; I'll babysit for Jessie,' said Rhys quickly, which was the most he'd said since he'd got there apart from mumbling 'No WiFi' a few times.

'Thanks, mate,' said Zach.

'Aw, but I'm big now. Why can't I come?' Jessie pouted.

'Because it finishes late, and if you're not in bed when Santa comes he won't—'

'Okay. I get it,' said Jessie with a huge grin.

'Is it far away?' asked Emily, without making eye contact. Lottie wondered if she had done the pregnancy test yet. Something flashed through her stomach – a physical memory – and she tried to ignore the pain in her own past. This was different; Emily had Zach, assuming she got around to telling him.

'No, the church is about a fifteen-minute walk. It's probably the only time they have a full house. Loads of people come from both villages: Dumbleford, which is at the bottom of the hill, and Henbourne on the Hill, which is, well, on the hill,' explained Lottie.

'Count me in,' said Emily, and Zach slipped an arm around her waist. The way he was looking at Emily warmed Lottie's heart. She hadn't seen him look at anyone that way since Melissa. Lottie shook her head: the thought of Zach's wife had made more skeletons rattle around her mind. Zach gave her a look and she froze. All this time, she had never revealed Melissa's secret, and she wasn't about to now.

'I'd like to go,' said Bernard. 'Not sure my steed is up to the return journey though.' He patted the arm of his wheelchair. Going down the hill was fine, but getting back up stretched the battery to its limit. He had been known to stop the traffic by zigzagging up the middle as the gradient was a little on the steep side. The puzzled looks on the faces of the queuing tourists was always entertaining.

'I'll drive you, Uncle Bernie,' offered Daniel. Nicola gave him daggers which he merely shrugged at.

'Thanks, Daniel. I missed it last year. I wasn't too good, health-wise.'

Lottie waited for him to say that this year would be his last Christmas, but he didn't. She and Zach exchanged bemused looks. There was still plenty of opportunity for him to mention it, and he surely would.

Lottie was cheered to see her family interacting; so far there had been no arguments, which was probably some sort of record. She sat back with a happy sigh and enjoyed the peace while it lasted.

Lottie had left everyone to a game of Ludo and was concentrating hard as she iced the Christmas cake. She had made it straight after the funeral and it had looked great when she'd taken it out of the oven, but shortly afterwards it had developed a big dip in the middle. She'd been pouring brandy over it for a few days and had put a big slice of marzipan in the dent and covered it all in icing in the hope that nobody would notice. As she went to the dining room to retrieve the old cake decorations to distract attention from the cake's failings, she caught Zach creeping out of the drawing room backwards like a cartoon burglar – all he needed was a stripy top and a bag with SWAG emblazoned on it. He took his time to shut the door carefully.

'What are you up to?' she asked, loudly. It had the desired effect; he jumped and held his hand to his chest.

'Bloody hell! Don't do that.'

'You're up to something. Come on, spill.'

'What? I'm not doing anything.' Lottie gave him a well-practised look – it was the one she reserved just for her brother and had perfected when they were kids. 'Okay.' He held up his hands. 'You got me. I was trying to find that little car ornament of Nana's. I was going to ask if I could have it to remember her by, seeing as you and I weren't left anything in the will.'

Lottie eyed him suspiciously. 'It's in her bedroom. If you give me five minutes, I'll come up with you.'

'I can go,' he said.

'Actually, I've not been in her room since . . .'

Lottie felt foolish, but ever since Nana had died, she couldn't bring herself to go into her bedroom. It felt like she was intruding, which was silly, but it was the thought of all her things still being there and her not.

'I understand. Of course we can go together.' He gave her arm a squeeze. She loved her brother and she knew he loved her too. They had been through a lot and had always been there for each other. Now that Nana had gone, he was the one person she knew she could rely on.

Lottie followed Zach upstairs and they paused outside Nana's bedroom door. 'You ready?' he asked, and Lottie nodded. She took a moment to compose herself; it was just a bedroom, there was nothing to fear, and yet all the times she'd thought about going in she'd found a good reason not to. Zach gave her a reassuring smile and opened the door. It was dark and he flicked on the light switch. They peered inside. This was the biggest bedroom: the walls were papered with tiny pink flowers dotted about on a fresh white background, and there was a large antique sleigh bed in the middle of the far wall, a painted blanket box at its foot. The bed covers were ruffled as if Nana had just got up and was maybe pottering about the kitchen in her dressing gown.

Whilst Lottie viewed the room from the safety of the doorway, Zach strode over to the dressing table. Lottie reckoned Nana was one of the few people still to have one and actually use it. A walnut jewellery box sat on top with a bottle of Samsara next to it – Nana's favourite perfume. Zach opened a drawer and chuckled. He held up four pots of Nivea face cream.

'Do you think she was expecting a siege?'

'More likely they were on two for one,' said Lottie. Nana loved a bargain.

Zach started opening and closing the drawers either side of the dressing table. Lottie didn't like the sensation it gave her. She felt like a grave robber. These were Nana's things – her private things.

She stepped into the room. 'Stop.'

Zach saw her expression and paused. 'I know this is tough, but someone needs to go through everything. And when we finally find a buyer we'll need to get the whole place emptied.'

Lottie felt like crying. This was all horrid. The world, and most notably her family, moved on regardless, and it shocked her. The sad thing was that she knew Zach was right – and after Christmas she'd be left to sort it all out on her own. She should be seizing the opportunity for some help. Zach went back to checking the drawers.

What would Nana say? 'You've got a backbone – so let's see it.' Lottie straightened her shoulders. 'Will you give me a hand with these bed covers?' She marched over and began taking off the pillowcases. She should have stripped the bed weeks ago.

'Yeah,' he said, sounding distracted. 'Looks like Nana did her Christmas cards early.' Zach held up a wodge of envelopes. He joined Lottie at the bed and flopped down on it, sorting through the pile. 'Here you go,' he said, handing her an envelope with her name on.

Lottie took the envelope and studied the handwriting. Nana's tiny perfect lettering stared back at her. It was the sort of writing that people often commented on – neat and uniform, but with a distinct style, very like Nana herself.

Zach found his envelope and ripped it open. He didn't look at the front of the card, which Lottie knew Nana would have carefully chosen. He read the inside and she saw him jolt like he'd driven over a speed bump too fast.

'You okay?' she asked.

Zach looked at his sister. 'You'd better open yours.'

Chapter Seven

Lottie stared at the front of the pretty card for a moment before she opened it. She was surprised to see the inside cover filled with Nana's writing.

My dear, dear Lottie,

There is no easy way to tell you this, hence I have taken the coward's approach and decided to write it in this card. I am sorry to tell you that I don't have long left to live. I have cancer and the doctors have told me that I have about three months. That is very hard for me to write and would be even harder for me to say to your face.

I don't want to dwell on my health. I can't stand it when old people constantly go on about what's wrong with them. If I get like that you have my permission to shoot me.

I have loved having you home for the last few weeks but I don't want to be a burden to you, so when the time comes I will be going into a hospice – please don't challenge me on this. I have my pride.

There is also something I want you to do for me – talk to Joe Broomfield. Life isn't easy and we make the decisions we do with the best of our knowledge and with the best of intentions, but keeping secrets is like a cancer and if you don't sort it out it will eat away at you.

I intend to make this Christmas a very special one. Here's to a happy family Christmas and a prosperous New Year for us all.

With love,

Nana

X

P.S. Seize every opportunity that comes within reach. They are often fleeting, so go with your gut.

Lottie felt Zach's arm across her shoulders and she quickly closed the card. She could no longer see properly thanks to the tears streaming down her cheeks. She hadn't been aware that Nana had known she was ill until now. Clearly it wasn't the bolt from the blue they had all believed it to be; Nana had been keeping the biggest secret of all. Although looking at the pile of cards addressed to each of the family, Lottie surmised that Nana had intended to hand them out and tell everyone before Christmas. In the end, she didn't get the chance.

Lottie pulled a tissue from her pocket and blew her nose. Zach's card was open and she read it on the sly. Most of it was very similar, but what she had asked of Zach was for him to hold Melissa in his heart yet open up his life to love again; both for his sake and Jessie's. Zach caught her looking.

'What did yours say?'

'Same,' she said, without making eye contact.

'Wise old bird, wasn't she?' he said with a chuckle. 'What should we do with these?' he tapped the card on the top of the pile.

'I guess you hand them out.' Lottie was already wondering what advice Nana had imparted in each of the other cards and was itching to find out.

'Who am I? Postman Pat?'

'There's a touch of ginger in there,' said Lottie, playfully tugging his hair. 'And if Mother visited Yorkshire, she'd most likely have slept with everyone in Greendale.'

'Ew, you have a sick mind.' He gave her a shove.

They fell silent. 'Maybe wait for a good time?' Lottie suggested, although she feared that with their family this might be a very small window to spot.

Emily had found herself sitting in the huge room that she would have called a lounge, but the family called a drawing room. She'd not been good at history at school, so she wasn't sure what a drawing room was for. Whatever they called it, this was a beautiful room: high ceilings, ornate cornicing and a proper chandelier in the middle of the ceiling – not a Downton Abbey-size one but still rather impressive. Perching on the sofa, she'd found a rare spot in the manor with okay signal, so she fired off a few last-minute emails from her phone. She loved her job in corporate recruitment and was close to getting a promotion. She'd worked all hours the past few weeks to land a new client and she was determined to get January off to a good start too.

Dayea joined her and sat on the same sofa. The two women smiled at each other politely. Emily decided to break the silence. 'Hi, I'm Emily.'

'I am Dayea. I am the carer for Bernard.'

Dayea was leaning forward as if expecting a similar job title from Emily. 'I'm Zach's girlfriend.'

'Yes, Lottie, she tells me about you.' Dayea did a lot of

smiling and nodding but it didn't quell the unease her statement had triggered in Emily.

'Oh, um. That's . . . what did she say?'

'She tells me she is very much wanting to meet you. Zach has said . . .' Dayea was looking at the ceiling as if trying to recall something. 'Zach has said "buggerall".' Dayea seemed happy with her recall.

'He hasn't said much about his family to me either. Do you know them well?' Perhaps this was an opportunity to get the inside track from someone outside the family.

'I know Bernard very well. He is a kind and funny man. His family they just see an old man in a wheelchair. I see a lifetime of stories and a good heart.'

'That's lovely. What about everyone else?'

'I also knew Rose. She was my friend. She was a lovely lady, very smart.' Dayea tapped her temple. 'She knows all the things that go on in the family.' Dayea moved her hands as if shuffling imaginary cards on a table.

'And what might they be? The things that are going on.' Emily loved a bit of gossip.

'They are like all families. They love each other but they don't always show it.' Dayea let out a giggle. 'Rose would say they are like a good cake – sweet, full of zest, and with plenty of nuts.'

Lottie had spent the next hour preparing the Christmas Eve meal, which had helped to take her mind off Nana's card for now. She rang the hand bell, a boot sale find from years ago. It was far less grand than it sounded, but came in useful in a sprawling house where shouting rarely worked. She started ferrying food to the large dining table as she heard doors opening upstairs and people approaching.

Dayea had fixed Bernard something earlier so whilst he

was taking a nap in the drawing room everyone else took a seat at the table and eyed the spread with interest. Zach unscrewed the wine and started filling glasses. 'Right. There are fresh rolls,' said Lottie, as Rhys leaned over and grabbed one, then dropped it because it was red hot, 'but be careful. They're straight out of the oven,' she said pointedly at Rhys, who gave a smirk in response. 'There's spaghetti Bolognese. Then cheese, crackers and Nana's chutney. And sausage rolls and mince pies.' She pointed to the latter items just in case people weren't sure, because they were homemade and had come out looking quite odd. She had been too generous with the sausage filling and it had escaped at both ends, plus they were slightly overdone.

'They look like poo,' said Jessie, covering her giggles with her hands.

'Hey, cheeky,' said Lottie, ruffling her hair, but the child did have a point. In their defence they had a lovely glaze, so 'shiny poo' would have been a more accurate description. 'Tuck in everyone.' And on cue, chatter started and arms came at the food from every direction. This was what Nana enjoyed – feeding her rabble of a family.

'I helped make things,' added Jessie over the chatter and Lottie kissed her head.

'Is there no ham?' asked Uncle Daniel, scanning the table from end to end.

'It's in the pressure cooker,' said Lottie. Daniel looked disappointed and helped himself to a pile of spaghetti.

'Is the Bolognese meat-free?' asked Angie.

'Er, no,' said Lottie casually. A penny rolled around her mind and finally dropped. 'By any chance are you vegetarian, Scott?' she asked.

'Vegan,' he said.

Bum, thought Lottie. She glared at her mother in an

attempt to convey her murderous thoughts. 'Mum, I wish you'd—'

'Reminded you?' butted in her mother. 'She often forgets that I'm vegan.' Everyone glanced in her direction and there was a brief pause in noise levels. Lottie wanted to call her out. Since when had her mother ever been a vegan? Or vegetarian? Or even keen on vegetables for that matter? Her mother appeared to be trying to communicate but her eyebrows weren't moving. The Botox was still doing its job. Despite this, Lottie got the message: *please don't out me as a committed carnivore.*

'Silly me,' said Lottie, slapping her palm to her forehead. 'Anyway I'm sure the spaghetti is vegan friendly and I think Nana has some jars of tomato sauce in the cupboard. There's also bread, cheese and hummus.' Veggie crisis averted, for now. She'd worry about Christmas dinner later.

'But is it *vegan* cheese?' asked her mother, peering at the cheese selection accusingly.

'No . . . it's not vegan cheese, but,' she checked the label on the tub of hummus, 'the hummus is fine.' She almost shouted, 'Hooray for the hummus!'

'I'm looking forward to your mince pies,' said Angie to Jessie, picking up one of the misshapen delights. Lottie wondered at the speed with which the food was disappearing around her.

'Auntie Lottie made those,' said Jessie. Angie gave Lottie a pitying look.

'Any suet in them?' asked Scott. Lottie nodded. 'Not vegan, Angie,' he said. Angie tried to look nonchalant but failed.

Oh well, thought Lottie. 'Happy Christmas Eve, everyone,' she said, raising her glass.

Lottie took her seat opposite Emily and helped herself

to some food. She noted that Emily was joining Jessie in having orange juice rather than wine and she wondered if that meant what she thought it did. It was clear she knew Lottie was watching her and she concentrated on her plate.

'Scott, what sort of thing are you into?' It was Lottie's thinly veiled attempt to discover if there was anything in the house she could subtly wrap up as a gift for him. Even though it was her mother's fault for not telling her, she couldn't bear the thought of Scott realising he wasn't on the guest list.

'Your mother,' he said, with a soft look at Angie. Uncle Daniel almost choked on his spaghetti, and embarrassed splutters echoed around the table.

'What's funny?' asked Jessie, frowning at the grown-ups.

Lottie gave up; they were worse than children. 'Nothing, sweetie, they're just being silly.' Lottie glared at Uncle Daniel and he thumped his chest.

'Went down the wrong way,' he said, smothering another fit of the giggles.

'What do you do for a living, Scott?' asked Zach, and Lottie silently thanked him for stepping in with her relieved expression.

'Trimmer,' said Scott and he carried on eating.

'What do you trim?' asked Zach.

'Someone's bush?' asked Daniel and the giggling started up again.

Scott chuckled, but thankfully seemed to have missed that the joke was on him. 'I'm a classic car trimmer. I replace interiors in vintage cars.'

'That must be a very skilled job,' said Lottie, glaring at the worst offenders.

'I don't know about that, but I do love it. It's great to

74

have the chance to work on something really old and make it feel new again.'

Uncle Daniel opened his mouth but the scowl Lottie shot him made him shut it again. 'You like old cars then?' asked Lottie.

'Oh, yeah. I like anything really old.'

That finished Daniel and he burst out laughing. Scott didn't seem to get the joke. 'Ignore them,' said Angie, through pursed lips.

'Lottie, how's *your* love life?' asked Uncle Daniel, once he'd recovered.

Lottie inwardly sighed but outwardly lifted her head high. 'All over, thanks. Anthony and I split up.'

'He never listens,' said Nicola. 'I told you about this. Anthony was having an affair with a solicitor? Barrister?' She looked to Lottie for confirmation.

'Barrister,' Lottie confirmed, ignoring the embarrassed faces around the table as they all tried their hardest not to look at her. She concentrated on her dinner.

Nicola continued, undeterred. 'Lottie dumped him and he sacked her. Understandable really. Far too difficult to work together after that.'

'And Lottie has more pride than that. She doesn't need a man like Anthony. Or any man for that matter. She's always been someone who can stand up to life on her own,' said Angie. Lottie blinked at her mother and her rare show of support. Angie gave a brief nod of understanding.

'What are you doing for a job now?' asked Nicola, turning to Lottie. All eyes followed.

'Nothing at the moment. I'm thinking I might retrain.' Her marketing degree had taken her firmly down the corporate route and she needed a change. The only positive of splitting up with Anthony was that it had enabled

Lottie to spend time with Nana, and as it turned out, that time had been particularly precious, as nobody except Nana knew those would be her last few months. During that time Lottie had relaxed and taken time to reassess a few things. At twenty-seven she had thought herself set on a path; Nana had seen it from a different perspective. She had made Lottie feel that she was young enough to change her mind. That she had plenty of time to strike out in a different direction; to reinvent herself, if that was what she wanted to do. Lottie had decided that it was what she wanted, although sadly Nana had died before they had managed to work out exactly what that different direction might be. And that was the really tricky bit – her path was as undecided as a butterfly's.

'When you say retraining, does that mean you're thinking of going back to uni?' asked Zach.

'Good idea,' said Nicola. 'Because when we sell the house, you'll need somewhere to live.' Zach was glaring at her. 'What? I'm just being practical.' She buttered her roll diligently.

'A place like this will take ages to sell,' said Zach, giving his sister a reassuring smile despite the death stares from his mother and uncle.

'I hope so,' said Lottie. 'I'm not sure about the practicalities yet – I've a few ideas but nothing firm. But talking of uni, how are you getting on, Rhys?' She was keen to turn the attention away from herself. He was studying Archaeology at Cambridge, as Aunt Nicola liked to drop into conversation at any and every opportunity.

Rhys seemed to freeze as the spotlight turned on him. 'Okay, thanks.' He bit into a sausage roll and that seemed to be the end of that conversation.

'He's too modest. Aren't you, Rhys? He's on for a first.

I mean, a first from Cambridge and he'll have the world at his feet.'

'Mum!' Rhys appeared to be shrinking with embarrassment.

'You should be proud,' she said. Nicola took a sip of wine and studied the glass. 'These are pretty.' Nobody engaged. 'Daniel, we need new wine glasses.'

'Why? Did you wear the others out?' asked Daniel and an amused titter rippled around the room.

Someone at the front door tugged at the bell pull, and Lottie and Rhys both breathed a sigh of relief. Lottie got up to answer it, but Bernard must have been woken by the bell as he and his speedy wheelchair beat her to it.

Lottie was pleased to see that it had stopped raining. Standing on the step was the estate agent.

'Hello,' said Lottie. 'Did you want to come in?' It was still bitterly cold outside.

'No, thanks. I'm not stopping. You're on my way home and I've just taken a call so I thought, as it's Christmas, I'd deliver the good news direct.'

'Good news?' Those words seemed to her to be in opposition. Lottie was aware of the others joining her and Bernard in the hallway.

The estate agent straightened his shoulders. 'We've had an offer on the house. Full asking price.' His eyes shone with glee as he spoke. 'Cash buyer so there's no chain. This place will be off your hands in no time.'

'That's fantastic news,' said Angie, clapping her hands together.

'No chance of anyone else being interested? An opportunity for a bidding war?' asked Uncle Daniel and the estate agent twitched a fraction and shook his head. 'Oh, well.'

'Shall I confirm that you've accepted their offer?' The

estate agent was leaning precariously forward in antici-pation.

'Yes,' said Angie and Daniel together.

Lottie struggled to find her voice. 'Who's bought it?'

'I think it's a company. I've only got a contact name. We'll sort out all the paperwork in the new year and we'll know a bit more then. Right, I'm off. Merry Christmas.'

Everyone seemed to be congratulating each other and they moved off to the drawing room. Lottie heard a cork pop and a cheer go up. She didn't move; she was in shock. Apparently it was the day for shocks. Uncle Bernard buzzed his chair forwards and shut the front door, reversed back and took hold of Lottie's hand. 'It'll be okay, Button. You'll see. Fresh start for all of us, hey?'

She dug deep. If Uncle Bernie could be positive when he was facing being homeless at seventy-two, she knew she should be making more of an effort. Although it wasn't the fact she was going to be homeless that had winded her; it was the thought that this house – Nana's house – would be lost forever. The one constant thing in her life would be gone.

Angie put her head into the hallway. 'Did you say some-thing about making mulled wine?'

'It's for after the carol service,' said Lottie, a little snap-pier than she intended.

Angie pouted. 'I'll have to stick to the Prosecco then.' Another cork popped behind her. How could they cele-brate losing the house?

'Hang on. That's for tomorrow,' said Lottie going after her mother. Thank goodness she'd kept some bottles in reserve.

Angie offered Lottie a glass. 'Oh, do lighten up, darling.'

Chapter Eight

Emily was trying to make herself useful by clearing the dinner table, but she'd reached the point where she didn't know where things went, and if she started opening cupboard doors she'd look like she was snooping. The dining room was a long room with pelmets and sweeping pale-green drapes at the window. The top half of the walls was covered in a shiny embossed wallpaper, with dark wood panelling to the bottom half, and there was a large redundant fireplace with an ornate gold-framed mirror above, which bounced back the light from the chandelier. Near the door was a beautifully carved clock case; on cue it chimed out six o'clock. It all seemed very grand to Emily.

She collected up the tablecloth and admired the table top. She'd not seen a table like it before. It had comfortably sat all of them around it in matching dark wood chairs. This place was a revelation to her. Of course she'd seen houses like this before – even checked a few out on the internet, dreaming about what she'd spend a lottery win on – but she'd never been inside one. Zach hadn't given her any inkling that his family had a place like this. But then why would he? He didn't seem to think it was a big deal. If he'd said they'd had a mansion she'd have thought he was showing off; or worse still, lying.

Lottie came in, looking paler than she had before. She looked around at the tidy room. 'Thanks,' she said. 'You didn't have to clear away.'

'I wanted to help,' said Emily, holding the place mats aloft. 'Where do these go?'

'Sideboard. End cupboard.' They exchanged hesitant looks.

'It's a lovely house. I can understand why you don't want to celebrate it being sold.'

'Thanks,' said Lottie. 'I just thought I had more time, that's all. I thought the same with Nana too.' Lottie gazed out of the window, although Emily wasn't sure what she was looking at as it was dark outside.

'I wish I'd met her,' said Emily.

Lottie turned to look at her. 'Nana was a force of nature. I honestly thought she was invincible. I know it sounds crazy, but she never acted old and I never considered a time when she'd not be here. I suppose I didn't want to think about it.'

'Zach said she practically brought you and him up.'

Lottie bobbed her head. 'Yeah, I guess she did. We were here on and off for most of our childhood. It's what's made this place feel like home.'

Silence claimed the space between them. Lottie went back to looking out of the window whilst she folded the tablecloth.

Emily needed to say something because the elephant in the room was so vast its trunk was up the chimney and its bum was hanging out of the window. She pushed the door to. 'I didn't know you worked in the shop.'

'I don't. Well, not really. The shop was going to be sold

80

so some locals set up a community project to save it. We all work an hour or two for free to keep it open for everyone to use.'

'That's a nice idea,' said Emily, wondering what to do with her hands. She wasn't sure how to bring up the tester kit. She knew she'd already said far too much in the shop to be able to pass it off as a purchase for a friend. She straightened her back. 'Thanks for not saying anything about . . .'

'Oh, don't worry. It's okay. It's none of my business.'

'Wow, you are a nice sister. Mine wouldn't think that. Any opportunity to stick her beak in my business she'd take it, especially if she could make me look bad or herself look better. Sorry, I'm sure you're not like that.' She hated it when her mouth went off without her brain getting on board.

Lottie smiled. 'I hope not. I just want Zach to be happy. He's been through a lot.'

'I know. And I don't want anything to mess up what we have. This whole missed period thing has taken me by surprise.' Lottie had such a kind and genuine face that Emily couldn't help but confide in her.

Lottie put down the folded tablecloth. 'Does Zach know?' She held Emily's gaze.

Emily shook her head. 'I didn't want to worry him if it's nothing, and I've not had a chance to do the test yet.' Every time she'd gone in search of a toilet it had either been occupied or Zach had intercepted her, and there were only so many times she could say she was going for a wee before he'd think she had something seriously wrong with her waterworks. The one time she had managed to dash in the loo she'd forgotten her bag – and therefore, the tester.

Lottie looked surprised. 'Are you putting it off?'

'I guess,' admitted Emily.

'Why's that?'

'I don't know. Bit scared I guess.' Although there was some comfort in not knowing. When she didn't know, she didn't have any decisions to make or anything to tell anyone – ignorance really was bliss.

Lottie tipped her head towards the door. 'No time like the present.'

Emily ran her bottom lip through her teeth. Perhaps she had put it off long enough.

'Time to decorate the tree!' hollered Jessie, running in and grabbing their attention. Jessie took Emily by the hand and she saw another opportunity to put off the inevitable for a little while longer.

Everyone was gathering in the drawing room to decorate the Christmas tree. Other decorations were up and scattered throughout the house, but the tree was always done on Christmas Eve. They formed a human chain and boxes and boxes of decorations were passed down from upstairs until they were all set on the floor in front of the large windows that dominated the main room, along with their lush gold drapes. Uncle Daniel was standing on a chair rearranging the lights and tutting to himself. Zach flicked the switch on the socket. The lights in Daniel's hand lit up and he nearly fell off with the shock.

'Bloody hell!' he shouted, wobbling violently and grabbing the tree for support.

'Nooo!' shouted Lottie, having visions of the whole lot going over. Uncle Daniel stabilised and returned to adjusting and tutting. Jessie skidded across the room and managed to halt her stockinged feet just short of the tree.

She was grinning broadly. Lottie remembered being that age and brimming over with the excitement of it all. She loved witnessing Jessie's enjoyment of Christmas. She didn't see her niece as much as she'd like, as Zach didn't live nearby. Time with Jessie always had an odd effect on Lottie – she enjoyed every minute, but each of those minutes was a stab in her heart that she herself didn't have a child.

'Come on, Button. Let's get cracking,' said Uncle Bernie, dragging her from her thoughts. Lottie took the lids off all the decoration boxes. This was Nana's prized collection, which she had lovingly added to over many years – she'd had a story about every bauble. Lottie wished now that she had taken the time to write the stories down because already, she was staring at an ornate peacock-patterned decoration and struggling to recall the tale that went with it.

'Okay, choose a box,' said Lottie, refocusing her mind on totting up how many they had. They were one box short. 'Mum, can you and Scott share a box?'

'Of course,' said her mother. 'As long as I get first pick.' Her mother studied the boxes and chose the one with the big glass baubles.

'You next,' said Lottie to Jessie, who went for the animal-themed decorations as Lottie knew she would. 'Okay, help yourselves.' She ushered Emily forwards: she seemed somewhat bemused by the process. Sometimes family traditions that made perfect sense to you were baffling to anyone else.

Lottie had the odds and sods box – baubles which had no real theme or dominant colour, but were pretty just the same. She breathed in the smell of the fresh pine tree. The smell transported her back to all those other

Christmases where she had done this exact same thing. She loved having a real tree, and this one was a beauty.

Everyone took the task seriously and found the perfect spot for their selection of baubles. They each took their time, apart from Jessie who had rushed to put all her animals around the lowest branches.

When they'd all finished moving and adjusting, they stood back to admire their handiwork. Lottie carefully unwrapped an ornate star.

'This star, Nana bought in Norway in 1978. It was the first Christmas decoration she bought for her new home, here at Henbourne Manor,' said Lottie. She addressed Emily and Scott, who were new to this, and thankfully were standing near each other. 'We have a family tradition that the youngest person always puts the star on the top of the tree. We've all taken our turn,' she said, looking at Zach and Rhys.

'Some people did it more years than others,' mumbled Zach loud enough for Lottie to hear. He'd never really forgiven her for only being two years younger than him.

'Hey, we mostly alternated until Rhys came along,' said Lottie. 'Here you go, Jessie.' She reverently handed her the sparkly star and Jessie took it, her tongue sticking out of her mouth in concentration. Zach lifted his daughter up and she tried to secure it on the top of the tree, but each time the weight of it made the top sway precariously.

'Too heavy,' said Zach.

'What happens now?' asked Jessie, handing the star to her father.

'We have a backup plan from when this happened a few years ago,' explained Lottie, returning the star to the box and getting out the stand-in.

'Whoa, what's that?' asked Scott.

Lottie felt defensive. 'It's our Christmas angel.' She passed the doll to Zach.

'Looks like vintage Barbie,' said Scott with a chuckle.

So does my mother, thought Lottie. Zach and Jessie placed the angel on the top of the tree. The doll's alarmed expression was perfect, given she had a Christmas tree shoved up her nether regions. Lottie glanced at Emily, who blinked away a confused look and swapped it for an encouraging one. Lottie knew the scrawny doll looked a bit weird, but it was their angel; and maybe this Christmas she was who they needed to watch over them. Lottie started a little round of applause and everyone joined in. She stood and looked at the tree for a moment. It was beautiful; the fairy lights twinkled rhythmically, making each bauble sparkle, each of them one of Nana's special memories, there for them to share. Lottie's eyes danced from one ornament to the next: the drummer boy Nana said reminded her of Zach; the puppy with a stocking in its mouth she'd known Jessie would love; a glass spiral she'd paid a fortune for but had to have; a hand-painted bauble she'd bartered for at the local Christmas fayre.

The lights suddenly went out. Lottie gasped.

Zach's head popped up from behind the tree. 'We're going out, and this is a fire hazard.' How to break the spell, thought Lottie.

Chapter Nine

Joe flicked through the TV channels and tried to ignore the little dog whimpering at the door. Everything on television was sentimental, or soap operas with long complicated stories that were now building to a dramatic festive climax, but were lost on anyone just tuning in. He sighed and switched it off. Being on your own on Christmas Eve sucked. Why he'd thought now was a good time to return to cold, wet Britain, he couldn't think. He'd been spontaneous and rash. Right now, he could have been in Florida at a friend's place enjoying sunshine and a cold beer. He'd been watching the updates on Facebook with increasing envy.

He was also bothered by the fact that things hadn't gone as he'd hoped with Lottie. He hadn't expected her to welcome him back with open arms – far from it. But he had hoped she'd react in some way. Of all the scenarios he'd run through in his head, her emotionless expression was not what he'd envisioned. He had thought at the very least she would have been shouting and throwing things at him – *anything* to show that she felt something, even if it was anger. But her complete lack of emotion told him all he needed to know. He was someone from her past, and he had the distinct feeling he should have stayed there.

The dog barked at him and it brought him back from his troubled thoughts. looked at the clock: a long evening stretched in front of him. And after that, the whole of Christmas. The scruffy little dog made eye contact and wagged his tail. Joe knew the dog wanted to go out, but he couldn't walk him without a collar and lead. Joe gave the dog a scratch round his ears. He was a sweet little chap, but sadly nobody had been in touch to claim him or register him as missing.

Joe went to have a root about. He didn't have a lot of stuff, he'd always travelled light, not feeling the need to have much in the way of possessions, so there was little point checking the things he'd brought from America. There was a cupboard in the kitchen which had a mixture of things that the owner had said he could help himself to as they'd been left behind by previous tenants. He went to check and the little dog scurried along with him, his claws sounding on the lino floor.

Joe scanned the cupboard shelves: clingfilm, mustard. Yuck. That stuff was disgusting. In the cupboard under the sink he found string, a Spider-Man football and a pink skipping rope. Joe had an idea.

After a bit of work with some scissors, his rusty knowledge of knots from Boy Scouts and a very patient little dog, Joe managed to fashion a harness out of the skipping rope.

'Right, little fella. Let's test this out in the garden first.' Given how the dog had run off earlier Joe wasn't about to risk losing him again, and he had no idea how he would behave on the makeshift leash.

The dog pulled as soon as Joe opened the back door,

but the harness held firm. It was around his chest and secured on top, so it wasn't going to hurt him even if he did pull. The rain had stopped but it was still blowing a gale and bitterly cold, and Joe pulled his coat tighter around him. They set off around the garden in the light from the kitchen window, and the dog seemed very happy to be outside; he bounced about frantically sniffing at the strange plants. It lifted Joe's spirits to see it.

This was why he loved animals. Despite how crap their life might be, they always took pleasure in the simple things. They lived in the now, not worrying about what had happened or what the future held, but enjoying the moment – despite everything. People could learn a lot from them.

Once the initial excitement had worn off and they were seeing the hydrangea for the sixth time, Joe's four-legged companion had settled into walking quite sedately at his side, although he was now looking up at Joe as if questioning why they were lapping the small garden.

'Okay, boy,' said Joe. 'Shall we test this out on a proper walk?'

Once he'd uttered the key word, the dog was back to bouncing up and down like he was on a trampoline. 'I'll take that as a yes,' said Joe.

They were soon heading down the hill into Dumbleford. This was where he'd gone to school. Henbourne had been too small to have its own primary school, and so was Dumbleford really, but together they'd made up the numbers to keep Dumbleford village school going. Joe did a lap of the large village green, while the dog managed to wee at every other of the little white posts that held up the looped chain fence surrounding it. He took in the hotchpotch of houses lit up by streetlamps, and remembered who had lived in them all, wondering to himself if those people were still around. The tearooms was still there, but the grocer's and pet shop had been turned back into homes. The Christmas tree stood grandly in the middle of the green, although he could only see its multi-coloured lights, flashing manically as if trying to hurry him along. Joe looked longingly at the pub. Its disturbing sign made him remember all the times he'd tried to get the name, the Bleeding Bear, into conversations with his mum and dad, as it was the closest he could get to swearing without getting into trouble.

The thought of his parents made him draw up his shoulders and increase his pace. He strode back up the hill, past Mr Bundy's cottage, towards Henbourne. He had known coming back would mean facing his past, and he was ready to do that. Thanks to the American predilection for therapy he had had more than his fair share, some of which he had found helpful. It had certainly made him consider coming back to England more than once, but in the end, it hadn't been a therapy session that had made him pack everything up and get on a flight.

Lost in thought, he found himself nearing the church. The sound of jolly voices drew both his attention and the dog's, who pulled at the skipping rope.

The vicar was standing at the lychgate welcoming people, wearing more decorations than the village green Christmas tree. As Joe approached, the church bells started ringing in greeting. He glanced at the clock tower: it was coming up to eight o'clock.

'Good evening,' said the vicar, a middle-aged man with a beard and a happy face.

'Hello,' replied Joe. 'Any chance you've seen this dog before? He's a stray.'

'Oh, now let's get a good look at you,' said the vicar, crouching down and making the dog pull to get a lick of his face. 'She's a lovely little thing, but I'm afraid I don't recognise her.'

'It's a boy,' said Joe, feeling he had to explain on the little dog's behalf.

'Right. Why don't you come in? It'll be a full house tonight, and you never know, it might trigger someone's memory.'

Joe faltered. It was a good idea, but he wasn't a church-goer. He had been, once upon a time, but too much had happened and his faith had been challenged to its limit.

'It's the candlelit carol service, nothing too heavy,' said the vicar.

Joe could feel the seconds ticking in his head as he took far too long to decide. It was like being in a game show as the time ran out.

'Joe!' someone shouted from up the hill. Joe looked to see Zach striding towards him with some of the Collins family, including Lottie, following behind.

Zach greeted Joe warmly, pulling him into a hug. 'Good to see you, mate.'

'You too,' said Joe.

'Ah, Lottie,' said the vicar. 'Perhaps you can convince this young man to join us.'

Lottie came to an abrupt halt and patted down her hair. 'Everyone's welcome,' she said. *More of her dismissive attitude*, thought Joe, watching her bend down to greet the dog, who was pulling hard to jump up at her. Joe knew her tights wouldn't last two seconds against claws and tightened his grip on the lead.

'You should join us. Carols on Christmas Eve – what's not to love?' said Zach. 'And there'll be mulled wine back at the manor afterwards if you fancy it. And for you too, Vicar,' added Zach, turning to address him.

'Very kind, but I have a date with a turkey that needs stuffing,' said the vicar, and he went to greet some new arrivals. The rest of the Collins clan arrived and all greeted Joe warmly, making him feel like a returning hero – a completely different vibe to the one he was getting from Lottie. Zach and the others headed into church, leaving Joe with Lottie still petting the dog at his feet.

'That's a special lead you've got there,' said Lottie, standing up and eyeing the pink skipping-rope handle wrapped round Joe's wrist.

'The latest from the Paris catwalk.' Both the dog and Lottie gave him a look.

'Still not tracked his owners down then?' asked Lottie.

'No, I wondered if they might be in there.' Joe indicated the church.

'Come on, Joe. You joining us?' called Zach, from the church doorway.

'Yeah. I think I will, if that's okay?' He directed his question at Lottie.

'Then we'd better go in before it's standing room only.' She turned and walked away, and Joe followed.

Inside the church, the bells were still audible. The dog started to bark, making all heads turn in their direction. *Nothing like making an entrance*, thought Joe.

'At least we know everyone's seen him,' said Lottie.

Joe noted the mixture of surprise and intrigue on people's faces, followed by muttered comments and a few pointed fingers.

Joe picked up the dog, who stopped barking, and the heads turned back to face the front. It seemed quite a few people had recognised Joe, but no one came to claim the dog.

Bernard had manoeuvred his manual wheelchair to such an angle as to block off the front row pew. He was shooing other people off it whilst simultaneously signalling to get Lottie and Joe's attention.

'Do we have to sit right at the front?' asked Lottie. 'There's space over there.' Lottie indicated Shirley waving to them, her white hair dancing in time.

Bernard huffed. 'I'm not sitting with her.'

Joe looked to Lottie for an explanation whilst he returned Shirley's frantic waves of greeting. She'd always seemed lovely; a little forthright, but kind-hearted – fairly typical of local residents, he remembered.

'Shirley was chosen to play Father Christmas at the Christmas fayre instead of him,' whispered Lottie.

Joe shrugged and tried to hide a smirk. 'She does have a moustache any wing commander would be rather proud of.'

'Bloody WI and its equal opportunities,' mumbled Bernard forcefully, ushering Lottie and Joe into the pew. They ensconced themselves at the front and, after a bit of a sniff around, the dog settled down between Joe's feet for a snooze. Joe took in his surroundings. The church was pretty much as he remembered it, although being Christmas there was lots of holly on the higher ledges and a number of decadent floral displays in deep reds and golds dotted down the aisle, cascading over the tops of their stands. Along every ledge there were large candles and, although they were lit, it wasn't that noticeable with the church lights up.

Joe studied the Nativity scene. He leaned towards Lottie to whisper to her and she flinched.

'You okay?' she asked.

'Yeah, but the Nativity scene is missing a wise man.'

Angie leaned in from the other side. 'Isn't that always the way?' she said, with a short cackle. She put her hand to her mouth as if the sound had surprised even her.

'Sorry,' said Lottie. 'She's been drinking.' She pointed at the Nativity. 'A wise man was stolen. It was front page news in the local paper.'

After a while the vicar came to the front and introduced himself, welcomed everyone and made an appeal for information about the little dog. Dutifully, Joe held him up at the right moment, triggering a chorus of *ahhh*s, but nobody rushed over to claim him. The vicar said a prayer and the lights dimmed. Joe lowered his head in respect and failed to stop thoughts of his parents creeping in. He was grateful when the vicar announced the first hymn: 'O Little Town of Bethlehem'.

When he looked up to sing, he took in the beauty of the church swathed in candlelight: the flickering flames casting shadows; the congregation bathed in a warm glow. It felt Christmassy and, at last, so did he. It had him belting out the words of the song, and the little lost dog joined in, barking through the chorus.

The more carols they sang, the more Joe relaxed. Seeing Bernard take a crafty swig from a hip flask and watching the way Lottie nervously adjusted her hair clip, he was flooded with memories of the warmth and love of the Collins family, which had been such a big part of his childhood. It was an unexpectedly nice way to spend Christmas Eve, and Joe felt that he had ticked another box on his journey to acceptance as he left the little church with good wishes ringing in his ears.

Joe had decided he should give the mulled wine at the

manor a miss. Lottie hadn't seemed keen to meet up again – she'd said the right thing, she always did, but her eyes told him something different. Aside from their exchange at the start, she'd barely said a word to him during the service, despite sitting next to him. Then again, what was there to say? They'd already spent far too much time apart. He knew the way he'd left all those years ago had been far from ideal, and his need to cut all ties with his former life must have been hard for Lottie to understand. With hindsight, he could see that he could have handled his departure far better. Hopefully someday Lottie would give him a chance to explain, but tonight definitely wasn't the moment.

'Joe, you're coming back, right?' asked Zach, falling in step with him as they reached the lychgate. Lottie was up ahead, and as the rain started again she guided her swaying mother in to the back of her uncle's car while he was busy wrestling Bernard's wheelchair into the boot. Joe wavered. He had nothing waiting for him back at the cottage apart from his own thoughts, which were always a dangerous thing to be alone with, and he supposed if things got awkward with Lottie he could simply leave. The dog gave a tug towards Henbourne as if trying to influence his decision.

'Sure. Why not?' And he started chatting to Zach whilst the little dog trotted along happily on his skipping rope.

Chapter Ten

Lottie was pleased to get back into the warm and dry. She pulled off her boots as Rhys met her in the hallway.

'Hiya Rhys. How did the babysitting go?'

'Really easy, thanks. Jessie spent most of the time playing with the Christmas tree.' Lottie's head shot up in alarm. 'Chill, it's fine. She said it was a magic present tree.' He gave a chuckle. 'She took herself off to bed not long ago because she wanted to make sure she was asleep before Santa came.'

'Great. How's the new house share going at uni?'

'Oh, you know. A bit messy in places but otherwise fine.'

'I can't believe in eighteen months you'll be graduated and probably working. Imagine that. My little cousin.' She reached up to ruffle his hair and he dodged out of the way.

'I've got a job already,' he said, his expression furtive.

'Oh great, doing what?' Lottie had been a part-time waitress when she was at university, and although the pay was rubbish, the tips had been pretty good.

'Car sales,' he said, with a grin.

'Blimey. How did you swing that?'

'Look, don't say anything to the rents. They don't know yet.'

'No, of course I won't.' Lottie understood, they'd only worry about whether he was spending enough time studying.

'Thanks Lottie. You're sound.'

'Thanks,' said Lottie. It was meant to be a compliment, but somehow it made her feel old. Playing to how she felt, she added: 'Make sure your degree doesn't suffer. All right?'

She hung up her coat and didn't pay much attention to Rhys's slightly confused expression. Her mind was focused on heating up the mulled wine and getting the nibbles into bowls. Angie joined her in the kitchen.

'So what's going on with you and little Joe Broomfield?' asked her mother, pinning her with her gaze.

'He's hardly little any more.'

'Don't deflect the question.'

'There's nothing going on. He left and now he's back.'

'Back with you?' Angie tipped her head forward in question.

'No. He's just back.' Lottie wanted to add that they were just friends, but right now she wasn't even sure of that.

'Well, I'm pleased you're not bothered,' said Angie. 'Any chance of a sandwich?' she asked, opening the fridge and scanning the shelves.

'I could do you a bacon sandwich.' She waited for the reaction.

Without hesitation Angie's face lit up. 'Marvellous.'

Lottie shut the kitchen door. 'I knew it. You'd no more turn vegan than wear cheap make-up. What are you up to?'

'Come on, Lottie. Scott is completely right for me in

every way.' Lottie raised an eyebrow. 'Apart from him being a committed vegan.'

And half your age, added Lottie in her head. 'But you lied to him. That's not a great start to a relationship is it?' She put the mulled wine on a low heat and started stirring.

'It's only a white lie.'

'There's no such thing. If he loves you, he won't care that you like to chow down on a lamb shank.'

'Shhh,' hissed Angie, checking over her shoulder. 'It's like a religion to him. Come on, I'm starved. Your spaghetti was bloody awful.'

'Thanks.' Lottie checked her to-do list. She wasn't past bartering. 'If you get the presents off everyone and put them under the tree, I'll make you a bacon sandwich after we've done the mulled wine.'

'Deal.'

'And make sure Jessie doesn't see the presents or you'll spoil everything.'

'Of course. I'm not completely heartless,' called back her mother as she left the kitchen.

Thankfully, Lottie had got the mulled wine ready before they went out, so it only needed heating and pouring into the punch bowl, which was waiting on one of Nana's best trays alongside a stack of ornately decorated mugs that Nana had brought back from one holiday or another. She took the lid off the saucepan and breathed in the smell; the mix of wine and spices was enticing. She was about to check the temperature when a scratch at the back door distracted her.

She opened the door and the Duchess shot in, but for the second time that day, she wasn't alone. She was carrying something small and brown in her mouth as she leaped onto the worktop. 'Duchess!' shouted Lottie, fearful that the soup disaster was going to be re-enacted with the mulled wine. She cornered the cat next to the large saucepan and scooped her up into her arms. *Phew, that was close,* thought Lottie. But as she lifted the Duchess up, the cat let out a meow of protest and promptly dropped the mouse into the mulled wine.

'Eek!' squealed Lottie and the mouse together. Lottie hastily put down the cat, grabbed a mug from the tray and scooped out the mouse. In two strides she was in the utility with the wine-soaked mouse skidding around the mug as he tried to escape. She tipped him into the mop bucket, put the lid back on and heaved a giant sigh of relief. The Duchess twirled around her legs proudly.

'Where's the mulled wine?' asked Angie, popping her head around the door. 'I don't think I can hold them off much longer.'

Lottie would have to sort out the mouse later.

It was almost ten thirty when Lottie entered the drawing room. The family was gathered and Angie was making final adjustments to the pile of presents now crowded around the base of the Christmas tree. It was a perfect picture of Christmas. The Duchess came to have a sniff, in a blatant attempt to identify her gift. Bernard clapped his hands together and Lottie heard the front door open as the walkers arrived back from church. Almost immediately there was the sound of frantic claws on wood and the little dog came hurtling into the room.

'Hey!' Joe shouted, somewhat belatedly.

The Duchess instantly puffed up to the size of an overinflated beach ball and took off at high speed across the nearest sofa. The little dog was in hot pursuit, his skipping-rope lead bouncing behind him, now somewhat redundant.

'Someone grab him!' called out Lottie.

'Get the rope!' shouted Joe, narrowly missing snagging it with his foot as the dog rushed past him.

A frenzied game of chase ensued, until the Duchess careered across the presents and dived up the middle of the Christmas tree. The dog followed, sending presents flying in all directions.

'My piles,' complained Angie, surveying the chaos.

'What's happening?' mumbled a sleepy voice from the doorway. Everyone froze. Jessie yawned and rubbed her eyes. They widened in disbelief as she took in the festively wrapped parcels scattered around. 'He's been,' said Jessie, a huge grin spreading across her face as she spotted something in the middle of the presents. 'My puppy!' she shouted, and she skidded up to the tree and wrapped the dog in a hug.

The dog seemed to consider whether to continue his tree ascent after the cat, but the draw of a cuddle proved too much and he returned the little girl's attention with doggy kisses.

'Oh, no,' said Zach, leaping in, 'he's not for you, Jessie.' It felt like everyone winced.

Jessie hugged the dog. 'But he's with the presents. Santa has delivered him,' said Jessie, matter-of-factly.

The scene Jessie had walked into would indeed reinforce her belief. 'Yes, but . . .' Zach seemed to be struggling to find a robust answer, 'sweetheart, he's not yours.' Zach's face was crumpled with the effort of breaking the bad news to his daughter.

The little dog was now snuggled in her arms, although he still had one eye on the cat stuck halfway up the Christmas tree. Jessie looked around at the assembled faces. 'Did anyone else ask for a puppy for Christmas?'

They all shook their heads. 'Then he *must* be mine,' she said, emphatically.

Zach's chin hit his chest. 'Can someone please get me a very large mulled wine?'

'Ah – about the mulled wine—' started Lottie, as pictures of the mouse doing an Olympic dive into it raced through her thoughts; but she was cut off by the cheer that went up when Angie walked in with the tray. Before she could say any more, Emily and Scott began ladling it into the mugs.

'Who wants one?' asked Emily, happily offering out a mug.

'But . . ' Lottie couldn't find the words as everyone crowded round.

Emily handed Lottie a mug. 'I thought I'd help.' Lottie stared at the mulled wine. A few moments ago a small mouse had been doing backstroke in it. 'Have I offended you?' Emily looked aghast.

Lottie gave herself a mental shake, Emily was trying to help. 'No, it's fine.' The mouse had only been dipped in it for a nanosecond. 'And thank you, that was kind.' Emily's smile returned and she pressed the mug on her.

Joe joined Jessie and Zach on the floor by the tree. 'Hiya, I'm Joe. I'm a vet. Do you know what a vet does, Jessie?'

Jessie nodded. 'You look after sick animals. He's not sick is he?' She looked alarmed.

'No. He's not sick, but he is lost. I think he might have a family somewhere. Maybe he was a stowaway on Santa's sleigh.' Jessie's mouth made a perfect 'O' shape. 'What I'm thinking is that he really needs someone to take good care of him over Christmas, but then he'll need to go home. Do you understand?' Joe gave the dog's head a pat.

Jessie's face was stony and Lottie thought she was going to cry. 'Sooo I get to have a dog, but only for Christmas?'

'I'm afraid so, sweetheart,' said Zach.

'Can I name him?' asked Jessie, her jaw tight. Joe shrugged, but Zach was shaking his head. 'I'm calling you Dave,' she told the scruffy little dog, who looked up into her eyes like he'd found the love of his life.

'Dave?' questioned Lottie, handing round more mulled wines.

'It's the name of her favourite minion,' explained Emily. 'It's a cartoon character,' she said to Uncle Bernard, who was looking puzzled. Lottie smiled inwardly. It said a lot about Emily that she knew this about Jessie. Although Zach had been keeping Emily to himself, it seemed they must have been spending quite a bit of time together, as Lottie had already noted that Jessie seemed very comfortable in Emily's company.

Lottie poured grape juice for Jessie and another on the quiet for Emily, just in case, and they all stood around the Christmas tree chatting and drinking. The Christmas cards flashed into Lottie's mind and she went to get them. She steeled herself and entered Nana's room on her own, keeping her mind on her task. As she picked up the cards, she noticed that Zach had left the bottom drawer open on the dressing table. She went to close it as she passed and something inside caught her eye. She bent down and picked up the car ornament Zach had been looking for earlier. How had he missed that? Popping it in her pocket, Lottie switched off the light and left.

Zach was coming out of the blue room and put a finger to his lips. 'I've put Jessie back to bed.'

'Without Dave?' said Lottie with a smile.

Zach looked momentarily confused and then recovered.

'Joe managed to convince her that the dog would be better staying with him tonight and he'll bring him back in the morning.'

'Christmas Day?' Lottie couldn't hide the alarm in her voice.

Zach shrugged. 'Clearly he has nothing better planned.'

Great, thought Lottie. *You don't see someone for nine years and then they're everywhere.*

They walked downstairs together. 'Here you go,' said Lottie, handing the car ornament to Zach.

'What do I want . . . oh yeah, great. Thanks,' he said, putting it in his trouser pocket. It wasn't the joyful response of someone who had been searching high and low for something. Lottie's suspicions of what Zach had been up to in the drawing room earlier increased.

'I thought it was probably time to hand these out,' she said, waving the cards.

As they approached the drawing room, they met Joe in the hallway. He was leaving with the dog under his arm. 'Me and Dave are off now,' he said.

'You don't have to go,' said Zach, looking at Lottie to back him up.

Joe looked conciliatory. 'I think we've caused enough chaos for one night.'

'Did you want to stay for lunch tomorrow?' asked Zach.

Joe looked at Lottie. 'I guess that's up to the chef.'

She could hardly rescind Zach's invitation. When she thought about it she'd rather know in advance if she had another one to feed, and she'd feel better knowing one way or the other if Joe was going to be there all day or not. 'It makes sense to eat here if you've got to walk back up with Dave,' she said.

She could see he was thinking about it. 'Thanks. I'd love to.'

'Great,' said Zach, slapping him manfully on the arm. 'See you tomorrow.' He headed for the drawing room.

'Night, Dave,' said Lottie, still amused by Jessie's name choice. She gave the dog some fuss.

Joe brushed his fingers through his hair and looked awkward. 'Look, you know we—'

'Not the time, Joe,' said Lottie. 'Night.' And without a backwards look, she followed her brother.

Lottie handed the cards to Zach, who gave her a long-suffering look as he saw the buck pass in his direction. She busied herself refilling people's glasses. The mulled wine had gone down a treat and there appeared to be no immediate ill effects from it having briefly been a mouse Jacuzzi.

'Can I have your attention for a minute?' announced Zach. Everyone stopped talking and looked at him. 'Lottie and I found some Christmas cards that Nana wrote before she . . . left us. It looks like she knew she didn't have long left and she's explained that in the cards.' He handed them around.

'She added a few words of wisdom to mine and Zach's and we're kind of assuming she's done the same in all of yours.' Lottie scanned the faces. They didn't seem quite so keen to rip them open now.

'You can open them in private, if you want to,' said Zach, giving Lottie a look.

Lottie sat down on the arm of the sofa next to her mother and hoped very much that she was planning to open hers now. Lottie sipped her mulled wine, eyeing her family over the rim of her mug. She noticed that Uncle

Daniel and Aunt Nicola had separate cards, which intrigued her. Rhys took his, stuffed it in his back pocket and carried on scrolling through his phone. Emily was watching too as, like Scott, she didn't have one to open.

'Aren't you going to open it?' Scott asked Angie. Lottie leaned back slightly so she was at a good angle if Angie opened the card.

'It's just a Christmas card,' said Angie, but Lottie could tell she was wary of what message might be inside.

Uncle Bernard opened his card and Dayea read it over his shoulder, which Lottie thought was a little impolite.

'Lottie, have we got any more of that fizzy stuff?' asked Uncle Bernard.

Lottie wanted to hang on to what they had left for Christmas dinner, so she was trying to form a response when her mother answered for her. 'I've seen four bottles in the utility, Bernie. Shall I get them?'

Bum, thought Lottie. 'They were actually for tomorrow.' Lottie didn't want to be a killjoy, but she liked a glass of fizz with her Christmas dinner. 'There's plenty of wine.'

'But we need fizz for a toast,' said Bernie, focusing on Angie, who was already on her feet. She duly returned with the bottles on a tray and a hotchpotch of glasses, as most of the appropriate ones were already in the ancient dishwasher. Lottie sent up a silent prayer to the god of domestic appliances every time she set the thing off.

Scott popped the cork on the first bottle and Lottie tried hard not to sulk whilst glasses were filled and passed round.

Bernard cleared his throat. 'It's a blessing to have all of you here this Christmas, and these cards from Rose show that she would have whole-heartedly agreed with me on that. She also offers a reminder that life can throw you unexpected curveballs; some good, and some bad. She's advised me to enjoy my old age and to squeeze every drop of joy out of it that I can. So I'd like to offer two toasts. Firstly, merry Christmas, Rose, wherever you are.' He held up his glass.

'Merry Christmas, Rose,' everyone chorused, and sipped their drinks in unison.

'And secondly, whilst we're together, there's something I wanted to tell you all,' said Bernard, and the family exchanged concerned glances. 'I'm conscious of the fact that I'm not a well man . . .'

'Here we go,' whispered Zach to Lottie. '*This'll be my last Christmas,*' he said, mimicking Uncle Bernie's voice, and Lottie dug him in the ribs to shut him up.

' . . . so I've been thinking seriously about my future,' continued Bernard. 'And I want to take matters into my own hands—'

'Not, not,' began Daniel, clicking his fingers as if trying to summon the word, 'that place in Switzerland.'

'Dignitas?!' said Lottie, her fingertips rushing to her lips with the shock of what this meant.

'That's it,' said Daniel, giving Lottie a congratulatory nod.

'No, you can't, Uncle Bernie.' Lottie was shaking her head and Zach put an arm around her shoulders to comfort her.

'Well I, for one, think it's very sensible,' said Aunt Nicola. Daniel shot her a look. 'What? If it's what he wants.'

Bernard cleared his throat again, but it was more of a half-chuckle. 'You lot do jump to some funny conclusions. I know I'm not in the best of health, but I'm not at death's door either. Lottie, love, cheer up.' He smiled at her. 'I'd like to announce . . .' He looked furtively at Dayea, reached out, took her hand and drew her closer to his chair. 'I've asked Dayea to be my wife and she said yes!'

It was as if someone had pressed a pause button: the whole room froze, with the exception of Scott, who popped the cork on the remaining bottle of fizz, sending the cork flying into the Christmas tree and scoring a direct hit on the Duchess who was still hiding there. With a screech of a meow she fell out of the tree and shredded a few presents in her haste to get away.

'Congratulations!' cheered Scott, and a mumbled echo ran around the roomful of stunned relatives.

Lottie downed her fizz in one go, fervently hoping tomorrow would be a less eventful day.

Chapter Eleven

It had been an odd evening: partly a normal Christmas Eve and partly an engagement party for Great Uncle Bernard and Dayea. Lottie had to admit that they seemed very happy – neither of them had stopped smiling since the announcement, which was lovely to see – but the looks that had been exchanged between the other family members conveyed their concerns. Dayea had been his carer for a while, but their burgeoning relationship had gone under everyone's radar.

As the old clock nudged midnight, Lottie was hand-washing the glasses. She was startled when her mother dashed into the kitchen. 'Did you know about Bernard?' she asked, her words tumbling out extra fast.

'No,' said Lottie, over her shoulder. 'And even if I did, it's not exactly any of our business.'

Her mother leaned back against the worktop and watched Lottie. 'It is our business if that woman thinks she can wheedle money out of Uncle Bernie or out of this house.'

'Ah, that's what's got you worried. You think she's after the inheritance?' Lottie shook her head. Her mother was so predictable; not really concerned for her elderly uncle, merely worried that she might, in some way, lose out financially.

'Not at all. You read about this sort of thing in the papers.'

'Do you?' Lottie doubted that you did.

'Yes. Poor confused elderly people being cheated out of their money and home.'

Lottie snorted a chuckle. 'He's not confused. And I'm pretty sure there's no way she could get the house, because the deeds are with the solicitor. Poor Bernard has already had his home sold from under him.' *Just like me*, she thought. Lottie washed the last glass and placed it on the drainer. 'Plus, I think you're overlooking the fact Dayea is lovely. She dotes on Uncle Bernard.'

'It's not right though. An age difference like that.'

Lottie's eyebrows rose and stayed put. There was no way she could let that one go. 'What, like the age gap between you and Scott?'

Angie pulled her head back like a threatened tortoise, giving herself a triple chin. 'That's completely different, as you well know.'

'No, it's not. You're old enough to have breast-fed him.'

'Rubbish. There's only single figures between me and Scott.'

'If you believe that, then you're either delusional or very bad at maths.'

Angie chewed her lip. 'It's single figures, because he thinks I'm forty-two, so—'

'He's the one that's bad at maths.' She waved a tea towel at her mother, but when she ignored the gesture Lottie started drying up.

Angie moved towards Lottie and she thought, for a moment, she was about to lend a hand but instead she hoiked herself up to sit on the worktop. 'Did you read your Christmas card?'

'From you? Yes, I said thank you,' said Lottie, deliberately misunderstanding her mother's question.

'No. The one from Nana.' Angie's expression was brooding.

Lottie was a terrible liar, so she deflected the question, in the hope that her mother wouldn't probe any further. 'Yep. Did you open yours?' Her mother nodded. Lottie paused the drying up. 'And?'

Angie shrugged. 'It said she knew about the cancer and she wanted me to be happy.'

Lottie watched her mother closely. It was likely she had inherited her useless lying ability from her. 'And what was her advice?'

Angie glanced over Lottie's shoulder and her expression changed.

'Here you are,' said Scott, from the doorway. 'Everyone's going to bed. Shall we?'

'I was just giving Lottie a hand, but I think we're nearly done now.' She hopped down from the worktop and kissed Lottie lightly on the cheek. 'Night, darling,' she said.

'Thanks for an ace evening,' said Scott.

'You're welcome.' She watched them snuggle together as they walked away. She couldn't help but marvel at her mother's unfailing conviction that this next guy might be the one, and that, if it turned out he wasn't, she would still believe her perfect man was out there somewhere, she merely had to hunt him down.

Maybe Lottie wasn't cut out for relationships. For some reason the men she fell for found her really easy to walk away from. She knew she couldn't face a lifetime of being hurt; she wasn't as resilient as her mother. She took things to heart, she always had.

Zach strode in carrying more glasses. 'These were on the windowsill.'

'I asked if that was all of them,' said Lottie, feeling tired and a bit irritated.

'Hey, I've just sat and blown up umpteen balloons. Packets of the things.'

'Ta,' she said, ticking balloons off her list, but she lacked enthusiasm.

'You need a hand?'

'No, Mum's been helping me.'

'Really?' His eyebrows registered his surprise.

'No, not really.' She plunged the glasses into the suds. 'Sorry, I'm tired and . . . you know . . . Joe's back.' She held his gaze for a moment and some level of understanding passed between them.

Zach picked up a tea towel. 'You not pleased to see Joe?'

Lottie paused, her hands covered in bubbles. 'Pleased?' She pondered the word. 'I guess I'm pleased to see him. But then I remember him leaving and that makes me sad. It feels like everything's been turned upside down.' She huffed and rubbed at her mother's lipstick stain on the rim of a glass. 'I'd packaged up everything about Joe and pushed it into a dusty corner of my mind. I've moved on.' She checked Zach was still paying attention. 'But you must be pleased he's back.' Zach and Joe had always been close as kids – both football crazy and big on dinosaurs.

'I am. I like that I'll still have a reason to visit Henbourne after this place is off our hands.'

'Don't say it like you'll be glad,' said Lottie.

He gave a sheepish grin. 'You see right through me. No, honestly, I'm really going to miss the old place. Not as much as you, but still. Are you going to stay around here or . . . ?'

Lottie turned to face him whilst drying her hands. 'Rent is high around here, so I doubt it. Number one priority is finding a job – and that could take me anywhere.' To some people that would be an exciting prospect, but not to Lottie. She wanted to stay cocooned in Henbourne Manor where she felt protected. But what she wanted and what was practical were two very different things. In a few weeks the sale would go through and she'd be homeless. She needed to get a job fast.

'Maybe you could find something local? I got mates rates on the rent for Joe's place so—' Lottie's head jerked up and she almost dropped the glass she was about to put away.

'*You* sorted out the cottage for Joe?' There was a hard edge to her voice.

'Er, yeah. He messaged me on Facebook, asked what I thought. You know, about coming back. And if I could help him find somewhere.'

'You knew he was coming back and you didn't think to warn me?' Lottie put down the glass with a thump and they both recoiled at the sound.

'Don't be miffed.'

Miffed came nowhere near to how hurt and cross she was. 'Zach. Think back. Do you remember how I was when Joe left?' She could feel unwelcome emotions bubbling, and she had to concentrate to keep them at bay.

Zach scratched his head. 'It was a long time ago, Lottie.'

Her eyes widened incredulously. 'And what? Time heals?'

'You couldn't have stopped him coming back.'

Always one for the facts, was Zach. She knew he was

right, but seeing Joe that morning had shaken her more than she wanted to admit, and dug up long-hidden feelings she was scared to be reacquainted with. 'But forewarned is forearmed,' she pointed out. That's what Nana said, too, and it was true.

Zach's thoughtful silence was irritating Lottie. She washed out the suds from the sink with jerky movements, refilled it with hot water and stomped off to the utility to retrieve the turkey, mulling over whether she could make battering someone with a frozen turkey look like an accident. She spotted the mop bucket and remembered the mouse.

Zach followed her. 'You cleaning at this time of night?'

'No. The Duchess invited someone round for a sleepover.' She took off the lid and they both peered inside. The tiny mouse was curled up on an old cloth.

'Is it dead?' asked Zach.

Lottie saw its whisker twitch. 'No, he's sleeping off a massive hangover.'

'Ri-ight,' said Zach, looking thoroughly confused.

'I think I'll leave him until tomorrow.' Lottie put the lid back.

'I know you were upset when Joe left and everything . . .' Zach began. She shook her head and heaved the partially defrosted turkey into her arms.

'Upset?' She hugged the icy poultry and pulled an exaggerated grimace. 'Try "totally devastated" and you won't be close.' She dropped the turkey unceremoniously into the sink. Half the water sloshed out and all down her front. Zach sniggered and she twisted to glare at him, although she could see the funny side too. Some of her annoyance at Zach abated. Her shoulders slumped in defeat. 'You only had to tip me off, that's all I'm saying.

Seeing him this morning brought it all back at a hundred miles an hour and kinda gave me memory whiplash.'

'I didn't say anything because you had enough going on with Nana. I figured Joe was coming back whatever your feelings on the matter, so you were going to have to face it. Why have the worry beforehand?'

It felt like he had considered her feelings, but she still wished he'd mentioned it. At least that would have taken the shock out of her early morning encounter.

Lottie took a deep breath. 'Okay. But for future reference a heads-up would be welcome.'

He stood up straight and saluted her. 'The next time you have an ex-boyfriend about to move back and I happen to get prior notice, I promise to tell you before his flight lands.'

He was incorrigible. 'Gee, thanks. Now clear off – you've been about as helpful as Mum.'

'Harsh.' He grabbed a Santa hat she'd left on the table and threw it playfully at her. 'Night, sis.' He walked to the door and paused. 'And merry Christmas.'

'You too.'

Lottie was about to put away the glasses when she realised what Zach had forgotten. She sighed – the glasses could wait. She pulled on the Santa hat and went to do her last job of the day – or the first one of Christmas Day, depending on what way you looked at it.

Emily had finally got her chance to go to the bathroom, but now she wasn't sure she wanted to do the test any more. It would change everything, and Emily didn't want her life to change. Things with Zach had been going really well. He'd wanted to take things slowly at the beginning, and that suited her. Their relationship had grown steadily

113

and she was happy. Work was going brilliantly, she was on track for promotion, and for the first time there was an opportunity to earn more than her sister. This was something she'd been striving for, and for so long it had eluded her – the opportunity to be better than her sister at something. She was on the cusp of winning.

The blue room was in darkness because Jessie was asleep, so Emily felt her way around and gathered up her washbag and night things. She wasn't a fan of the dark. She wasn't scared of it, she just wasn't used to it – she lived in a town full of streetlights. Out of the window, she noticed it was pitch black – no light pollution at all. She pulled the curtains tightly closed – talk of ghosts earlier had made her a bit jumpy. The only sound was Jessie's steady breathing.

'Your turn,' whispered Zach, returning from his night-time routine.

Emily went to the bathroom. She hurried about washing her face and brushing her teeth to buy herself a little time. She didn't want Zach wondering why she was taking so long. She unwrapped the pregnancy test and speed read the instructions – it was pretty straightforward.

She slumped against the wall. This wasn't how she'd expected this moment to be. She'd thought that one day in her future she'd have a family. When she was ready. When she was at the peak of her career, and comfortably ahead of her sister. But was that ever going to happen? Each time she got close to beating her sister, something happened. Either her chances were derailed or her sister got some accolade. Emily was tired. Tired of the endless battle, the constantly moving goal posts. She studied the tester kit. If she was pregnant, that was it – the end of the race. Her sister was going to zoom into the lead and stay there.

Emily hadn't expected this. She wasn't a thoughtless teenager, she was a responsible adult who had taken precautions. A baby did not feature in her plans right now.

She closed her eyes and turned the little box over in her hand. If this was it – the moment she'd find out she and Zach were going to be parents – then shouldn't he be here too?

Zach was already in bed when Emily returned from the bathroom, so she scooted in next to him. She stared into the darkness and pondered what to do.

'Zach?'

'Hmmm.' He sounded sleepy.

She didn't know what to say. 'It's okay. Forget it.' She wriggled under the covers.

'Is something worrying you?' he asked. She was impressed by his perceptiveness. This could be the opportunity she'd hoped for, a chance to share the situation with him. 'Because you know the whole ghost thing is a legend. None of us have seen it. Well . . . apart from that time Granddad swore blind someone tapped him on the shoulder when he was in the loft.'

'Right, yeah, the ghost,' said Emily, blinking into the darkness and failing to see much at all.

'There was also the shadow that Nana saw on quite a few occasions, but we put it down to her cataracts. And the time the bathroom door slammed twice but no windows were open. But, you know – an old house like this makes odd noises.'

'Okay,' said Emily, beginning to feel not very reassured at all. 'Anything else?'

Zach leaned in closer and she could make out his

features. 'You know that sensation that someone's watching you?' Emily nodded. 'I get that here a lot but when I look there's no-one there.'

Emily shuddered. 'Do you think there's a ghost?'

'Who knows? Night,' he said, placing a kiss on her cheek before turning over.

Emily pulled the covers up a little higher, her mind now fully occupied by the ghost stories. She gave herself a mental shake: there were no such things as ghosts. At least it had taken her mind off the pregnancy test for a while. She turned over to face the door, shut her eyes and listened to the rhythmic sound of Zach's breathing. She'd just started to drift off to sleep when she heard a creak. It was faint but it made her eyes snap open. Darkness swathed the room. A flicker of dim light appeared fleetingly at the bottom of the door. Emily froze. She watched shadows moving in the hallway; heard another creak. Her breath caught in her throat. The light faded.

'Zach,' she whispered. There was no response. She stared at the bottom of the door for a moment until her attention was pulled further up, where the handle was slowly turning. Her heart started to race; she could barely breathe. The door gradually opened. A shadowy figure loomed in the doorway. Bright red demon eyes flashed, slightly out of sync. Emily screamed.

'Em!' Zach shot upright.

'Daddy!' came the sleepy cry from Jessie.

Someone flicked on the light. Emily stopped screaming. She blinked at the figure in the doorway. Lottie was standing there wearing a Santa hat and her flashing Christmas earrings – she looked quite cross. Emily was confused. Why was she creeping into their bedroom?

'I didn't mean to startle you,' said Lottie, holding something behind her back.

Zach hopped out of bed and went to Jessie. 'It's just Lottie saying goodnight. Come on you, back to sleep.' Jessie didn't need telling twice; she slumped back onto her pillow and closed her eyes. Zach turned back to Emily and gave her the same cross look that Lottie was wearing.

Why did she feel like she was the crazy one? 'I'm sorry. I thought it was the ghost.'

Lottie held up a bulging Christmas stocking and passed it to Zach, who silently placed it at the foot of the bed, mouthing 'thank you' to Lottie. Realisation dawned on Emily. She felt like a prize idiot.

Lottie switched off the light and left the room. Emily blinked in the darkness. At her side, she felt Zach turn over huffily. She sat for a moment, waiting for her heart rate to settle. This was turning out to be a Christmas she wouldn't forget – for all the wrong reasons.

Lottie laid out her outfit for Christmas Day, something she'd done every Christmas Eve since she was a child – apart from the Christmases where Nana had said 'You'll be fine in your pyjamas', which was code for 'You're getting some new clothes'.

She finally got into bed and shivered at the chill of the cotton. She wriggled about to try to warm herself and the covers up. It didn't work. She thought about the rest of the family all cuddled up with their partners. Even Jessie had gone to bed cuddling a much-loved teddy. Only she and Great Uncle Bernard were sleeping alone, and he wouldn't be doing that for much longer. She let out a sigh.

Every time she tried to clear her mind, Joe popped up like a sexy jack-in-the-box. She kept having the same row with him in her head over and over again: where she would demand an answer to his behaviour nine years ago, and he wouldn't have a good enough excuse. It was exhausting. On top of that, she was worrying about whether the turkey would defrost in time, *and* her feet wouldn't warm up. It was useless. Lottie got out of bed, padded down to the thermostat and moved it up a few notches – she was fed up with being cold.

She went to the kitchen and refilled the turkey's bath with fresh hot water. A scratching sound drew her attention to the utility and the little mouse imprisoned in the bucket. She got some cheese from the fridge and placed a tiny bit next to the mouse. 'It's not vegan,' she told him and he sniffed it cautiously.

Lottie desperately wanted everything to be perfect for Christmas Day. She checked her to-do list again, which freaked her out more. A giant yawn escaped. She really did need to try to get some sleep, and there was no more she could do tonight, so she trundled back to bed.

Lottie felt like she'd just drifted off to sleep when she was woken with a start by what sounded like distant gun shots. What on earth was happening? She was out of bed and onto the landing when she realised the noise was coming from downstairs. Her heart picked up its pace as her sleep-addled brain tried to figure it out. Zach stumbled onto the landing rubbing his eyes, and there was another rapid burst of bangs. They looked at each other and exclaimed simultaneously: 'Balloons!'

The siblings raced downstairs and Lottie flung open the drawing room door to a symphony of popping. Zach pulled open the curtains in a dramatic movement. What were left of the inflated balloons lay amongst the scattered debris of shrivelled rubber. He put his hand on the radiator and flinched.

'This is red hot. That's what's made them all pop.'

'Bumholes,' said Lottie, and a giggle escaped. Another balloon gave a sudden bang.

'What idiot turned the heating up?' he asked, good-humouredly.

'What idiot put all the balloons next to the radiator?' retorted Lottie, starting to pick up the colourful confetti of popped balloons.

'I'm not blowing any more up,' said Zach.

Lottie gave him a look that disagreed. 'Top drawer.'

Zach's shoulders slumped forward and he went to get them like a recalcitrant teenager. They spent the next half an hour chatting amiably, sharing memories and blowing up more balloons – thanks to Nana's love of a buy-one-get-one-free offer, they had a lot. When they were out of puff they stood up to leave and surveyed the room. The tree still looked magnificent, a colourful pile of presents at its base – despite some torn wrapping thanks to Dave and the Duchess – and beyond that, the carpet was covered with multicoloured balloons like a haphazard rainbow.

'I could just jump on all of those,' said Zach.

'Don't you dare,' said Lottie, giving him a thump. 'Bed, or Santa won't come.'

'Santa's already been and scared the crap out of my girlfriend, thanks very much.'

'Sorry,' she said, shutting the door on Christmas, but she was grinning from ear to ear.

They crept upstairs, but at the top a noise coming from down the corridor stole their attention. They both tiptoed closer until the sounds were clearer. They were met by a rhythmic *boinging* noise, similar to an over-enthusiastic gymnast on a dodgy trampoline, accompanied by their mother's voice giving encouragement to Scott. Zach and Lottie looked at each other, their faces matching pictures of horror.

'More balloons?' suggested Zach.

'Definitely,' said Lottie, and they raced back downstairs.

Chapter Twelve

Christmas Day

Jessie opened her bedroom door and announced in a loud voice, with more than a passing resemblance to Noddy Holder, 'It's Chriiiiiiistmas!'

Lottie rolled over and squinted at her alarm clock. 6.23 a.m. Even though she knew it could have been much worse, she groaned. It had been another hour after they overheard her mother's amorous antics before she'd dared to venture back upstairs. But she couldn't laze about any longer: she had a date with a turkey the size of an overfed pterodactyl. She prayed to the Christmas dinner fairy that the beast of a bird had defrosted overnight.

It was Christmas Day. She shook herself awake: it was her favourite day of the year, and a big smile spread across her face. Then she remembered that she'd be spending most of it with Joe and her smile faded. People talked about the elephant in the room – but today she'd be spending her time trying not to get trampled by a whole herd.

Doors started to open and she dragged herself out of bed and pulled on her Chewbacca onesie. She'd had to put her old dressing gown in the wash after Dave's antics the morning before. She pulled up the hood, shoved her feet into her old *Star Wars* slippers and shuffled onto the landing. A piercing scream jolted her to full consciousness.

'Mum!' yelled Lottie, pulling off her hood and grabbing her screaming mother by the arm.

'You scared the life out of me, dressed up like that,' scolded her mother.

'Why? Who did you think would be coming out of my bedroom apart from me?' The scream was still ringing in her ears.

Her mother bristled. 'I don't know.' Lottie tilted her head, expecting a better answer. 'A bear. Or bigfoot?'

'In Henbourne?' Lottie shook her head and plodded downstairs. She was tired and grumpy. She knew she had to get over that quickly or she'd spoil Christmas; probably not for everyone else, but certainly for herself.

She filled the kettle and fired up the coffee machine. Angie joined her in the kitchen.

'Coffee?' offered Lottie.

'No bucks fizz?' Angie pouted elaborately.

'There's buck but no fizz. You drank all the Prosecco yesterday. Remember?' Lottie let out a giant yawn and didn't cover her mouth.

'Goodness. I saw all your fillings,' said her mother, looking repulsed. 'I thought you were joking about the fizz. Surely you can conjure some up from somewhere?' Angie's tone had changed to simpering.

'I'm not bloody Harry Potter,' said Lottie. She was kicking herself for not getting more Prosecco, but usually everyone stuck to wine. 'We have wine and lots of sherry.' There had been quite a bit of sherry in the order Nana had placed. Lottie suspected that maybe that was how

Nana had managed to get through all of Christmas with a smile on her face.

'Sherry?' Angie recoiled. 'I'd rather drink bleach.'

'We have plenty of that too.' Lottie pointed to the utility. Angie marched over to it. 'I was joking,' said Lottie.

'I'm seeing what wine you've got. Scott and I won't drink anything cheap, we have . . . arghhh!'

Lottie stuck her fingers in her ears. 'Will you please stop screaming? It's like living in a horror movie, except nobody's died a painful death. Yet.' She gave her mother a pointed look.

Angie scurried out of the utility. 'There's a mouse!'

'Ooh yes, there is – and now that the Duchess is tucked up asleep I'll release it back into the wild.'

'The wild?' Angie recoiled as Lottie retrieved the bucket, swinging it under her mother's upturned nose on purpose.

'Yes. Have you seen the state of the back garden?' Lottie opened the back door, took a few steps outside and gently tipped the mouse out in some long grass. She came back in wishing she could escape that easily too. Having Joe there all day was a daunting prospect and one she wasn't sure she was equipped for.

Angie was giving her a sideways look. 'Has it gone?'

'Yes, he's off to tell his friends what an ace sleepover he's had and how much he enjoyed the non-vegan cheese.' *And about the time he peed in the mulled wine*, she thought.

Angie turned, her flowing nightie billowing theatrically as she stormed out. Lottie chuckled to herself; she was feeling less grumpy already.

After coffee and toast, both of which Angie complained about, they were ready to open the presents. Lottie sneaked into the drawing room ahead of everyone, sipped a glass of sherry to steel herself for the day ahead, and switched on all the fairy lights. She took a moment to savour the scene before the family descended. She wanted to remember this; capture it like a photo in her mind. *My last Christmas morning at Henbourne Manor*, she thought, and a sad sigh escaped.

'Auntie Lottie, can we come in now?' came Jessie's eager voice from the hallway.

'Ta-dah!' said Lottie, swinging open the door. Jessie ran in and came to an abrupt stop in front of the tree. Balloons bobbed at her feet. She turned back to Lottie and beamed at her. No words were needed – Lottie felt exactly the same. This was the magic of Christmas.

Everyone gathered in the drawing room and the sound of excited chatter was warming to the soul. Lottie heard the back door open and close and within seconds they were joined by the scruffy little dog, although he now had a rather fetching yellow bow tied around his neck.

'Dave!' shouted Jessie as the little dog jumped all over her making her giggle wildly. Lottie stared at the door, preparing herself to see Joe.

She didn't have to wait long. The door opened and Joe tentatively peered in. The sight of him made her stomach flip, though that could have been the sherry she'd gulped down. She hadn't been expecting him quite this early.

'I'm bearing gifts.' He handed her two boxes of mince pies and a nice bottle of Prosecco.

'Ooh, fizz,' said Angie, but Lottie hugged the bottle protectively to her chest and glared at her mother.

'Thank you,' Lottie said to Joe. 'You didn't have to.' He gave a weak smile and she returned it. His smile spread into a grin and she wondered why until she glanced down – she was still wearing her Chewbacca onesie. She shrugged and tried to act nonchalant. They never got dressed until after presents, and she wasn't changing to impress Joe – those days were long gone.

'Presents!' shouted Jessie.

'Right, Jessie, you can go first,' said Lottie. Jessie didn't need telling twice; she was already in a paper ripping frenzy.

'It's a unicorn!' she yelled, holding up a box with a large white fluffy toy inside. 'Thanks Emily.' The little girl threw her arms around Emily's neck and kissed her. Lottie and Zach exchanged looks. Lottie had the distinct feeling Zach was trying to communicate something, but she couldn't be sure. Perhaps she was reading too much into it. Jessie began reading labels and handing round presents. The room's volume escalated in line with Jessie's excitement, and before long they were drowning out Michael Bublé – Nana's favourite.

After a few minutes, the months of shopping, buying and wrapping had been reduced to a sea of shredded wrapping paper, ribbons and bows. Lottie surveyed the devastation surrounding them. The Duchess had already found a bow she liked the look of and was batting it about happily under the watchful eye of Dave, who was held firm in Joe's strong hands.

Jessie had a pile of stuff, as every child should – including a Hungry Hippos game, which Lottie was looking forward to playing. Aunt Nicola was cooing over the latest in robotic hoovers and Uncle Daniel was telling anyone who'd listen how much it had cost. Angie and Scott were giggling over the underwear they'd bought each other, and a pair of dinosaur socks. She was sure Zach wouldn't miss the socks she'd originally bought for him. Scott seemed genuinely thrilled with them and she saw

Zach eye them appreciatively. Oh well, she could always get Zach a pair for his birthday.

Joe was looking like the little boy who Santa Claus forgot. She felt bad that he was the only one without something to open. If she'd realised he was going to be there for present opening, she would have hastily relabelled another of Zach's presents. Despite everything that had happened between them, it was still Christmas. Perhaps there was something she could do instead.

'Watcha get?' asked Zach, leaning over her. Lottie was very pleased with her present haul.

'Thanks for these,' she said pointing at the new *Star Wars* slippers she so desperately needed. 'Smellies, chocolates and gift cards mainly. I got this from Uncle Bernie.' She held up a woolly hat with Yoda ears. 'And a nice top from Fat Face.'

'You shouldn't call Mum that,' he said in mock horror and she laughed.

Apart from her mother bundling up the extra-long hot water bottle Lottie had bought her and muttering something about Lottie trying to ruin her sex life, everyone seemed happy and that was all Lottie was really aiming for.

Emily had opened her things from her mum and dad in between watching Jessie open her presents.

'Right,' said Zach, drawing everyone's attention. 'Emily's turn.'

Emily felt uncomfortable as all eyes turned on her. Something squirmed in her stomach as she wondered what he'd got her.

He handed her a beautifully wrapped box. 'This isn't your main present.'

'Oh, okay. Thank you.' She opened it hastily. 'It's that hand cream I liked.' She smeared a little on – it smelled divine. 'Thanks,' she said leaning over to give him a kiss.

She waited for him to produce the second gift, but he was sitting there looking apprehensive.

'Your other present is in the tree,' he said, and they both looked at the large spruce. 'You need to have a hunt to find it.'

'O-kay,' said Emily slowly. This was unusual. She had no idea what she was looking for, but she suspected some sort of joke present. She got up, smoothed down her dress – still feeling a bit conspicuous for not being in her pyjamas like most of the others – and knelt in front of the tree. She moved the ripped paper out of the way and looked about the base of the tree. Nothing. No more presents left. She gave Zach a questioning look.

'Look in the branches,' said Zach, moving to the edge of his seat.

Emily peered into the middle of the tree. Everyone was watching, so she didn't want to snag her hair on the branches. She carefully leaned in. The smell of pine was more intense and the tiny lights flickered around her face. She blinked and traced methodically along the closest branches, with no idea what she was looking for. There was nothing there. She tilted her head up and scanned the higher branches. Still nothing.

'Emily?' asked Zach. 'Have you found it?'

'Nope.' She stuck her head out from under the tree. 'How big is it? Is the paper the same colour as the tree, by any chance? Because I can't see anything.'

Zach gave a jaunty raise of his eyebrow. 'It's not wrapped. And it's quite small.'

'Oh, okay,' said Emily, trying not to convey her disappointment that he'd not bothered to wrap this present. Apparently it was wrapped in a tree.

A couple more minutes passed, and people started to chat amongst themselves. Lottie joined Zach on the sofa. 'I'm sure when you pictured this it was a lovely idea, but . . .'

'I can't find it, Zach,' she said, pulling her head out and catching her hair in the branches. 'Ow.' Emily reversed from under the tree and sat on the floor.

'I'll help,' said Zach, and he dived inside the Christmas tree.

Joe sat down in Zach's vacated seat on the sofa. 'Has charades started early?' he asked, indicating Zach's bum sticking out from under the Christmas tree.

'Missing present,' said Lottie.

Zach crawled out from under the tree. 'I need a word,' he said to Lottie, with a grimace, and they left the room together.

Emily felt like she was in a parallel universe. Nothing made sense. Christmas with her family was far more straightforward. She'd missed not having scrambled egg on toast in bed – that was one of their Christmas treats. And presents were a simple affair where people handed them to each other and unwrapped them one at a time. This was all rather strange.

Jessie was playing with her new toys, and everyone else was sipping drinks and having a closer look at their presents. Emily looked at hers. She had a colouring book for adults from Jessie and a book titled *Don't Feed the Monkey Mind* from her sister – she feared it wasn't a joke present. There was a pretty hand cream set from Lottie, and a small cheque from her mum and dad with a note not to cash it until the end of January. She shuffled herself along the sofa to where her drink was and remembered that she'd chosen orange juice, which was more than a disappointment – she'd prefer something a little stronger. Great Uncle Bernard was puzzling over four tins of tuna someone had bought him and Angie was checking if anyone had batteries – although Emily couldn't see any gifts that needed them. Spending Christmas with someone else's family was proving to be an odder experience than she'd expected.

Chapter Thirteen

In the chilly hallway Lottie waved her arms as if she was directing a plane onto an aircraft carrier. 'Slow down, stop gabbling and start from the beginning.'

Zach took a deep breath. 'I hid Emily's present in the tree yesterday and—'

'Why?' This seemed like an odd thing to do.

'Because I read it somewhere and thought it sounded romantic and now *it's* gone and—'

'What's gone?'

'The present.' Lottie tilted her head with the level of menace only a younger sibling can muster. 'I don't want to say what it is because then it spoils the surprise.'

'She's not five, Zach. And it's not my surprise, so you can tell me.'

Zach's brows knitted together, and he drew in a long, slow breath. 'Okay,' he said, reluctantly. 'But I swear if you breathe a word to anyone . . . you remember the flowerpot incident?' Lottie flinched. 'Right. Then we understand each other.'

'Well?' Lottie was growing impatient.

Zach looked furtively around the entrance hall and lowered his voice. 'It's a diamond engagement ring.'

'Squeeeeeeeeeee!'

'Shhhhhhhhhhh!'

The drawing room door opened and Rhys came out. Briefly wrong-footed by the welcome party in the hallway, he held up his Christmas present – a state-of-the-art metal detector. 'Going to put this upstairs. Thanks for the cash Uncle Zach and the Nando's gift card Auntie Lottie.'

'You're welcome,' they chorused, looking very suspicious as they grinned at him and followed his progress all the way to the top of the stairs. They stayed silent until they heard the box room's door creak shut.

'Oh my gosh! This is so exciting!' Lottie clapped her hands together like a toy monkey with new batteries. Tears filled her eyes. She was beyond happy for her brother, and she flung herself forward and hugged him tight.

'Ooft! Okay, calm down. I hope Emily reacts half as well as you. Do you think she'll say yes?'

The pregnancy test flashed into Lottie's mind and she struggled to form a sentence. Perhaps now was a bad time for him to ask Emily. Perhaps she would say yes for all the wrong reasons. Lottie's mouth opened and closed.

'Well, that's hugely reassuring. Thanks, sis – I'm really glad you're on my team.' He shook his head.

'Sorry. Of course she will. But for now we need to focus on finding the ring. Where did you put it exactly?'

'In the tree,' he said deliberately, as if talking to someone a bit slow on the uptake.

'I know it's in the tree, but *where* exactly?'

'Third branch up. Nestled against the trunk and right next to a fairy light that lit it up perfectly. But it's not there now.'

'And when did you put it there again?'

'Yesterday afternoon.' He lowered his guilty eyes. 'When you caught me sneaking about.'

'Ah, I knew it. No wonder you weren't interested in the little car. You're a rubbish liar.'

'Can we please get back to my crisis?'

'Okay. You hid it late afternoon. Jeez Zach, anything could have happened to it since then.'

She scanned her memory, playing back the events of the previous day as if on fast rewind. Her eyes widened and so did Zach's as they hit on the same moment at the same time.

'Dave,' said Lottie and Zach together.

'That scruffy mutt has eaten it!' Zach started marching up and down the hallway running his hands roughly through his hair.

'We don't know for sure. It might just be on the floor. But if he has . . . Then the bright side is you should get it back sometime tomorrow.' Zach gave her a look that didn't need any words.

Lottie popped back into the drawing room and whilst tidying up bits of paper around the tree had a thorough check to see if the ring was on the floor. It was nowhere to be seen. She returned to Zach, who was pacing in the hallway.

'Nope. I can't find it,' she said.

'Bloody Dave has eaten it.'

'Maybe Joe could X-ray Dave, then we'd know for sure?'

'Oh what, with his portable X-ray machine he brought with him?'

Lottie was nodding until Zach's sarcasm registered. 'Hmm, good point. But he's a vet. He might have some other ideas for removing an engagement ring from a dog?'

'This is such a mess.' Zach shook his head and Lottie

felt sorry that his romantic plans had gone awry. He slumped against the wall, nudging a photograph of a long forgotten relative. Lottie made the picture level and leant against the wall next to him.

'It's still lovely that you want to marry Emily.'

Zach was staring at his feet. 'You like her, don't you, Lot?'

'Yeah. I mean I don't know her that well, since she's not been able to visit because we've all been so ill for such a long time.' If Lottie had worn glasses she'd have been looking at him over the top of them.

Zach's head snapped up. 'I was hoping you'd not noticed that. I just wanted to be sure before I introduced her. No point in scaring her off early.'

'She seems like a lovely person, and she's thoughtful towards Jessie too. And if she's not scared off by our weird family then I'd say she's a keeper.'

'Thanks, that means a lot.' Zach gave her a friendly nudge.

They went silent for a bit and contemplated the situation. At the same time their eyes looked skywards as the floorboards creaked above them. They looked at each other and nodded – they'd had the same idea.

They took the stairs two at a time. 'Rhys?' Lottie rapped her knuckles on the box room door.

There was no immediate response so Zach joined in. 'Rhys!'

The door opened a fraction and Rhys's face appeared with one earphone lifted, a question mark of an expression on his face.

'Do you think we could borrow the metal detector, just for a mo?' asked Lottie.

Rhys's eyebrows showed his surprise. 'We'll only be a few minutes. We'll look after it. Promise,' added Zach.

Rhys shrugged, disappeared for a few moments and reappeared. 'I think these dolls are reproducing. There weren't this many last year.' He opened the door and Zach recoiled at the sight of the fixed expressions staring back from every surface.

'Blimey, it's the Botox queue at Pins and Needles,' said Zach with a chuckle.

'Sorry about the dolls.' Lottie bit her lip. 'Detector?'

Rhys thrust the detector through the door. 'According to the instructions it emits a high . . .'

'Thanks,' said Zach as Lottie grabbed the device and they both went thundering back downstairs.

Lottie slipped into the drawing room and tapped Joe on the shoulder. When he looked up she pointed at the dog and beckoned him into the hallway.

'What's up?' asked Joe as he joined them, clutching a wriggly Dave.

She gave Joe a rushed summary of the situation, explaining that Dave had likely eaten Emily's present – but not that it was an engagement ring. The fewer people who knew, the better.

Joe put the dog on the floor. 'What's the plan?'

Zach switched on the metal detector and held it aloft as it gave a whistle. 'This will tell us if he's eaten it.' Dave was instantly enthralled by the whistling machine and appeared to be barking his thoughts on the matter as he pogoed to try to grab the end of it.

'I'll take that,' said Joe, seizing the detector.

'Good idea, you'll know where to aim it,' said Zach. 'Shall we put him on the kitchen table or what?'

'Neither. Are you two insane? You can't run a metal detector over a dog.'

'Why?' asked Zach.

'Will it hurt him?' asked Lottie.

'No, but would you like it?' She detected the merest hint of a scold in his tone. They both shook their heads. 'And the chances of it giving you an accurate reading are pretty slim.' He switched it off and Dave stopped barking.

'How do we find out if he's eaten it?' she asked.

'He has,' said Zach. 'It's the only explanation. Can you operate on him?'

Joe squeezed his eyes shut. 'Bit drastic, mate. And all I've got is my basic kit and no working premises.'

'Could you ask another vet if you could use theirs? I mean they won't be working Christmas Day?' Zach was starting to sound desperate.

'Not really, no.' Lottie could tell that Joe was hoping Zach wasn't serious.

'X-ray then?' said Zach.

'Don't happen to have one of those on me either, or an ultrasound, before you ask. X-ray would give the best results, but he'd need an anaesthetic whereas with ultrasound the animal doesn't have to keep perfectly still so there's no need to knock him out.'

Lottie threw up her arms. 'Farmer Giles.'

Joe sniggered. 'Is that a condition you suffer from?'

'Not rhyming slang for piles.' She was trying her hardest to stay cross with him. She gave him a hard stare and continued. 'Giles Hutton. He was in Zach's year at school. He went to agricultural college and now he's into mating animals.' Joe cheekily raised one eyebrow. 'Husbandry,' she explained, but he was still grinning. Lottie ignored it. 'He was in the Bleeding Bear a few weeks ago showing off this portable ultrasound he'd been using to check sheep to see if they were carrying lambs. He was actually using it to see which of the rugby lads was storing the biggest

135

fart in their bowels—' why was she talking about farts? '—but anyway. He'll be home for Christmas. It's worth a shot?' Joe was nodding.

Zach didn't look so sure. 'I still say we open him up.'

Lottie ignored her brother and made the phone call and was soon relaying the information to them. 'Giles is home and nursing a hangover, but he has the ultrasound and we can borrow it.'

'Hi. Is everything all right?' asked a concerned-looking Emily, exiting the drawing room. The other three stood stock still, looking at each other.

Zach stepped forward. 'Yeah, it's all fine. Look, I'm afraid you're going to have to wait a bit for your main present. Bit of a hitch.'

'That's okay. I'm happy with my hand cream.' She turned to Lottie. 'Can I help with dinner?'

'Crap! Yes, you can,' said Lottie, running for the kitchen. Thanks to all the lost ring drama she'd completely forgotten about dinner, and now she was behind.

Emily followed Lottie as she skidded through the kitchen and began unpacking crates of veg.

'Nana ordered all this, and I added some more to be on the safe side,' said Lottie, clutching a bunch of carrots.

At last Lottie handed Emily the final stalk of Brussels sprouts and they surveyed the mountain of food now on the table.

'There's a possibility I may have over-ordered,' said Lottie, with a pout.

Emily wasn't sure how to answer; she'd only ever seen that many vegetables in a supermarket. 'Always better to have more than you need.'

'True,' said Lottie, waving a pointed finger at the potatoes. 'But I think we only have one peeler.'

'How about I do the cauliflowers? They don't need peeling.' Emily picked up one of the five from the table. 'Are some of these for tomorrow?'

Lottie blinked. 'I have absolutely no idea. Nana used to do it all. I wish I'd asked questions; paid more attention. Or insisted on helping when Nana shooed me away. Can you cook?' Desperation stared out from Lottie.

'I'm more of a salad or stir-fry kind of person. My family's not big on veg, so one cauli would do four of us. Shall I do three?'

Lottie started picking up and putting down random vegetables and muttering incoherently under her breath. Emily wished Zach would join them; she was fearing for Lottie's sanity. 'Lottie. Shall I cut up three?' She waved a cauliflower in front of Lottie's face.

'What do we do with this?' Lottie waved a pineapple at her. Emily dodged out of the way for fear of losing an eye. 'Pineapple. Where does that feature in Christmas?' Lottie was frowning hard. 'I've got to conjure something up for vegetarians. No, they're vegans. Vegetarian would have been *too* easy.' She rubbed her forehead with the heel of her hand.

'They should be okay,' said Emily, indicating the vegetables heaped on the table.

'What's this?' asked Lottie, holding up what on first glance looked like a large nut.

Emily leaned closer. 'Nutmeg,' she said, feeling quite proud of her identification.

'You're right. Nana put some in the Christmas pudding. But dessert is sorted. So what the hell is it for?' Lottie appeared to be expecting an answer, but Emily just shrugged. Lottie rushed over to the fridge, had a rummage and produced a carton of buttermilk. 'And this. What's this for?'

Emily didn't know. 'Hot chocolate?' It was a guess.

'Oh my gosh. I don't know what I'm doing,' said Lottie, pulling out a chair and sitting down with a thud. 'I thought it would just turn out all right on the day. That it would be obvious what I was meant to do; but it's not. I literally don't have a clue what I'm doing.' She waved her hands about as if trying to cool herself down, even though the kitchen was quite chilly.

'Ask your mum?' suggested Emily, and she could have sworn she actually saw the colour drain from Lottie's face.

Lottie shook her head. 'Oh, no, no, no. That's a very bad idea. There are things you need to know about our mother. Firstly, you should never *ever* show any sign of weakness.' She was counting them off on her fingers. 'Secondly, she's never cooked anything more complex than a ready meal in her life and thirdly . . .' Lottie paused and stared at the mound of potatoes. 'This is my mother we're talking about, so whatever level of disaster I'm facing right now she will be able to take it to DEFCON one.'

Emily found herself nodding, although she was quite unsettled by the tirade. 'I guess we can't all be worthy of *Masterchef*.' Emily gave a little giggle to show she was trying to lighten the mood, but Lottie was still looking panicked.

'We should have gone to the pub. Is it too late to go to the pub?' Lottie's eyes pleaded.

'I think so. All you can do is your best.'

Lottie was shaking her head. 'There's a million people in there expecting me to cook them a perfect Christmas dinner.' She was getting paler. 'They want more than my best. They want a Nana Rose Christmas. But I'm not Nana.'

Emily smiled through clenched teeth. 'It's okay. Nobody's expecting it to be perfect.' Lottie's head shot up and she looked hurt. 'Let me rephrase that,' said Emily, wondering where the hell Zach was. 'What's important is everybody getting together. Nobody really notices the food. It's just a roast dinner.'

Lottie took a sharp intake of breath and Emily knew she'd said the wrong thing again. 'Just. A. Roast. Dinner?' Lottie's voice was quiet.

'That's what my mum says. People get all het up about it, but she does one every week and says it's super easy and—'

'Can you get her on the phone?' asked Lottie, blinking rapidly.

'Sure, if you think it'd help?'

Lottie nodded and already looked a little brighter.

Emily had already had a brief word with her mum to wish her a merry Christmas before she'd lost signal. She'd felt strange not being at home with them all. In an odd way she was even missing her sister's sniping. Sometimes they'd had Christmas at her aunt and uncle's, and she'd worked a couple of years, but she'd never spent it with people she hadn't met before. It felt a bit like cheating on her parents, although they had seemed fine about it – but that had only made her feel more homesick. They were always supportive of whatever she did, even if it was something they didn't really agree with. The whole late period thing wasn't helping either. She wished she was at home. Sometimes all you needed was a hug from your mum. Although she was starting to understand that a hug from Angie wouldn't do the trick for poor Lottie.

Lottie cleared her throat, pulling Emily from her thoughts. She fumbled with her phone and dialled home. As she'd expected, her mum was more than happy to help. Lottie hung on to her every word, asked a multitude of questions and wrote down copious notes including a running order for what went on the hob or in the oven and in what order. Her mum was even able to tell them that the nutmeg and buttermilk were probably for making bread sauce, which they had unanimously decided nobody really liked and would take too much effort, so it had been scrubbed from the menu.

They ended the call with lots of thanks and an open invitation from Emily's mum to call any time if they got stuck. 'Your mum's a lifesaver,' said Lottie and Emily felt quite proud. Her mum was brilliant; but then didn't everyone think that about their parents? 'Thank you,' said Lottie, giving Emily a quick squeeze. Emily smiled; it was a lovely gesture and went a little way to making her feel accepted. 'Right. We have our orders. Let's get to work,' said Lottie, picking up the vegetable peeler and attacking a very large parsnip.

Chapter Fourteen

Lottie quite enjoyed preparing the veg with Emily, sharing giggles over oddly shaped carrots. It helped to get things in perspective, and Emily was good company. It was also an opportunity to learn a little bit about her. They both managed to steer clear of the possible pregnancy – she didn't even know if Emily had done the test or not. Lottie supposed she would have to say something before the day was out, especially with a proposal looming; assuming that Dave coughed up – or 'deposited' – the ring at some stage.

'So you and your sister have a bit of a competitive relationship then?' Lottie had been picking up vibes.

'Understatement. She's made one-upmanship an Olympic sport. I put decking in my garden – she gets decking and a pergola. I buy Mum and Dad a voucher for afternoon tea – she buys them a holiday in France.' Lottie couldn't hide her astonishment. 'She drives me crackers.' Emily pulled a Christmas cracker from the nearby box.

'Crumbs,' said Lottie, dusting down the worktop. Emily giggled. 'I thought Zach was a pain in the bum, but he's nothing like that. He was annoying when we were kids.

You know, the usual stuff: Chinese burns, blaming me for trumping, telling tales. But as an adult he's great. Still a bit annoying, but I know he'd always be there if I really needed anything.'

'My sister's not all bad . . . as kids we used to have fun, in between the squabbling. We'd make dens and pretend we were lost fairies. And she gave me a ride home on her bike when I cut my knee – but then she *had* pushed me off a swing, so technically . . . But now it's just the squabbling.'

'Where did it go wrong, do you think?' Lottie was chopping carrots.

'When my sister got my parents what they really wanted.'

'Which was?' Lottie paused the chopping frenzy.

'A police officer for a daughter.' Emily's cheek twitched.

'Ah, tricky. Mum's never been interested in what me or Zach do for a living. Although she was keen for me to work on the cosmetics counter at Boots so she could use the discount.'

They both sighed and carried on chopping with increased vigour.

Emily slid her carrots into a saucepan. 'What was Melissa like?'

The question made Lottie freeze; she had to employ her best acting skills to look natural. Any mention of Melissa always put Lottie on edge; this was what secrets did. 'Melissa was lovely,' said Lottie, and she returned her attention to the parsnips.

'I'm sure she was, but what was she like as a person?'

Lottie swallowed and had a little think about how best to word it. 'She was ambitious, very focused. A good person.'

Emily seemed to be biting her lip. 'A lot to live up to then.'

Lottie wasn't sure how to reply. 'We all have our talents,' she said. 'Sadly, mine isn't cooking.' She nodded at the sliced parsnips, which she now realised she should have cut into chunks.

The turkey seemed to have defrosted overnight, and Lottie put it in the oven, according to Emily's mum's instructions. After an internet search, she was delighted to find a picture of a vegan Christmas wreath, which was basically a veggie sausage roll made into a circle shape and decorated with cranberries and basil to look like sprigs of holly. She and Emily had made their own version using the leftover slab of ready-roll pastry Lottie had bought for the sausage rolls and which she was thrilled to discover was vegan friendly. They made their own filling of mushrooms, garlic, cranberries and onion with a good grating of nutmeg. They had no idea how it would turn out, but at least her mother couldn't say she'd not made an effort. She hoped it was edible, for Scott's sake.

'Do you want to get changed?' asked Emily, glancing at Lottie's onesie.

Lottie looked down at herself. She didn't know where the time had gone. 'If you're okay here?' she asked, feeling like Emily was now very much part of the team.

'Of course. Go!' And she shooed her from the kitchen.

Lottie was showered and changed and heading back downstairs when she heard giggling coming from the bathroom. She stopped and listened. It was her mother and Scott. She shook her head, she didn't want to think about what was going on in there. The voices stopped, the bathroom door opened at speed and her mother's face appeared.

'Tut, tut, tut, Lottie. Looking through keyholes?' The squeaky floorboards must have given her away.

She heard Scott chuckle behind her. 'No, I was . . .' She stopped herself; she didn't have to explain herself to her mother. And she wasn't going to let her wind her up today. She turned away.

'Hang on. Don't go. Have you got any batteries?' asked Angie, sounding a little anxious.

'What size?' asked Lottie.

Angie giggled. 'Big ones.'

Lottie was suspicious. 'What for?'

'Goodness Lottie, what's with the Spanish inquisition?'

'I'll look in the messy drawer.' Lottie went to leave but Angie spoke again.

'Erm . . .' her mother paused. 'How's dinner going?'

Angie had sailed through every Christmas doing the bare minimum and this year was to be no exception. 'Fine, thanks. I've got things to do,' said Lottie.

'Oh, so have I, darling. So have I,' she said, with a sultry wink. Lottie shuddered and sped off.

When she reached the hall, Zach and Joe were coming in through the front door. Dave was trotting happily at their heels and they seemed to be in high spirits. 'How did it go with Giles?' asked Lottie.

'We couldn't see anything really. So it looks like I'm on poo patrol for the next twenty-four hours,' said Zach with a chuckle.

'You seem happy about that.' There was no getting away from their jolly manner.

'We popped into the Bear for a swift one,' said Joe.

'We got more fizz,' said Zach, waving about two bottles, which Lottie intercepted.

She narrowed her eyes. 'You're both drunk.'

Zach waved his hands rapidly, palms down, as if he was worshipping her. 'Shhh. Keep your voice down. And no, not drunk. Just the right level of merry for Christmas.' With that, he and Joe started to laugh, proving beyond doubt that they were definitely drunk.

'I only had one,' said Joe, undoing Dave's skipping rope. The dog made a dash for the stairs and Lottie grabbed him.

'Oh, no you don't. The Duchess is up there snoozing.' She held on to the dog and turned towards Zach. 'Good luck sorting poo in your state.'

'Not my fault,' said Zach. 'The new landlady was too welcoming.'

'She's got a young English Mastiff. Gorgeous dog,' added Joe.

'Tiny is an unconventional pub dog, but he has become a bit of a local favourite,' agreed Lottie.

'This fella could be a guard dog.' Joe fussed Dave and the dog wagged his tail furiously. With his mouth lolling open he looked like he was laughing, too.

'Oh, yeah. He's terrifying.' Today she felt far more awkward around Joe than yesterday. Perhaps the shock had worn off, taking some of the anger with it. Now she was facing the day-to-day reality of him being back. She needed to tackle that situation head on. And as Nana would say, there was no time like the present.

'Can you take Dave in there?' she asked Zach. Before he could answer, she'd thrust Dave into his arms, guided him into the drawing room and shut the door.

She turned to Joe. 'We need to talk,' she said, grabbing her coat and opening the front door.

Joe looked resigned as he turned up his collar and went

outside. They started walking in silence while Lottie ordered her thoughts. The sky was bright but there was still a bite to the wind that cut along the ridge the house stood on.

'Here's the thing,' she said, shoving her hands deep into her pockets. 'I understand why you left when you did, but I had no idea you weren't coming back.'

'I'm back,' he said, in a jolly voice.

'Joe, I want to have a proper discussion about this. Clear the air. If you're not capable of that . . .'

'Sorry. You're right.' There was a long pause. 'I guess even I didn't know I wasn't coming back. Not when I first left. I just needed to get away. There was a tentative offer of a university place in the States and I wanted to get as far away from Henbourne as I could.' He twisted to look at her. She was watching him closely.

'I know. You said that in your note.' She'd read and re-read the note she'd found on the doormat so many times she could recall it even now. How he didn't want to hurt her, but felt he would go mad if he stayed and that she was most definitely better off without him. The feelings of that day, so deeply buried, began to resurface and churn in her gut. Her mouth went dry. 'Joe, you had people who cared about you here and you shut them off. You shut me off.'

'Had?' repeated Joe, not looking at Lottie. 'I *had* people who cared. But not any more. Eh?'

His challenge sparked anger inside her. 'Yes, *had*. You've been gone for nine years!' Her voice was rising. 'Did you expect me to put my life on hold for you? Did you think I had nothing better to do than sit here twiddling my thumbs waiting for you to come back? You didn't call. You didn't write. I had no idea where the hell you were.

And you clearly didn't care about me!' She was shouting through the tears and she roughly wiped them away with her sleeve.

She took in a few gasps of icy air and lengthened her stride. She'd been a mess when he'd left. That was meant to have been *their* summer. Their last few weeks together before they went to separate universities. They had festival tickets and a week booked in a caravan in St Ives, as well as a ludicrous amount of parties and barbecues lined up. They'd pledged to keep their relationship going, to be committed to the long-distance thing. But that had been when they thought the distance between them would be from York to Bath, not England to America.

Joe caught her up and placed a hand on her arm. She halted, and he faltered, looking up at the dull sky. Eventually he spoke. 'I guess when my . . .' There was another long pause and Lottie realised that even after all these years he couldn't speak about what had happened. He took another deep breath. When he spoke, the deep sadness in his voice held her attention. 'I think I must have had some sort of breakdown. I don't know for sure. I didn't see a doctor or anything. I couldn't face any of it. Couldn't cope. It was like I had to shut my old life into a box. Lock it up and throw away the key.'

It took the wind out of Lottie's sails. Until now, whilst she had understood what had driven Joe to leave, she hadn't appreciated the full impact on his mental health. She let what he'd said sink in.

Her anger subsided. 'I wish you'd stayed. You didn't have to face it alone.'

'I did,' said Joe emphatically. 'I couldn't drag anyone else down. Least of all you.'

'You left me . . .' she started. His eyes were locked on

hers, but he stayed silent. She wanted to tell him what she'd had to deal with alone – what she'd been through – but she couldn't, and perhaps she never would. She understood what he meant about shutting things in a box and throwing away the key – she'd done exactly the same thing. But that was something she couldn't share with him, with anybody.

The wind picked up and Lottie shuddered. Her coat wasn't a match for the December weather. They had been on a bit of a route march. When he didn't respond, she put her head down and headed back towards the manor.

They walked in time and in silence until they reached the driveway, where Joe halted abruptly. Lottie slowed to a stop and turned to look at him. His head was low. He slowly looked up. 'I am truly sorry for what I put you through, Lottie, but I still think it was the right decision.'

She didn't answer him. She wasn't sure what he wanted from her, but she couldn't bring herself to say it was all okay – because it wasn't. When she didn't respond he gave a nod of understanding and walked past her up to the house.

She waited there for a minute, watching him disappear up the drive. He was standing by his decision. His decision to leave Henbourne; to leave her. Fine, at least now they both knew where they stood. The sooner she got away from here, the better.

When Lottie came inside, there was no sign of Joe. The smell of the cooking turkey was a welcome assault on her nostrils; she breathed it in deeply. She checked her face in the hall mirror, marvelling at how blotchy it could get from a few tears. She ran her fingers through her short hair, redid her special Christmassy hair clip and straightened her shoulders. She only had to get through today, then she could forget about Joe Broomfield and move on with her life – something she thought she'd done nine years ago.

Zach came into the hallway, his eyes alight with mischief. 'I think I know where I've seen Scott before.'

'Great.' Lottie put her hands on her hips.

'Don't sound so enthusiastic. You're going to love this . . . What's wrong? Have you been crying?'

Lottie closed her eyes. She didn't want to cry again. It was silly, but she couldn't help it.

'Hey. Is it dinner? Because I bet we can get someone to open up the village stores and get a load of pizzas. I quite fancy pizza.'

He wasn't even joking. She gave him a shove and rubbed at her eyes. 'No. Dinner is fine.' Although she did need to go and check on her timings. 'It's Joe.'

Zach had the look of every confused male. 'What's he done?'

'Nothing new. He just said that he felt leaving me was the right decision. And it hurt a bit. But I'm fine.' To prove her point, she slapped on a fake smile, which Zach seemed to take as genuine.

'Okay. Great. Let me tell you about Scott.' *Are all men completely insensitive, or simply oblivious?* thought Lottie.

The drawing room door opened and Dayea came out, heading for the stairs. She stopped, turned around and approached Lottie. 'What's wrong?' she asked, her eyes seeming to reflect Lottie's sadness.

'I'm fine. But thanks for checking,' said Lottie, trying her best to sound bright.

Dayea took her hand. 'Thank you for inviting me. I'm having a very lovely Christmas.'

'I'd hold fire with the compliments until after lunch, if

I were you, Dayea,' joked Zach. He received glares from both women in response.

'You're one of the family now,' said Lottie.

'That is a kind thing to say but then you are a kind girl.' Dayea patted her hand before continuing upstairs.

Zach led Lottie down the hall nearer to the kitchen. He held up his hands to big up his revelation. 'I thought I'd met Scott somewhere before. It turns out I haven't, but I have *seen* him somewhere before.'

'Right. Where?' Lottie was losing interest and the cauliflower cheese was calling her.

'In a porn film!'

'What?' Lottie's mouth had fallen open. She shut it again. 'Are you sure? You have been drinking.'

Zach waved her words away. 'Certain. The whole trimmer thing was probably code, or a cover story or something.' Zach was nodding excitedly. 'He's definitely a porn star. You didn't need to get him a present – you could have given him coal. He's a very naughty boy.' Zach was giggling.

'How sure are you about this?'

'Certain. Trust me, I've seen him in loads of porn films.'

The sound of someone dropping something in the kitchen drew their attention. They both peered around the door to see Emily looking shocked. Lottie was pleased that it wasn't her mother. That would be no way to find out that your new partner was a porn star.

Emily was staring wide-eyed at Zach. He was still grinning, but his smile dropped at Emily's stony expression. 'I don't usually watch porn,' he said, directing his words to Emily but twisting to look at both women. Emily stormed out of the kitchen and upstairs.

'Shit,' said Zach.

'I think you've got some explaining to do.' Lottie pointed after Emily. 'Go after her, you dunderhead.'

'Right. Yes.' Zach at last jogged off down the hallway. 'Em, wait! I can explain.'

Chapter Fifteen

Lottie busied herself in the kitchen and was pleased with how dinner was coming along. It was slightly worrying that everything seemed to be under control – it probably meant she'd forgotten something vital. She checked her plan and timings. It was all on track. As per Emily's mum's instructions, she liberally basted the turkey with goose fat and reverently returned it to the warmth of the old cooker.

Angie's head popped round the door. 'Did you find those batteries?'

'No, sorry, I've only got the little ones. I think Zach used the last big ones for one of Jessie's new toys.'

'Great, which toy?'

Angie's enthusiasm had Lottie suspicious. 'That noisy robot thing. Why?'

'No reason,' said Angie and she was gone.

Lottie had no sooner turned back to the cooker than a bump and bang announced Uncle Bernard powering into the kitchen, catching the doorframe on the way in. 'I've come to check on the ham,' he bellowed. He'd been on the sherry since breakfast, which definitely impacted on his driving skills and probably wasn't wise on his medication.

'It's in the fridge. We don't need it until teatime,' said Lottie.

'What time is dinner?' asked Daniel, strolling in with his eyes glued to his phone.

'Usual time. Why?' asked Lottie, as she hopped up to sit on the worktop to avoid being run over by Uncle Bernard, who was now lapping the kitchen.

'Thought I might . . . um . . . pop out afterwards. Or possibly before.' Uncle Daniel pulled out a chair and blocked Lottie's route to the cooker. 'Have I got time before dinner?'

Lottie was getting flustered; she was meant to be making the stuffing. 'That depends on where you need to be and how long you're staying for.'

'Ah, yes. I suppose.' Daniel returned to his phone.

A door banged and the sound echoed down the hallway. Someone wasn't happy. Zach appeared in the doorway. 'That didn't go well,' he said, all saggy-shouldered.

Lottie didn't have time to comfort him now. 'I'm sure Emily will come around.' She reread the ingredients and instructions for the stuffing for the fifth time.

'Should I slice the ham now?' Uncle Bernard had his head in the fridge – Lottie wasn't sure if he was asking her or not. 'It'd be all ready to go into sandwiches then.' He hummed 'Jingle Bells' as if pondering his options. 'Where's the electric knife thingy?' he asked, spinning his chair ominously in Lottie's direction.

A vision of a Christmas Day massacre as Uncle Bernard careered around in his out-of-control wheelchair brandishing the electric carving knife shot into Lottie's mind. She couldn't risk that. 'I think it died,' she said. She couldn't look him in the eye; he'd know she was lying.

'That's a shame.' Uncle Bernard looked sad.

'I'll have a check later,' said Lottie, relenting. 'I might be wrong.'

'Where's the robot? I can't find it and Jessie has disappeared,' said Angie, marching in with her hands on her hips.

'Enough!' said Lottie, and they all jolted at her raised voice. 'I can't concentrate if everyone is asking me questions.'

'Should we go, Button?' asked Uncle Bernard.

'Yes, please,' said Lottie, composing herself.

Angie had a face like she'd swallowed holly. 'But I just need—'

'Shoo,' said Bernard, and he ran her out of the kitchen with his wheelchair on its highest speed setting.

'Thank you,' called Lottie. She was grateful to Uncle Bernard, although she feared the day could still end in a hail of bullets – or her mince pies, which could probably do a similar level of damage.

Lottie made the stuffing using step-by-step instructions from Emily's mum. It was much easier now everyone had disappeared. She moved back to view everything bubbling merrily on the stove and breathed a little sigh of relief. She hoped it wasn't tempting fate, but she seemed to be on track.

She scanned her list. Next up: lay the table. Their Christmas table was always something special, and this year was no exception. Lottie had sat down weeks ago with Nana and they had chosen the colour scheme, so she wanted to make sure it was just right.

She was rummaging in the sideboard when Jessie popped her head around the door.

'Watchya doing?' Jessie asked.

'I'm laying the table. Do you want to help me?'

'Yeah. I've got something for the centre.' Jessie ran off and returned shortly afterwards with something green and red made from papier mâché.

'Oh that's impressive,' said Lottie.

'It's holly,' said Jessie, proudly placing it in the middle of the table. It was quite big but at least it could stand up on its own. It was one large bulbous holly leaf with two oddly shaped red berries at the base. Lottie studied it. Now it looked like a giant green knob with red balls.

The door opened and Joe's face appeared, his expression uneasy. Lottie went into 'everything is completely fine' mode. Even though it wasn't.

His eyes alighted on the phallic centrepiece. 'Wow. That's . . .'

'Holly,' said Jessie.

Joe narrowed his eyes and appeared to be stifling a laugh. 'Of course it is. Anyway, I'm going to pop back down to the pub. I wondered if Jessie wanted to come with me?'

Jessie and Lottie exchanged confused expressions. 'I think Zach's trying to cut down her alcohol consumption,' said Lottie, trying overly hard to sound breezy. Jessie giggled.

Joe shook his head and she noticed a little colour spring to his cheeks. He seemed awkward around her too. Was this how things would be for the rest of the day? Uncomfortable and cautious?

'Sorry. Let me try again. Petra from the pub said she can let me have a sack of Tiny's food, but I'm not carrying it up the hill. So I'm going in the car to pick it up. I thought Jessie might like to meet Tiny.' Jessie was pulling a face. 'Tiny's a dog, by the way,' added Joe, and Jessie's

155

face lit up. She ran for the door. 'I'll take that as a yes,' he said.

'Hang on,' said Lottie. 'I don't mean to be judgemental but didn't you have a skinful earlier?'

'Nope. I had half a pint. It was Zach who was downing them. And I wouldn't dream of driving under the influence.' His expression was serious.

At least he hadn't changed on that score; she'd always admired his strong moral compass. 'That's okay then.' She busied herself with some serviettes.

Joe rubbed his chin. 'Actually, that reminds me: is Zach okay? Because he wouldn't elaborate, but back at the pub he kept saying something like Emily wouldn't be his girlfriend for much longer.'

'Erm, I'm sure he will explain when the time is right,' said Lottie, biting her lip. It was tricky, but she could hardly give away the secret that Emily was about to be upgraded from girlfriend to fiancée.

'Come on, Joe!' called Jessie from the hallway.

'I'd better go.'

'Make sure you're both back in time for dinner, or there'll be trouble.' Lottie was back to fake jolly mode. Joe gave a short nod before he disappeared. When she heard the front door shut, she let out a sound like a punctured bouncy castle. It was taking so much effort to interact with him. She missed their carefree relationship.

Lottie finished laying the table by herself. Underneath everything else was the thick table protector – as per Nana's instructions, it always went on first, just in case the heat of the dishes or an accidental spillage damaged her precious antique table. Next, she had used the thick white tablecloth that Nana kept for best, overlaid with a pretty, shiny cloth, deeply embroidered with bright red poinsettias and deep green holly leaves. Nana had brought it back from a German market many years ago. Either side of Jessie's phallic holly centrepiece were two large candles which promised scents of cinnamon and clementine, surrounded by pinecones and real ivy that Lottie had collected from around the village. It was tasteful apart from the bright red crackers on each place setting; but then you had to have crackers.

Lottie stepped back to admire her handiwork. The table was the picture of Christmas. She hoped Nana would have approved.

Just as Lottie returned to the kitchen, two timers went off simultaneously and the sprouts went volcanic and spewed all over the ancient hob, extinguishing the gas. She began to regret banishing everyone else from the kitchen. She pushed her hair off her face with her hand, forgetting she was wearing oven mitts, and wondered how on earth Nana had managed Christmas dinner – for nine or more – on her own for all those years.

Lottie decided that unless she wanted a disaster on her hands – and all over the kitchen – she needed help. She straightened her apron and strode down the hallway. A cacophony of voices and barking grew in volume as she drew closer to the drawing room. The muddle of fraught voices, interspersed with the dog's insistent howls, made her realise that what she'd left behind in the kitchen may have been the calmer of the two situations.

She gripped the brass doorknob and was about to steel herself for what lay inside when the butler's bell began to echo around the manor house. Someone was at the front door. Lottie dropped her hand and claimed the visitor as a temporary escape; she'd tackle the family in a moment.

She hurried to the oversized door, opened it and was hit by a sudden rush of icy air. She braced herself against the cold and faced the woman standing on the steps, her petite face framed by the fur trim of her hood.

'Happy Christmas!' Lottie chimed, before she clocked the young woman's tense expression.

'Nicola?' the woman asked, appraising Lottie in a way that made her shiver more than the chill winter's air had.

'No. I'm her niece, Lottie. But come in, I can get Aunt Nicola for you.' Lottie ushered the woman inside; the front door gave a tired creak as Lottie shoved it closed and led the way. She was beginning to feel uneasy at the thought of eking out the turkey any further; although if the visitor was vegan, she was in luck.

'Sorry, I didn't catch your name?' asked Lottie, as they reached the drawing room. It still sounded as though a football match were taking place inside. The woman ignored Lottie, opened the door and strode in.

Inside, the family appeared to be conducting at least three simultaneous arguments: Angie was trying to get Jessie's robot off Zach, Daniel was pressing buttons on the robovac whilst Nicola shouted out the instructions, and Uncle Bernard was arguing with his wheelchair. Dave was bouncing up and down by the windowsill whilst the Duchess clung precariously to the curtain top with unsheathed claws. Lottie opened her mouth intending to yell 'shut up', but the woman was already shouting.

'Dan!' Her voice commanded instant and total attention; the noise dwindled away and everyone, including the animals, turned to look. Uncle Daniel's habitual high colour drained to white and he rushed forward, bumping his shin on the antique coffee table in his attempt to intercept the woman as quickly as possible.

'Daniel?' Aunt Nicola's voice sliced through the room. She twitched a smile at the young woman but directed her question at her husband who was now halfway across the room, vigorously rubbing his bruised shin. 'Who is this?'

Daniel started to speak but there were no distinguishable words, only a jumble of incomprehensible burbles. His gaze pivoted from Nicola, to the young woman, and back to Nicola's increasingly fierce face.

The woman pulled down her hood to reveal long, golden hair. She was exceptionally pretty.

'I'm Rebecca,' said the woman, before Daniel could answer.

Chapter Sixteen

'I don't think it was a good idea to come here, Rebecca,' said Daniel, his voice barely a whisper, his expression one of stunned mortification.

Rebecca lifted her chin. 'But you said you would spend this Christmas with me,' she said.

'Daniel?' snapped Nicola. When he didn't answer, she walked calmly over to Rebecca. The heads in the room swivelled like they were watching match point on centre court at Wimbledon.

Rebecca straightened her spine and the two women weighed each other up.

Lottie cleared her throat. Daggers were hurled in her direction for interrupting the floor show, but she continued anyway. 'I think this might be a discussion you'd like to have in the snug?' she suggested, opening the door and hoping the three key performers would exit. Nobody moved.

'I'm leaving now, Dan. Are you coming?' asked Rebecca. Lottie held the door open and watched the cool draught from the hallway waft the tinsel as everything else in the room stayed still. Duchess saw her opportunity, jumped down from the curtain and darted through the open door;

Lottie shut it quickly to halt Dave's chase. Rebecca looked momentarily startled. 'Sorry,' said Lottie. 'They can't be in the same room or they fight.'

'Like some other people we could mention,' said Bernard. 'What?' he said to the looks that were fired in his direction. 'We're all thinking it.'

'Can we just talk about this?' asked Daniel. Nicola and Rebecca both spun in his direction, making him jolt at his obvious mistake. 'I mean . . .' He looked from one to the other.

'I'm done talking,' said Rebecca. 'No more empty promises.' Her voice cracked and Lottie immediately wanted to comfort her.

'I've certainly got some things *I'd* like to say,' said Nicola, eyeballing her husband, her voice laden with sarcasm.

Daniel cupped his chin; or perhaps he was protecting his throat, Lottie couldn't be sure. Whichever, it seemed a guarded gesture. 'Nicola, I didn't mean for you to find out like this. I—'

Nicola let out a hollow tinkle of a laugh. 'Oh, don't for a moment assume this is a big surprise, Daniel. You've been acting strange for weeks. Always late home, constantly on your phone. You're not exactly MI5 material.'

'Nicola, don't . . . it's not what you think,' said Daniel.

Nicola's eyes locked onto her husband. 'I think it's exactly what I think. What's it to be? Me or her?' She turned slowly back to stare, unblinking, at Rebecca.

'Dan. Aren't you going to say something?' Rebecca's lips formed a hard line.

Uncle Daniel was running both his hands over his head where his hair used to be. 'I . . . um . . .' He blew out his cheeks and shook his head. 'You see . . . the thing is . . .'

'Fine. I'm leaving.' Rebecca marched to the door. Lottie faltered as Dave was nearby. She muttered an apology for blocking Rebecca's exit, scooped up Dave and stepped aside.

'Goodbye. And sorry everyone for interrupting your Christmas.' There were mumbles and coughs in response. Rebecca gave Lottie a tight smile as she opened the door for her, and the young woman strode out with her head high.

'Well, that was tawdry,' said Nicola, picking up a glass with a shaky hand and pouring herself a large brandy. 'Can you believe her chutzpah?'

'I bet you're good at Scrabble,' said Scott, and Angie gave him a nudge.

Daniel, who appeared to have been in a state of suspended animation, suddenly bolted for the door. 'Rebecca. Wait!'

For a second Nicola looked like she was going to vomit. Instead she finished the brandy, returned the glass to the silver tray and followed her husband from the room. There was a brief moment where the others exchanged looks, and then Angie scurried out the door, keen not to miss the next act. The rest followed quick on her heels, with poor Bernard bringing up the rear after he got a wheel caught on the sofa.

Emily grabbed Zach's arm and pulled him to one side as they exited the drawing room. His eyes followed the row in full swing at the open front door as she dragged his body towards the kitchen.

'Zach.' Emily's tone wasn't unlike Nicola's: it made them both jump. Zach's head snapped around and he gave her his full attention. 'Sorry. I don't think we should intrude,' said Emily, embarrassed to have witnessed what had just unfolded.

Zach's face fell. 'You're right, of course.' He paused for a moment, listening to Rebecca's raised voice. 'But this is literally the most exciting thing Uncle Daniel has ever done. *Ever*. And by like a trillion miles.' Zach emphasised the words with his hands.

'Zach . . . I don't know them and I feel really awkward.'

'None of us know Rebecca,' he said. She glared at him. 'Okay, okay. You're right.' He turned his head for one last glimpse of the argument before he let her tug him away. They walked through to the kitchen, where the smells of Christmas dinner greeted them. The Duchess slunk into the utility and curled up on a new mophead.

Emily faced Zach and with a renewed sense of purpose she looked him in the eye. 'We need to talk.'

Her words seemed to slap him. His expression changed from childlike mischief-maker to undertaker. 'What is it, Em?' His eyes searched her face. 'Is it the porn?' He shook his head. 'Of course it's the porn. I am telling you the God's honest truth. Like I said I can get Clarky to tell you himself. That man has no shame. He was watching it for most of the stag weekend. I couldn't avoid it. And I did try.' Emily tilted her head on one side. 'Okay, maybe I could have tried a little harder, but I swear I told him to switch it off but he wouldn't. If I turned it off he switched it back on again. He had paid for some bumper package so he wanted to get his money's worth.'

She opened her mouth to speak but it was difficult to get a word in.

'The thing is if Clarky hadn't been on a porn marathon I wouldn't have found out about Scott. I *knew* I'd seen him somewhere before. I remembered because I said to

163

Clarky "Since when did Mark Antony have a tattoo?" He was playing Antony in *Cleo-Pant-Tra.* He clicked his fingers and his face lit up. 'And he was Barnum in *The Great Tits Showman.*'

'Are you making those titles up?' Emily didn't want to be distracted but she couldn't stop the corners of her mouth lifting.

'No, seriously. It was the worst porn I've ever seen. *Poke-Her-Hontis* was very badly acted.' Emily's eyebrows rose and with them Zach's hands. 'Not that I've watched loads you understand. This is reject porn. That's what Clarky called it. This stuff is so bad it's got a bit of a cult following.' He shook his head. 'Apparently *Fantastic Breasts and Where to Grind Them* won some awards.'

'I don't want to talk about porn.'

'No. Of course not. Sorry.' His brow furrowed. 'Then what did you want to talk about?'

Emily took a deep breath. *Here goes nothing.* 'I want you to come to the bathroom with me.'

Zach's eyes sparkled and he pulled her to him. 'Comfier in the bedroom. Jessie will be gone for ages if there's dogs involved.'

'Zach, I'm not suggesting sex.' He looked disappointed. She pushed her hair behind her ears and tried to buy herself a moment's thinking time. She should have thought this through. She couldn't seem to conjure up enough words to make the sentence she needed to say. Instead she took his hand and led him back into the hallway, past the quarrelling threesome and their assembled audience and up the stairs. She caught Lottie watching them as they passed and she was buoyed by the warm smile she gave her. Emily clutched Zach's hand tighter and hoped she was doing the right thing.

'Hang on. I can't miss this,' said Zach. 'You go on up, I'll be there in a minute.'

Nicola, Daniel and Rebecca were all outside on the doorstep spitting venom at each other while the rest of the family skulked behind the half-open door. Rebecca started off down the steps.

'Oh, leaving so soon, Rebecca?' said Nicola, the name sounding oddly acidic on her tongue. 'I'm sure we could stretch the turkey to one more. Make it a proper family *affair.*'

'Right,' said Rebecca, spinning on her heel and marching back up the steps to face Nicola. Nicola stood her ground and Daniel clapped his hands to get their attention.

'Let's not do this. I can explain,' he began.

'But you're not,' said Rebecca, throwing her arms up. 'You're ashamed of me. Aren't you?'

'Well, *obviously,*' said Nicola, drily.

'Will you shut up?' snapped Rebecca. 'My God you're vile. Why the hell he stayed with you instead of my mum I'll never know.'

'Her mum too?' said Angie with a gasp.

'Shhh,' said Bernard.

Nicola stepped back. 'Who's your mother?' she asked. Rebecca didn't answer so Nicola tilted her head at Daniel. When he spoke he spoke to his shoes. 'Elaine.'

Nicola let out a startled, tinkling laugh. 'Elaine? Your old PA?' Daniel nodded. 'Well, of course, I knew all about *that.*' Nicola straightened her shoulders.

'It was years ago,' said Daniel. 'It's been over since—'

'Since she had me,' cut in Rebecca. 'I'm his daughter.'

'Ahhh,' came the chorus of realisation from the family, still watching from inside.

165

Daniel seemed to deflate. 'Do you see the hopeless situation I'm in?'

'No, I see the situation you've put this poor woman in.' Nicola uncrossed and recrossed her arms. 'Rebecca, I am truly sorry for the misunderstanding, and for what I've said. However, my first priority is to our son. Rhys doesn't need to be upset by something like this. It's an important year for him.'

Rebecca was shaking her head. 'He's had a father for nineteen years. I've only just . . . I've . . .' but her voice cracked and she couldn't continue. She strode off towards a battered-looking VW Beetle. Nicola turned back towards the house, and the group huddled at the door all pulled away in unison having been caught spying.

'What's going on?' asked Rhys as he joined them in the hallway. The group stared at him guiltily. He pulled off his headphones and leaned in front of Lottie to look out of the window. 'Who's that then?' he asked, pointing at Rebecca's car reversing erratically across the grass as Daniel jumped in his car and took off after her.

'It's, um. Well, she's . . .' Lottie faltered. She'd wanted one last happy family Christmas, but right now she'd settle for one where they got to the end of it without someone being murdered.

'Can I smell burning?' asked Rhys.

As if in reply, the smoke alarm began wailing.

'Dinner,' said Lottie, almost shouting, and she fled towards the kitchen, thankful to be literally saved by the bell.

As Lottie charged into the kitchen, the Duchess charged out in a blur of fur, and Lottie found herself alone in the smoke-filled room. The shock of it made her take a large breath and she immediately started to cough. Black fumes were billowing from the oven. She had to hold her hand over her nose and mouth as she opened it. A wave of black smoke met her and she blinked hard as it stung her eyes. The turkey was ablaze. Still coughing, Lottie pulled on the oven gloves and rescued their dinner from the oven, dropping the roasting tray unceremoniously onto the kitchen table. As she let go she realised the flames had spread to the oven gloves. She yelped and wrestled them off.

Joe appeared as if from nowhere, grabbed a tea towel, stuck it under the tap and spread it over the now fully aflame oven gloves, putting out the fire instantly. He then went through the kitchen opening all the windows. The back door was already swinging open from where he'd dashed in. Jessie was standing on the step outside watching. Joe snatched up another tea towel and took up position underneath the fire alarm, frantically waving until it finally stopped shrieking.

'Oh dear,' said Angie, who had come to see what all the commotion was about. She was now peering at the turkey. Flames were still dancing across its charred surface. Lottie could see it was taking all her mother's self-control not to dissolve into hysterics.

'There's nothing to worry about,' said Lottie. This was enough to cope with without her mother's unhelpful commentary.

'Oh, I'm not worried,' said Angie. 'I'm a vegan. Remember?'

Lottie could feel her blood beginning to boil. She was almost as hot as the turkey. 'I hope you're not hungry because the *vegans*,' she made inverted comma signs in the air, 'are going to have to share with everyone else.' A quick glance into the open oven reassured her that the vegan wreath Emily had helped her with earlier had survived the blaze. She picked up the charred oven gloves.

'It's like *Carry On Christmas*,' said Angie with a hoot.

'Showing your age, Mother,' said Lottie.

Joe escorted Jessie through the still-smoky kitchen into the hallway, waved Angie away and shut the kitchen door. He and Lottie stared at the blackened turkey together. 'It's completely ruined,' said Lottie, failing to hide the dismay in her voice.

'You might want to cross "chef" off your list of possible new career paths,' joked Joe.

He took a carving fork from the drawer and gave the turkey a prod. He wasn't helping. 'Don't do that, Joe. It's definitely dead.'

'And cremated.' Joe was nodding.

'Too late for last rites.'

'We should probably put it in an urn or scatter it on a rose bush in the garden.'

'Bugger,' said Lottie with feeling, as Joe inspected the turkey closely.

'Actually, I don't think it's ruined. It must have been the fat that was burning and not the actual turkey, otherwise by now it would be a lump of charcoal.'

Lottie picked up a sharp knife, nudged Joe out of the way and made a small slice into the breast meat. Underneath the dark skin the turkey was indeed fine. Utter relief washed over her. Joe rummaged in the cupboards and without saying anything handed her a roll of aluminium foil. This was clearly where she had gone wrong. She wrapped a large sheet of foil over the turkey and flung it back in the oven.

Now alone, Joe and Lottie glanced awkwardly at each other. A shiver came over Lottie and she busied herself with shutting the back door. She'd need to leave the windows open a while longer, because the smell of the

168

burning fat was still strong. Goodness knows what Nana would have said, although come to think of it, Lottie was sure Nana would have seen the funny side – and hopefully, eventually, she would too.

The silence between them was thick. Dave trotted in and made himself comfortable on the mophead that the Duchess had recently vacated.

Joe was scanning the kitchen – it was the proverbial bombsite. 'What's the motto here?' he asked with laughter in his voice. '"Cook like you're not cleaning up"?'

'Except I'll be doing that, too, unless I frogmarch people in here.' Lottie sighed. It was like being a lone soldier on a battleground surrounded by the enemy – but worse, because she was related to these people.

'I'll give you a hand.' Joe rolled up his sleeves and began filling the sink with water.

'Thanks,' she said, and she readjusted her hair clip. Joe smiled and then looked away.

'Did you get the dog food?' This was the level she needed to keep it at with Joe – mundane and perfunctory.

'Yeah, I wasn't sure I was going to get Jessie away from Tiny. She's proper bonkers about dogs. But then I was the same at that age.'

'I remember,' said Lottie, failing to hide the sadness the memories brought to her eyes. She snatched up a Pyrex jug. They needed gravy, and she needed a distraction. She hastily tugged at the foil on a chicken stock cube, and as the foil gave way, the cube inside exploded in her face.

'Ow! My eye,' said Lottie, dropping the rest of the cube and feeling it crunch underfoot.

'Here, let me look.' Joe took her arm and guided her to the light of the window. 'Head up.'

She struggled to look at him through her good eye, she

wasn't good at winking but she could see he was smiling. 'Open your eye then.'

'This isn't funny,' she remonstrated. 'It's really stinging.'

He gave a jolly snort. 'Only you could get injured by a stock cube.' There was pure affection in his voice. Or perhaps she was imagining it. Joe was so close he could have kissed her. For a moment she wondered if he was going to. Her pulse quickened. 'Blink,' he instructed. He tore off a piece of kitchen roll, wet it and gently dabbed around her eye.

'Is it okay?' she asked, continuing to blink with her mouth open in what she knew was a particularly unattractive manner – but she couldn't help it. And at least that would kill any romantic notions.

'Yeah, a dash of water and that's the gravy done,' he quipped. 'It's nothing a roast potato can't fix.'

Chapter Seventeen

Emily wandered into the kitchen. 'How's it going?' she asked.

Lottie squinted at her through one eye. 'Not great.'

Joe was drying up a saucepan. 'She got gravy in her eye,' he said, with a smile.

'Gravy?'

'I was attacked by an exploding stock cube,' explained Lottie.

Emily was puzzled as to how a stock cube could explode exactly. 'O-kay. Can I help?'

'Here.' Joe threw the tea towel to her as he passed. 'I need to make some happy Christmas phone calls to the States.'

Emily caught the tea towel and set to work.

'Did you and Zach sort things out about the . . . adult films?' asked Lottie.

'Yeah. It was his mate who paid for them. I guess if there's free porn on TV most men are going to watch it. And to be honest, it does sound like it was hard to avoid – they were sharing a room. And, you know, stag week-ends,' said Emily with a shrug.

'Hen nights aren't much better. People go a bit crazy.'

'I prefer a nice spa,' said Emily. 'I'd love a massage right now.' Lottie's lips twitched. 'Oh, not that I don't want to be here. I'm having a nice time.'

'How are you finding it so far?' asked Lottie. 'It's okay. I know what a complete nightmare this family is – and that's from someone on the inside. I can't begin to imagine the horror it must seem from your perspective.'

Emily tried not to blush, but it was impossible. She turned to face the draining board. She didn't want Lottie to see her when she lied. 'No, it's lovely. They're all very . . . lovely.'

The laughter that came from Lottie was one step away from maniacal villain. 'No, they're not. It's okay, you don't have to lie to me.'

Emily relaxed a fraction. 'I guess they are a bit quirky.'

'Quirky? I'd like to say they put the "fun" in "dysfunctional" . . . but they don't.'

Emily checked Lottie's expression. She seemed like an honest and open person; this wasn't a trap. Emily relaxed her shoulders. 'You're right; they're a nightmare. How come you're still sane?'

'I'm not. I just look good next to them. It's all relative. In this case, literally.' They laughed together and any final barriers between them were down. Lottie sidled over and pushed the kitchen door shut. They needed a little bit of privacy for a good gossip.

'I like Bernard. You looked surprised when he announced his engagement,' said Emily.

'I think we all were. But I'm happy for him. Dayea is lovely.'

'I'm sure she is; but there *is* a bit of an age gap. You don't think maybe . . .'

'She's after his money? It's okay, I think we all thought

it. But I'm sure she's genuine – and if she's going to make him happy, I can't see the harm really.'

'And your mum's going out with a porn star.' She laughed, saw Lottie's expression change, and instantly felt bad. 'I'm sorry. That's probably not quite as funny from your perspective.'

'No, it is funny. It's also typical of my mother. She has a really bad track record with men. And, despite everything, I do worry about her. I think she really likes Scott, so the inevitable breakup is going to hurt. This time she won't have Nana to pick up the pieces.'

'And I couldn't believe it when that woman turned up. It was like Christmas Day in Albert Square,' said Emily.

'There's less drama on *EastEnders* – and at least they have some light relief. But I guess we have alcohol, and that helps a bit. Not that I'm advocating it for everyone.' Lottie's eyes momentarily scanned Emily's midriff. Emily tensed up as Lottie spoke again. 'I saw you and Zach go off together earlier.' The unspoken question hung in the air.

This was the conversation Emily could not avoid. Part of her didn't even want to any more. She needed a friend right now, and Lottie seemed to fit the bill, even if she was her boyfriend's sister.

'I didn't do the test,' said Emily. Lottie looked surprised. 'I decided it was something Zach should be there for and I told him we needed to talk.' Lottie began nodding and Emily relaxed. 'But when I went upstairs, he stayed down here to watch the live episode of *EastEnders* playing out on your doorstep.' She sighed at her foiled plan.

'Typical bloody Zach. He's rubbish at picking up vibes. You kind of need to spell it out to him.'

'It's really difficult with the family around us all the time.'

'Yes, you'd think in a house this size you'd be able to escape, but you can't. Summer is better here. The gardens are vast, so there are lots more opportunities to be on your own.'

'Outside loo?' asked Emily, only half joking. Lottie shook her head. 'Then even the gardens aren't ideal for doing a test,' pointed out Emily.

'True,' said Lottie, with a smile. 'You know you're just putting it off now. Right?'

Emily liked that Lottie told it how it was. 'Yes, I know. But I'm terrified of the result.'

Lottie's eyes widened. 'Don't you want kids?'

'I do want children,' said Emily, putting down the tea towel and leaning against the sink. 'But I want to make the decisions in my life about what I do and when, and right now this is not part of the plan.' The thought of slipping off the career ladder worried her, as well as her sister's smug face.

'Sometimes that's not possible. Nana used to say that everything happens for a reason and I truly believe that.'

Emily rubbed her tummy. She wished her period would kick in and then everything could go back to normal. She couldn't believe she'd got herself into this pickle. She was usually so careful. 'I really don't know how this happened.' Lottie tilted her head. It made Emily smile. 'Well, apart from the obvious.'

'But you don't know for sure it *has* happened until you do the test.'

This was the simple fact – Lottie was right. 'It's just a late period right now, and that's no big deal. But once I do the test then it could be a pregnancy and I really will have to face it. And I'll have to face Zach.'

'It is his fault too, you know.' Lottie's expression was

warm. 'You shouldn't have to go through this on your own. Nobody should.' She seemed to pause for a moment. 'And I know he's my brother, but he's also a decent bloke. If you ignore the nightmare family, of course.'

'Maybe I was wrong about doing the test together. If I do it and it's negative then there's no drama.'

'And if it's positive?'

Emily took a deep breath. 'Then perhaps it would be best if I got my head around it first.'

Lottie was nodding her agreement. 'I think that sounds like a good plan.' She checked her list on the table, looked at the clock and then set a kitchen timer. 'No time like the present,' she said. 'Do you want me to come with you?'

For a second Emily almost dismissed the offer out of hand, but there was something so kind and genuine about Lottie that made her feel she needed her around. 'Maybe just outside the door,' she suggested.

'Of course. And we can play this however you want to with Zach. I'll never breathe a word.'

'Okay.' Emily stood up straight. 'Let's do this.'

Upstairs, Lottie waited outside the bathroom door and felt uber conspicuous. If anyone came, she was the wrong end of the corridor to make a dash for her room, so she'd have to come up with some sort of an excuse for being there. She'd given Emily a hug before she'd gone inside the bathroom and that had been a few minutes ago, although it felt like a lot longer. Lottie tapped on the door. 'You okay?' she whispered.

'I can't go,' came back the hushed response.

'Ah,' said Lottie. Having a wee was critical and doing it quickly was equally so. Lottie's nerves couldn't cope with the subterfuge of hovering outside the bathroom. If Zach came up she'd probably spontaneously combust. 'Put the tap on. And think of Niagara Falls.'

After a pause she heard the tap start inside. She waited some more. *Oh come on, Emily*, she thought. The suspense was killing her and now, thanks to the sound of running water, she needed a wee too. She was quite excited. She didn't know if she'd ever get to do this herself, so it was nice to share in someone else's milestone – even if they weren't ecstatic about it.

A door opening downstairs had her on red alert. She did a high-speed tiptoe across the landing like a cartoon thief and was poised to dart into her bedroom if anyone should come up. She heard a scrabbling sound, and Dave appeared. Someone must have let him out of the drawing room but not thought to supervise him. He trotted up to Lottie and she gave him a pat. 'Shhh,' she told him, for no apparent reason, and then crept back to resume her position outside the bathroom with Dave in tow.

'How's it going?' she asked in a stage whisper.

'Good.'

What did that mean? The Duchess slunk out of Lottie's bedroom and Dave bolted towards her. Lottie snatched him up and he began barking furiously. In the struggle, Lottie fell against the bathroom door with a bang. A yelp came from inside.

'What's happened?' asked Lottie through the closed door. There was no answer. The Duchess hightailed it downstairs and the fight went out of Dave. He let out a yelp similar to Emily's. 'Emily, are you all right?'

The lock turned and the door opened a fraction. 'You'd better come in,' said a dejected-looking Emily.

'Whatever's wrong?'

Emily pointed at the toilet bowl and Lottie cautiously

peered over the rim. Dave, still in her arms, had a look too and wagged his tail. There, floating in the toilet, was the pregnancy tester.

'I dropped it when there was a bang on the door,' said Emily, her eyes somehow seeming bigger.

'Oh, sorry. That was me. And him.' She turned Dave to face her; he was partly responsible too. They all stared at the white plastic stick floating in the loo. 'Are you going to fish it out?'

Emily took a slow breath. 'Ew,' said Emily with feeling, reaching into the toilet and retrieving the tester. She dropped it by the sink and began washing her hands.

'What did it say?' asked Lottie.

'It won't work. The toilet's full of loo Bloo.' Frustration was evident in Emily's voice.

A few seconds passed before Emily picked it up by the very tip and held it so they could all see. Dave was particularly interested and was sniffing wildly in the stick's direction. Lottie focused on the little window.

'What does two blue smudgy lines mean?' asked Lottie.

Emily snatched up the packet from the side of the bath and checked the pictures. 'Positive. It means I'm pregnant.' Emily was rapidly turning the same colour as the pristine white towels behind her.

'Or does it mean it's been dropped in loo Bloo?' asked Lottie. They had no way of knowing.

Emily sat on the edge of the bath with a thump. 'But what if it still worked?' Emily looked at her with frightened eyes.

'Don't worry, not all of the madness in the family is hereditary,' said Lottie.

* * *

Lottie vigorously rang the handbell and herded everyone into the dining room, careful to tuck her toes out of the way of a high-speed Bernard. 'Sorry, Button,' he said, with a wave.

'Do we have to sign a waiver form before eating, so we can't sue you if the food kills us or something?' asked Zach, chuckling along at his own joke. Lottie stuck her tongue out at him.

The sound of the front door opening and closing made everyone pause. Uncle Daniel slunk in and took his seat. Lottie was pleased to see he had come back.

'Everything okay?' she asked.

He wobbled his head. 'I managed to catch her and we've had a bit of a chat. It's all a bit of a mess. But the situation's not irretrievable.'

'That's good,' said Lottie, watching everyone else take their seats. 'No, sorry Scott your place name is over there.' Lottie indicated the opposite side of the table to Angie – her attempt to divert him from cosying up to her mother. Angie gave her the look of a sulky teenager but sat down in the right place.

'Where's Aunt Nicola?' asked Lottie, which was answered by a series of shrugs. Lottie handed the oven gloves to Emily and started a quick search for her aunt. She grumbled to herself when there was no sign of her on the ground floor. The food would be getting cold. She dashed upstairs and could hear sniffling as she reached the top. She tapped lightly on her aunt's bedroom door. 'Aunt Nicola, it's dinner time.' Inside Nicola blew her nose loudly and came to the door. Lottie gave a sympathetic smile when she opened it. 'Are you coming down for some turkey?'

Nicola's face was red and blotchy and Lottie softened at the sight of her. Her aunt may not have been the warmest of characters, but she didn't deserve the Christmas she had had so far.

'I don't think so. I've had to tell Rhys he's not an only child.'

'How did he take it?' asked Lottie.

'He doesn't seem bothered. He just kept saying if Rebecca's twenty then it happened ages ago so it's "no biggy".' Lottie had to smile at Nicola using Rhys's turn of phrase.

'If he's okay, that's a big hurdle over. Don't miss out on your Christmas dinner.'

'I'm not sure I could stand the smug looks,' said Nicola.

'It won't be like that. I promise. They'll all be far too busy inspecting the meal I've produced and worrying if it's going to land them in A&E.'

Nicola didn't smile. 'You all think I deserve it.'

Lottie shook her head. 'No one thinks that.' Nicola gave her a knowing look.

'Really. Nobody deserves to be cheated on. And they certainly don't deserve to be confronted with it on Christmas morning.' Aunt Nicola was lots of things: she was a snob, a social climber and not the most sensitive of people, but she was not a bad person.

'Thank you. Do you want to know a secret?'

Lottie wasn't sure she could cope with any more secrets, but despite this she said, 'If you want to share, of course.'

Nicola's expression was unreadable. 'I didn't know about Daniel's affair. Not a clue. I just said I knew all about it so he'd not think he'd won. But I found out at the same time as you all did when she . . . Rebecca, walked in.' Nicola's voice was steady, defying the tears which were silently running down her cheeks. 'I know it happened a long time ago but I can't just dismiss it.'

Lottie pulled her aunt into a tight hug. 'Come on,' she said, stepping back. 'You've never been one to hide away. Remember it's Uncle Daniel who's in the wrong here.'

This seemed to galvanise Nicola. She straightened her shoulders, strode onto the landing and shut the bedroom door behind her. 'Then what are we waiting for?' she asked, blotting her eyes and smoothing down her hair. This was more like the Aunt Nicola Lottie was used to.

When they entered the dining room everyone was sitting in the right places, which was a feat in itself. Jessie was chatting happily to Scott and they seemed unaware that everyone else in the room had fallen deathly quiet. Lottie was thankful that someone had put on some Christmas music. A few eyes darted in their general direction but quickly refocused on piling their plates high with the bounty of food, which Emily must have ferried to the table in Lottie's absence. Nicola took her place opposite Daniel. Lottie wished she'd thought to move one of them, but it was too late now to do anything without it turning into *the* most awkward game of musical chairs ever.

She lit the candles and took her seat on the end so she was near the door for a quick exit to sort out the pudding. She noted that most plates were full but there was still plenty of food on the table, meaning she had catered for twice as many people, just like Nana used to do – although there were no pigs in blankets left for her, which was hugely disappointing. Lottie stuck her fork into a large roast potato and felt the crispiness of the outside. A little bud of pride blossomed inside her.

'What is that?' asked Rhys, pointing at Jessie's papier mâché creation, unable to hide his grin.

Bernard raised his eyebrows. 'Looks like a giant—'

'Holly! It's holly. Leaf and berries,' explained Lottie, outlining the shape in the air and immediately wishing she hadn't. 'Jessie made it.' Everyone congratulated Jessie, and Bernard smothered his dinner in gravy, still chuckling under his breath.

'Here you go,' said Bernard, passing the gravy boat to Angie.

'No thanks,' she said, picking up her cutlery.

Bernard looked more shocked than he had at the Rebecca revelations. 'No gravy? What on earth is wrong with you?' he asked.

Angie kept her eyes on her plate. 'Nothing.'

'But you always have gravy – and loads of it!' He put a finger in the air as if a thought had struck him. He caught a drip of the gravy and tasted it. 'It's okay. Lottie's done a fine job.' He offered the gravy again.

'No, thank you,' said Angie more firmly this time.

'You're worrying me now, Angie. What's the matter?' Bernard plonked down the gravy boat and studied his niece with genuine concern.

'Nothing is wrong. I'm a vegan,' she said, in almost a whisper.

Bernard gave a hearty chortle. 'Well you weren't five minutes ago when we were stealing those pigs in blankets.' Angie's eyes were wider than a bush baby's sitting on an ant's nest. For a moment everyone at the table paused apart from Jessie, who was simultaneously eating a carrot whilst peering down the end of her cracker.

Scott gave a half laugh from across the table, but when Angie didn't look up he put down his knife and fork. 'Angie? He's joking right?'

'Not at all,' said Bernard. 'She couldn't scoff them down quick enough.' He started another chortle but glanced around the table and seemed to notice the discomfort in everyone's body language.

'You're not a vegan?' asked Scott, confusion distorting his pretty features.

'Is she heck as like. She's always been a committed carnivore, has this one,' said Bernard proudly. Bernard turned and clocked Angie's expression. 'Angie? What's up?'

Angie dropped her cutlery onto her plate. The clatter made Jessie drop her cracker and splatter gravy across the tablecloth. 'All right. I may have fallen off the vegan wagon for a moment. It's not an actual *crime*.' She aimed her words at Scott.

Poor Scott appeared genuinely surprised. 'Being a vegan isn't like going on a diet. It's a long-term commitment.'

This would be something alien to Angie – her only long-term commitment was to her honey-blonde hair colour. Other than that, everything else, including her children, was a passing phase.

'And I am prepared to make that commitment. I want to, I really do,' said Angie, her voice softening. Lottie wasn't sure her mother was still talking about being a vegan.

Lottie cleared her throat. 'Could you pour the wine please, Zach?'

Zach did as he was asked. He was quieter than usual. 'You okay?' mouthed Lottie. He gave a nervous nod. What did that mean? Did he know about the pregnancy test? Or was he still fretting about the jewellery making its way through Dave's colon?

'Sorry,' said Scott, realising everyone had stopped eating.

'No need to apologise,' said Daniel, kindly. Nicola's head jerked up at the sound of his voice and for once he met her gaze straight on. Lottie froze. It was like witnessing a prey animal suddenly turn predator. 'I should apologise,' said Daniel. The tension in the room was palpable and everyone looked like they were taking part in a mannequin challenge – all stock still. 'I'm very sorry about the outburst this morning.' Nicola opened her mouth but he continued. 'And my behaviour in general.' There were embarrassed mumbles around the table.

'Um.' Lottie tipped her head in the direction of Jessie, who was watching intently, and Daniel gave the briefest of nods. She'd been out with Joe at the time of the showdown and the less she knew about it the better.

Daniel looked contrite. 'That wasn't how I wanted to introduce Rebecca to the family.' More mumbles followed.

Joe mouthed to Lottie, 'What's going on?'

'Tell you later,' she mouthed in return. Their ability to read each other's lips was still there.

Everyone tucked into their meals. Watching them eat was like the Hungry Hippos game had come to life.

'Is it cracker time?' asked Jessie, mid-mouthful.

'Yes, I think it is,' said Lottie, wiping her mouth on her serviette feeling thankful for the distraction. Jessie grinned.

A frenzy of cracker pulling and bangs followed and laughter filled the room. Hats were put on, cracker prizes swapped and pun-filled jokes read out. Lottie had a brief sense of satisfaction as she watched her mad, lovable family interacting. For a moment all tensions were forgotten – or at least were put on hold.

Zach looked pleased with his cracker prize. He winked at his sister.

'This meal is lovely,' said Joe, pointing his knife at his plate. A chorus of agreement rippled around the table and Lottie felt her cheeks colour. This was what she'd been striving for. Despite the arguments, interruptions, revelations and chargrilled turkey, she'd done it: she'd made her first-ever Christmas dinner.

'But no bread sauce?' asked Bernard, scanning the table.

Lottie rolled her eyes. 'Not this year. Sorry.'

'Oh, that's a shame. Christmas highlight that is,' said Bernard, and Dayea rubbed his hand in condolence. 'Always have bread sauce at Christmas.'

'Nobody really likes it though,' said Lottie, feeling defensive.

'*I* like bread sauce,' said her mother; and there were a few nods of agreement. Lottie shook her head – there was no pleasing some people.

'Can't say I've missed it,' said Joe. Lottie was grateful for the support, but it felt uncomfortable that it was coming from him.

'I shouldn't think you've missed much. America has all the stuff we have, *plus* a million other better things,' said Rhys.

Joe swallowed his mouthful. 'There's a couple of things I missed.' He gave the briefest of glances in Lottie's direction and her stomach flipped.

'Marmite?' suggested Zach, and the conversation flowed merrily as they compared the differences between the two countries, largely focusing on food. Everyone was eating and chattering, and it felt like Christmas.

Cutlery was placed on empty plates and contented sighs abounded, which was Lottie's cue to clear the table.

'Please can Dave come in now?' asked Jessie.

'Not yet,' said Lottie, but as soon as she opened the dining room door, Dave shot in anyway, performing a quick sweep of the room like a highly trained sniffer dog before grabbing something from under the table and racing off.

Most of the plates had been cleared into the kitchen, and Emily had run out of ideas for ways to help between courses. She found herself sitting at the dining room table with the warring couple. Nicola was glaring at Daniel, who was staring at his phone. The looks between them burned with unspoken arguments. Emily thought her family had disagreements, but this was on a whole new level. The uncomfortable silence was too much for her: it gave her time to think about her own situation, and she really didn't want to do that.

She needed to get things straight in her own mind. Seeing the two blue lines on the pregnancy test had affected her differently to how she'd expected. Rather than terror or devastation, there had been a surprising pop of something else. She reluctantly had to admit that maybe a tiny part of her would be okay with being pregnant. She didn't fully understand it. Perhaps she just wanted the silly competition with her sister to be over. Or maybe motherhood was something she'd put to one side for too long?

'The manor house is lovely. Did you used to live here?' she asked Daniel, in a desperate attempt to break the silence.

'Yeah. We moved here when I was about four. Actually, Nicola also lived here for a bit.' He glanced at his wife. She was laser beaming him with her stare.

'Did I? When?'

Daniel put his phone down. 'After you fell out with the university mates you were sharing a place with.'

'Oh. Yes. I remember.'

Daniel leaned forward and narrowed his eyes. 'Come to think of it I remember something else about that, too.' He turned his attention to Emily, as if telling her the story.

'One of them was a bloke, and he kept turning up here. And relentless phone calls too. He was desperate to talk to Nicola. What was his name?' Daniel clicked his fingers as if trying to conjure up the name as he might summon a waiter.

'Nigel,' said Nicola, her tone snappy.

'Yes, Nigel. I always wondered about Nigel, if maybe he and Nicola had been more than just friends,' he continued to speak to Emily. 'But I decided not to pursue it. Because Nicola was with me, so whatever had gone on didn't matter. It was in the past.'

'Right,' said Emily, wishing she could slink away without being noticed.

'I mean I've often wondered exactly what happened between Nigel and Nicola; but I let it lie. Didn't go on about it.'

Nicola slapped a palm on the table, giving Emily a start. 'Fine, Daniel. If we're getting all the secrets out on the table – I kissed Nigel. Okay? Well, we kissed each other after too much cider, and it was all rather awkward. It wasn't an affair and there was no resulting child.'

'Ah!' pounced Daniel. 'But a kiss is still a betrayal isn't it?' he asked Emily.

'Um. I suppose . . .' They were both staring at her now. She swallowed hard.

'I've been helping,' announced Jessie, returning to the room with Uncle Bernard close behind her.

'Ooh good idea. I should help too,' said Emily, quickly getting to her feet, as she spied her chance to leave. She'd heard of being caught between a rock and a hard place, but that was like being under a landslide.

'We should help too, Daniel,' said Nicola and they followed Emily from the room. There was no escape.

Everyone had been very keen to help clear the table, so Lottie found herself in the kitchen surrounded by helpers, leaving only Jessie and Bernard in the dining room. She figured they'd all spotted an opportunity to look and feel like they'd helped with Christmas dinner by chipping in with the bare minimum. Oh well, it meant she could focus on the pudding while they squabbled over how best to stack the dishwasher. And squabbling they were.

'Dad, you can't put the saucepans in or there's no space for the plates,' said Rhys.

'We'll need to wash the plates by hand,' said Daniel.

'But that's loads,' said Nicola. 'Far easier to wash a couple of pans,' she added, taking them out of the dishwasher. Rhys and Daniel started adding the plates.

'I'll leave these to soak,' said Nicola putting the pans in the sink. It didn't take a genius to work out who would be washing those up.

'If you put the plates in the other way round I can put these mixing bowls in,' said Emily hovering nearby. There were huffs in response but they made the changes so Emily could add the bowls.

Joe waved a full cutlery holder about. 'Where does this go?'

The dishwasher crew all stared at the full machine and sighed in resignation.

Jessie's scream ripped through the house. Everyone rushed to the dining room, Zach in the lead. Lottie dashed in behind Joe to see the table on fire: a funeral pyre of their Christmas. The smoke alarm screamed into life in the hallway, which added to the panic. Zach was shielding a tearful Jessie.

'Open the window,' yelled Joe, scooping up the flames

187

in the table protector and charging towards Lottie with the flaming bundle as wine glasses crashed to the floor. She flicked the catch and flung the window open, just in time for Joe to hurl the ball of flames through it. It gave a satisfying and reassuring hiss as it hit the wet ground outside.

The smoke alarm stopped. The buzz of Bernard's wheelchair grew closer and he appeared in the doorway and surveyed the scene. The panicked faces all turned in his direction. 'I only popped to the loo. What the devil's going on now?' he asked.

'You okay?' Zach asked Jessie, his face full of concern as he checked her over for any signs of damage. Emily joined him and wrapped the child in a hug; it was an instinctive gesture and despite the drama it brought a brief smile to Lottie's lips.

Jessie nodded and sniffed back a tear. 'I thought I could put the candle out with the tablecloth like Joe did when the oven gloves were on fire.' Lottie thought back to Joe throwing a wet tea towel over them. 'It all caught fire at once,' she added, the horror of the moment in her wide eyes.

'That's the end of Rose's special German tablecloth,' said Bernard, peering out of the window.

'Nana bought that years ago. I doubt it was subject to any fire-retardant guidelines,' said Lottie, joining him at the window and surveying the smoking mass. She turned back to see Joe was wincing. She looked down at his hands. 'Bloody hell, Joe. You've burnt yourself.' It probably wasn't the thanks he would have liked.

'It just needs cold water,' he said, squeezing past Bernard's chair and exiting the room. Lottie followed him.

In the kitchen Lottie ran the cold tap and thrust Joe's

hands under it; he didn't protest. She hastily emptied the contents of the ice tray into a bowl – Angie would have to do without any in her G&T. 'Let's have a look,' said Lottie, holding out her hands. Joe placed his dripping wet fingers in hers. Despite everything, the intimate contact made her stomach tumble over.

Lottie concentrated her attention on Joe's hands. 'Left one is okay,' he said, and she agreed. The right one however was very red and already blistering on the palm.

'Here,' she gently put his right hand into the bowl with the ice. 'Keep it in there for as long as you can bear. It'll help reduce the damage.'

'Thanks.' He looked a little sheepish.

'You were really brave back there,' said Lottie, finally giving him the credit he deserved for acting so quickly.

He shrugged. 'I just got there first.' Typical Joe, always modest.

They both stared at his hand, distorted by the water. For a moment they glanced up at the same time and then hastily returned their eyes to the bowl.

Lottie looked away and realised they had an audience. A number of faces were at the kitchen doorway.

'Right. Show's over. Back to Christmas.' Lottie clapped her hands. She was not going to let this Christmas get derailed – not even by a tablecloth inferno.

Chapter Eighteen

Lottie managed to shoo everyone out of the kitchen except for Joe, who was still soaking his burned hand. She busied herself with getting dessert ready, avoiding Joe's gaze, which she knew was on her.

'I was worried about coming back,' said Joe.

Lottie concentrated on turning out the hot, steaming Christmas pudding; she didn't want to get burned too. 'That's to be expected.' *After nine sodding years*, she added in her head.

'But stepping back into the manor house it's like I've never been away.' When Lottie paused to look, Joe was wearing a soppy smile.

She gave the upturned bowl a firm tap as she'd seen Nana do, and lifted it up. The plate was bare apart from a dribble of juice, and the pudding was still firmly in the bowl. 'That's nice, Joe. I'm glad.' She plonked the bowl back down with a thud, partly for the pudding and partly for Joe, but he didn't react.

'Nothing has changed,' he was looking idly around the kitchen, 'apart from your hair colour.'

Lottie peeked under the bowl. No sign of the pudding. She slammed it down and noted with satisfaction that this time Joe jumped. 'Not a single thing,' she said. 'Everything is exactly the same, just as you left it.' *Apart from me*, thought Lottie, *I've changed. Before you left, I knew what I wanted in life but then I lost my drive. I've walked blindly into a dull career and lurched through a series of unsuitable relationships.* She gave the bowl another hearty whack.

'You okay?' asked Joe.

'Me? I'm fine.' Lottie glared at the disobedient pudding bowl.

'Maybe this was what I needed all along?' Joe was watching her but sounded somewhere far away.

She rubbed her forehead, ignored the fact she'd smeared pudding juice across her face, and focused on the Christmas pudding. She held the bowl tightly through the charred oven gloves and lifted. Still no pudding. 'Argh!' She slammed the bowl down and the serving plate broke in two with a loud crack. 'Bugger it!' She lifted the bowl to reveal the bottom half of the pudding straddling the two halves of the plate. She drew in a slow breath. Why was everything so hard?

'Pudding smells good,' said Joe, sniffing the air like a Bisto kid. He seemed unaware of the undercurrent. 'Did you make it?'

She couldn't take the credit. 'Nana did. I sort of helped. She always made them weeks in advance.' *All I had to do was heat it and get it out of the sodding bowl and I can't even do that right*, she thought. Tears pricked her eyes and she blinked them away. She wasn't going to let Joe see her cry, especially not over a pudding.

She moved the half-pudding to another plate and checked for any shards of china – the last thing they needed was another injury. She took a knife from the drawer, prised out the rest of the pudding and plonked it on top. It looked like a mole hill dug by a very amateur mole. Oh well, it would have to do. Hopefully no one would notice once she'd poured the brandy on it.

Lottie warmed the brandy, poured it over the lumpy-looking pudding and quickly put a lit match against the surface. The match burned but the pudding didn't. She moved the match over the surface, but it still didn't catch light before the match burned out. She sighed, went to rummage in a drawer and found the candle lighter. She held it up, pulled the trigger, and to her surprise a flame appeared. 'Hurrah!' she said, aware she looked like a crazed scientist.

She stood by with the candle lighter, repeated the brandy heating, poured it over the pudding and immediately put the flame to it. Nothing. She frantically waved the candle lighter over the whole pudding. Nothing. The pudding wouldn't light.

'The one thing that's meant to be on fire.'

Joe chuckled. 'You're not getting cross with a pudding. Are you?'

Lottie pulled back her shoulders. She was cross about a lot of things. 'How's the hand?' she asked.

He took it from the iced water and inspected it. 'Okay, I think.'

She offered him a clean towel to dry it on. 'I'm giving up on lighting the pudding.'

'Maybe we've seen enough things overheat today.' His tone was soothing and they exchanged weak smiles.

Zach slunk in from the garden and shut the door. 'You okay mate?' He nodded at Joe's hand.

'I'll live,' said Joe, and he went to join the others in the dining room.

'Did Dave do his business?' asked Lottie.

'Nope. He's peed on everything out there though. I swear he's holding on to it on purpose.' He watched his sister, who was using two serving spoons to try to squish the pudding into more of a dome shape. 'I've got an idea,' said Zach, a twinkle in his eye. He pulled a bright green plastic ring from his pocket and held it under her nose.

Lottie looked at the tacky toy ring and then at her brother. 'You're never going to propose with that. Are you?' She hoped her screwed-up expression conveyed her thoughts.

'Listen. It's genius. We hide this in the pudding. Because why would I put a diamond ring that cost a grand in—'

'*How* much?' said Lottie, pulling her head back in surprise.

Zach waved the question away and continued. 'She finds this one in the pudding. I go down on one knee. Everyone swoons. She says yes. Then I can tell her she can have the real one later.'

'You think she'll say yes, to that?' She pointed at the plastic ring.

'Definitely,' said Zach.

'I'm not sure.'

'Trust me. It's delightful and Christmassy.'

'Not cheap and tacky?' Lottie gave the ring a sideways look.

'No.' Zach looked hurt. 'It's better than waiting for Dave to poo out the real one. This way she doesn't even need to know it's been through a dog's digestive system.'

Lottie could see how that would be appealing. 'What if Emily chokes on it?'

'You're being negative. If we put the pudding on top, she won't actually scoop it up and eat it.'

Lottie shrugged. 'On your head be it.' She picked up the

top bowl, put the ring in the next one and replaced the top one so it couldn't be seen.

She carried through the Christmas pudding and Zach brought in the tray with everything else, including ice cream for Jessie.

'You not lighting it?' asked Rhys, disappointedly eyeing the puddingy mass.

'I think we've all seen enough flames for one day.'

'Well we've seen enough people getting burned, for sure,' quipped Scott, but nobody laughed.

Jessie looked sheepish. 'Sorry.'

'Don't worry. At least you're safe,' said Lottie, putting down the pudding and kissing the top of Jessie's head. 'There's ice cream for you, Jessie.' She knew that would hold her attention so she'd not notice the green ring sitting in the next bowl. Lottie served hers and moved on.

'Pudding?' Lottie asked Emily, trying to sound nonchalant. She could see Zach watching out of the corner of his eye.

'Erm . . .' Emily was studying the lumpy-looking mass.

If she didn't have any, that would scupper Zach's plans. 'Oh don't worry about how it looks. Nana made it so it'll taste great.'

'I want some,' said Angie; Lottie noted Zach's concern.

'Not your turn,' scolded Lottie. 'Emily is a guest. Emily, you'll have a little won't you?' Lottie scooped up some pudding, placed it neatly on top of the green plastic ring and passed it to her.

'Okay, just a little then.' Emily rubbed her tummy and Lottie had to concentrate not to stare. Was that because she was full of dinner or growing a baby?

Emily took the bowl and Zach relaxed back into his seat. Lottie really hoped this went to plan. Another ripple of excitement went through her that her big brother was doing this. Such a big life milestone, and she was here to witness it. It would be the injection of happiness this Christmas needed. She served everyone else whilst keeping a check on Emily, who poured over some cream but waited to start until everyone else had theirs. *Lovely manners*, noted Lottie.

When everyone was served, Lottie tucked into her Christmas pudding. The taste of brandy was strong. Zach was eating his, but he was watching Emily with every mouthful. People were quiet apart from the odd mumble of appreciation. Nobody made a Christmas pudding like Nana. The sweetness of the fruit and the moistness of the pudding with a hint of bitterness made it a classic combination. This was Nana's last pudding, and Lottie knew she'd never written the recipe down. She'd have to have a think and see if she could remember the ingredients. It was sad to think it could be lost forever.

Lottie took a surreptitious glance at Emily's bowl. She would reach the ring soon.

Jessie had finished her ice cream and was watching her father. 'Daddy,' she asked sadly, 'why don't you want Emily to be your girlfriend any more?'

Chapter Nineteen

Zach stiffened like he'd been whacked on the head with a newspaper. Emily had stopped with her spoon halfway to her mouth. A tiny speck of green plastic was visible in her bowl. Zach giggled nervously. 'Don't be silly. Of course I want Emily to be my girlfriend.'

Jessie shook her head. 'No, I heard Joe telling Auntie Lottie that you said you didn't. And that makes me sad because I really like her.'

Joe went pale. 'Ah, well . . .' began Zach.

Emily was still holding her spoon aloft. She looked questioningly at her boyfriend, who was visibly squirming. 'Zach. Did you say that?' asked Emily, her voice almost a whisper.

'Technically,' everyone was watching him closely, 'technically, yes. But—' Zach didn't get to finish his sentence. Emily had dropped her spoon and rushed from the room. Zach slumped back into his chair. 'That didn't exactly go to plan.'

'What's going on?' asked Angie, eyes flitting between her children.

'Nothing,' chorused Lottie and Zach together.

'Jessie, you shouldn't listen to grown-up conversations; and you certainly shouldn't repeat them,' said Zach.

'Sorry,' said Jessie with a shrug. 'Can I have more ice cream, please?'

'Can you serve her, Mum?' asked Lottie. 'I'm going after Emily.' Lottie handed the ice cream scoop to her mother, who eyed it like it were a lit firework.

Lottie left the room and immediately encountered a dancing Dave. She put her head back round the door. 'Dave wants to go out again.'

'Bloody Dogzilla,' said Zach, screwing up his serviette.

Lottie heard the front door slam. She grabbed her own coat and Emily's and ventured into the cold after her. She could see Emily walking away and jogged to catch her up, struggling to put her coat on as she went. She shivered as she did it up. The bite of the wind had quickly chilled her.

'Emily, wait!' called Lottie.

Emily stopped, and as Lottie reached her she could see she was crying. Lottie didn't think; she just wrapped her in a hug. Emily's body gave way to sobs.

When Emily pulled away Lottie gave her her coat. 'Thank you. You're so thoughtful.'

'Unlike my brother.' They exchanged looks. 'It's not what you think.'

'Not wanting me to be his girlfriend is pretty clear.' Emily pulled a tissue from her coat pocket and wiped her eyes.

There was no way for Lottie to explain without giving the game away about his planned proposal, and he'd go mental if she did that. 'Things get lost in translation when they're overheard. Please trust me – I know he definitely still wants to be with you.' Emily didn't look convinced. 'Assuming you still want that. Now you've met the family, nobody would blame you for wanting to run for the hills.'

At last there was a snort of a laugh from Emily. 'It's like being in a drama series. I keep wondering what the next revelation will be.'

'Rhys is a champion Morris dancer,' said Lottie, her face deadpan. She could see Emily wasn't sure. 'Nah, I'm kidding. Come on, let's have a walk. We'll see if the others can stop arguing long enough to add the bowls to the dishwasher.'

Lottie pulled her coat tighter and linked an arm through Emily's. 'Welcome to the madness of the Collins family. You'll get used to us eventually.'

They strolled down the hill and Lottie couldn't help but take a peek through windows at other people enjoying their Christmases. She wondered if they were wrestling with issues like her family, or whether they were passing round the chocolates and watching telly.

'The meal was lovely,' said Emily.

'Thanks for your help with it. Your mum was a life saver.'

'I think I need to be with my mum,' said Emily, as if thinking out loud.

'I know it must feel like things are falling apart, but if you can just hold out for another day everything will slot into place. I promise.'

Emily nodded. 'I hope you're right.'

They reached Dumbleford Green, where people were coming in and out of the pub like a shift change.

'Merry Christmas,' called Shirley, her party hat lopsided as she clutched her tartan trolley and zigzagged her way across the green.

'Merry Christmas,' called back Lottie. 'Dumbleford's oldest resident,' she explained to Emily. 'I think she arrived with the pub foundations.'

'It's nice that you all know each other.'

'It is.' The thought of leaving tugged at her heart.

A large dog bounded over and almost took Emily out. 'Whoa!' said Emily, startled.

'Tiny, calm down,' said Lottie, as the English Mastiff bounced up and down around them. 'It's okay, he's harmless. He's no idea he's the size of a small horse.' The dog charged off and began circling the Christmas tree on the green. A young boy chased after him.

'Maybe Dave isn't so bad after all,' said Emily.

Lottie was pleased that she'd managed to reduce Emily's worries a little, but Zach really needed to pull his finger out before some serious damage was done to his relationship.

Back at the manor Emily decided to go for a lie down. Lottie left her to it. She'd had a spark of an idea, and if the timing was right, she was going to sneak off again.

'Dad. Can I have a word?' asked Rhys, as they met at the bottom of the stairs.

Daniel's troubled expression left him. 'Of course, son. What is it?'

Rhys held up his metal detector. 'Fancy seeing if there's buried treasure in the garden?'

'Or an escape tunnel. I could do with one of those right now.'

Rhys patted him on the back. 'I'll bring a shovel,' he said, a cheeky sparkle in his eye.

Having checked everyone was settled and the dishwasher was gurgling away, Lottie had put her coat back on. Shhh,' she said, holding the door for Daniel and Rhys as they all left the house together. She slung a cloth bag over her shoulder and checked the coast was clear.

'Are you up to something?' asked Rhys.

'Kind of. But it's a nice something.' She patted the bag. 'Not a word.'

Lottie walked speedily to the cars parked on the drive and Rhys and his father set about using the metal detector nearby. The light was fading so Lottie got straight to work.

'So, what's up?' Lottie heard Daniel ask his son. Lottie didn't like eavesdropping but they knew she was there, so it wasn't entirely sneaky listening. She concentrated hard on her task but it was impossible to tune out Uncle Daniel's voice. 'I'm guessing it's the mess I've made of everything.'

'I love you *and* Mum. I don't want you not seeing Rebecca because you think it'll upset me, because it won't.'

'Thanks, Rhys. That's incredibly mature of you. The truth is, Rebecca was a huge shock. I only found out she existed a couple of months ago – and even then I thought it was a scam. Or a joke.'

'So you've not been keeping her a secret for twenty years then?'

'Goodness, no. I can barely keep quiet about what we've bought people for Christmas, let alone something like this. I ignored the Facebook messages at first and then I realised there was a distinct possibility she was telling the truth. But I couldn't tell you or your mum about Rebecca without owning up to . . .' Daniel tailed off.

'Having an affair,' prompted Rhys.

'It was never really an affair. We flirted at work and then we landed this big client, went out and got drunk and ended up in some dodgy hotel for the night. We both knew it was a mistake. And then Elaine phoned to say she couldn't work for me any more. And she quit and I never saw her again. I swear.'

'It's okay. I believe you, Dad.'

'I've barely thought about her until Rebecca got in touch. And it all seemed to go a bit crazy.' Lottie popped her head up to see Daniel rubbing his hands over his shorn hair.

'It certainly went crazy today. Mum's really upset.'

'I know and I'm so sorry, Rhys. I never meant for anyone to get hurt. It's hard to explain but—'

Rhys waved his words away and slung the detector headphones around his neck. 'What I wanted to say was: what do you always say to me?'

Daniel sounded puzzled. 'Call your mother? Eat something other than beans on toast? Start revising early?'

Rhys chuckled. 'You do say all of those things, but no. You tell me to do what makes me happy.'

Daniel rubbed his chin, floored by the simplicity of his son's logic. 'It's not that simple, I'm afraid.'

'I think it is. If you want Rebecca to be part of your life, then you need to commit to it. Not keep her at arm's length.'

'But your mum . . .'

'When she's calmed down she'll be cool,' said Rhys.

Daniel's gaze rested on the house. 'Your Nana would have had something to say about all this. She would probably have given me a thick ear too. And I'd have deserved it. I've been an idiot.' He looked back at Rhys and put his arm around his shoulders. 'I'm so proud of you, Rhys. You've got a wise head on those shoulders and an excellent future ahead of you. Don't bugger it up.'

Rhys shuffled his feet on the gravel, looking embarrassed. 'Yeah, about that . . .'

Father and son walked off around the house and Lottie returned her full attention to the job in hand. She just hoped everything would turn out okay.

Chapter Twenty

Lottie rubbed her cold hands together when she came indoors. A high-speed Duchess shot past her into the relative warmth of the hall. The cat wrapped her fluffy tail around herself and Lottie wished she had one of her own, as the cat looked at her from behind it like a belly dancer behind a veil. 'I know, it's cold,' said Lottie, interpreting the cat's glare. The new owners would have to sort out the hallway's dodgy radiator and the poorly fitting windows, thought Lottie with a shiver.

She was hanging up her coat when Zach came through from the back of the house with Dave at his heels. 'Has he been?' asked Lottie.

'Nope, I swear he's holding on to it on purpose,' said Zach. Dave trotted off, happily wagging his tail.

Lottie commiserated with her brother. 'Hopefully not much longer to wait.'

'What for?' asked Emily, appearing at the top of the stairs.

'Star presents! Come on,' said Lottie, beckoning Emily down.

'Okay,' said Emily, looking a little brighter. 'What's a star present? Is it like a prize for the best present?

Because I think whoever bought Bernard the tuna wins that one.'

'Nope, you'll see.' Lottie ushered her through to the drawing room, where Jessie was playing with her unicorn, Joe was chatting to Scott and Bernard was snoozing in his favourite armchair.

'I found this,' said Jessie, holding up a neatly wrapped present. 'It was under the sofa.'

'Ooh, is it mine?' Emily asked Zach hopefully. Zach shook his head.

'And there's this label for . . . The Duch-ess,' said Jessie, reading it slowly. 'I don't know if they go together.'

'Open it and see,' said Lottie, coming to kneel by the tree.

Jessie ripped off the paper, pulled out a CD and scrunched up her features in disappointment.

'Alfie Boe. The Duchess will love this,' said Lottie, trying to keep a straight face.

'Will she?' asked Scott, looking amazed.

'No,' said Lottie with a chuckle. 'This must be Uncle Bernie's and he's got the cat's tuna.'

'Ahhh,' said Emily, taking a seat nearby.

'Star present time,' chimed Lottie. Jessie gasped and dropped her unicorn. Emily and Scott exchanged confused looks as the rest of family became animated. 'Right,' said Lottie. 'I know this may be something only the Collins family do so I'll explain. This is a present from the star on the Christmas tree to the whole family.'

'Ri-ight,' said Scott, not sounding convinced.

'But it's a fairy,' said Emily, looking at the tree as if to check.

'But usually it's the fancy star thing,' said Bernard.

'Nana used to do it. It's a special present that brings us

all together,' explained Zach. 'Like last year it was tiddly-winks. We had a real laugh playing with them.' He seemed to ponder this. 'I guess it was Nana's way of getting us to stop fighting and enjoy each other's company.'

'The year it was marbles, I nearly broke my bloomin' neck on the blessed things,' said Bernard.

'Was that 2008?' asked Angie.

'Noooo,' said Zach. '2008 was Crappy Shitmas – the year we all got diarrhoea.'

'That's not a nice present. I hope it's not that this year,' said Scott. It was hard to tell from his expression if he was serious or not.

'Do you remember the year we got Twister?' Lottie was already laughing at the memories.

'That was the funniest,' said Angie.

'I swear I strained my groin playing that,' said Zach.

'More likely it was playing with Hazel Johnson that did it,' said Angie, with an old-fashioned look.

Emily's ears pricked up.

'A very ex-girlfriend from uni who dumped me on Boxing Day,' he explained. 'I blame you lot.' Zach jokingly pointed at Lottie and his mother.

'Come on,' pleaded Jessie, who was jiggling up and down, powered by pure excitement and anticipation.

'I wonder what it is.' Lottie gave the box a little shake and widened her eyes at the sound.

'Did you buy it?' asked Emily, her forehead puckering.

'Nana used to buy it,' said Zach, 'but I'm guessing this year . . .' He looked at Lottie.

She shook her head. 'No, I found it in the cupboard when I was looking for the star box.' She held it aloft.

'You mean it's not actually from the star?' asked Jessie, full of disappointment.

'Sorry,' said Lottie, pulling an apologetic face at Zach; he may have some explaining to do later. She read the tag. '*To the Collins family, with love from the Star*. I guess that's really appropriate, given Nana was the real star in our family.'

'And now she's gone to be one,' chipped in Jessie, making a lump form in Lottie's throat.

Lottie fixed her gaze on the present. 'Right,' she said, concentrating on not getting sentimental. She put the box on the floor and lifted the lid. Jessie shot forward and grabbed the first thing. 'It's a bicycle pump.'

'No, it's a balloon pump,' said Zach, taking a large pack of modelling balloons out and handing Lottie a small instruction book.

As usual, Nana had struck gold. The modelling balloons were a huge hit with everyone. It was something everybody could get involved in, and infectious laughter ensued, caused mainly by failed modelling attempts and the fact that everybody jumped each time a balloon popped. Joe was concentrating hard as he wrestled with a long pink balloon protruding from between his legs.

'Oh my,' said Angie, going all coy. 'What are you pumping up there?'

Joe quickly moved the balloon to under his arm. 'It's meant to be a flamingo,' he said, with the briefest of looks in Lottie's direction. It was still enough to make her heart leap. Flamingos were her absolute favourite. She loved their rich, unusual colour. It was sweet that he'd remembered. It took some effort to drag her eyes away from him.

'There you go,' said Scott, proudly handing Angie his creation.

'Ooh, it's a monkey,' she said, taking it from him and looking genuinely pleased.

'Is it a vegan monkey?' asked Zach under his breath. Lottie gave him a playful punch.

'You're up,' said Lottie, pointing at Dave who had trotted over to the door.

'Bloody hell,' said Zach, getting to his feet. Lottie followed him as far as the kitchen.

'You need to say something to Emily soon. She's really upset.'

'I know. I have tried. But once I've got the ring back from this constipated canine everything will be sorted.' He picked up a trowel from the utility and took it, along with his disgusted expression, into the garden.

By the time Zach returned, Lottie was busy making cups of tea and arranging mince pies on one of Nana's best plates. He simply shook his head as Dave raced past him into the house. 'Here,' said Lottie, passing him a laden tray. He took it dutifully. 'Christmas film time,' she added, but it didn't seem to lift his mood.

Zach followed her through to the drawing room. He put down the tray and people perked up. Lottie stepped over Joe, who was still tying up balloons, and offered around the mince pies. Bernard took two. Lottie drew the curtains, put on the television and sat down near the fire at a safe distance from Joe.

After a family squabble that was worthy of their own reality show, they finally all settled down to watch Jessie's choice of *Home Alone*. Lottie looked around the room at her family wearing paper hats at varying degrees of wonkiness. Dayea had a dining room chair pulled up close to Great Uncle Bernard's armchair and they were holding hands. It was a very different sight to Aunt Nicola and Uncle Daniel, who were sitting as far away from each other as possible: him setting up his new phone and her staring intently at the instructions for her robovac. Angie and Scott were at least on the same sofa, but with Jessie and Dave squeezed in between them. Emily was looking forlorn and Rhys was looking bored.

Lottie couldn't imagine Christmas without them all. It didn't seem right that next year they would all be scattered. Families were meant to be together, even if they wanted to murder each other – surely that was the spirit of Christmas?

She snuck a glance at Joe, who was sitting on the floor fiddling with his flamingo, and he looked up sharply as though he'd felt her watching him. She quickly turned her gaze back to the TV. She was still drawn to him – however hard she tried to fight it.

Bernard startled to shuffle forward in his seat. 'You okay?' asked Lottie.

'Just need my inhaler,' he said, rubbing his chest.

'I will get it,' said Dayea, and she dashed from the room.

'No, I'm going to the loo as well,' he called after her, followed by a huff when she didn't come back.

'I'll get the wheelchair,' said Lottie, getting up.

'I don't need the blessed wheelchair – I can make it that far,' he said, hauling himself to his feet as his knees creaked in protest. His bony hand gripped the chair tightly.

'Please let me help,' said Lottie, but he waved her away.

'No, I'm no invalid.' Lottie wished Dayea would hurry up and come back because he listened to her. He started to make slow progress, and Lottie sat down again. All eyes returned to the film.

Bernard gasped as he fell crashing into the coffee table, shattering it and a number of cups. Everyone leaped up. He was fighting for breath. Zach lifted Jessie into his arms and exited the room while Joe took charge. Lottie could see Bernard's leg was bleeding. Dayea came in, dropped Bernard's inhaler to the floor and began speaking very fast in her native language and holding her face in her hands.

'Dayea, can you get me clean towels, please?' asked Joe. She hurried off still talking to herself, clearly distressed.

'Shall I call an ambulance?' asked Lottie.

'Yes,' said Joe.

'No!' said Bernard forcefully, trying to right himself.

Joe rested a hand on his shoulder. 'Steady, Bernard. It's best if you lie still. I'll try to stem the bleeding while we wait for an ambulance.'

'Don't you touch me!' shouted Bernard uncharacteristically as he slapped Joe's hand away.

'He's not a doctor but he's the best we've got,' said Lottie, trying to smooth the situation. A vet wasn't going to be anyone's first choice for human medical care, but he was better than nothing.

Dayea came rushing in, thrust the towels at Joe and knelt next to Bernard, brushing the hair off his forehead. 'Don't let him touch me,' Bernard pleaded with Dayea.

'He is helping you,' she said.

Bernard challenged Joe with his gaze. 'We all know what your father did, and I'm not ready to go yet.' Joe looked shocked.

Lottie took a deep breath. 'Bernard, this is Joe. Not his father. He's trying to help you.'

Bernard mustered all his strength and stabbed a finger at Joe. 'His father was a murderer!'

Emily gasped and Joe turned in her direction, then back to Lottie. He handed the towels to her. 'Use that to put pressure on the wound,' he said, guiding her as to where to place it.

'Murderer?' Dayea's eyes were wide with alarm. Lottie's heart went out to Joe.

Bernard was gasping for breath. His gaze was firmly on Joe. 'You *must* have known.'

Joe ignored Bernard and focused on Lottie. 'More pressure, Lottie. Lean on it. Use your weight.' Alarmingly quickly, Lottie could feel the dampness of the blood that had soaked through the towel. Joe passed her another.

'Well did you?' continued Bernard through a rasping breath.

'You need to relax, Uncle Bernard,' said Lottie. His agitation wasn't helping.

'Where's the bloody ambulance?' muttered Joe. On Christmas Day the Cotswolds wasn't likely to be swarming with them. Bernard was looking pale and he began pulling pained expressions.

'Bernard?' said Joe. 'Is it your chest?'

Lottie didn't like to point out that it was quite obviously his leg that was the main problem, feeling the same damp sensation as the blood made it through another towel.

Bernard suddenly went rigid and then completely floppy. His face was an unhealthy colour.

'Bernard!' Joe raised his voice. 'He's not breathing.' He put his fingers to Bernard's neck. 'His pulse is weak.'

'What's wrong?' asked Lottie as Joe shunted her out of the way.

'It could be a heart attack,' said Joe. The words hit Lottie like a punch to her gut. Joe started mouth-to-mouth. The room fell silent as he worked. Bernard lay motionless. Lottie hugged Dayea to her as she sobbed silently.

Eyes flickered to the window at the sound of a distant siren, but everyone was glued to the horror in the room as Joe worked tirelessly on Bernard's still and pale form.

Bernard seemed to move slightly and Joe paused to take his pulse again as the sound of the siren screamed into the driveway. 'He's back,' said Joe. He sat back on his haunches. The door opened and two paramedics hurried in.

Joe filled them in and they got to work quickly. Within minutes Bernard was in a stretcher chair being wheeled to the ambulance with Dayea clutching his hand.

Lottie and Joe followed them out and stood on the steps. Everyone else was at the window. 'Do you think he'll make it?' asked Lottie, feeling the chill through her dress. 'Honestly,' she added, in case he was planning on fobbing her off.

Joe shuffled his feet. 'A heart attack at any age is never a good thing. He's generally not in the best of health. But he's with the professionals now, so he has the best possible chance.'

Lottie was grateful for a realistic view; she could manage her own expectations that way. Far better to be prepared for the worst – and hopefully be pleasantly surprised – than to be shocked, as she had been with Nana. 'Thanks for being honest, and for everything you did back there. You saved his life.'

'Anyone would have done the same.'

'Maybe, but after what he said you'd be forgiven for not wanting to help him.' She was embarrassed by Great Uncle Bernard's outburst. The ambulance lights began to flash, followed by the sound of wheels on gravel and in another moment, it was gone.

Joe stared at his feet. 'He was right though. Wasn't he? It won't ever go away. It was always the danger of coming back here. People have long memories.' He turned to go inside and Lottie caught his arm.

'Not everyone thinks like Bernard. I know the truth.'

'Do you?' asked Joe, a deep crease appearing on his forehead. 'Are you sure?'

She had been sure until now.

Chapter Twenty-One

Boxing Day

Boxing Day dawned like the sequel to a movie Lottie wanted to forget. She actually groaned as she opened her eyes and the flashbacks of the previous day swamped her consciousness. The Duchess, who was dozing by her feet, opened an eye, gave a cursory glance around and went back to sleep. Lottie wished she could do the same. She checked the clock – it was six o'clock; too early to get up. But not too early to call the hospital and get an update on Great Uncle Bernard.

After being passed around a few wards she was finally talking to the nurse treating Bernard.

'Are you his next of kin?' she asked.

'Erm.' Lottie knew her mother was officially his next of kin, and then it was Uncle Daniel. Neither of them had shown any major signs of emotional upset yesterday at the sight of the old man being whisked away in an ambulance. Lottie concluded that if 'next of kin' meant 'the person in your family who is closest to you' then it wasn't that big a lie. 'Yes. I think I am.'

'He's had a good night and he's doing as we would expect at this stage.'

Lottie wasn't sure what that meant. 'What happens next?'

'We monitor him until he's fit enough to come home.'

'Wow. So he's going to be okay then?' A happy tear took her by surprise. She'd been expecting the worst. 'He doesn't need any operations or anything?'

'A coronary artery spasm is usually treated with medication but that's up to his consultant.'

'Can we visit?'

'Yes. Afternoons between two and four and evenings six until eight thirty.'

Suddenly Boxing Day looked a bit brighter.

She was still yawning as she wandered downstairs. The house was silent. There was something comforting about knowing the rest of her family was safe asleep under the one roof; they'd all be leaving tomorrow, and Christmas would never be quite the same again.

Another thought struck her. Nothing would be quite the same now that Joe was back in Henbourne.

Joe. Images of him flashed through her mind, culminating with the one of him tucked up on the sofa last night. Everyone had been a bit subdued and they'd attempted to take their minds off events with a round of board games. Zach and Emily had teamed up to win most of them and thankfully they seemed to have recovered from their earlier upset. After everything that had happened, she'd cracked open the brandy and she, Zach and Joe had chatted into the night. The brandy had helped to relax the tensions between her and Joe – a brief armistice. Seeing Joe save Uncle Bernard's life had pushed the hurt to the back of her mind. Joe and Zach had drunk a fair bit and she'd ended up helping them both to bed. Zach had suggested the sofa for Joe and offered him a pair of shorts he'd been given as a present.

Lottie wasn't entirely sure why she felt the need to check on Joe this morning – he was a grown man, and he wasn't hers to check on any more – but old feelings had left their mark. A quick look to check he was alive was the least she could do. Anyway Dave was in there too, and he'd need a wee by now.

Lottie opened the drawing room door as quietly as the old hinges would allow and slunk inside, looking around furtively for Dave. She didn't want him making an escape and going after the Duchess, who had slept soundly all night. Which, when Lottie thought about it, was unusual for her – maybe Christmas Day had worn her out too.

She closed the door behind her as quietly as possible. She had only taken two steps before she realised something was very wrong. She spotted Dave on a cushion at the far end of the room. He made a groaning sound and rested his head on his paws. Joe stirred slightly on the sofa. Lottie looked about her. There was a trail all around the room – across the oak flooring, the cream wool rug and the Christmas tree mat. It was a trail of poo, smeared generously across every surface like a faeces racetrack. The smell was a shock to the nostrils. Lottie followed the path of poo with her eyes – no sign of the engagement ring – until at the end of the trail they came to rest on the culprit – Aunt Nicola's robovac.

Although the original source of the poo was obviously Dave she could hardly blame him for how it had now been liberally distributed. For a little dog he delivered a whole lot of poo. Joe was sleeping with his arm draped over his eyes. The blanket was only half covering him; his chest was bare and covered in a light dusting of hairs. She sneaked a look, tracing them down his body until they

214

disappeared inside his borrowed shorts. Lottie caught herself with a sharp intake of breath. What was she doing?

Her mutinous heart was begging her for another peek. She tiptoed across to Dave like a cat burglar, being ultra-careful where to place her new slippers, and picked him up. Dave responded with lots of happy kisses and an incredibly waggy tail. She could tell he was relieved at not being told off, poor thing. *And I thought 2008 was a Crappy Shitmas*, she thought.

She decided to leave Joe sleeping. He had a bellyful of brandy to sleep off and he'd been a hero yesterday, so he deserved a lie in. She planned out her route and daintily made her way through the poo maze back to the door.

Once safely in the kitchen, Lottie set off the coffee maker, tied on Dave's skipping rope and ventured into the garden for him to have a wee. It was cold and blustery outside. Dave did a lot of sniffing about and then decided to relieve himself against Nana's statue of Buddha. Lottie wondered if that would bring more bad luck but surely they'd already had more than their fair share?

Dave sniffed about some more and squatted down. Lottie sighed. She wasn't sure there could be any more poo in the little dog. And of course it was bound to happen when Zach was passed out upstairs sleeping off his brandy excesses. She certainly wasn't going to check through it for the engagement ring. Dave made a big show of scraping up the grass around his deposit until he was finally happy he'd done a good job.

She shut him in the kitchen, grabbed a plastic ziplock bag and steeled herself for the task. She covered her hand with the bag and reached down, only half looking to check she was on target. What she saw stopped her in her tracks, and she ran back inside with her hand still inside the plastic bag.

She rushed into the drawing room, halting herself just in time as she remembered the robovac's handiwork. The door swung open and Joe sprang awake. Looking disorientated, he tried to stand up and achieved it on the third attempt.

'Stop!' She held out her plastic bag-covered hand in a stop sign. 'Don't move a muscle.'

His eyes widened in alarm. 'What's wrong?'

'There's a problem with Dave.'

'So I can see,' said Joe, scanning the room and shaking his head.

'No. Not here, in the garden. I think he's bleeding. Could it be that the present's got stuck?'

'I'll come and check.' He tiptoed his way carefully across the room like a scantily clad *Crystal Maze* contestant, carrying his clothes with him. 'Great, you'll be needing this,' said Lottie, passing him the plastic bag gleefully. Then she remembered poor Dave and the joviality passed.

In the kitchen, Dave was sitting by the back door. His tail began wagging at the sight of them. 'Oh, you poor thing,' she said, picking him up and hugging him gently. She'd very quickly become attached to Dave, almost without noticing. It had only been a couple of days and he had slotted into the family so easily. Everyone seemed to love him – with the obvious exception of the Duchess. Lottie really didn't want there to be something wrong with the little chap. She wondered if this was why someone had dumped him. Sadly, some people didn't care enough and even for those who did, vet bills were expensive.

'Let's take a look at him.' Joe took Dave and placed him

on a kitchen chair. He had a cursory look around his nether regions. 'No sign of blood there.'

'It's in his poo. And there's loads. It's all red.' She knew that could only be a bad thing for poor Dave. She picked him back up and hugged him some more.

'Where is it?' asked Joe, pulling his jumper over his head and opening the back door.

'About three strides past Buddha and to the right. You'll need to bag it because Zach will need to check it for Emily's present.'

'Right.' Joe disappeared. Lottie hugged Dave to her and wondered at how far he'd come since Christmas Eve. The once-manic little dog was now more sedate and he seemed to enjoy the cuddle. He still tried to lick her face, but not in a frenzied way like before. There had been a change in him. She felt bad that she'd not noticed that he was calming down.

Joe came back in with a twist of a smile on his face.

'What?' she asked still feeling apprehensive. 'What's wrong with him?'

'Serviette,' said Joe.

Lottie barely registered what he said. 'Is it serious?' She hugged the dog a little tighter.

Joe broke into a broad smile. 'No, it's not serious. He's eaten one of the red serviettes from dinner. Someone must have dropped one on the floor. It probably smelled of gravy or meat so he's gobbled it down.'

'A paper serviette?'

'Yep.'

Lottie held the dog up to her face. 'You total numpty,' admonished Lottie. 'You really had me worried there.' She put Dave down and turned to Joe. 'So he'll definitely be all right? Now it's out?'

'It's unlikely there'll be any lasting effects. I've left the bag on the back step if Zach wants to play lucky dip.'

'Thanks Joe. Coffee?'

'Yes, please. We put away quite a bit of brandy last night.'

'I didn't have anywhere near as much as you and Zach, but I'm tired.' She flopped into a kitchen chair, she felt drained and it was still early.

'Any news on Bernard?'

'He's doing okay. Thanks for asking. It wasn't a heart attack, it was a spasm.'

'That's good. No damage and easier to treat.' They eyed each other awkwardly and then both looked away.

'Does it smell funny in here to you?' asked Joe.

Lottie sniffed the air. It smelled a whole lot better than the drawing room did. 'Still smells a bit like Christmas dinner.' It was a smell she liked – a familiar smell. Then she remembered something. 'Stuffing!' She leaped to the oven and pulled open the door. On a baking tray at the bottom sat a number of small, round pieces of charcoal that had once been balls of stuffing, painstakingly made.

Joe peered over her shoulder and chuckled. 'New balls, please.'

'I *knew* something was missing.' She'd left serving up the meal to hunt for Aunt Nicola. Emily had taken over and somehow the stuffing had been forgotten. She plonked the tray on the kitchen table with a clatter. Lottie poked one of the cremated stuffing balls with her finger – it was rock solid.

'Nobody else noticed,' said Joe.

'Unlike the bread sauce. I spent ages on these though. What an idiot to have forgotten them.'

'You're too hard on yourself, Lottie. You always have been.'

'Thanks.' She wasn't sure what else to say. He was right. She knew she was her own worst enemy when it came to beating herself up. She fingered a burned stuffing ball.

'You did a great job yesterday. Rose would have been proud. It was a really lovely meal.' He looked self-conscious and shoved his hands into his pockets. 'I mean it would have been better with stuffing and bread sauce, but otherwise it was great.' He gave her a friendly smirk.

She pulled a stuffing ball off the tray and hurled it at him.

'Hey! They hurt!' He picked it up off the worktop and threw it back, hitting her shoulder.

They giggled like children as they flung the stuffing balls across the kitchen. One hit Joe in the chest and exploded in a cloud of black dust. Joe held his chest like he'd been shot, and slumped against the cabinets. 'You got me,' he croaked. 'Goodbye, cruel world.'

'Well that's in very poor taste, I must say,' said Angie, from the doorway.

Joe almost fell over in his attempt to stand up straight. He looked guilty but didn't say anything.

'It's nothing to do with Bernard, if that's what you're thinking,' said Lottie. 'Oh, and since you ask: your uncle has made it through the night.' It was Angie's turn to look guilty.

'If you gave me a chance, I was going to ask you exactly that.'

'Ask me? Not planning to call the hospital yourself then?' Lottie shook her head and turned away. She heard her mother stalk off towards the drawing room.

'Shouldn't you warn her about . . .' Joe pointed after her.

'The visit from the Christmas crapper?' she asked, and he nodded. 'She'll find out soon enough.'

'Oh my dear God,' came her mother's voice, a couple of octaves higher than usual.

'There you go,' said Lottie, feeling smug.

'I think I should probably get going,' said Joe. He rubbed his palm across his stubble. 'I must look a fright.'

She let her gaze rest on him for a moment. He didn't look a fright. A little dishevelled perhaps. A couple of creases around his eyes. A light tan on his skin. Possibly broader at the shoulders. A little more muscular in his arms. He'd matured nicely. Something flickered inside her. 'No, you look fine,' she said, wondering where that wave of sentiment had come from. She turned away.

'I'll round up the hound. And then I guess I'll see you about.' He glanced at her.

'But you'll be coming to the duck race?' The words tumbled out and she disliked how desperate they sounded.

'Do they still do that?'

'Of course, it's tradition. See you there?' Lottie tried to sound nonchalant but failed.

'Yeah. Okay.' He seemed a little hesitant.

'And you're welcome to come back for dinner.' She threw another incinerated stuffing ball at him and he deftly caught it.

'I can't impose on you again.'

'It's only leftovers, and I'm guessing you've not got much on,' her eyes involuntarily shot to his bare thighs, 'I mean *in*. Food-wise.' She felt the blood rush to her cheeks at the faux pas. 'Not got much food in,' she repeated just to be clear.

'You're right; I haven't.' Joe seemed to realise he wasn't wearing much on his lower half and scooted round to the other side of the table. 'So, yeah, that'd be great. See you at the race.'

Angie appeared in the doorway. 'Have you seen what that dog has done in there?'

'No, that was entirely Aunt Nicola's doing,' said Lottie and she heard Joe splutter a laugh behind her.

'Aunt Nicola did that?! What are you talking about?' Lottie and Joe began giggling like school children.

Everyone else seemed to come downstairs at the same time, so she told them all that she wasn't clearing up the mess in the drawing room. She countered all of Aunt Nicola's arguments with the simple phrase, 'Your robovac.' Eventually Aunt Nicola went in search of cleaning materials and Lottie went off for a long soak in the bath. Hopefully, if the start of it was anything to go by, Boxing Day was going to be a doddle compared to the stress of Christmas Day.

Chapter Twenty-Two

Lottie was waiting for her bath to fill. She was watching the masses of bubbles multiply, idly wondering whether she'd maybe added too much bubble bath, when there was a tap on the door. Typical. Why did someone always need the loo when you were about to have a bath?

'Use the one downstairs,' she called.

'Lottie, it's me,' said Joe, through the door. 'I don't need the loo.'

She thought he'd already left. 'What is it?' she asked.

'Can you open the door please?'

Lottie looked down at her naked self. 'Er, no, not really.'

'I take it that's your handiwork all over the back of my Land Rover?'

Lottie had almost forgotten her secret mission of yesterday afternoon. While Uncle Daniel and Rhys had been chatting, she had been busy painting a variety of animal footprints over the back of Joe's Land Rover, as well as carefully adding 'local vet' on both doors. She couldn't tell from his voice if he was happy or not; although he didn't sound furious, which was something. She grabbed a towel, wrapped it around herself and opened the door a fraction.

'It might have been me.' She gave him her best cheesy grin. 'I didn't like you not having a Christmas present.'

'That's kind. I just wanted to say thank you.'

'Do you like it?' she asked. She wanted to see his reaction.

'I love it. You are really talented. You know, I always imagined that you'd made a career out of your drawing.'

It was odd looking at him through the crack in the door, but it also acted like a shield. 'I kind of lost the desire for it. I think you really need that to make a success of being an artist.'

She could tell by his expression that he didn't want to ask what had triggered her to lose her interest in something she had been so passionate about. 'I had better head off. I'll catch you later. Thanks again, I love it.' Joe broke eye contact.

'Okay, bye.' She went to shut the door and suddenly remembered something she needed to say. 'Joe!' She pulled the door open swiftly and lost her grip on the towel. He spun around as the towel hit the floor. She quickly snatched it up and tried to cover herself with it, but it kept bunching up and it took her too long to hide her nakedness.

'Yes?' She could hear the mirth in his voice. He was studying his car keys. She was grateful to him for pretending he hadn't seen her naked.

'I can paint on your mobile number if you like? Just let me know what it is.' She said it all in a hurry, flung herself back into the bathroom and shut the door quickly. Had she just flashed him and then asked for his phone number? She threw the towel on the radiator and smacked her palm to her forehead.

* * *

The Boxing Day duck race was a tradition Joe remembered fondly, although images of his parents in happier times danced through his mind, tingeing his memories with melancholy. He strolled up the hill with Dave trotting alongside him. He could picture his last duck race like it was yesterday: the contrast of the brightly coloured toy ducks against the stark winter outfit of the village; Zach, Lottie and the other village kids all excitedly racing along the banks of the stream shouting the numbers of the front-runners. The race started in Henbourne and the stream wove its way down the hill in a roundabout fashion until it reached Dumbleford, where the finish line was the ford across the road.

He reached the top of Henbourne Hill and carried Dave over the stile towards the bridge where the race would start. There had been a sharp frost and the drop in temperature meant it was still crisp underfoot. He'd missed the cold. He hadn't realised it when he'd been enjoying year-round sunshine, but there was a lot to be said for proper seasons. He joined the crowd of locals already amassing near the tiny bridge made of Cotswold stone. A waft of something delicious sparked a memory of Lottie's Nana's sausage rolls, and he turned to see Lottie opening a foil packet and offering some round. She saw him looking and came over. The frost between them seemed to be thawing and he was grateful.

'Sausage roll?'

'Please. I was just thinking about these.' He took one and bit into it. It was a bit burned on the bottom and the filling was spilling out at both ends, but otherwise it wasn't bad at all. 'They're good,' he said, and Lottie gave him her look that said she knew he was lying but she didn't call him on it. 'Each time I see you I'm surprised that your hair colour is the same,' he said, thinking out loud.

'I don't dye it any more, Joe. That was all a long time ago.' He felt the sadness connect them. All the time lost. All the things they'd shared, trapped in the past. She adjusted today's sparkly hair clip and walked away. He watched her disappear into the crowd to be greeted warmly by locals and visitors alike. Something about Lottie drew people to her. She was the kindest soul he'd ever known: completely unique and so very special.

Petra from the pub appeared with trays of mulled wine at a reasonable price, and just like that Joe felt festive again. He found a good spot not too close to the start, but near enough to see the ducks released. There were quite a few dogs about, and they all seemed to be off leads but behaving themselves impeccably. He looked at Dave, and Dave looked hopefully at him.

'Sorry, boy. I can't risk you running off.' Dave lay down grumpily as if he'd understood. Joe hung the skipping rope over his arm as he juggled his sausage roll and mulled wine. Some local children, all wrapped up in too many layers, excitedly rushed to the front as the announcer started counting down. The crowd joined in and a huge cheer went up as the ducks were released: a mass of yellow plastic tumbled over the little bridge and into the water. A few of the dogs barked and Dave jumped up excitedly. As the flash of yellow ducks bobbed past, Dave dashed through the many assembled legs, wrenching the rope from Joe's arm and disappearing into the crowd.

'Dave!' shouted Joe, and a couple of people turned to look but most of them were watching the scruffy little dog, who had launched himself into the water and was now chasing up the middle of the stream after the lead ducks. Joe dropped his sausage roll and hastily thrust his drink into Shirley's hands.

'And a happy New Year to you!' she called after him, before downing it in one.

Joe found himself in the middle of a group of children all running along the banks of the stream trying to keep up with the ducks as Dave raced along in the shallow water trying to grab one in his mouth.

'For goodness' sake, Dave,' shouted Joe and the boy next to him giggled.

'Is he yours?' asked the boy, waving his phone in Dave's direction.

'No,' panted Joe, although it was entirely his fault that this was happening.

'Shame. He's awesome.'

Joe paused thanks to a stitch in his side – he blamed the sausage roll – and a few more followers caught them up: a particularly windy bit of the stream's course had slowed the pace down. Dave was having the time of his life as more ducks caught up and surrounded him, bobbing in every direction as he pounced on them. 'Dave!' Of course the dog didn't look up. It took longer than a day and a half for a dog to learn a new name. There was nothing for it: Joe was going to have to go in after him.

Joe sprinted ahead to buy himself a couple of minutes before the ducks reached him. He pulled off his socks and trainers and slid down the muddy bank into the icy water. The cold took his breath away. He saw the lead ducks coming towards him with Dave in hot pursuit.

'Come on, Dave,' he called, in the hope of encouraging him to leave the ducks and come to him.

'Come on, Dave!' shouted the boy who'd spoken to him earlier, still pointing his phone in Dave's direction. And just like that the other children joined in. Then a few adults, then more, until the chorus echoed up the banks. 'Come on, Dave!'

The dog was oblivious. As he neared Joe he made a well-timed lunge for the duck in front, clasping it firmly in his jaws and giving Joe the opportunity to grab the skipping rope harness and haul Dave from the water, his little legs still running in mid-air.

The crowd cheered their delight, most likely thanks to the mulled wine, and carried on their way after the remaining ducks. Joe flopped down on the grassy bank and tried to take the duck from the dog's jaws, but Dave whipped his head away.

'That better not be my duck,' said a gruff voice.

'Or mine,' chimed in a few more.

Back to being public enemy number one, thought Joe, clasping the cold, wet wriggling dog to his chest. Dave had a firm hold on the duck and from his determined expression he wasn't planning on relinquishing his prize any time soon.

Someone loomed over Joe. He looked up warily. 'Sausage roll?' asked Lottie, failing to hide her grin.

He was pleased to see her smile, even if it was at his expense. 'I could do with a large brandy. This dog is possessed by the devil.'

'You love him really,' said Lottie, crouching down to ruffle the fur on the top of Dave's head, and coming quite close to Joe in the process.

'I must admit he's growing on me.'

'Me too,' said Lottie, and their eyes fixed on each other until discomfort made them tear them away.

Lottie had watched the performance play out and had been cheering Joe on from the bank. She'd almost run up to him at the end, but had managed to make herself saunter instead. And now here she was, standing close to him and feeling all self-conscious again. Especially after flashing him earlier.

'Did poogate get resolved?' he asked, standing up.

'After much moaning, arguing and a bit of shouting from me, yes.' They fell in step as everyone converged on the finish. They were a few strides away when a huge cheer went up. Lottie couldn't see who had won, but they would put the numbers up on a chalk board soon enough. They continued at a more leisurely pace with Dave trotting along beside them, his duck held proudly in his mouth.

'Did they find the engagement ring?'

'Shhh. And how did you know?' Lottie swivelled her head to check nobody nearby was listening.

'Something he said last night after a few too many brandies. Plus I figured if Emily's present was socks, Zach wouldn't be fretting this much.'

Lottie checked Emily wasn't nearby. 'No sign of it. Zach is really starting to panic. He's missed Christmas Day, so today is his last chance to ask her before they leave the manor tomorrow.' She ran her lip through her teeth. 'I guess I won't be far behind them.' She was thinking out loud. 'The new owners will want the place emptied as soon as possible.'

Joe was looking doubtful. 'Have they said that?'

'No. But it was advertised as no upward chain, so they won't want to hang about.' She stifled a giant sigh. 'It's probably for the best. The longer I stay, the harder it'll be to leave. Although it'll be weird being completely alone in the house.'

Joe gave her a worried look. 'I'm sorry. Has he got worse since this morning?'

'Oh, no. Bernard is still hanging in there; but when I spoke to Dayea earlier she was talking about him moving in with her. Which makes sense. No point him coming back to the manor only to have to move out again.'

'Where does she live?'

'You know what – I have absolutely no idea. Apart from that it's near Stow, I think, but I could have got that wrong.' Lottie made a mental note to find out more about Dayea; their superficial exchanges were fine before, but if she was going to marry Great Uncle Bernard and be a proper part of the family, then Lottie felt she should get to know her better.

Christmas Day had given Lottie a lot to think about. She'd known Joe wasn't in a good place when he'd gone to America, but she'd always thought of it as him running away, rather than him trying to preserve his mental health – his perspective had put a whole new spin on things. She felt selfish for thinking he'd left her. Now she better understood that he had to get away from everything associated with the village – and that just happened to include her. His timing had been exceptionally bad, but he wasn't to know that, for one simple reason – she'd never told him. Nana was right: keeping secrets was like a cancer. But when you'd held a secret for so long, how did you even begin to share it?

Something else had been playing on her mind as well. 'Joe, what did you mean yesterday when you asked if I was sure I knew what happened with your mum and dad?' She could instantly sense his discomfort.

Shirley interrupted the conversation by waving them down like a traffic cop. Joe quickly diverted towards her and they obediently slowed. 'Now don't you make a lovely pair?' said Shirley.

'Oh, no, we're not . . .' Joe pointed a finger at Lottie and then back at himself. His mouth remained open. Lottie felt warmth in her cheeks. He clearly didn't want Shirley to get the wrong idea about them. In fact, he seemed overly bothered that she might.

'I know, I know,' said Shirley. 'I'm just teasing you.' Joe gave a weak laugh and dropped his gaze to his shoes. 'I hear some actor has bought the manor, is that right?' asked Shirley, leaning in to catch every word of Lottie's reply.

'Then you know more than me, Shirley,' said Lottie, trying and failing to laugh it off. 'Even the estate agent doesn't seem sure about who has bought it – he said something about it being a company.'

'Well now. That is interesting.' Her eyes widened as she spoke, but that may have been the amount of mulled wine she'd consumed. It was widely known that Shirley liked a tipple. 'Very interesting indeed,' Shirley added.

Lottie didn't think it was interesting at all. She didn't want to think about what was going to happen to the manor after it was sold. It was all too raw. It felt as if she was selling her memories of Nana along with the house, and it was like a physical pain inside her. *Can you get homesick for somewhere you haven't actually left yet?* she wondered.

'And what's this I hear about an ambulance at the manor yesterday?' continued Shirley.

Joe seemed to take that as his cue to respond. 'Bernard had a fall and it triggered a heart spasm. He's okay though – in hospital recovering.' Shirley pulled her head back in surprise.

'Oh my. He's no age!'

Both Joe and Lottie looked puzzled. 'He's seventy-two,' said Lottie.

'Like I say. No age,' said Shirley. Lottie guessed age was all about perspective.

'Sorry Shirley, but I need to get back and feed the hordes. It was lovely to see you. Bye now.' Lottie gave her a kiss on the cheek.

'Okay. Keep me posted on the manor house. Especially if it's that Ryan Reynolds who's bought it,' called Shirley, and she waved them off.

Joe matched Lottie's pace but the atmosphere between them was different.

'You wanted my phone number,' said Joe, getting out his phone.

'For the Land Rover. Yes.' Lottie felt she had to clarify it wasn't exactly for her.

They exchanged numbers and walked on in silence. Lottie didn't like to ask the question about his parents again, and it seemed that Joe wasn't going to offer up an answer willingly. They began to walk up the hill, and neither of them spoke. Lottie was relieved when Zach jogged to catch them up and broke the silence. 'Can we talk?' he asked, giving a sideways look at Joe.

'Don't mind me,' said Joe, striding on ahead, and Dave quickened his pace until his little legs were almost a blur. Lottie watched Joe for a moment and then pulled her attention back to her brother.

'What's up?' She could tell there was something wrong. She always knew.

He huffed a bit before speaking. 'It's Melissa.' The words almost tripped Lottie up.

Chapter Twenty-Three

Lottie took a moment to compose herself. 'What do you mean exactly when you say *Melissa*?' Just saying her dead sister-in-law's name out loud had an odd effect on Lottie. Guilt crept all over her like a rash. After all these years keeping her secret, it was still difficult for her to bring Melissa to mind.

'I don't know,' said Zach. 'It's this whole engagement thing. I was so sure, so certain. Now with everything being delayed and all my plans going wrong it seems like some sort of omen.'

Lottie thought of Dave peeing on Buddha and then banished it from her mind – Zach's problems had started way before that. 'No,' she said firmly. 'It's not a bad omen. Sometimes things just don't go to plan.'

'But maybe they don't for a reason. I can't help wondering if . . .' he tailed off. Lottie studied him: his expression was pained. Her heart went out to him. This was more than a wobble.

'What?' she asked.

'If Melissa would approve.' He shook his head. 'I know it's crazy – because why would she approve of me getting a new wife? She wouldn't. Right?'

This was the moment. The opportunity to explain. The chance she'd been waiting for for nearly five years. She could solve Zach's problem, tell him the truth about Melissa – but if she did that, would it tear his memories apart?

She took a deep breath. 'Zach, there's something you need to know—'

'Ah, both my children together. That must mean you're plotting,' said Angie, slotting in between them both and putting her arms around their shoulders in an uncharacteristically affectionate gesture.

'Not at all.' Lottie made an effort not to look guilty and only partly succeeded.

'Come on. I know you two. What's going on?' Her mother had some sort of sixth sense when they were keeping things from her.

Zach shot Lottie a 'don't you dare' look. 'We were wondering who's bought the house,' said Lottie, thinking on her feet. She could see Zach relax out of the corner of her eye. 'Shirley reckons it's some famous actor.'

'Huh,' said Angie with a snort. 'Typical village gossip. I bet you'll be glad to escape it. Won't you?'

'No – I love it here.' Lottie swallowed down the unexpected emotion that accompanied her words.

'Oh, Lottie. My little homebird. You need to spread your wings, explore the world, embrace the excitement and the danger.' Angie's eyes widened dramatically as she spoke. 'Break some rules, live a little; like I have.' Both Zach and Lottie failed to hide their smirks. 'What? I've travelled.' Angie removed her arms from their shoulders, the public show of affection was over.

'Do you include getting chucked off a train to Cardiff in that?' asked Zach.

'How was I supposed to know you weren't allowed to plug in hair straighteners? There weren't any signs.' Angie was indignant. They laughed together and Zach's dilemma was forgotten – and with it, Lottie's chance to unload the secret she'd been keeping.

Emily found she was walking next to Joe. He was someone she hadn't spent much time with, and she had only picked up a few snippets of information from Lottie, who seemed to be very awkward around him. She was intrigued by what Bernard had said yesterday about Joe's father being a murderer – but it wasn't really a good conversation opener.

'So you've known the Collins family a long time then?' she asked.

Joe was nodding. 'Yeah, like forever. I was born here and me and Lottie went to school together. My parents were always busy – they both worked non-stop. So I spent a lot of time up at the manor.'

'Oh, so you must know them all really well.' Questions she wanted to ask were already forming in her mind.

'I did.' His demeanour changed. 'I moved away nine years ago. It seems so much has changed,' he looked up and Emily followed his gaze, which was resting on Lottie. He turned his head to take in the surroundings. They were just coming up to the church on the left-hand side and a small row of chocolate-box cottages on the other, 'and yet almost nothing has.'

His head dropped and she feared he was going to clam up on her. 'America, wasn't it?' she asked. 'Whereabouts?'

'Gainesville.' She shook her head; geography had never been her strong subject. 'Florida,' he added. 'It's about a two-hour drive from Walt Disney World.'

She nodded. 'Oh, okay. And you were working as a vet out there too?'

'Yeah. I worked at an emergency animal hospital.' She could tell he wasn't keen to talk, but she persevered.

'That sounds exciting.' He didn't comment. A thought struck her. 'How do you tell if an animal is pregnant?'

'Really depends on what sort of animal; but enlarged nipples are a general sign in mammals. Why?'

'Oh, no reason. I was just thinking that they can't take a pregnancy test.' She had to concentrate hard not to think about her nipples and she self-consciously adjusted her clothing.

'We can tell for sure from blood samples. And an ultrasound at a few weeks in.'

'Right.' Neither of those was helpful to her. He was giving her an odd look now, so she changed the subject quickly. 'What's the weather like in Gainesville?' she asked.

'Sunny and hot mostly. Look, Emily, I don't want to make you uncomfortable, but has Lottie said anything to you about me?'

The question – and his intense gaze – took her by surprise. 'Um, no. She hasn't. I don't really know her well enough for her to confide in me.' *Although I've confided in her*, she thought. 'Zach said you two were crazy about each other when you were younger.' She figured telling him that wasn't breaking any confidences.

He smiled briefly. 'Yeah, we were. Wasn't a day we didn't see each other.'

'That's pretty intense.'

He was watching Lottie again. 'It didn't feel that way. It felt right.'

Emily felt warm and fuzzy at his words. She knew exactly what he meant. 'Did you come back for Lottie?'

He blew out his cheeks, looked at her and away again. 'I came back for me. It's the only place I've ever truly belonged. But Lottie and the Collins family are a big part of why I feel that way.'

'It's a shame the manor is being sold. I guess the family won't have a reason to come back here any more.'

'I guess not,' he said.

'The end of an era, Zach called it.'

'It's certainly the end of something.' He zipped up his coat all the way to the top with a firm action and rammed his hands deep into his pockets. Emily did the same; it had definitely turned colder.

When Lottie got back to the manor Aunt Nicola was in the hallway.

'I have cleaned up that horrid little dog's mess.'

'Your robovac's mess,' said Lottie.

Aunt Nicola ignored her. 'I threw out the rug – it was beyond saving.'

'Oh, that's a shame,' said Lottie. She remembered a series of family photos of newborn Collins babies all snapped on that rug – including one of herself.

'Well it's the sort of thing we'll be chucking away soon anyway.' The words came like a slap to Lottie. The house was like a giant keepsake box, safely storing her precious memories. But what Nicola was saying was true: most of the furniture was old, but not old enough to be antique. Nobody would want it, not even the charity shop if it didn't have a fire-resistant label, so it would get dumped. The thought of all Nana's treasures in a skip loomed in her mind. Aunt Nicola was giving her an odd look.

'Are you all right?' Lottie asked, because despite her

spiky exterior Aunt Nicola had a lot on her plate. 'I mean, after yesterday.'

'I might look calm, but in my mind I've already murdered him a dozen times and hidden the body parts.'

'Right,' said Lottie, not sure how to respond; but she was reassured by the answer – it was typical Aunt Nicola.

'You've been in this situation. You know how it feels. There's not really any recovering from betrayal.'

'I'm not sure it's exactly the same,' said Lottie, an unwelcome picture of the night she'd caught her ex racing through her mind. Her situation was still quite fresh. 'This thing with Uncle Daniel was a very long time ago.'

'But I've just found out. He's kept it secret all this time. He's not the man I thought he was.'

'Have you had a chance to talk to him about it?' It was none of her business, but after the conversation she'd overheard with Rhys it did seem that the affair was ancient history.

'Not properly. I swapped with Rhys last night and slept in the box room. I say "slept" but those dolls gave me nightmares, so I was awake for most of it.'

'Sorry,' said Lottie.

'It's fine,' said Nicola. 'But you're right, I should talk to him.' She snapped off a rubber glove, making Lottie jump.

Lottie dished out instructions for someone to light a fire in the drawing room and snug before she set about making lunch. She felt more Christmassy today than she had yesterday, it was odd. Perhaps it was the fun of the duck race, or the relief of not having to cook a full roast dinner – *or*, a little voice inside her head cut in, *it's being around Joe again*. No. She banished that little voice and decided it must be that she had overdone the mulled wine. Yes, that would be it – too much alcohol and not enough to eat, that would certainly make you feel jolly.

Lottie could hear a kerfuffle coming from the drawing room, but she chose to ignore it, deciding that if it was something important someone would come and get her. She set about carving up the ham. It was a huge joint, and it would take ages if she was going to slice it thinly like Nana used to do.

'Have you seen the pen I bought your mother for Christmas?' asked Scott, appearing in the doorway.

Lottie racked her brains. 'Not since she opened it, no.'

'She's lost it.'

Lottie could hear her mother's dramatic performance coming from the other room. 'Could it have got caught up with the wrapping paper, perhaps?' she suggested.

'Great thought!' Scott punched the air. Bless him, he was so excited about everything, thought Lottie. Then she thought of the porn films and sniggered. He frowned at her as he went past so she turned it into a fake cough and his smile returned.

Eventually her mother's dramatics reached the kitchen. 'It's gone! My Swarovski pen has gone! I was going to finish writing my autobiography with it, but I can't find it anywhere.'

Lottie carried on battling with the ham.

'Lottie!' Her mother stamped her foot. 'Why aren't you searching for it?'

Lottie openly sighed at her mother's lack of perspective. Yesterday poor Bernard had almost died and she had barely noticed; today she'd mislaid a sparkly pen and was declaring Armageddon. 'It's not gone,' said Lottie, carefully putting down the carving knife. It was always safest not to handle sharp objects when she was arguing with her mother.

'It has.'

'You've just mislaid it.'

'But I've checked everywhere,' wailed Angie. 'I don't know what I'll do.' She slumped onto a kitchen chair and dropped her head to her chest. Lottie stared at the ceiling and counted to ten. 'Lottie. Did you hear me?'

'Yep. But other than suggesting you check again, there's not a lot I can do.' She picked up the carving knife. 'Are you openly eating meat again?' she asked. One less vegan to cater for would at least mean she wouldn't be eating ham for the foreseeable future.

'No, I'm a vegan.' Angie swished her hair.

'No, you're not. You're play-acting for Scott.' Poor Scott; he seemed quite sweet really, and completely different to anyone her mother had dated before – which was most definitely a good thing. 'Why can't you just be yourself? Why do you hide behind this . . .' she waved the carving knife and put it down hastily, ' . . . this act, all the time?'

Angie looked affronted. Her mouth dropped open and she pulled her body back into the chair. 'Me, acting? What about you?'

Lottie froze. She didn't know where her mother was going with this. Her own secret, Melissa's secret and Zach's engagement plans all whizzed through her mind. 'What about me?' She felt like an ant under a magnifying glass watching a cloud move away from the sun.

Her mother's cheek twitched; she hated that Angie knew she'd hit on something. 'You've been keeping secrets.' Angie narrowed her eyes but kept them firmly fixed on Lottie.

Lottie's skin began to prickle. 'What secrets?' She raised her chin defiantly.

'Oh. My. God!' said Angie, each word getting louder. 'Daniel!' she yelled. 'Daniel, come here.'

Daniel came into the kitchen with an irritated look on his face, closely followed by Zach, Joe and Emily. 'What's going on?' Daniel asked.

'No idea.' Lottie shrugged and tried to remain calm. 'Ask her.' She stabbed a finger in Angie's general direction. She couldn't make eye contact with her brother or Joe. Was this the moment she'd been dreading for years? Her cheeks were burning. She didn't want Joe to witness this, but what could she do?

Angie stood up and addressed her audience. 'She knew.' She pointed at Lottie and gave a fake sob. Lottie's stomach plummeted. 'She knew our mother was dying and she kept it to herself.'

That wasn't what Lottie was expecting. Relief mixed with indignation washed through her. For now, her secrets were safe. As usual her mother had gone off down the path to crazyland and she would have to coax her back.

'What? Nana didn't say anything to me. Honestly, I didn't know. Nobody knew,' said Lottie. Angie was shaking her head. Daniel was frowning hard at Lottie. 'I had the Christmas card, same as the rest of you.' She struggled to stop her voice from rising to a shout. 'If I'd known, then Nana wouldn't have had to write me a card.'

Angie pushed out her bottom lip. 'Proves nothing. You could have hatched the card thing up together.'

'For crying out loud,' said Lottie. She heard Nana in her words and it galvanised her resolve. 'What would I possibly have to gain from keeping that secret?'

'My mother,' snapped Angie. 'You always wanted her to yourself. You did everything you could to get between us.'

Lottie threw up her hands in frustration: this was madness. 'How could I get between you and Nana when *you* were never here?' Lottie shouted.

Zach stepped fully into the kitchen and strode over to stand next to Lottie. 'Mum, that's enough. Lottie didn't know about Nana.'

'How could you possibly know that?'

'Because I know Lottie and she's the most honest and trustworthy person I know.'

'She was always Nana's favourite. She always favoured Lottie over you, Zach.' Angie was calmer now, and because of it, more dangerous. 'You don't think those two are capable of making a pact not to tell anyone else?' She stared, unblinking, at Zach.

'No,' he said, calmly. 'I don't.'

Daniel was shaking his head. 'Angie, you know what Mother was like. Stiff upper lip to the end. She wouldn't have wanted any fuss or upset.' He turned to Lottie. 'And most of all, she wouldn't have wanted to see you upset.'

Angie opened her mouth, but stopped when Scott came in from outside, bringing a gust of winter through the door with him. Lottie glanced at Scott and her breath caught in her throat when she saw what he had in his hand. Her eyes shot to Emily who, from her wide-eyed expression, Lottie guessed had spotted it too.

'What's that?' asked Angie.

'That's what I was going to ask you,' said Scott, holding the pregnancy tester box aloft. 'I found this inside the packaging of the perfume I bought you. Have you got something you want to tell me?' Lottie realised that Emily must have found the packaging in the bathroom and used it to conceal the evidence before putting it in the outside bin. She wondered where the actual test had gone.

It was Angie's turn to look nervous. She got to her feet and moved towards Scott. 'Darling, what do you mean?' She went to take the box from him, but he snatched it away.

'I'm guessing you thought you were pregnant.' He turned to address the kitchen. 'We're hoping to have a baby.'

Zach coughed out a laugh and Lottie nudged him. Poor Scott, he really had no idea how old their mother was. Scott turned back to Angie. 'Well, are you?' he asked, his face hopeful. Emily was looking terrified and Lottie's heart went out to her. She liked Emily, and she loved her brother. This was not how this information was meant to be shared.

'No,' said Angie. 'I'm afraid I'm not. The test's not mine.'

'You're forty-eight,' blurted out Zach. Scott looked like he'd been hit with a pan; or at the very least, a cremated stuffing ball.

Angie looked panicked as she strode over to Scott and snatched the test box from him. Trying to move the conversation on as quickly as possible, she spun around to look straight at Lottie. 'But this means *someone* here thought they were pregnant.'

Lottie stiffened with alarm. She opened her mouth and said the first thing that came into her head. 'Scott's a porn star!'

Chapter Twenty-Four

'A porn star?' Angie's laugh tinkled merrily – until she saw the look on Scott's face. Angie put down the pregnancy test box on the kitchen table. Lottie stepped in front of it, silently picked it up and put it in her back pocket.

Angie turned to Scott, who was looking uneasy. 'What's she talking about, Scott?'

Lottie was about to usher everyone out of the kitchen until she realised that they'd only be listening on the other side of the door, so they might as well stay.

Scott's eyebrows were working overtime. His usual smile was replaced with a thin line. 'You remember I told you I'd been an extra in some low budget films?'

'Ones that never made it to the cinema,' said Angie, in a very small voice.

'You don't get *those* sorts of films at the local Cineworld,' whispered Zach, who appeared to be enjoying the show so much he just needed a bucket of popcorn. Lottie shot him a glare.

'I'm sorry—' began Scott.

'How many p . . . How many films?' asked Angie, a hardness creeping into her voice.

Scott opened his mouth and closed it a few times. 'I

really don't know.' Angie continued to stare at him. He held up his palms.

'Ten?' she asked.

'Fifty? A hundred maybe.'

Despite the Botox, Angie's eyebrows shot upwards. 'A hundred porn films! Bloody hell. Thousands of people could have seen them.'

'It's not likely. They're not that good,' cut in Zach. Scott and Angie both scowled at him and Lottie gave him another poke in the ribs. 'What? I was trying to help.'

'I've been doing it for years, on and off—' said Scott.

'On and off,' sniggered Zach.

'—whenever I needed the cash. But I haven't done one for months, and definitely not since we've been together.' Scott's eyes were pleading. 'I'm really sorry I didn't tell you the truth, but it's not something I brag about.'

Angie's head tilted. 'Do they pay well?'

Scott nodded. 'A day on set equals a month as a trimmer. But I promise I'll not do any more. I'm getting kind of old for it now anyway. And while I'm thinking about age . . .'

'Ooh, nice segue,' whispered Zach to Lottie.

Angie shook her head and turned away from Scott. Everyone else suddenly tried to look busy. 'Right. Show's over. You must have better things to do.' She tried to shoo Lottie out, but Lottie picked up the carving knife and pointed at the ham – she was busy. Zach got out of his mother's way and disappeared into the hallway with Emily and Joe.

'You're forty-eight?' Scott seemed to be trying to work something out.

Angie let out a tinny laugh. 'Zach was always rubbish

with numbers. He failed his Maths GCSE first time. Don't take any notice of him.'

Lottie kept her head down and prayed Scott didn't think to ask her.

'I thought we were trying for a baby,' said Scott, his voice gentle and full of hurt. He leaned back against the cupboards.

Lottie concentrated on slicing the ham super thin. She wished she could escape with the others, but she really did need to get this job done otherwise there'd be no lunch.

Angie pushed her hair behind her ears and gave him a soft smile. 'Oh, my dear Scotty. We *were* trying. We still are.' Lottie didn't want to think about that. 'But the thing is, I think I'm going through an early menopause.' *Not that early*, thought Lottie.

'Early menopause. You poor thing – why didn't you tell me?' Scott took her hand.

Angie went all coy. 'I wasn't sure. And it's the sort of thing that has most men running for the hills.'

'You know I'm here for you, right?'

'I do. And who knows? We might strike lucky. I'm happy to keep trying if you are.' Lottie wished she had some earplugs. She was staring at the ham so hard she thought her eyes might bleed. Now seemed like as good an opportunity as any to put a few things straight.

'Scott.' His head jerked in her direction. 'My mother is frequently misguided. Her vegan deception is a prime example. She was trying to impress you.' Before he could respond, she turned to her mother. 'And you really need to learn to be yourself. You always try to be what you think others want you to be. It never works, because eventually the real you comes out. People should accept you as you are. Both of you.'

Angie was blinking back her surprise at Lottie's words. Scott slunk an arm around her waist and they silently smiled at each other. It gave Lottie a warm feeling to witness the acceptance. Maybe her mother was getting better at choosing men; she'd had enough practice.

Angie pulled Scott close and kissed him. It was barely on the right side of public decency and Lottie nearly lost a finger when the carving knife slipped.

'Shit. Bugger me that hurt,' said Lottie, and the kissing couple pulled apart.

'Let's take this upstairs,' suggested Angie, all doe-eyed. She led Scott from the kitchen and they left Lottie to sort out her cut finger on her own.

Lottie wrapped a piece of kitchen towel around her bleeding finger and dashed outside to do a proper job of disposing of the pregnancy test box. She hoped that for now that was very much forgotten.

Lottie was adding the final touches to lunch when Emily came into the kitchen. There was an Everest of ham sandwiches, a separate platter of ham slices and ham and cheese on cocktail sticks. She'd made tomato and hummus sandwiches for Scott and put a big label on the plate with his name on it. There was also the last of the cheese board, Dayea's lumpia, crackers, sausage rolls, crisps and a pineapple – she still wasn't sure what she had been meant to do with the pineapple, but it made quite a nice table ornament. She figured the spread should keep the ravenous horde at bay until dinner.

'Thank you for earlier,' said Emily. 'I really thought the game was up. I owe you.'

Lottie waved her thanks away. 'It's fine. But watch out because my mother's memory is better than an elephant's.

She is preoccupied now, but she'll be back on the case later. I guarantee it.'

Emily looked concerned, and rightly so. 'Where's she gone?'

'Her and Scott are making up so she'll be busy for a while. Thankfully.'

Emily flopped down on a kitchen chair. 'This is turning into such a mess. I'm sure Zach knows something is wrong. He's acting all odd around me. Do you think he'll guess the test was mine?'

'No. The good thing about having an overdramatic mother is that you automatically assume anything like that is her trying to draw attention to herself. So you're good on that score. Also, he's a man. They're notoriously slow on the uptake on things like this.'

'Thanks. I don't want anything to spoil what I already have. Although I'm still a bit worried about what Jessie heard him say to Joe yesterday. I love Zach and Jessie.'

The fact that there was no pause between their names told Lottie all she needed to know. Anyone who Zach was considering proposing to needed to take him and his daughter as a package and it was clear that Emily did.

'Then really that's all that matters,' said Lottie.

'You're right.' Emily took a slow breath.

'You seem to be getting on well with everyone.'

'Joe's nice,' she said.

'He is . . . very nice.' The thought of him made Lottie smile.

'What was that all about yesterday? Bernard said something about Joe's father being a murderer.'

Lottie paused with the clingfilm hovering above a plate. 'It's true . . . but it's not that straightforward.'

'But murder,' said Emily, looking uncomfortable.

'Joe's mum was dying of cancer. His dad was the local GP. She was in her last few days and he gave her something to hasten the inevitable.'

'Poor Joe.' Emily scrunched up her features.

'Poor all of them. His dad was arrested shortly after. He died in custody and I swear it was from a broken heart.'

'That's so sad.'

Lottie nodded. It was indeed the saddest thing she'd ever witnessed. Talking about it flooded her mind with memories. She'd known them so well. It had been awful to see Joe's mum deteriorate and watch Joe trying to cope with it. When she had died and the police had taken Joe's father away, the small village had been besieged by press, and Joe had taken refuge at the manor. Shortly afterwards, he'd written her a note and left without saying goodbye. She'd not seen or heard from him again – until two days ago.

'Right. What have I forgotten?' Lottie scanned an eye over the food. She needed to keep her mind in the present. Her memories were too much of a minefield to wander through.

'Can I help with lunch? Ah.' She looked over the table and seemed to notice that lunch was already a done deal. 'Or dinner later?'

'Thanks.' Lottie was making a prawn curry tonight so she could fill everyone up with lots of rice. She just had to think of something to put in a vegan version. 'Is sprout curry a thing?' asked Lottie.

Emily wrinkled her nose. 'Not something I've heard of, and certainly not something I'd fancy.'

'No, me neither,' admitted Lottie. 'I might have to get something from the shop.'

'Could you get me another tester while you're there?'

'Sure.' Lottie hated seeing the worry in Emily's eyes. 'Whatever the result is, you'll deal with it. And it'll be okay. I promise.' Lottie hoped she sounded reassuring.

'Thanks. I don't know what I would've done without you these last couple of days.' Emily put out her arms and they hugged. Lottie felt quite emotional. She knew that whatever happened between Emily and Zach, she'd found a friend.

Lunch was the usual organised chaos that Lottie loved. It felt depleted around the table without Great Uncle Bernard and Dayea, and with Angie and Scott still in their room making up. Aunt Nicola and Uncle Daniel were being civil to each other – which was a big development, although it was all still quite awkward – and Jessie was excited, because Rhys was going to take her out for a go with the metal detector after lunch. Joe was quiet, Dave was restless and Lottie hadn't seen a glimpse of the Duchess since before poogate. She made a mental note to have a proper look for her after they'd been to see Bernard.

Peace descended while everybody ate. 'So who's coming to the hospital with me?' she asked. There were no immediate takers, so she dropped a steady gaze on Uncle Daniel who eventually looked up.

'I could come if you like?' He was almost as unfeeling as his sister. Lottie would save a seat in the car for her mother, but she suspected she would have some hugely plausible reason for why – whilst she would love to – she couldn't possibly come.

She hoped Uncle Bernard was going to be all right, but he wasn't a healthy man. She knew from Nana's friends that it was often the way – they were perfectly fine until one thing went wrong with them, and then there was a domino effect. Before you knew it you were at their funeral wondering what happened.

'I think I'll come too,' said Aunt Nicola, and Lottie noticed Uncle Daniel's shoulders sag. It appeared Aunt Nicola was keeping a close watch on her errant husband.

'Great. Uncle Bernard will be pleased. The more the merrier,' said Lottie. Although a trip with her aunt and uncle was not one she'd be looking forward to.

'I'll drive,' said Uncle Daniel.

Nicola looked pointedly at his empty wine glass. 'I don't think that's wise.'

'I think I've already proved that I'm not wise. But one glass doesn't make me a drink driver.' He dropped his serviette on the table and stood up. 'What time do you want to leave, Lottie?'

Lottie felt put on the spot, and she checked the clock. 'Visiting is from two o'clock. So about ten to?'

Daniel nodded. 'I've got some things to do. I'll be out the front at ten to two.'

'Perfect. Thanks,' said Lottie, and she returned to her ham sandwich.

Not two minutes had passed before Aunt Nicola was on her feet making excuses to follow Daniel. Rhys watched his mother go. Despite his age, Lottie could see the situation with his parents was affecting him. He was a sensitive lad – quiet and a bit distant, like most teenagers, but far more aware than they gave him credit for. Watching his parents hurt each other was a horrible thing for him to witness.

She could feel she was being watched. Joe was studying her with a faint frown. She wondered what he was thinking.

250

She had frequently thought of him over the years. At first he had dominated her thoughts, but over time he had been relegated to the occasional memory. Now he was back, taking up more headspace than she would have liked. He was back – but she was leaving. Everything was changing, and she wasn't sure she was ready for any of it.

'Who wants leftover Christmas pudding?' she asked. She was met with a round of mumbled nos.

Joe helped Lottie clear the table and followed her through to the kitchen. There was a charged silence between them; or maybe that was in his imagination. Lottie wrapped a ham sandwich into a neat foil parcel. Joe stacked the plates by the sink and, once she was finished, Lottie joined him. She started filling the sink with suds.

'I've been thinking about what Bernard said,' said Joe.

'Oh, Joe. Please don't dwell on that. Nobody else thinks you were involved.' Joe gave a slow, disbelieving blink. 'Okay. Maybe some in the village do. But most people don't – so does it really matter? *I* know you had nothing to do with it.' She gave him a reassuring smile.

He held up a hand to stop her. She thought she knew, but she didn't. 'You deserve to know the truth.'

Lottie's smile faded. She switched off the taps and gestured for him to sit at the table. 'What's up, Joe?'

Joe took a steadying breath. What he was about to say could change his relationship with Lottie forever. She already thought badly of him for leaving. His next revelation wasn't going to improve things, but he had to tell her the truth. 'Bernard's right. I did know what my dad was doing.'

Lottie's eyes widened briefly. 'You knew he was planning to . . .?' She didn't need to finish the sentence.

'Deep down, I knew,' admitted Joe, and Lottie seemed to relax a fraction. 'He didn't explicitly say what he was planning, but he didn't have to. I knew.' Lottie reached out and put her hand on his. It was good to feel her touch; to know she still cared. 'It broke my heart to see my mum fade the way she did. To see her in pain. Each day it got harder to put on a brave face when I saw her. I'd cry on Dad's shoulder every night.' He paused as the memories flooded back, catching him off guard by how vivid they were.

'You gave her the strength to fight for as long as she did,' said Lottie, giving his hand a squeeze.

'Dad said he couldn't let us both suffer indefinitely. I should have realised then what he intended to do. Maybe deep down I did, and that was what I wanted to happen. I certainly wanted her to be at peace.'

'That's what we all wanted. Nobody could blame you for wanting that. She was in a great deal of pain. The medication wasn't working. Lots of people would have done the same as your father if they had had the means.'

'But he did it for me as much as for her.'

'Your father was a kind and gentle man. What he did, he did out of love for both of you,' said Lottie.

'But I knew, Lottie. And I didn't stop him. That makes me culpable.'

'Joe, you didn't know for sure. Unless he explicitly told you what he was planning,' she left a pause and Joe shook his head, 'then you couldn't have stopped him.'

'Maybe I could have done something. Said something.'

'You were only eighteen. I don't believe there's anything you could have done, Joe; however hard you'd tried.'

'But I didn't try. And the price I paid was to lose them both.' Tears welled in his eyes and he blinked them back.

'It may all seem to fit together now, but I don't think you saw it so clearly at the time. Time does strange things to our memories and emotions. If you'd had the slightest inkling, would you not have talked that over with someone?' she asked.

Joe lifted his head and smiled. 'I'd have told you.'

'That was kind of what I was getting at but I didn't want to appear big headed. Back then we told each other everything. We talked all the time. And remember,' she pushed her thumb against his, 'no secrets.'

Joe chuckled. 'I'd forgotten our secret sign.' As kids they'd had a secret club and met in an old shed on the manor land. They'd had a motto and a secret sign, which had stayed with him and Lottie into their teens: a code they lived by as their romance blossomed.

'I saw your face the day your mum died. That wasn't the face of someone who knew.'

Joe stared at the floor, composing his breathing, trying to keep his emotions in check. 'Thanks, Lottie. That means so much.' He wiped a stray tear away. 'Bloody hell, I feel better now than I did after any therapy session in the States. And it was a lot cheaper.'

'You've not had my bill yet.' She squeezed his hand.

'You're funny.' He studied her face. Her dark brown eyes, the delicate blush of her lips. 'I've missed you, Lottie.'

'I've missed you too, Joe.'

Tentatively he leaned forward. He watched her breathing speed up. At last their lips touched ever so gently at first. They shared their first kiss in nine years and it felt like coming home.

Chapter Twenty-Five

'Anyone coming to the hospital?' shouted Uncle Daniel into the hall.

Lottie pulled away from Joe. For a second their eyes met, and everything was all right with the world. The last time she'd kissed Joe, she kissed the boy, but here was the man. There were many reasons why she shouldn't have kissed him, but right now she couldn't think of a single one. The connection between them was still there.

A smile spread across Joe's face and something lit up in Lottie's heart. It was like the years of hurt had been dissolved by his kiss. But life wasn't that simple – she knew there were a million things to sort out. In this moment, though, she felt the tiniest spark of hope that they might actually be fixable.

Uncle Daniel shouted something inaudible and Lottie got quickly to her feet. 'I need to go.' She pointed at the door and then touched her lips. She held in the childish giggles of joy that were bubbling to the surface. Pure happiness was coursing through her.

'Of course, go,' said Joe. 'And I need to take Dave for a walk. But let's get together some time tomorrow after everyone's gone home?'

'Yes.' She couldn't control the grin on her face, and she could barely wait for tomorrow.

'Bloody hell. I'm not a sodding Uber!' hollered Uncle Daniel.

'Coming!' yelled back Lottie, and she grabbed up the foil parcel from the table and almost skipped from the room.

Jessie met her in the hallway. 'Lottie, my robot has stopped working,' she said, her face glum.

'Let's take a look.' Lottie slid off the battery cover to reveal an empty compartment. 'I think I know what the problem is. Wait there,' she said.

Lottie bounded upstairs and rapped on her mother's bedroom door. She heard a scuffle inside and her partially clad mother appeared at the door. 'Is it lunchtime?'

'No, it's visiting time, and you need to get dressed. But before you do, can you return the robot's batteries?' Lottie held up the toy. Angie burst out laughing, and so did Scott in the background.

'Seriously. Do you want me to tell Zach what you've stolen them for?' Lottie gave her mother a hard stare.

'You're such a killjoy.' Angie shut the door and Lottie waited. She heard something buzzing followed by spluttered giggles. She nearly put her fingers in her ears. Eventually Angie opened the door and stepped out, fully clothed.

'Here,' she handed over the batteries. Lottie put them in the robot and headed back downstairs, Angie following after her.

'Do you think I could have them back when Jessie goes to bed?'

'No!' Lottie handed Jessie her robot at the bottom of the stairs and she skipped off happily.

* * *

255

As they got in Uncle Daniel's car, Lottie passed her mother a foil-wrapped ham sandwich. Angie didn't query what was in the sandwich; she just ate it. Lottie managed to bagsy the front seat, on the grounds of getting a wee bit carsick if she sat in the back, and surprisingly Angie and Nicola both let it go unchallenged. Being in the front meant it wasn't as easy for her mother to question her either, which was good because she had a lot to think about. She snuggled into the large leather seat. Uncle Daniel flicked a switch and the seat gently heated up under her bum. It matched the growing warm sensation inside her.

Lottie rolled her lips together. Joe's kiss had taken her by surprise. Her heart felt lighter for it, like something had been unlocked and set free. She took a deep breath and tried to steady her racing thoughts. This didn't change the past, but it certainly provided a whole new lens through which to view the future. Joe was back and he'd kissed her. There was the nine-year gap they needed to sort through – and the big messy bit before that too – but that was all history. She wanted to focus on how she was feeling right now. A small thread of happiness was uncurling inside her and it felt like she was coming to life after a lengthy hibernation.

Nicola brought a frostiness to the car. She tutted when Uncle Daniel crunched the gears and he glared at her via the rear-view mirror in return. Thankfully the journey was uneventful and fairly quiet, apart from Angie telling Nicola how amazing Scott was and what a bonus it was that he was a porn star. Nicola said nothing. Zilch. Not a thing. And all the while, Lottie and Uncle Daniel exchanged glances and a variety of raised eyebrow combinations.

* * *

When they got to the hospital, visiting hours had already started, and as expected, Dayea was at Bernard's bedside holding his hand. Bernard was a bulky man, but lying in the hospital bed with tubes and monitors attached to him, he seemed quite frail. His skin was ashen – he looked poorly to Lottie. They said their hellos to Dayea and pulled up chairs.

'How's he doing?' asked Lottie.

'He is sleeping,' said Dayea, with a tired smile.

'Yes, but how bad is he?' asked Angie. Even Nicola tutted at her lack of tact.

'Oh. The nurse says he's doing fine. But they may do an autopsy,' said Dayea, struggling with the medical terminology.

Lottie had to double-check Bernard was breathing. 'I don't think you mean an autopsy,' she said, trying to ignore the tittering from Daniel and Angie behind her. They had no respect. 'Possibly a biopsy?'

'Yes. That is it,' said Dayea, pointing at Lottie in agreement. 'The nurses will explain better. They are lovely,' she added.

'I'm sure they are. And they do such a brilliant job. Have they talked about when he might be able to come home?' she asked.

'No. I asked, but they are not able to say. I think we may need a nurse at home to care for him.'

Angie shot forward and almost fell off her chair. 'If you're talking about a private nurse, that sort of care costs a lot of money. Surely he'd be better off staying here.'

'He can come to live with me,' said Dayea, jutting out her chin at the end of the sentence. Lottie was pleased to see her standing up to Angie.

Angie turned to Daniel. 'That might be helpful for

agreeing a completion date for the sale of the property.' Daniel nodded along. They were bloody unbelievable.

'It's okay, Dayea,' said Lottie. 'You don't need to think about that right now. We just need to focus on Bernard getting better.' She shot a look at her mother and uncle, but neither seemed bothered.

Dayea looked tired. Her usually bright complexion was washed out and she had dark circles around the eyes.

'Have you slept?' asked Lottie.

Dayea nodded. But Lottie wasn't convinced, and it probably showed on her face. 'A couple of hours maybe.'

'I brought Bernard some things from home. And his new slippers I bought him for Christmas.' Lottie opened the bag to show Dayea.

Lottie could see Angie was getting fidgety already. She picked up the menu off the side. 'Roast chicken; cottage pie; herb-crusted salmon,' she read out. 'This sounds quite good. At least he'll get a decent meal in here.' She tipped her head at Lottie as she laughed at her own joke.

'Do they have a vegan option?' asked Lottie. 'Because you could always join him.' She gave Angie a murderous look and her mother put the menu back.

They all sat and stared at Bernard. Lottie found she was breathing in time to the rhythm of his monitor. If she wasn't careful she was at risk of nodding off herself. This was the trouble with hospital visits. They were always too warm and, when the person you'd come to visit was asleep, there wasn't really much to be said.

However, it appeared that the elderly gent in the next bed was quite chatty. 'Hello, there. Merry Christmas,' he said, swinging his legs out of bed.

'Hi, Merry Christmas,' said Lottie, being polite. She had a bit of an issue with saying this on Boxing Day, but she'd let it go – the poor chap might not know he'd missed it.

'Nice to meet you; I'm George.' He offered a hand to shake, which Lottie and Daniel both took.

'Family outing, is it?' asked George, with a chuckle. Lottie responded with a small smile. 'He's better than he was when they brought him in.' He pointed at Bernard. 'Woke me up, they did, but I don't sleep too well in here anyways.' He put his slippers on. 'Best place for him though.' He sighed. 'Dodgy ticker, but he's okay now,' he added, with great authority.

'Yes, that was a relief,' said Lottie, feeling that someone really should answer the poor man.

A nurse came over and began checking George's monitor. George leaned forward conspiratorially to Daniel. 'Yesterday, this nurse checked me down there and said I was circus sized,' he said, proudly.

'No,' said the nurse. 'I said you were circumcised.' She shook her head and George looked thoroughly deflated. Daniel belly laughed and George gave him a grumpy glare before forcefully pulling round his curtains. Lottie couldn't help but snigger. Poor George.

Angie stood up and leaned over Bernard. 'Uncle Bernard, it's Angie. Can you hear me?'

'Angie what are you doing?' asked Nicola.

'I'm seeing if he knows we're here. Because if not, then . . .' Angie tapped her watch. Lottie gave her mother her best death stare and Angie huffed and sat down again. She was worse than a toddler.

The nurse moved on to check Bernard and they all watched her intently; especially Dayea. Lottie hadn't thought of it before, but it must be quite odd to do a job where you were constantly watched by others. *A bit like always being on stage*, she mused. The nurse jotted something in a folder at the foot of the bed.

'How's he doing?' asked Lottie.

'He's stable. He's only sleeping. You can wake him up if you like.'

Lottie was relieved to hear this. 'Thank you.'

'Any questions, just ask,' said the nurse with a friendly smile, and she moved on.

'Shall I wake him?' Lottie asked Dayea, who nodded.

'Not much point in visiting if we don't,' said Angie.

Lottie ignored her mother. 'Uncle Bernard,' said Lottie, patting his hand gently. No response. 'Uncle Bernie. We all came to visit you.'

'Wake up Bernard, for heaven's sake.' Angie gave his shoulder a good shake.

Poor Bernard jolted and let out a loud fart. Daniel got the giggles again. 'What? What?' said Bernard, blinking rapidly and looking alarmed. Lottie watched his monitor with trepidation.

'It's okay. We came to say hello,' said Lottie.

Bernard's features settled into a warm smile. 'Button,' he said, reaching for her hand. His expression tightened. 'Have you brought Joe?' He glanced rapidly around the bed.

'No.' She kept her irritation under control, he wasn't a well man.

'Right. There's a possibility that I may have overreacted yesterday.' He glanced at Dayea, who was nodding.

Lottie couldn't let it go that easily. 'Joe saved your life.'

'So I hear. It was just that all I could think about was what Joe's father did. These medical people have your life in their hands. He nearly got away with it you know. The murder.'

260

'But he didn't, did he?'

'I guess not.' Bernard looked contrite.

'And more importantly, it was nothing to do with Joe.'

Bernard pouted but didn't say anything. It was too much to hope he'd changed his opinion of Joe overnight.

'Good to see you looking better,' said Daniel, leaning over and patting Bernard's shoulder.

'Thanks. I'm feeling better too,' said Bernard, shuffling himself up on the pillows. Now he was awake, his colour was improving. 'I'll be out of here in no time,' he said, and Lottie saw him squeeze Dayea's hand. Lottie was pleased he had someone like her to care for him. Dayea failed to stifle a huge yawn.

'Dayea, he needs you fit and well. You should go home and get some rest.'

Dayea shook her head. Lottie remembered Dayea's car was still at the manor because she'd gone to hospital in the ambulance with Bernard. 'Let us drop you home. There's room in the Range Rover.' Uncle Daniel nodded his confirmation. 'Then that's settled. You need to rest and you need to eat.' Lottie could have got rid of the rest of the ham sandwiches if only she'd thought.

Lottie updated Uncle Bernard on the duck race, including Dave's involvement, and it was lovely to see him laugh. The change in twenty-four hours was quite remarkable. When she'd run out of things to tell him and her mother's twitching had reached a level where the nurse was paying attention, they said their goodbyes.

They managed to persuade Dayea to let them give her a lift, although Lottie felt sure she would have a quick shower and change and then get a taxi straight back to the hospital. But in a way, that was reassuring. She didn't like to see her great uncle this unwell, but she did enjoy witnessing the love they clearly had for each other. Dayea loved Bernard – that was obvious.

Lottie was also glad of the excuse to see where Dayea lived, especially if she was serious about having Bernard move in with her. Not that they needed Lottie's approval, but she did care where Bernard went, unlike most of the rest of her family. Dayea sat in the middle seat in the back and gave directions by way of pointy fingers next to Lottie's right ear. She directed them to Bourton-on-the-Water, one of Lottie's favourite villages.

They drove through the main street, with its little stream running alongside the road, perfect footbridges dotted along it. The ducks were huddled together in groups. *Not many tourists about to feed them at this time of year*, thought Lottie. The small shops were all closed, but with their pretty bay windows all done up for Christmas, they looked enticing.

'Here,' said Dayea, forcefully pointing across Lottie. Daniel took the next left turn into a wide road with elegant houses. 'At the next lamp-post. Stop, please,' said Dayea, and Daniel did as instructed. Everyone peered out to get a look. The house they were outside stood back from the road, like its neighbours, and was built in warm yellowy Cotswold stone. It was beautifully symmetrical with three large windows on the first floor, a central door painted grey and a large sash window either side.

'This is nice,' said Lottie.

'Yes, who lives here?' asked Nicola.

'Me, I live here,' said Dayea, giving Nicola a look that said that was a very dumb question.

Angie exited first so that Dayea could get out of the middle seat, and she had a good nose around the driveway. 'There's a caravan,' called back Angie delightedly.

'Yes,' said Dayea. 'I sleep in it. But it has plenty of room.'

Lottie leaned over to see the tiny caravan, with neat curtains, bunting at the windows and its wheels lodged on bricks. 'It looks lovely,' she said, and Dayea smiled at the compliment.

'Who do you live here with then, Dayea?' asked Angie, eyeing the big house.

She got the same look as Nicola. 'Just me who lives here.' She pointed at the caravan.

'Right,' said Angie, and she shook her head as she got back inside. 'She's a sandwich short of a picnic, that one,' she mumbled.

'Talking of which; did you enjoy your *ham* sandwich?' asked Lottie. Her mother shut up.

Lottie lowered the side window and Dayea came up to it. She could barely see inside – she was so tiny compared to the Range Rover. 'If there's anything at all we can do, please call the house. Okay?' said Lottie.

'Thank you, Lottie. You are a very kind girl.' Dayea went on tiptoe and leaned in through the window. 'Thank you, Mr Collins. You are kind too,' she said to Daniel. She glanced at Nicola in the back. Then, as if remembering something, she added to Daniel, 'But you are also a massive *ass hat*.' The women in the car erupted into giggles as Dayea turned and walked up the driveway.

Chapter Twenty-Six

'Well, that was interesting,' said Angie from the back seat, as they set off back to Henbourne. 'I wonder how come she's staying there.'

'Maybe it belongs to another elderly gentleman with unstable health,' said Nicola.

'Or perhaps the caravan was left to her when someone died,' said Angie.

'Not really any of our business, though, is it?' said Lottie.

'If she's got designs on ripping off Bernard then I'd say it is,' Nicola chipped in.

Lottie looked around to see Angie nodding enthusiastically. 'You're right. She's even keener now he's in hospital. I suspect she's thinking she'll get her hands on his money sooner than she thought.'

Lottie was outraged. 'You're wrong. Anyone can see that Dayea adores Bernard.'

'And his money,' said Angie. 'Lottie, you're very sweet, but do you really think she'd be interested in a cantankerous old man if he didn't have two pennies to rub together?'

'Well . . .' Lottie didn't like that she was thinking this over. They were making her question things.

'Let's just say it how it is. She's a gold-digger,' said Angie.

'Don't judge others by your standards,' said Lottie.

'I think we should investigate Dayea a bit more.' Aunt Nicola's tone was serious. 'You do hear about people befriending the elderly and then bumping them off for their assets.'

'Okay, ladies,' cut in Daniel, 'this is Bernard's choice. I don't think we should get involved. Whether we're against them getting together – or for it,' he gave Lottie a look, 'I think we should all stay out of Bernard's affairs.'

Lottie was stung. 'You would say that. You don't care what happens to him as long as he's not living at the manor and he doesn't get in the way of the sale.' *And you don't care what happens to me either*, she thought.

It was quiet in the car for a while. Lottie fumed silently and stared out of the windscreen. She didn't like being lumped in with her unfeeling mother and aunt.

'Did you open your card from Mother yet?' Angie asked Nicola.

'Yes. It said something about there coming a time when you have to let go and move on to the next chapter. I'm not sure what she meant. What did yours say?' asked Nicola.

'Oh, nothing significant,' replied Angie. Lottie could tell her mother was lying. 'Daniel, have you opened yours?' asked Angie.

'Yeah. It said something about there never being a wrong time to do the right thing . . .' His voice tailed off.

They returned to a thoughtful silence, mulling over the cards and messages that Rose had sent them. Lottie watched the countryside zoom by as the Range Rover hurtled down the narrow lanes, taking every bump, puddle and pothole in its stride. She wished she could be a bit more Range Rover.

'Can we stop at the village shop, please?' asked Lottie as they neared Dumbleford. It would save her a trip out later.

Uncle Daniel gave a little huff. 'Yeah, okay.'

'We're going to drive right past it. You can drop me off if there's something you need to get back for.' But what that could possibly be, she had no idea.

He softened a little. 'It's okay, I'll wait. As long as you're not doing a full week's shopping.'

'At those prices?'

'I'll pop in too,' said Angie. Lottie rolled her eyes. That was all she needed. She wouldn't be able to get the pregnancy test for Emily if her mother was spying on her.

'No need. Let me know what you want and I'll get it,' offered Lottie, as casually as she could manage.

But her mother wasn't going to let it go. 'No, I'd like a nose around to see what's changed. What do you need anyway?'

'Something vegan for Scott's dinner.' She had dismissed the sprout curry out of hand.

'Oh, well then, I should definitely come. I can advise you.'

Lottie balled her fists and thrust them under her thighs. She felt like a teenager – she could easily have gone off in a strop had she not been in a moving vehicle. This was what her mother reduced her to. 'I'm getting butternut squash, if they've got any, to make a curry.' The village stores' stock was not the most glamorous, but they had all the basics, as well as things requested and bought regularly by the villagers. Lottie had quite a good insight into the lives of the locals via their purchases. Shirley liked a granary loaf and was particular about her sherry, which she bought quite a lot of; Lottie wondered if it was acting as a preservative, as she was pushing ninety and still going strong. The vicar had a major Curly Wurly habit and Maureen from the tearooms went through enough pickled eggs to sink a flotilla of battleships – or, alternatively, to gas the occupants.

Daniel pulled up by the village green and put on his hazard warning lights. Lottie figured it was more a gesture to her that he wasn't planning on stopping long, rather than a warning to other drivers. Lottie hopped out and headed for the little shop without waiting for her mother. Inside, there were so many women chatting near the till that it was like a WI meeting. They gave a chorus of warm welcomes as she entered, and she realised that buying the pregnancy test on the quiet really wasn't going to be possible whether her mother was there or not. While she scanned the vegetable section, the entry bell announced her mother's arrival. The women turned to look, but then carried on their conversation.

'Do they have any curly kale?' asked Angie.

'Nope. And anyway I'm doing butternut squash curry.' Lottie was emphatic. Her mother followed her to the freezer. Lottie pondered the ice creams and sorbets.

'He can't have anything cream based,' said Angie, haughtily.

'I know,' said Lottie, barely managing to keep her cool. She would be glad when her mother went home tomorrow. She hoped they were booked on an early train. 'And I'll get some almond milk, too, so you can have porridge in the morning.'

'Porridge? Darling, I know you don't watch your weight, but how many carbs do you think there are in porridge?'

'More than there are shreds remaining of my patience,' she said slowly.

'If you're going to be passive aggressive, I'm going to wait in the car,' said Angie huffily, and she stomped out of the shop, making the door chime work overtime. The gathered ladies went on hold for a moment to watch her dramatic exit. The door closed and the chatter resumed. Lottie calmed herself.

The entry door chimed again, the ladies paused their conversation and, fearing her mother had returned, Lottie's hackles rose. She needn't have worried. A woman Lottie didn't recognise walked in and headed to the wine section. Lottie picked up the raspberry sorbet and checked the ingredients, aware that the ladies had resumed their conversation, although now it was hushed, with a decidedly excited tone.

The stranger's phone rang and she answered it. 'Hi . . . Yes, Megan speaking . . . No.' She had a strong American accent. 'Tuesday latest. Can you do that? . . . Okay. Bye.'

Lottie shut the freezer and glanced at the woman as she headed to the till. She was still studying the wines. She had olive skin and black hair, neatly tied back. Lottie couldn't help but notice that she was very slim: her waist was tiny; minuscule in fact. And she was dressed like she'd been to a wedding. Lottie smiled, but got no response.

Lottie paid for her items, said her goodbyes to the assembled women and exited the shop. Outside, she did a double take: pulled up in front of Uncle Daniel's car was an almost identical Range Rover. She clambered into the passenger seat of her uncle's car and did up her seatbelt. 'Did you see who got out of that car?' she asked as Daniel pulled away. Lottie could see a man sitting in the driver's seat.

'Meghan Markle!' shouted Angie and she slapped her hand on the window.

'What?' said Daniel, making the car swerve a fraction. 'Bloody hell, Ang,' he added, full of irritation.

Lottie swung her head around to see a glimpse of the American woman coming out of the village stores. It was difficult to tell, but she did definitely bear a passing resemblance to Prince Harry's wife.

'Oh my God. I can't believe it.' Angie was jigging about with excitement. 'Did you see her in the shop, Lottie?'

'Yeah.' Lottie was trying to process it as best she could.

'Did she speak to anyone?' asked Angie.

'No, but she did answer her phone.'

'Did she have an accent?' asked Nicola. It was like being interrogated.

'Yeah, a sort of Texan drawl.' Squealing erupted from the back seat like a classroom full of teenage girls. Lottie turned in her seat. 'It can't be the Duchess of thingy. She won't be here for Christmas,' said Lottie, totally unconvinced.

'What did she say, Lottie?' asked her mother, an edge in her voice.

Lottie sighed. 'She answered the phone as Megan, but—'

Her mother let out an excited screech. 'It was her! It really was.'

'Go back, Daniel,' instructed Nicola.

Daniel turned into the driveway of the manor. 'No way. I'm with Lottie. I don't think it was her. And anyway, she'll be gone by now.'

'Lottie, you want to go back too, don't you?' wheedled Angie.

'Nope. I think it was one of those lookalike people.'

'In a brand-new Range Rover?' asked Nicola, incredulously.

Daniel parked next to Joe's Land Rover; it was dwarfed by the enormous car. He got out and shut the door. 'He's such a killjoy,' said Angie. She slammed the door and studied Joe's car. 'Oh, now look at this.' She pointed cheerily at Lottie's artwork.

'It's very imaginative,' said Nicola. She peered closely at the letters. 'It's not a vinyl stick-on thing either.'

'I did it,' said Lottie. She felt partly proud and a little embarrassed. It was a long while since she'd painted anything at all. This hadn't exactly stretched her, but it was a start.

Angie straightened and Lottie braced herself for the thinly veiled insult. 'Oh. I quite like it.' Lottie couldn't have been more shocked if all of Santa's reindeers had pirouetted across the drive.

Chapter Twenty-Seven

Emily had just made a round of teas when the hospital visitors returned in a flurry of excitement. Angie, with some help from Nicola, retold the story of the American woman in an elaborate and dramatic way.

Lottie coughed. 'Great Uncle Bernard is doing okay, by the way.' She gave each of them a hard stare.

'That's good,' said Zach, and Scott nodded.

Angie was shooting her daggers for interrupting their story. '*Anyway*, we were this close to meeting royalty.'

Emily had been rapt by the tale. 'So was it really her?' she asked.

'Definitely,' said Angie, clasping her hands in front of her and flopping into Great Uncle Bernard's armchair.

'Doubtful,' said Daniel, pulling the lid off the Quality Street. 'What on earth would she be doing round here?'

'Didn't they get a place in the Cotswolds?' asked Emily. She thought she remembered reading something in a magazine about it. 'Chippen or Chipping something?' Uncle Daniel passed her the Quality Street.

'Chipping Norton?' suggested Zach, leaning over and taking a green triangle from the tin.

'I think so,' Emily said, hunting for a purple one. They'd all gone.

'That's it then,' Angie's excitement went up another notch, 'it must have been her.' She twisted to look at Lottie. 'I told you it was. How did you not recognise her?'

'Because she didn't look like her.' Lottie threw up her hands, looking frustrated.

Her mother puffed out a breath. 'Why are you always like this?' Angie asked.

Lottie chuckled. 'Like what?'

'If I say it's black, you say it's white. It obviously was Meghan Markle, so—'

'Isn't she Meghan Windsor now?' asked Emily. She shrank away from the glare that Angie gave her for butting in whilst she was berating her daughter. 'Sorry.' She took a strawberry cream and passed the tin to Lottie.

'Duchess of Sussex,' said Zach, and Uncle Daniel raised his eyebrows. 'What? I remember stuff like that.'

'How far is Chipping Norton?' asked Scott.

'Not far,' said Angie, walking around to have a rummage in the chocolate tin.

Scott was watching Angie closely. She pounced on a green triangle. 'Ooh, I love these.' She held her prize aloft, but her happy smile slid away when she saw the look Scott was giving her. 'They're not vegan friendly, are they?'

'I'm afraid not, darling,' said Scott. Angie dropped the chocolate back in the tin and Lottie pulled it away from her mother, grinning broadly.

Angie jumped up. 'We should go to Chipping Norton.'

'We are not stalking some poor woman on Boxing Day because she looks a bit like the Duchess of . . . of . . .' Lottie nodded at Zach.

'Sussex,' he said, on cue.

'Anyway,' said Lottie, checking the clock, 'it's time for the stocking game.'

Kill me now, thought Emily. This family had the weirdest traditions. She had thought that everyone's Christmas was roughly the same: turkey, crackers, pudding, presents. But the Collins family took it to a whole new level. Why couldn't they just eat chocolate and argue over TV like any normal family? She really liked Lottie and didn't want to let her new friend down, so when she looked her way, Emily gave her a big smile. But she was already dreading the stocking game – whatever it was. Things were feeling weird between her and Zach. They'd not had a moment to themselves away from Jessie, so they hadn't been able to discuss anything, and the second present he'd mentioned seemed to have been forgotten.

'Are you up for the stocking game?' Lottie asked her.

'Joe and Jessie have taken Dave for a walk. Should we wait for them to get back?' asked Emily. *Anything to delay the stocking game*, she thought.

'Yeah, we should really,' said Lottie. 'Actually, do you want to give me a quick hand with something?' she asked.

'Sure.' She felt a flutter of anticipation at Lottie having managed to get her another pregnancy test. And she followed her out to the kitchen.

Lottie shut the door. 'I'm really sorry. I couldn't get the test. The shop was full of locals and Mum came with me too.'

Emily's shoulders sagged. 'Don't worry. Thanks for trying.' She rubbed a hand over her face. She looked tired.

'Are you sleeping okay?'

'Not great.' There seemed more hidden behind her words.

'Is it the not knowing?'

273

Emily sighed slowly. 'Last night Zach was muttering in his sleep. Most of it wasn't audible, but he said "Melissa" a couple of times.'

Lottie wasn't sure how to respond. 'Ah. That's unsettling.'

'It is. Really unsettling. Here's me wondering if I'm carrying his child, and his mind is full of the wife he loved. The perfect wife.'

'Hmm.' It was an involuntary noise, and it conveyed too much. Lottie regretted the sound as soon as she'd made it.

Emily cocked her head in a way not dissimilar to Dave. 'What does that mean?' There was hope in her voice. Lottie felt that familiar guilty sensation begin to weigh her down.

Emily was about to question further but the back door swung open. In came a bouncy Dave and a worn-out-looking Jessie. 'We've walked miles and miles,' she said, and she flopped onto the floor and began tugging at her wellies. Joe followed her in and shut out the biting cold. The sight of him made her stomach flip. It felt as if their kiss was still fresh on her lips.

'Did you have fun?' asked Emily, automatically crouching to help Jessie with her boots.

Jessie nodded. 'I think Dave knows his name now, but Joe wouldn't let him off the lead.'

Joe was shaking his head. 'Best he doesn't get lost before we find his owners.'

Jessie's face dropped. 'But I thought we were keeping him.' She looked pleadingly at Emily.

'It's likely he has an owner somewhere. Maybe even a little girl like you who loves him.'

Jessie's bottom lip was on the wobble. 'But he loves *me* now.'

'I know, sweetie.'

Dave pawed at Jessie's jeans and she gave him a hug. 'See? He loves me.'

Emily was looking at Lottie for help.

'Emily's right. We need to do absolutely everything we can to find his owners.'

'What if we don't find them?' asked Jessie, scratching Dave's tummy when he flopped on the floor like a hopeless drunk. She pinned Lottie with a hopeful stare.

'Then he'll need a new home.' Emily's eyes widened and Lottie shrugged, she couldn't lie to her.

'Can I have him then?' asked Jessie, her head swivelling around to look at each of the adults in turn in the hope of a positive response.

'I'll be looking after him while we try to track his owners down. So you can always visit him while he's with me,' said Joe, with a broad smile.

'Maybe he's Meghan Markle's dog,' said Emily, with a giggle.

Joe was looking puzzled. 'What's this? Royalty?'

'Oh, it's a really long and very fanciful story,' said Lottie. 'Trust me, you don't want to know.'

The front doorbell sounded and Lottie went to answer it. Her mother beat her there, which in itself was a huge surprise as Angie usually did absolutely nothing more than she had to. But when Angie opened the door and the visitor was revealed, Lottie knew why her mother had raced to open it.

The Meghan Markle lookalike was on the doorstep. Angie stepped forward and performed an elaborate curtsey. Lottie couldn't contain her laughter. 'Honoured to meet you, Ma'am,' said Angie.

The young woman was wearing what looked like an

expensive pale cream coat with a sumptuous matching fur collar. Lottie hoped it was fake fur. She was strikingly pretty, but up close it was even more obvious to Lottie that she wasn't the Duchess of Sussex. It really was a 'Should have gone to Specsavers' moment.

'Hello,' said Lottie, joining her deluded mother at the door.

'Lottie,' snapped Angie, and she waved at her to join her in a curtsey.

Lottie ignored her. 'How can we help?' She knew her grin looked a bit manic, but she simply couldn't dilute it. It was one of the funniest things she'd ever witnessed; and more importantly, it would provide a lifetime of amusement as she would never let her mother live this down.

The woman dragged her eyes away from Angie, still bent low mid-curtsey. 'Hi. I'm not sure if y'all can help me, but I was told you might know where I can find Joe Broomfield.'

Lottie's grin vanished. A million questions flooded her head. 'Er, um . . .' The woman was still waiting. Lottie pulled herself together. 'Yes. Of course. Joe is here. Come in.' She pulled the door wide open. 'Oh, do get out of the way, Mother.'

Lottie heard the kitchen door open and turned to see Joe walk into the hallway. He froze mid-step.

'Joey!' shouted the American, and she strode towards him on her very high heels.

'Megan?' Joe couldn't have looked more shocked if the Queen herself had cartwheeled up the hall. 'Megan. Hi.' She threw herself into his arms.

'Surprise!' said Megan, stepping back to appraise him.

'Yes. It's definitely that,' said Joe, colouring up.

An unpleasant shiver went through Lottie, and she belatedly shut the door as Angie, at last, stood up straight.

'So Joe knows the Duchess of Sussex?' whispered Angie, looking more than puzzled.

'Bloody hell, Mother. How many times? She isn't Meghan sodding Markle,' said Lottie. But she did want to know exactly who she was.

Chapter Twenty-Eight

In the kitchen, Emily got Jessie a glass of squash and listened as she recounted her dog walk in fine detail. She was a lovely child, full of enthusiasm and zest for life, like her father. She thought of Zach. One of the many things she loved about him was his honesty. She'd never had any reason to doubt that what he'd said about his wife was completely true. Zach had always made her out to be a brilliant mother and a wonderful person, but now Lottie had sown a tiny seed of doubt in Emily's mind. Perhaps Lottie had a slightly different perspective on Melissa, or even more likely, Zach had chosen to forget any non-perfect qualities. That frequently happened when people passed away, especially if they died young and tragically as Melissa had. But she could recall Zach saying that Lottie and Melissa had been the best of friends, so surely Lottie had no axe to grind. In which case, it was even more odd that Lottie would cast doubt on Melissa's being flawless.

She wished Lottie would tell her. She didn't mean to be unkind, but to know that Melissa wasn't perfect would make her feel a whole lot better. It felt like she had set a standard Emily could never live up to. Of course she had

had partners who'd had significant exes before, but those conversations had been brief and easily forgotten. A quick share of their pasts, and then they'd focused on the now. But Melissa was different: she kept popping up, and she was always going to, because she wasn't an ex – she would forever be a huge part of Zach and Jessie's life. Melissa was Jessie's mother, and Zach was keen to keep her memory alive for Jessie's sake – which Emily totally understood, and 100 per cent agreed with. But right now, she wasn't entirely sure how she would cope with it.

Zach was a great dad, there was no question about that, but however hard he tried he was never going to fill the space Melissa had left in Jessie's life – quite simply, nobody could. Jessie had been a baby when her mother had been killed, so she had no recollection of her at all. Emily's heart ached for the little girl. She couldn't imagine growing up without a mother. Emily and her own mum had a close relationship; they always had, but now she was an adult they were more than mum and daughter, they were friends too, and Emily couldn't imagine not having her there through all the trials and tribulations of life. Just being apart from her this Christmas, with everything that was going on, had been hard.

Emily watched Jessie telling the story of Dave tying Joe up in the skipping-rope lead. Her pretty, pale-blue eyes sparkled as she re-enacted the scene, her glossy dark hair bouncing around her shoulders. Jessie looked like her mother; Emily knew this from the many photographs she'd seen in Zach's house. *She must be a constant reminder to him of Melissa*, she thought. A little mini-Melissa keeping his wife's image alive.

Emily didn't like to consider how Jessie would feel about having to share her father. It would be exceptionally hard for her. It had just been the two of them for the last five years. A new sibling often had a big impact on a child.

And how would Zach feel about being a father again? He'd never mentioned wanting more children. Did that mean he didn't? She'd not steered the conversation in that direction. It had never been something either of them had brought up for discussion. Although just because she hadn't raised the subject, it didn't mean she didn't want to be a mother some day; it just hadn't been near the top of her priority list. Right now, though, it was the only thing on her list, written in red and underlined many times.

They had all been rubbing along quite happy with how things were. But now the carefully woven patchwork of their life had a loose thread. Emily feared the whole thing was going to unravel, like a cheap cardigan.

Lottie had gone rigid as she watched Megan hug Joe again. A klaxon was going off in her head. She coughed quietly and Joe's head snapped around. 'We're going to go and start playing the stocking game.' She knew it sounded ridiculous, but she didn't know what was going on, so carrying on as normal – well, normal for the Collins family – seemed like the best course of action. 'It's a Boxing Day tradition,' she explained, although she probably didn't need to. Megan was scrunching up her pretty features. Lottie wasn't sure whether that was due to confusion over what the stocking game was or at the way Lottie was staring.

Megan let go of Joe and strode over to Lottie with such gusto that Lottie took a step back. Megan came to a halt in front of her. 'That was so rude of me,' said Megan, placing both hands on her own chest. 'I'm Megan.'

Lottie didn't like to say, 'Yes, I'd gathered what your name was, but what the hell are you doing here hugging my Joe?' so she said, 'I'm Lottie,' and offered her hand to shake. She was hardly going to hug the woman.

Megan's hands sprang up. Lottie winced in case she was going to hit her. 'Oh, I've heard so much about you. All the crazy things you and Joey got up to as little kids. It is a delight to finally meet you.' She flung her arms around Lottie and squeezed her far tighter than was necessary. Lottie glanced through Megan's elaborate fur collar at Joe, who was rubbing his chin, the way he did when something was bothering him. Good – at least he had the decency to look unsettled.

'That's nice,' said Lottie, disentangling herself and adjusting her hair clip.

Angie stepped forward. 'I'm Angie. Has anyone ever told you that you are the spitting image of Meghan Markle?'

'Now aren't you the sweetest?' said Megan, kissing her cheek. 'I love your home,' she said, waving an arm around. 'It's so cute and British. Just like Joey.' She turned to gaze coyly at an uncomfortable-looking Joe.

'And how do you know Joe exactly?' asked Lottie. There, she'd said it. She'd taken the bull by the horns and draped it in fairy lights.

'Why, Joey's my partner.' Megan said it as if it was the most obvious thing in the world.

Lottie felt as if the ceiling had fallen in on her. 'Shocked' didn't cover it. She looked to Joe, but he was staring at the floor. She had forgotten to take a breath when she needed it, and now she quickly breathed in, making an over-dramatic gasping noise. Really not the calm reaction she had wanted to convey.

'Oh, how lovely,' said Angie, clapping her hands together. Lottie wanted to slap her with one of the ham sandwiches. 'Are you moving to England too?'

Lottie froze. She knew she was staring wide-eyed at Megan but she couldn't help it. First Joe had upended her world on Christmas Eve and now, two days later, this woman had materialised and spun her back to front. It was like some weird form of extreme zorbing. Megan sauntered over to Joe and ran a fingertip seductively along his jawline. Joe had the decency to look embarrassed. 'That depends on whether or not he'll have me,' she said, her voice almost a purr.

Lottie's stomach turned over. She felt sick and humiliated. She wanted to escape the excruciating situation. She could hear Nana's voice in her head: 'You're stronger than you know, Lottie. Be brave.' She decided to pull herself together. She straightened her back and slapped a smile on her face. 'Right. That is lovely,' she said, the words leaving a bitter taste in her mouth like she'd bitten into a bad nut, 'I expect you'll be off to . . . to, um . . . catch up with each other.' Lottie had to wipe her mind of thoughts of what they might really be off to do. Imagining Joe and Megan in bed together wasn't going to help her already battered ego. 'So while you two do . . . that, we'll be off to play the stocking game.' She began nudging her mother in the direction of the drawing room.

Megan did something akin to jazz hands whilst bobbing up and down on her heels. 'That sounds like so much fun. Can I join in?' she asked, taking off her expensive coat and handing it to Joe. Joe and Lottie shared the same bemused expression.

'We'd love you to,' said Angie, flashing a scornful look at Lottie and showing Megan through to the drawing room.

The house seemed to be getting chillier. Only Lottie and Joe remained, standing at either end of the hallway. Lottie wrapped her arms protectively around herself. She stared at Joe. Hurt and anger vied for attention inside her. How the hell had he failed to mention that he had a girl-friend? In fact, Megan had referred to him as her 'partner' – that sounded even more serious than boyfriend and girlfriend.

A few short hours ago, she'd shared the most tender of kisses with Joe, and it had felt so right. She'd thought their kiss had meant something – but clearly only to her. Perhaps it was just nostalgia. She'd read somewhere that nostalgia literally meant 'homecoming pain' – how fitting that seemed now. All the old hurt had returned in truck-loads.

Joe opened his mouth and she held up her palm to stop him. 'No, Joe. I don't want to hear it. Not now. Not ever.' And she strode with purpose into the drawing room.

She could almost read the questions on everyone's faces when she entered the room behind Megan and her mother. 'This is Megan,' said Angie, her eyebrows dancing as she left a pause before adding. 'She's Joe's American girl-friend.' Lottie could feel her cheeks flush, but she had no idea why. Nobody knew about the kiss, thank goodness. She had nothing to feel embarrassed about. She'd had no idea that he'd had a girlfriend, or there was no way on earth she would have kissed him. She knew too well what it was like to be cheated on. It hurt her afresh that Joe had been so casual about kissing her when all the while he was in a relationship with Megan.

Zach was frowning hard and looking to Lottie for an explanation. She gave the tiniest of shrugs. At least Megan appeared to be news to him too. When Joe didn't follow her into the drawing room, Lottie closed the door behind her.

Scott was first on his feet. 'Hi Megan, I'm Scott,' he said, offering her his vacated seat and his usual broad smile.

'Scott's my partner,' said Angie, proudly popping up from behind Megan.

A round of introductions followed as Megan sat down. 'I love your accent,' said Emily. There were nods of agreement.

'Whereabouts in America are you from?' asked Angie. 'Lottie thought Texas.'

'Oh no. I'm from Lake Charles, Louisiana,' said Megan, an element of great pride in her voice.

'Beautiful part of America, Louisiana. Lovely people,' said Uncle Daniel.

'Well, aren't you all a delight?' said Megan.

'Yes, we are,' said Jessie.

'Oh, and you're the cutest,' said Megan. Jessie blushed at the compliment. It seemed Megan was making a good first impression with everyone except Lottie.

Megan regaled them with a brief history of her ancestry, which she proudly explained had origins in Africa and Ireland. Lottie watched her family, all entranced by her.

Zach poured Megan a glass of wine and topped up his own. He tilted the bottle towards Emily's glass and she shook her head. He paused as he put the bottle back. 'You not drinking?' he asked, looking puzzled.

'I'm okay at the moment. Maybe later,' said Emily. She glanced briefly in Lottie's direction, but Lottie didn't really notice; she had far too many other things on her mind now.

Chapter Twenty-Nine

Angie and Scott settled themselves by the fire whilst Lottie went to the sideboard, where family photos crowded together as if vying for attention, to find the prepared stocking. The door opened slowly as Joe crept in to join them. Everyone turned to watch what he did. He slunk over to Zach and sat on the arm of the chair next to him, a couple of seats away from Megan.

Zach's expression was stony. Despite no words being exchanged, Lottie appreciated his support.

Lottie handed out pens and a piece of paper to everyone. Usually the stocking game was her Christmas highlight, but right now, she felt like it was the last thing she wanted to play. She was the current reigning champion – four years in a row – but that was all going to change this year: she'd set it up, so she couldn't take part. 'This is the stocking game,' she said, holding up the classic Santa stocking like it were Exhibit A. 'Inside here are twenty mystery items from around the house: some Christmas-related, some not. The stocking is passed around everyone five times.' Scott was already looking confused. 'Each time, you are allowed to put your hand inside and feel the items. Any peeking will result in instant disqualification. With each pass, we speed things up, so your time with the stocking gets shorter and shorter.' She could feel Megan's intense concentration and Jessie's excitement. She glanced at Joe, who was staring at the fire. 'When it's been round five times, you have one minute to write down as many items as you can. The person with the most correct answers wins.'

'What's the prize, Auntie Lottie?' asked Jessie. She leaned towards Emily. 'Last year it was a chocolate orange.'

'Ooh my favourite,' said Emily, pulling Jessie to her for a hug. 'But if I win I'll still share it with you.'

'A. Chocolate. Orange?' asked Megan, pronouncing every syllable carefully.

Jessie opened her mouth to explain, but Lottie was already on it. 'Sorry. Different prize this year. It's a selection box.'

If anything Megan looked even more confused. Lottie retrieved it from the sideboard and held it up for her to see. 'Ooh, candy,' she said.

Lottie started the Christmas music they always used for this game and handed the stocking to her mother. 'Oldest person goes first, then we'll go round in seat order.' Angie gave her a murderous look and snatched the stocking from her. The first round always took a little while. To Megan's credit, she really entered into the spirit of it. Lottie watched Joe when it was his turn. His troubled expression made it look as though he was putting his hand into a bag of snakes, but Lottie knew it wasn't the game that he was concerned about.

He briefly turned in her direction and then immediately his eyes shifted to Megan; Lottie's stomach clenched. Every time she thought of Joe's kiss, pain ached in her heart. She didn't want to do this. It was too hard. She should just abandon the silly game and walk out. Then she saw Jessie mouthing to herself the items she thought were in the stocking so that she wouldn't forget before the time came to write them down, and she relented. Christmas was about children and about family, so for now, she would put her hurt pride and battered feelings to one side and finish the game.

'Come on, Joe. It's time to move on,' said Lottie, taking the stocking from him.

'Yes, Joe. It's time to move on,' repeated Megan, and the words were like daggers to Lottie's poor wounded heart.

Lottie took a rushed breath and thrust the stocking at her mother. 'Okay, faster this time.'

Mercifully the rounds got quicker and the game drew to a close. There was silence as everyone frantically jotted down what they thought was in the stocking and answers were crossed out and reinstated.

'Time's up,' said Lottie. They swapped papers and Lottie pulled out an array of items from the stocking one at a time to a series of cheers and groans. Everyone guessed the candy cane, but the donkey ornament that usually lived on a windowsill upstairs had them all stumped, as did the skiing yeti tree decoration.

She felt Joe's eyes on her. 'Tot up the scores and hand back the papers,' she said. She wished she could read Joe's mind because his expression was telling her nothing.

Scott was declared the winner. Lottie heard Zach whisper to Emily, 'He's got an advantage – I bet he gets to do a lot of rummaging around in stockings.'

'Shh,' said Emily, clearly struggling to suppress a giggle as she glanced at Jessie, who was looking interested in the conversation.

'That was so much fun,' said Megan. She sipped her drink daintily.

'It's silly really,' said Lottie, not knowing why.

There was a scratch at the door and a bark from the hallway. Megan recoiled. 'Is that a dog?' She looked to Lottie for an answer.

'No, I taught our cat to do really good impressions.' Lottie gave a sweet smile to mask her sarcasm and went to open the door.

'No!' Megan's voice was fraught. 'Don't let it in!'

'He's very nice,' said Jessie. 'I'm sure you'll like him.'

Megan was shaking her head. 'Yes, he's only little,' added Lottie, in case she was expecting a slobbering Saint Bernard.

'I'm highly allergic,' said Megan, getting to her feet and inching towards Joe. Lottie doubted this, considering Megan had been sitting where Dave had sat earlier and hadn't appeared to have any reaction. It was also more than a hurdle if she was in a relationship with a vet.

Joe got to his feet. 'I should probably be going anyway.' He aimed his words at Zach. He seemed to be struggling to make eye contact with Lottie.

Megan linked her arm in Joe's and Lottie looked away. The rip in her heart tore a fraction further. She bit the inside of her mouth to keep from crying: she had shed enough tears over Joe Broomfield for one lifetime. As he walked towards her she snatched open the door, forgetting who was waiting on the other side.

Dave dashed inside, pausing for a moment to spit something furry out of his mouth. His tail whirled like an errant propeller. He raced towards Jessie, but when Megan squealed he diverted towards her, his paws sliding on the polished wood floor. Lottie thought Megan was going to jump into Joe's arms and, she guessed from his alarmed expression, so did he.

'Dave!' called Jessie, and the dog pirouetted, dancing between them – torn by his desire to respond to Jessie and his innate curiosity about the new person. Megan's squeal hitched up a notch and she scurried behind Joe, clutching handfuls of his jumper. She did look genuinely terrified, but Lottie was lacking any sympathy. She marched over to retrieve the dog and reached forward at the same time as Joe bent down to grab him. Their heads collided and Lottie came off worse. For a moment, everything went black and pain shot through her temples. She toppled backwards and Joe caught her, steering her to the sofa. She opened her eyes to see him up close and concerned, with a frowning Megan looming over his shoulder.

Joe began. 'I'm so sorry—'

'No, my fault.' It was an automatic response. She put her hand to her head; already a swelling was forming. 'Are *you* all right?' She scanned his face for any signs of damage or growing lumps.

Joe smiled. A kind, heartfelt smile. 'I'm fine. Head like a brick,' he said, giving it a rub.

'Don't I know it,' said Lottie, feeling slightly queasy.

'Can you focus okay? You may be concussed.' Joe leaned closer and looked deep into her eyes. A waft of aftershave made her senses ping. Even though she knew his concern and closeness were purely for medical reasons, her treacherous heart leapt all the same.

'I think you're fussing,' said Megan. 'She's fine.' She peered a bit closer. 'You're fine, aren't you?' she asked, although Lottie got the distinct feeling it was more a statement than a question.

'You need ice on that,' said Joe, ignoring Megan.

Lottie felt awkward. 'No, I'm okay. Really.' She tried to get up to prove it, and a head rush had her sitting back down sharpish.

'Whoa,' said Joe. 'Come on. Let's get you some ice.'

Dave barked and Megan looked like she was going to faint. 'Joe! Joe! Stop him!' She deftly put Joe between herself and Dave.

'You should go,' said Lottie. However nice it was to have him fuss over her, it was only ever going to be temporary. Better to let him leave and go cold turkey.

Joe opened his mouth as if to protest, but Megan spoke first. 'You're right. It's been mighty fine, but we need to be getting along now. Don't we, Joey?'

Zach scooped up Dave, who strained to get a lick of Megan as he passed. 'Eurgh,' she said with a shiver.

Jessie looked to Emily. 'I don't like Megan any more,' she said loudly.

'Erm, you might want to see this,' said Zach, opening the door into the hallway further to reveal Megan's coat in a crumpled heap. Whether the collar had once been alive or not, it was definitely dead now, thanks to a good mauling by Dave. Lottie was starting to really love the little dog.

'My Max Mara!' wailed Megan, as Dave spat out another piece of the ravaged fur coat.

Joe said his goodbyes. He leaned down to give Lottie a fleeting kiss on the cheek, and he saw her flinch. Pain ripped through him like an arrow through air. He'd hurt her, and he hated himself for it. 'Can I leave Dave here?' he asked.

'I think you'll have to,' said Lottie, adding in a firm voice, 'for now.'

'Thanks.' He could hear Megan's foot tapping from the hallway. There were things he wanted to say to Lottie, but she turned away. Being under her family's spotlight wasn't helping either.

'Joey?' called Megan, her voice impatient.

'Bye, everyone,' he said. Zach was giving him filthy looks, so he decided against shaking his hand. 'Come on.' He ushered Megan out of the front door and closed it behind them. The sound of the heavy door shutting echoed through him. It had something final about it.

Megan made a big show of waving as they walked away from the house, but to be fair, most of the household were at the window watching them go. She walked over to Daniel's shiny new Range Rover. Joe unlocked his Land Rover and he watched Megan do a double take at the old vehicle, before slapping back on a Hollywood smile and waving to the Collins family.

Megan brushed down the passenger seat, even though it was clean, and got in. Joe didn't know what to say, so he said nothing. He started the car and allowed himself one last look back at the house. Lottie was just visible, standing behind Zach. Her expression was one that would haunt him.

And with that, he drove out of the gates and away from Henbourne Manor.

'Aren't you gonna say howdy?' Megan's voice was strained, as if it was taking a lot of effort not to shout.

'Why did you come here, Megan?' He glanced briefly at her. She was staring straight ahead through the windscreen and he caught sight of her in profile. She looked amazing. She was a striking woman – that was what he had immediately been drawn to when they'd first met five months ago.

'I came because there was no answer at the address you gave me. I went to the little stores and they said I'd likely find you at Lottie's.' He didn't like the way she said Lottie's name, almost like she was ridiculing it. It didn't sound right on her tongue. Joe didn't want to think about what rumours were already zooming through the village, spreading quicker, most likely, than one of Donald Trump's tweets.

Joe pulled up outside the rental cottage. Megan went to undo her seat belt and he put a hand on hers to stop her. She gripped his quickly and relief spread across her face. 'I've missed you, Joe.'

It was Megan who said the words, but he heard them as if spoken by Lottie: the same words she'd uttered only a couple of hours earlier. He shook his head to rid himself of the image.

'Don't you have any luggage?' He changed the subject.

'Oh, my driver has it. I had someone arrange a car for me. After he dropped me at . . .'

He wasn't sure if she couldn't remember, or didn't want to repeat Lottie's name. 'The manor house,' he said, filling the gap.

She nodded. 'After he'd dropped me there. I told him to go and wait for my call.'

Joe really didn't want to ask the question that was buzzing around his brain for fear of the answer, but at six o'clock on Boxing Day evening he needed to. 'Where are you staying tonight?'

Megan looked out of the passenger window at Mr Bundy's tiny cottage. 'Well, here, of course.'

'I don't think that's a good idea.'

'Joe, we need to iron a few things out. What could be better than cosying up in front of a real fire with a mug of cocoa and Christmas cookies, while we talk things through?'

Joe let out a resigned sigh. Of course she expected to stay with him and what could he do? She'd flown some four thousand miles, and he could hardly expect her to find a hotel on Boxing Day. He hated being forced into a situation, but Megan was a grade-A manipulator.

'Central heating,' he said.

'I'm sorry?'

'No real fire. It's radiators only. So don't expect any cosying up.' He got out of the car and slammed the door.

Chapter Thirty

Lottie found it was important to keep busy. 'Don't dwell on things you can't change' – that's what Nana would say. So now they were all playing charades from a new set Lottie had bought off eBay but, having already removed *An American Werewolf in London* and *Fifty Shades of Grey*, she was doubting its 'child-friendly' sticker. Her mother was up miming a song; she had spent the last minute jumping about like an idiot, with people suggesting everything from 'Smells Like Teen Spirit' to all the songs from *The Greatest Showman*. The doorbell rang through the house and Lottie went to answer it. Her heart thumped a little faster at the thought that it might be Joe. It was dark and the wind was fierce, so she held on tight to the door as she opened it. On the doorstep was Shirley with her tartan trolley.

'Hello, Shirley. Come in,' said Lottie, marvelling that the little old lady had made it up the hill in the high winds, and then wondering whether it was in fact the wind that had brought her here, Mary Poppins-style.

'I'm not stopping. I just called by to see how young Bernard was,' she asked, without a hint of humour in her voice. But then if you were pushing ninety, seventy-two was young by comparison.

'He's doing all right and he's getting the best nursing care. Hopefully he'll just need some medication and to take it easy. Thank you for coming to ask. That's really kind.'

Shirley waved the thanks away. 'You know how it works around here, Lottie. We all look out for each other. Most likely why someone dumped that little dog here. They knew someone would take him in.'

'Is that what you think happened?'

'Someone came in the pub with tales of a little dog being pushed out the back of a van a few nights ago.'

'Poor thing.' Lottie wanted to go and give Dave a hug. She still hadn't thanked him for shredding Megan's coat.

'Right, I best be off,' said Shirley, pushing her trolley for the door.

'Actually, Shirley, would you like to stay? We're playing charades – and I've got sherry.' Lottie had barely finished her sentence before Shirley's coat was off.

'I can't stop long,' she said, as she scuttled into the drawing room.

Lottie poured Shirley a large glass of sherry, but she was already on her feet taking her turn at charades.

'What was Mother's?' Lottie asked Zach.

'"Let Me Entertain You",' he said.

They watched Shirley mime her four-word book and film. She was pulling at her hair and making horn shapes with her fingers, prancing around.

'Mad hair!' shouted Jessie, who was trying to join in but obviously struggling.

'*Hellboy*?' asked Zach.

'Is it a dinosaur?' asked Daniel, to much tutting from Nicola. But at least they were in the same room and hadn't murdered each other; Lottie was buoyed by that. She'd hidden the sharp knives, just to be on the safe side.

'Dancing unicorn,' said Jessie, erupting into fits of giggles.

'Horny goat,' suggested Scott, and everyone else cracked up.

'Time's up,' called out Emily, and Shirley slumped into the chair by the fire and downed half her sherry in one swig.

'What was it?' asked Lottie.

'*The Devil Wears Prada*,' said Shirley, and everyone groaned.

The next hour flew by with everyone enjoying themselves, except for a worrying moment when Shirley almost lost her sherry while Jessie was acting out *Kung Fu Panda*. It had been lovely to see Shirley. She refused to let anyone drive her home or call her a taxi, insisting nothing ever happened in Dumbleford, which Lottie had to agree was true. Lottie had waved her off with the remains of the bottle of sherry tucked safely in her wheelie trolley, singing 'I'm just a teenage dirtbag baby' all the way down the drive. Perhaps the answer to a fun Christmas was to invite enough people to dilute the family to a bearable level, mused Lottie.

Lottie found herself standing on the landing looking out of the window at the trees being shaken by the wind. She couldn't straighten things out in her head. The Joe she had known wasn't a cruel person, but what he'd done felt unforgiveable. A bedroom door opened behind her, but she didn't turn around as her attention was held by one of the lower branches on the larger of two birch trees, which looked as if it was going to be wrenched away from the security of the trunk.

'Hey. You okay?' It was Rhys. He seemed pretty upbeat, given all that had happened in his family this Christmas.

'Yeah. I'm okay. How about you?'

Rhys rested the metal detector on the floor for a moment as he pondered. Lottie wondered if she was going to get a deep and meaningful conversation out of him. 'I'm . . . okay.'

Lottie smiled at the brief response. 'As long as you're sure.'

'Apart from Nana's doll collection freaking me out, that is.' He tipped his head towards the box room. 'I swear their beady eyes follow me around the room.'

'Sorry,' said Lottie. 'They creep me out too. That's why I gathered them all up and put them in there.'

'It's like a Chucky lookalike convention,' he said with a laugh. 'You want to find buried treasure with me?'

She wanted to say no, but there was something about his voice. He didn't sound like the nineteen-year-old man he was; he sounded far more akin to a child. She felt, despite his earlier response, that maybe this was a sign that he did want someone to talk to or at least a bit of company.

And if it gets my mind away from brooding over Joe, then it will help me too. 'Yes, Rhys. That'd be great.'

His face brightened and they went downstairs. They layered up and braved the bitter wind outside. Lottie gritted her teeth. He had better want to talk about something, because she didn't want to freeze her backside off in the dark so he could dig up long lost hair clips. Rhys led the way round to the Italian garden at the side of the house.

Lottie switched the garden lights on and scanned the ground. 'What's made you come here?'

'I've done a few patches on the main lawn and found nothing. But then when I thought about it, this side of the house is nearest the road.'

'Right,' said Lottie, having no idea what difference that would make. She pulled her woolly hat down over her numbing ears.

'That's a Roman road,' he said pointing left and right.

Lottie had a good look in both directions as if seeing it for the first time, even though it was a road she had walked along and driven up and down countless times. 'I did not know that. And that means what?'

'Doesn't *mean* anything,' said Rhys, with a one-shouldered shrug. 'But thousands of people would have travelled this road over the centuries, and when they stopped for the night it's likely they would just camp down at the roadside.'

'Oh, okay. That makes sense.'

'We could turn up the odd button, or even a coin.' He was the most animated she'd seen him all Christmas.

'That would be . . . exciting.' She gave him a pat on the shoulder and then thrust her gloved hands deep into her pockets, secretly hoping the detector would find something quickly and they'd be able to get back inside and warm up. The temperature had taken a definite plunge.

Rhys put on the headphones, checked a few things on the machine and then began methodically sweeping it over the grass. Lottie followed. They slowly made their way along the hedge line, Rhys pausing occasionally to give an area an extra sweep. Lottie was losing feeling in her toes when someone tapped her on the shoulder. She was surprised to see Emily.

'You've been missed. I was sent to find you.'

'By whom?' asked Lottie.

'Your mother.' Lottie raised one doubtful eyebrow. 'Well, she was asking when dinner was.'

'Yeah, that's not quite the same thing as being missed.'

'What are you doing?'

'Hunting for buried treasure,' said Lottie, while Rhys continued to look serious.

'Not avoiding people then?' said Emily, doing up her coat right to the top as the wind whipped around them.

'Whatever gave you that idea?'

'Oh, I don't know. Maybe a certain American who seems to have clicked her manicured fingers and made Joe come running.' It was an accurate description.

Perhaps Emily would be a good person to talk to. She had no preconceived ideas about her or Joe or what had happened in the past. Lottie checked Rhys wasn't paying any attention to them. 'Joe and I . . . Before I went off to see Bernard . . . We kissed.'

Emily stopped walking and gave Lottie a wide-eyed look. 'After all the . . . *stuff* that's happened?'

'That was before I knew he had a partner. And yes. Despite all the stuff that happened nine years ago it felt . . .' she tailed off as she thought back to the moment.

'How did it feel?' asked Emily, tentatively.

'Familiar. It felt right. It was like all the years and all the hurt were dissolved by that kiss.' Emily wasn't looking convinced. 'Okay, I know that's a bit much. But it did feel like nothing was insurmountable. Like we could move forward together.'

'But now there's Megan.'

'It would seem that Megan was always there. Joe just omitted to mention that he had a very attractive American girlfriend hidden away somewhere.' The thought of Joe with Megan was like a corkscrew twisting into her heart.

'He's a bit of a shit then.'

Lottie blinked at her turn of phrase. She didn't like

hearing someone talk about Joe like that but the hardest thing of all was that Emily was spot on.

They paused their walk as Rhys stopped to have an extra sweep of the metal detector over the currently dormant vegetable patch, where Nana used to grow her runner beans. There wouldn't be any next year, and Lottie couldn't help but wonder what might be in their place. If Shirley was right and it was a film star, perhaps this would be an extension, or a garage for luxury cars, or maybe even a swimming pool. Or, as her mother had mused, the whole manor house could be bulldozed, in which case this might be the front room of one of many houses with postage-stamp-sized gardens they would squeeze onto the plot. The wind whistled around the side of the house, and Lottie shivered.

Rhys pulled up one side of the headphones and grinned at them. 'We've got something.'

Lottie tried to muster some enthusiasm for the metal detecting. She strode over to Rhys and watched as he pulled a trowel from his pocket and scraped at the soil.

'What is it?' asked Emily, trying to restrain her hair behind her ears.

'Not sure. It was a strong signal though.' Rhys continued to scrape away the earth. Lottie couldn't help thinking that maybe he should dig it over a bit. It wasn't like he was uncovering something precious like the Blackfriars Mosaic. Emily was watching intently. Rhys's trowel pinged as it hit something metal and they all peered a little closer in the dark. He dug into the soil with the tip of the trowel. 'It's a nail,' he said. 'Quite a big one, though.' He pulled out the rusty metal and showed Lottie.

'I think it's a horseshoe nail,' said Lottie, pointing at the square end. 'That's quite interesting.'

Emily gave her a sideways glance and checked her watch.

'It could mean this was near a blacksmiths,' said Rhys, straightening up and surveying the garden.

'There'd probably be a lot more nails and horseshoes if it was,' said Lottie. Rhys seemed buoyed by the prospect: he replaced his headphones and carried on. Lottie and Emily huddled together. Lottie hoped Rhys would give up soon so they could go back inside.

'I don't want to speak out of turn, but . . .' Emily paused.

'But?' said Lottie, encouraging her to finish the sentence.

'Earlier, when I mentioned Melissa. You kind of implied by your reaction that maybe she wasn't entirely perfect. Or have I misread that?' Emily was watching her intently.

'Umm.' Lottie felt cornered.

'You see, from what I've heard about Melissa, she makes Snow White look like Miley Cyrus.'

Lottie chuckled and it faded as she remembered Melissa. They had been such close friends. 'She was a good person but, you know, none of us are perfect.' As soon as she'd said it, she wished she hadn't – Emily's reaction was like a hound picking up the scent of a fox.

'What did she do?' Emily was walking even closer to Lottie. 'I won't breathe a word to anyone. I promise.'

'I can't tell you that, Emily. I shouldn't have said anything.' This was something even Zach didn't know about Melissa – she could hardly divulge the secret she held to his girlfriend.

'That's a shame, because Zach's never going to tell me.' She was staring at Lottie. Lottie tried to look anywhere but at Emily. The silence between them lengthened. Lottie concentrated on Rhys, who had stopped again and was scraping at a patch of ground. 'Zach doesn't know that

Melissa wasn't Snow White. Does he?' Emily wasn't going to let this go.

Lottie eventually shook her head, half afraid of where this was leading, but at the same time thinking how good it would feel to share her burden with someone. 'I should have told Zach a long time ago. But I can't now.' She looked at Emily, waiting with bated breath.

'Why not? No time like the present and all that.'

'Because this secret will tear him apart.' *But keeping it locked inside has been tearing me apart for years*, thought Lottie.

Chapter Thirty-One

27 December

Lottie headed downstairs, letting out a noisy, Chewbacca-like yawn to match her onesie. She was slowly turning into a wookie. She'd made it to the twenty-seventh – everyone was going home today. Something caught her eye as she passed the landing window. It was still early and dark, but something made her reverse and take a good look.

Lottie blinked repeatedly at the scene outside. Everything was white. It was still windy, but it was now also very snowy. She rubbed at the glass with her sleeve in a vain attempt to change the picture.

'Bugger!'

She hurried downstairs, skidded into the hallway and pulled open the front door. A blast of icy air momentarily stopped her in her tracks. She watched as the snow drift which had been leaning against the front door toppled towards her in slow motion, covering her from the thighs down. For a moment, stunned, she stood still: a human snowman. She shook her frozen legs free and leaned with all her weight against the back of the door, trying to push the snow back outside with the door but, with the wind fighting back, it was almost impossible.

'Need a hand?' Zach appeared in the hallway and added his weight to her efforts. With a resentful creak the door finally closed.

'Thanks,' she said, looking in dismay at her sodden bottom half. Her Chewbacca onesie was suddenly a lot heavier. 'I can't believe how much snow there's been overnight.'

'I know.' His eyes glinted like a child's. 'It's awesome. I can't wait for Jessie to wake up.'

'But everyone is meant to be going home today.' She couldn't hide her despair at the thought that they might not be leaving. It had been lovely to have them all together, but it was definitely time for them to depart.

'Cheer up, Lottie. Today has to be the day Dave poos out the ring. And, anyway, snow is fun.'

Lottie shook her head at her brother. 'It's not fun when you've got to feed a warring family with a few crumbs.'

'If Jesus could feed the five thousand I'm sure we can rustle something up.'

'I don't have five loaves, and the vegans wouldn't eat fish even if I had any.'

'Come on, Chewie. Let's see what you've got.' He marched off towards the kitchen as Lottie stifled another yawn.

'Hang on two minutes – I need to change first. It feels like I've wet myself.' She left a soggy trail back upstairs.

A few minutes later she was changed into her jeans and plodding down the stairs again. Zach was in the hall, tying new rope onto an old sledge. 'How much snow is there?' She sent up a silent prayer. Lottie had only seen out the front of the house; perhaps the snow wasn't that bad everywhere else.

'Enough to go sledging and make a snowman!'

Lottie rolled her eyes – Zach was incorrigible. 'No sledging before breakfast.' She gave him a shove in the direction of the kitchen.

The two of them were the only ones up, and her mind raced back to her conversation with Emily. She had read and reread her card from Nana before she'd fallen asleep. Everything and everyone was encouraging her to come clean. Reveal the secret she'd been keeping all these years. She watched Zach happily checking cupboards. Now was probably a good opportunity; trouble was, she wasn't quite brave enough.

She switched on the kitchen radio and listened as a multitude of road closures and weather warnings were announced. She took stock, thinking back to yesterday. She'd used up most of the leftovers; everyone had hoovered them up like starving locusts. There was ham, and she knew she had some cream crackers left over, along with some eggs and lots of sprouts. She didn't much like the thought of what she could make with that. Instead, she looked at Zach, who was humming 'White Christmas' with his head in the larder. 'You've got loads of tins of tomatoes.' He popped his head out. 'Have you got any pasta?'

'Glass jar on the floor,' said Lottie, pulling out a chair and flopping down.

'Oh, brilliant there's loads. We could do pasta bake for dinner.'

'Not very exciting.' Lottie wrinkled her nose.

'What's the bread situation like?' he asked, and by opening the empty bread bin he answered his own question. 'I don't suppose you've got any strong flour and yeast by any chance?'

'Who are you, Mary Berry?' Lottie scratched her head. Nana used to make her own bread, although she hadn't done it recently. 'There's probably some somewhere.' She knew she sounded uninterested. She'd worked her Darth Vader socks off over the last few days, and she'd had enough. She'd done what she'd set out to do – she'd completed Nana's last wish and they'd had their last family Christmas at Henbourne Manor – and she'd been secretly looking forward to them all going home. She wanted to get to the stage where there was enough distance from the event that she could begin to remember it through rose-tinted spectacles. This definitely hadn't been the perfect last Collins family Christmas she had wanted – not even close. Bernard had had a heart spasm. Emily thought she might be pregnant, Scott was a porn star and her mother had been outed as a pretend vegan. Uncle Daniel had a secret lovechild, and there was still no sign of Dave delivering the engagement ring Zach had hidden in the Christmas tree. And the biggest shock of all, for her, was Joe turning up after nine years of living in America, closely followed by his Meghan Markle lookalike girlfriend. Lottie slumped her upper body onto the kitchen table. It was a mess. The Collins family was a mess.

Zach came back into the kitchen with armfuls of stuff. A puff of flour burst into the air as he dumped it all on the table. 'How about we make some bread?' He was clearly channelling his inner Paul Hollywood.

Lottie mumbled half-heartedly, 'They'll want breakfast first.'

Zach opened the fridge. 'Scrambled eggs?' He was far brighter than was necessary in the situation.

'Vegans,' said Lottie, making the word sound like she was swearing.

'Porridge with almond milk for them,' he said, shoving his head back in the larder. 'I'll even pop some raisins in it. I think we'll be okay for today. Let's hope the village stores opens up despite the snow, so we can get supplies for the next few days.'

Lottie shot bolt upright. 'Few days?' Lottie almost screeched. 'They're all leaving tomorrow if I have to dig a way out of the village with my bare hands.'

'I thought this was what you wanted? Everyone together.' He looked genuinely perplexed by her reaction.

'Not indefinitely. Just for Christmas. I've got things I need to sort out.'

'Like?' he asked as he rifled through Nana's cookbooks.

'My life.' Zach gave a sideways glance. 'I'm not being dramatic. I'm being factual. This place is sold. Assuming that all goes through smoothly, I will have nowhere to live in a matter of weeks. Someone has got to clear this place out and in case you hadn't noticed it's a bloody huge house. I also need to make a decision on what I'm going to do career-wise, and either return to the rat race or get booked onto a course.' She felt her shoulders sag. That was a mighty big list to do all on her own – especially without Nana in the background cheering her on.

Zach paused in the middle of weighing the flour. 'Can I help?' he asked.

'I don't know.' She slumped back onto the table.

'I will help you, Lottie. But first, I'm making a bread masterpiece.'

She watched him for a moment. 'Why are you so ridiculously upbeat today?'

He lowered his voice to a whisper. 'Because with any luck, Dave is going to poop out a ring.' He looked truly joyful at the prospect.

'Eurgh,' said Lottie.

'And that means I can finally propose to Emily.'

'And what wondrous way of proposing have you conjured up now?' she asked.

Zach's shoulders dropped and his happy bubble popped. 'I have no idea.'

The rest of the family joined them over the next thirty minutes and all expressed varying degrees of dismay at the weather. Scott checked the trains and most were cancelled, so Lottie definitely had the delight of her mother's company for at least another twenty-four hours. Uncle Daniel was confident of being able to get where he wanted to go in his Range Rover, even if he had to take it off-road. However, after checking the motorways, he was waiting for more snowploughs to be deployed to the area.

Eventually, they sat down to a cobbled-together breakfast. Lottie was quite pleased with the bubble and squeak she'd managed to rustle up using the rest of the Brussels sprouts and leftover potatoes, and everyone was tucking in.

The bell chimed through the house and Lottie went to answer the door. She very much hoped it wasn't Joe. She opened the door to Petra, the landlady from the pub, bundled up in a parka and wellies.

'Come in,' said Lottie, keen to shut out the blustery weather.

Petra stepped over the mound of snow at the door and gave her a hug in greeting. 'I just wanted to let you know that the lane is blocked out of Dumbleford, thanks to loads of snow and a truck that's been abandoned, and none of the cars can get up Henbourne Hill.'

'Ah. So we're a bit snowed in then.'

'A bit?' said Petra, with a laugh. 'A lot. Even Giles couldn't get his Land Rover up the hill this morning. And Shirley had to abandon her Morris Minor at the bottom. We've given up trying to dig out the cars at the pub.'

Lottie's shoulders rounded forwards. This was not what she wanted to hear. 'Okay. Thanks for walking all the way up here to tell me. You could have rung.'

Petra was shaking her head. 'Nope. The snow has brought down the phone lines, and I don't have your mobile number. But there is good news.' Lottie wasn't getting her hopes up. 'We have plenty of food at the pub, so we're doing a big buffet lunch today for ten pounds a head. If you want to brave the snow, we'd love to see you.'

'Petra, that is good news. Thank you.' At least she wouldn't have to cook a main meal today.

'Oh, and top gossip.' She leaned in close, almost scooping Lottie into her parka hood. 'Apparently Meghan Markle is hiding out in the village,' she whispered with a wink.

'No, she's not,' said Lottie, her gut tightening at the thought of Megan and Joe together. 'It's just a woman who looks a bit like her. She's Joe Broomfield's partner.'

'The vet?'

'Yeah, that's the guy.'

'He seems lovely. He was the talk of the pub on Christmas Day,' she said, giving Lottie a sideways look. 'You came up in that conversation too.'

Lottie rolled her lips together. 'Yeah . . . that was a long time ago, Petra.'

'Before my time,' she said, and she opened the door. 'Hope to see you later. Take care.'

'Definitely, reserve us a table for . . .' she counted them off on her fingers, 'nine.' A bark came from the kitchen, 'And one dog.'

'Consider it done.' And the door closed behind her.

So everyone in the village knew her past – and now they would have the next instalment of the story of Joe Broomfield. One that no longer included her.

Lottie puffed out a breath. There comes a time to let go and move on to the next chapter. Lottie had a feeling that now was that time.

Chapter Thirty-Two

The general mood was downbeat. The snow had scuppered everyone's plans, and no amount of refreshing the weather forecast was going to make the snow disappear any quicker. Lottie was keen that they didn't dissolve into their usual family bickering and that they somehow made the best of things – she just had to think of something to keep them occupied.

The first half of the morning was quite easy; Jessie managed to persuade virtually everyone to go outside to play snowballs and make a family of snowmen with her, with the exception of Rhys, who was still asleep, and Angie, who – according to her – didn't have anything appropriate to wear for snow. Dave had had a whale of a time chasing snowballs, but had been puzzled every time he'd tried to bite one and it had instantly disappeared.

Lottie made a vat of hot chocolate, and an almond milk-based version for Scott, who was very grateful; he just managed to stop her spoiling it by adding marshmallows, which apparently contained gelatin. She'd learned a lot about vegan food this Christmas, which might come in handy if Scott and her mother stayed together for a bit longer.

'Can we make more snowmen after this?' asked Jessie, spooning more marshmallows into what remained of her hot chocolate. There was a collective groan from around the kitchen table as everyone warmed their numb hands on their mugs.

Rhys meandered into the kitchen to mumbled greetings. 'What time are we leaving?' he asked, looking between his parents.

Nicola shook her head. 'For someone as intelligent as you, that is a very stupid question.'

Rhys turned to his father and Daniel pointed at the window. Rhys strained his neck. 'It's snowing.'

'Congratulations. The undisputed winner of the Stating-the-bleeding-obvious Award goes to Rhys Collins,' said Zach and he ruffled Rhys's hair. Rhys batted him away, and a good-natured boyish tussle ensued.

'Rhys, do you want to play in the snow?' asked Jessie.

'Maybe later,' he said, as his impromptu scrap with Zach ended. Jessie pouted.

Lottie handed Rhys a full mug. 'It's been made a while. Do you want me to microwave it?'

By way of an answer, he downed his hot chocolate and picked up his metal detector.

'You might find a horseshoe today,' said Emily, stifling a giant yawn.

'It felt like I was close yesterday,' said Rhys, pulling on the woolly hat he'd got for Christmas. Lottie snatched it off his head. 'Hey!' he said in protest. She snipped off the price tag and he smiled as she handed it back to him.

'Can I help?' asked Jessie, sounding a little dejected. 'Pleeeeeeeeeeease?'

'Erm . . .' Rhys looked to Lottie. Clearly he felt a flat refusal would be unkind.

312

'How about you and I watch Rhys,' Jessie's face fell, 'and we'll take trowels so we can help dig up the horseshoe when he finds one?'

'Yay,' said Jessie, tipping up her mug and adding to her already impressive hot chocolate moustache.

'She reminds me of someone with that moustache,' said Lottie to Zach as they watched.

'Cousin Paul?' Zach suggested. Lottie shook her head. 'Nicola's brother Stephen?'

'Nope. That's not it.'

'Aunt Pearl,' he said, triumphantly.

'Yes!' said Lottie, and she congratulated him with a high five.

Lottie found herself following Rhys round the garden again, wrapped up under multiple layers. Although just as cold today, it was a whole lot prettier outside. The snow had cloaked everything in a white sparkly blanket, and the manor house looked beautifully serene. Somehow the weather had given it an extra edge of magnificence, like it had been painted onto the landscape.

'Do you like Emily?' asked Jessie.

'Yes, I do. She seems very nice,' said Lottie.

'She is. I like her. I thought Daddy liked her too.'

'Oh, he does, sweetie.'

'Do you like Joe?' Jessie fixed her with a hard stare.

'Um, yes. I like Joe.' She could feel her cheeks burn despite the cold.

'I don't like that lady. She screamed at Dave,' said Jessie.

'He did eat her coat,' reasoned Lottie, smiling at the thought of Dave spitting out lumps of fur collar.

Jessie giggled. 'That was funny. Is Scott going to be your new daddy?' Lottie felt her eyes ping wide open.

313

'We've got something!' Rhys called over, digging frantically.

Lottie was grateful for the interruption.

'What is it?' asked Lottie as she reached him.

'Here,' he said handing her the headphones. 'Listen.' She put one to her ear and Rhys waved the detector over where he was digging – it let out a screech. 'It's something big.' He returned to digging.

'Probably a horseshoe,' whispered Lottie, passing the headphones to Jessie, who nodded her agreement.

'Right, let's dig it up,' said Rhys, and he and Jessie set to work with their trowels. Lottie folded her arms and hoped it was something a little more interesting than the rusty nail they'd found yesterday.

Jessie was an enthusiastic digger, if somewhat haphazard. Rhys had to guide her back to the hole a few times or she'd have tunnelled to Dumbleford. Finally, her trowel made a sound like she had stabbed it into a plate – it put Lottie's teeth on edge. Rhys put down his own trowel and dug his fingers into the ground to clear the earth away from whatever was there.

A few moments later, Rhys sat back on his haunches and stared into the hole they'd dug. 'It's definitely not a horseshoe,' he said, his face full of confusion.

Joe was at the kitchen table studying his accounts on his laptop when he heard the bedroom door open, and Megan appeared. He glanced in her direction. He'd heard her padding about between the bedroom and bathroom earlier, but this was the first time he'd seen her since last night. She was fully dressed in a striking red-and-white striped dress and matching heels. She'd had her driver drop off a ridiculous amount of luggage late the previous evening.

'Good morning, Joey,' she said, in her seductive drawl. He saw her look out of the window. 'An English village in the snow. Is there anything prettier?'

She was likely fishing for a compliment. 'No, there's nothing prettier,' he agreed.

'Where can I get a decent coffee around here?' asked Megan, leaning against the kitchen doorway and eyeing Joe.

'There's some instant by the kettle.' He didn't look up.

'A kettle? How British is that?' She sidled over and studied the ordinary-looking kettle. 'Fascinating.' Joe liked having a kettle again. He hadn't even noticed that he'd missed not having it in America, but he had. 'There must be somewhere I can buy a coffee and perhaps brunch?' She came up behind him and leaned against the back of his chair.

'There's the tearooms on the village green. You might want to try there. Or the pub.' When he was a kid, the tearooms had been a very traditional set-up with bone china teacups, saucers and flowery cake stands. It had been one where they went as a treat and wore their Sunday best. He had been looking forward to checking it out and seeing how it had changed – but not today.

'I don't know if I can be fussed to walk all that way.' She sighed into his hair making him freeze.

Petra had called by earlier to let him know they were doing food at the pub. He checked his watch. 'If you can wait a bit I think the pub is our best option.'

'What's this you're working on?' asked Megan, her manicured nail whizzing past his right ear and pointing at the laptop screen.

Joe shut the laptop lid. 'It's just my accounts.'

'Your accounts or our accounts?' She turned to perch

on the table next to him and watched his response carefully. 'Is there something I should know?'

'Megan, we talked this through last night.' His voice was weary. They'd not gone to bed until two that morning, and he was fed up of talking. Why did she always insist on going over and over the same thing? 'The practice here will be in my name and funded by me. It's what I want.'

She pouted. 'My Mr Independent.' She ran a finger under his chin.

'I need to sort out Dave,' he said, getting to his feet.

'Who's Dave?' She tilted her head in a way that reminded him of the little dog. The comparison, which would have so deeply offended her, made him smile.

'He's the dog that ravaged your coat.' He was still smiling at the memory.

'Eurgh.' She gave a shudder. 'I hope you're going to euthanise the horrid thing.'

His smile slid away. 'No, I'm going to make a couple of calls to local rescue centres and vets and see if he's been reported as missing over the holidays.' There was a good reason he'd kept Megan away from the caring side of his job – the two most definitely didn't mix.

'So where are you taking me for lunch?' she asked.

'The pub.'

She mouthed the word pub as if it was completely alien to her.

'Once I've made these calls we can brave the walk down the hill. You might want to swap your heels for some wellington boots.'

He tried not to take too much pleasure in the disgusted look on her face.

* * *

Lottie had grabbed a crate from the log store and Rhys and Jessie had carefully dug out their find, which was now on the middle of the kitchen table with the whole family staring at it, mesmerised.

'Is that all of it?' asked Daniel, his eyes fixed on the mud-covered artefact in the crate.

'I had a quick sweep round with the detector and it didn't register anything else,' said Rhys.

'How old is it?' asked Emily.

'It's not really my area. But I'd say it's about two thousand years old. Give or take a couple of hundred years,' said Rhys. All heads briefly turned his way. 'It's terra sigillata. It's almost certainly Roman.'

The heads turned back in unison to stare at the broken red earthenware pot nestled in the wooden crate, still caked in mud. Lottie marvelled at the faint flower pattern still visible. To think it had lain in their garden all those years and was only now seeing daylight again. Or the kitchen strip light, to be more precise.

'What's it worth?' asked Angie.

Rhys puckered his lips. 'If it was perfect, maybe a couple of hundred. In this condition not a lot. But a local museum would be interested.'

Jessie was pulling a face. 'Is the pot metal?'

'No, it's made from a type of red clay. When it was new it would have had a shiny glaze,' explained Nicola, always keen to show off her knowledge.

Jessie was frowning. 'Because Rhys said the metal dec-tor—'

'Dee-tect-or,' corrected Emily, snaking an arm around Jessie's shoulder.

'Dee-tect-or,' repeated Jessie. 'He said it beeped if it found metal. And it was beeping a lot.'

Heads swivelled around the table and, as simultaneous pennies dropped, Rhys reached for the pot.

'Be careful,' said his mother.

'Empty out the earth,' instructed Daniel.

Rhys used his trowel to carefully nudge the soil out of the top of the pot. He was almost halfway down before he paused. 'There's something there.' He looked back at the eager faces.

'Let's see,' said Jessie, voicing everybody's thoughts.

Rhys reached in and pulled out a lump of mud caked around a number of tiny green discs.

Zach lifted up Jessie so she could get a better look. 'What are they?' she asked.

'They're coins,' said Zach. 'Very old ones.'

Angie reached for one that was jutting out. She gently rubbed the soil off its surface and peered at it closely.

'Is it Roman?' asked Emily.

'Is it worth anything?' asked Daniel.

'Is it lunchtime?' asked Jessie, wriggling to get down from her father's arms.

'Clasped hands,' said Angie in a faint voice. She was frowning hard at the coin.

Rhys bent his head to get a better look. 'I think that denotes it was minted here.'

'What's that mean?' asked Lottie. 'Is it fake?'

'No. I think it's one of only a few coins minted in Britain by Carausius,' said Rhys.

'To think the house has been keeping that a secret for all these years,' said Lottie to nobody in particular.

'There's one of those coins on eBay for eighty quid,' said Daniel, showing round his phone screen at lightning speed.

'It's treasure-trove, Daniel. This needs to be declared to

the authorities.' Nicola turned to Rhys. 'This could be an important find. It's a wonderful thing for your CV once you leave university and—'

'I already left uni at the end of last term,' said Rhys, taking the coin from Angie, 'and I'm not going back.'

'What?' said Daniel and Nicola together – united for a change.

'I've got a job.' He turned towards Lottie. 'Lottie thinks it's a good idea. Don't you?'

Lottie's eyebrows felt like they were heading into space as his parents' glares turned on her.

Chapter Thirty-Three

Lottie refused to get involved and made a break for upstairs as a row of gargantuan proportions kicked off over the coins in the kitchen. Angie followed close behind her. As Lottie went into her bedroom, she realised that her mother hadn't gone past her, which she would need to do in order to get to her room or the bathroom. Lottie backtracked. She opened Nana's bedroom door to find Angie sitting on the bed.

Lottie was about to question her mother's motives for going in there, but something about the posture of her body stopped her. 'Are you okay?' asked Lottie from the doorway.

Angie tipped her head up. 'I'm not bonkers or anything, but I needed to check she wasn't here.' Angie chewed the inside of her mouth. 'That is bonkers isn't it?'

'Yep. Totally nuts.' Lottie went inside, shut the door and joined her on the bed. 'But I know what you mean. It's kind of unbelievable that she's not here any more.'

Angie's eyes filled with tears. 'Especially at Christmas.' Lottie put her arm around her mother and reluctantly Angie let her hold her, briefly. She sniffed back the tears and pulled away.

'I thought you hated the Christmas gathering,' said Lottie.

'I don't hate it. I suppose I'm not its biggest fan, but who likes being told what to do?'

Lottie hadn't really thought of it like that. 'It's tradition though.'

'Tradition? Or not wanting to let things change?' Angie fixed Lottie with a stare. She wasn't sure if the comment was aimed at her or Nana.

'There's something reassuring about both. I like that Christmas is always here, and that we all know what happens when. It's comforting.'

They sat in silence for a moment. 'Does life worry you?' asked Lottie. 'Making decisions that could send you in a specific direction, but not knowing if it's the right one.'

Angie gave her a quizzical look. 'Old age worries me. I swear the hairs on my top lip are thickening.' She leaned closer to Lottie so she could inspect them.

'What am I looking at?' asked Lottie, trying not to look too closely.

'Am I getting a moustache?'

'Don't be daft . . . Hercule,' said Lottie, and her mother gave her a light slap on the arm. 'I'm joking. Of course you don't look like Hercule Poirot. You look more like Aunt Pearl.'

'Same moustache. Stop it. I'm thinking of spending some of my inheritance on having surgery.'

Lottie regarded her mother. She was an attractive woman who had worn well. Yes, there were some tell-tale wrinkles around her eyes and neck, but overall she looked incredible. 'You look great for your age.' Lottie studied her mother's face. 'I don't think you should have any surgery.'

Angie looked shocked. 'Not my face! Down there.' She pointed between her thighs. 'It's meant to make sex even better. Not that we have a problem in that department. Although the last couple of days have been a bit sparse thanks to you stealing our batteries and relegating us to the bed from hell. I swear, every spring in that mattress has been imprinted on my—'

'Stop!' said Lottie, trying to block the unwanted pictures from her mind. She'd need extra-strength mind bleach to rid herself of those.

Angie looked taken aback. 'I thought mothers and daughters were meant to share things like that?'

Lottie was shaking her head. 'I don't think so. We share enough already.'

'Like what?'

'Insults and a genetic predisposition to choose the wrong men. Let's stick to those.'

'Speak for yourself. My Scott is wonderful.'

'I have to admit, he does seem nice.' Lottie paused, then decided to say it. 'Do something for me, Mum?' Angie twitched but didn't respond. 'Be honest with him. He seems like a decent guy and I think you two could have something good together. And most importantly, I don't want to have to look after you when you get old.' Lottie said it with a smile so her mother would know she was joking.

Angie rolled her eyes and looked across at Nana's dressing table. 'I guess we need to think about sorting her things out.'

'We do,' said Lottie, with a sad sigh. 'Do you want to give me a hand now?' Angie's face said she didn't.

'Won't it just all go to charity?' Angie gave the room a cursory sweep.

'I guess so, but . . .' Lottie was slightly thrown by the comment. It was true, there was very little that she would want to keep, but at the same time she couldn't give it all away. 'Come on, we need to do the important stuff. I'd rather do it with you than on my own.'

'Fine,' said Angie, and Lottie picked up Nana's jewellery box and handed it to her.

'This is all mine, so that's easy,' said Angie, closing the lid with a snap and putting the box next to her on the bed. She let her arm rest protectively around it.

'Oh. I thought it might be nice for me to have something of Nana's to keep. And Jessie too.'

Angie tried to hide her surprise. 'Well, um, okay. What was it you wanted?'

'Nothing expensive. Just something like her marcasite ring she wore if she was going out. And maybe her Saint Christopher for Jessie? Nicola might like something too.'

Angie snorted. 'Fine, but I'm not giving it all away.'

'I'm not asking you to.' Lottie was becoming irritated. Her mother could be so selfish sometimes. 'Here,' said Lottie, pulling out the bottom drawer of the dresser and setting it down on the bed the other side of Angie. 'Have a look through there.' Angie looked at it as if it might explode.

'We found the cards in there,' said Lottie, her mind returning to the words in hers.

'That was really odd wasn't it? That she'd taken the time to write in everyone's card when she could have just called us all together to tell us.'

'No. I thought it was very Nana. She didn't want a fuss. She said that in the card. This way everyone knows, but there's no big drama.' The avoidance of drama was probably what was foxing her mother, who had courted it her whole life.

'I guess.' She pulled out packet after packet of tights from the drawer. 'Did she even wear anything other than flesh colour?'

Lottie ignored her mother. 'What did your card say? I mean not a general interpretation. What did it actually say?' asked Lottie.

Angie put the tights down and cupped her hands in her lap as if thinking over how to respond. 'It said, "Spend time with your children – they are your greatest achievement."' Lottie was warmed by the words. Angie seemed puzzled. 'It's just another criticism. I do spend time with you when I can. But you know I'm busy. Don't you, darling?'

'Yes, Mum,' said Lottie, and she pulled out another drawer. The fact that Angie still hadn't asked what Lottie's card said spoke volumes.

'Your Nana always made me feel like she could do everything better than I could. Even bringing up you and Zach.'

'I'm sure she didn't mean to,' said Lottie.

'Daniel was academic and successful. I suppose I always felt I disappointed her.' Lottie could relate to that. Angie gave herself a shake. 'I probably imagined it all anyway. Because I *have* made a success of my life and I'm only halfway through.'

'What was that you said before about an early menopause? Are you okay?'

'Oh, I'm fine. It's wonderful. No need for contraception or sanitary products. It's saved me a fortune.' Angie looked genuinely delighted.

'There are worse things that are transmitted through having sex.'

'Worse than babies?' Angie flinched. 'Surely not.'

'Do you think the early menopause thing could be

hereditary?' Lottie bit her lip. She wanted to have children; it was frightening to think her time might be running out faster than she thought.

Angie shrugged. 'Why do you ask?'

Lottie shook her head. Her mother was unbelievable. 'Because it might impact me.' Lottie couldn't help her voice rising at the end.

'Oh. I see.' Angie seemed to give it some thought. She took Lottie's hand. Lottie felt unexpected emotion bubble inside her. Her mother was rarely demonstrative, so when she was it always took her by surprise. 'You know, darling; being a parent isn't all it's cracked up to be.'

'Mum!' Lottie's voice was louder than either of them expected. It made Angie jump.

'Oh, don't take everything personally. That wasn't a dig at you. I hate to admit it, but Nana was right. You and Zach are the best thing I've ever done. I know I've been an unconventional mother. But you know I love you. Don't you?'

It was lovely to hear her mother say it. 'Yes, Mum. I know.'

'That's good then.' She let go of Lottie's hand and returned to sorting tights.

Emily and Jessie were in the kitchen when a tired-looking Lottie appeared. Emily watched her take a deep breath and paste on a smile.

'Where is everyone?' asked Lottie.

'The boys have gone to watch TV,' said Emily, wrapping her arms around Jessie. 'And Nicola has gone to look for some book about Romans in the box room.'

'She could be lost in there forever. I'll give her half an hour and then send in a rescue crew. Or maybe the vicar because I'm fairly sure a couple of the dolls are possessed.'

'I'm bored,' said Jessie, her face glum.

'Shall we make cakes?' suggested Lottie. Emily loved how Lottie was always able to find a solution for everyone else's woes.

Jessie was already jumping up and down. Emily didn't mind what they did, as long as Jessie was occupied. This wasn't what anyone had planned for today. She'd been hoping that she and Zach would have some time to themselves, as Jessie had been meant to be on a pantomime trip with Rainbows, but it wasn't to be.

'Yeah, why not,' said Emily, trying to muster some enthusiasm. At least she wasn't at work.

'We're off to the pub for lunch, but the hordes will still want something come teatime. Thanks to one of Nana's WI cookbooks I've found a couple of vegan cake recipes that we've got the ingredients for,' said Lottie, swiftly tying an apron around a still-jumping Jessie. 'Right, my eager helpers; let's set to work.' Emily gave a weak smile as Jessie bounded off to the larder. 'You okay?' asked Lottie.

'Yeah . . . No . . . I guess so.'

'Doesn't sound conclusive,' observed Lottie. She opened out the cookbook and read out the ingredients to Jessie. Jessie was soon focusing hard on measuring flour, her tongue sticking out of the side of her mouth in concentration. Lottie guided Emily into the utility. 'Come on, out with it.'

'Does Zach seem . . .' Emily checked Jessie wasn't listening, '*all right* to you?'

'In what way?'

Emily shrugged. She was struggling to put her finger on exactly what was awry, but something definitely was. 'He's up and down more often than a hyperactive meerkat. He's usually so even.' It was something she loved about him. He had a reliable personality: always upbeat. And yet, over the last few days, he'd been all over the place. 'Is he just like this when he's with the family?' It would be a logical explanation, and would hopefully mean she could stop fretting that he was going to dump her. Emily was unable to shake what Jessie had said on Christmas Day from her mind, despite Zach's protestations.

'I'm always unsettled around my mother. She does that to me. One minute I'm fine, the next I'm rock bottom.' *That would explain it*, thought Emily. 'We always say our mother had postnatal disappointment.' Lottie chuckled and returned to Jessie at the kitchen table. Emily was thinking.

Emily bit the inside of her mouth. So perhaps it was the family causing Zach's mood changes then. 'Maybe I should talk to him again.'

'Aren't you going to wait until you know?' Lottie nodded at Emily's stomach before returning her attention to beating together the sugar and margarine that Jessie had carefully measured out.

'I'm hoping to pop in the shop when we go to the pub.' She chose her words carefully – Jessie looked like she was engrossed, but she didn't miss much.

'Good plan.' Lottie paused and held up a wooden spoon dripping with mixture. 'Actually, be careful of who's on the till. If it's Rhonda, the news of what you've bought will be around the village before you've stepped in the pub.' Emily could tell that the horror of this was etched on her face. 'It's okay. Any of the others are all right . . . apart from . . . Actually, I'll make you a list of who's likely to blab and who's not.'

'Great. Thanks. I think,' said Emily, feeling like she was about to embark on a James Bond-worthy expedition rather than a trip to the village stores. 'Do they wear name badges?'

'Actually, no, they don't.' Lottie pulled a face. 'You'll have to ask them.'

'Great,' repeated Emily, this time with even less enthusiasm.

'Here, Jessie. You need to give this a stir and then add in the flour,' said Lottie, putting the bowl down near her and holding it steady.

Jessie obliged and they followed the next steps of the recipe together while Emily watched. When they'd completed two batches of cakes – one vanilla and one chocolate – Jessie's attention span was exhausted. Emily wrapped her up in many layers and sent her off with Rhys and Dave to try and find more treasure in the garden.

Emily and Lottie sipped tea while they waited for the cakes to cook. The Duchess wandered in and flopped dramatically at Lottie's feet. 'You okay?' Lottie asked the cat. She looked how Emily felt: overfed and fed up. She watched as Lottie went to tickle the Duchess and the cat took a swipe at her. 'Hey, grumpy. What's with you today?' The Duchess got up and made a point of washing herself thoroughly where Lottie had touched her before disappearing again.

'What are you going to do about Joe?' asked Emily.

Lottie stared out of the window almost as if she hadn't heard her. 'Nothing I can do. It's out of my hands now.'

'You're just going to give up on him?'

Lottie twisted in her seat, her face pained. 'I'm not giving up.'

'Oh, okay,' said Emily, feeling pretty sure that doing nothing was exactly the same thing but she didn't know Lottie well enough to push her on it.

Lottie's expression softened. 'I'm sorry. I didn't mean to snap at you. I have been mulling it all over and there's really nothing I can do.'

'Is he not worth fighting for? If it was Zach I wouldn't walk away without a fight.'

Lottie opened her mouth, but instead of saying anything she sipped her tea and turned back to stare out of the window at the snow-painted trees.

When the timer buzzed, Emily helped Lottie get the cakes out of the oven. They had risen well, but mainly in the middle, so they all had a massive peak in the centre.

'They look good,' said Emily, kindly, feeling her stomach grumble.

'They're a bit pointy. They look like volcanoes.'

'Or perky breasts,' said Emily, giving them a sideways look.

Lottie hastily covered the naked buns with a clean tea towel and they left them to cool.

Chapter Thirty-Four

Zach grabbed Lottie while they were all putting on coats in the hallway ready to go to the pub for lunch. He pulled her in to the dining room.

'Emily's worried about you. She still thinks you're going to dump her,' said Lottie, before Zach could speak.

'That'll be resolved in the next couple of hours,' he said. 'I need your help.'

'Why?' Lottie was suspicious.

'Because I've had a brilliant idea. I need you to do something for me. Top secret.'

Oh dear, thought Lottie. 'I will if I can.' She wrapped her scarf round her neck twice.

Zach waved his hands animatedly. 'When we all go to the pub, you need to sneak off—'

'Hang on. Where will Emily be?' After her conversation with Emily, she was losing track of who'd be sneaking off where.

'With me, of course. Where else would she be?'

She couldn't answer that. He had a good point. 'Nowhere. Come on, tell me the plan.'

After Zach had relayed his instructions and Lottie had asked far too many questions, he joined the others and

Lottie made an excuse about needing to check everywhere was locked up. Instead, Lottie put on her wellies and headed out the back door where, as Zach had explained, she found a large sack. She peeked inside. As expected, it was full of holly branches. Lottie pursed her lips in thought. It was a lot of holly, but was it enough? She grabbed the secateurs and another sack and went to give the holly bush another severe pruning.

When she was happy with her haul, she locked up the house, picked up the sacks and began her trudge to the pub. It was gently snowing, and silent flakes were floating through the air serene and mesmerising. Within a couple of paces she identified a problem: no matter how she held the sacks they bumped against her, and because they were woven the holly easily poked through and spiked her. 'Ow! Stop pricking me!' she shouted at the sack when it grazed her for the umpteenth time. Somehow shouting at it made her feel slightly better. She wasn't usually a shouty person. Perhaps it was something she should do more often, rather than bottling up her anguish. She stopped, gave her scratched thigh a rub, rearranged the sacks and set off again. 'Ow!' It was no good. She was going to have to grit her teeth and accept it was going to hurt. *The things I do for other people's happiness*, she thought. Maybe one day karma would shine on her. She muttered a string of mild expletives and then decided to utter one with each jab the holly gave her. She soon got into a rhythm: 'Bugger, arse, damn, prick; bugger, arse . . .'

Halfway down the hill she stopped again and jiggled the sacks round. At this point her right thigh probably had more holes than a teabag. It wasn't too far now to the village green.

'Bugger,' she said as she set off. The sack spiked her in the bum. 'Arse.'

She concentrated hard on her goal, ignoring the door opening nearby. 'Damn, prick,' she said, loudly, as Joe stepped out of the doorway and into her path. He recoiled from her verbal assault. She blushed and was about to apologise and explain, but she caught sight of Megan and decided against it. Lottie skirted around them and continued down the hill. 'Arse.'

She focused on her goal. She had far more important things to think about today than Joe Bloody Broomfield. She neared the green and watched as the door to the village stores opened and a furtive-looking Emily came out. Lottie quickly slung the sacks into a hedge and kept walking. As anticipated, Emily looked around, saw Lottie and waved. She waited for Lottie to reach her.

'Did you get it?' asked Lottie.

'Yep,' said Emily, biting her lip and patting her bag at the same time. 'It was a nightmare getting away from Zach. I had to say I needed tampons before he'd let me out of his sight. I got some fizz,' she held up the bottles, 'in case we need to celebrate.' Lottie didn't like to ask which result they would be celebrating.

'Good idea. Look, I just need to . . .' She needed a reason to delay going to the pub with Emily, but her brain wasn't being terribly quick coming up with something.

'Need to?' prompted Emily, appearing concerned.

Lottie heard the crunch of footsteps behind her and a quick glance over her shoulder confirmed it was Joe and Megan. 'I need to speak to Joe about Dave,' she said, in a loud and deliberate voice, bringing Joe to a halt next to her.

'What's up?' asked Joe. He, Emily and Megan were all

332

staring at her. Megan was running a critical eye over Lottie's outfit. She didn't care. She was dressed for the weather, not a fashion parade.

'Could I talk to you in private?' asked Lottie, putting on her most serious face and focusing on Joe.

'Er, yeah. Okay.' Joe was hesitant.

'Are you going to the pub?' Emily asked Megan.

'Yeah, but—'

'Let's get in the warm.' And Emily guided a reluctant Megan away.

As soon as they were out of sight, Lottie grabbed Joe's arm and marched him back towards where she'd dumped the sacks full of holly. 'You might as well give me a hand with this.'

'What's going on, Lottie?' asked Joe.

'Oh, you know, just a traditional Collins Christmas full of secrets and cock ups.' She gave a forced smile and handed him a snowy sack. 'Be careful of the pricks,' she informed him, her face deadly serious.

He was grinning until he started to walk after her. 'Ow!' he said, giving his side a rub.

'I did warn you,' said Lottie, with a sense of satisfaction. She'd spent a few hours thinking how she'd like to stick pins in him. Who knew it would be so easily arranged?

Joe let out a more strangled 'Ow!', which made her turn round. 'Scrotum,' he whispered.

'Ouch. Pricked in your . . . Well, yes, that's going to hurt.' She turned away to hide her smirk and carried on. She heard his footsteps crunch on the snow behind her as he caught her up.

'Lottie, I need to explain—'

'No, you don't,' she cut in without turning around. 'You don't have to explain yourself to me.' She strode away so that he couldn't contradict her. She didn't want to hear his excuses.

When she reached the middle of Dumbleford Green she dropped her sack of holly onto the snowy ground and rubbed her hands together to warm them up. Joe did the same. 'Here's the situation: Dave hasn't delivered the ring, so Zach has come up with a new plan and we're it.' She pointed between herself and Joe.

'Okay,' said Joe, giving a furtive look in the direction of the pub as Lottie tipped the holly onto the snow.

'Come on, we're up against the clock on this one.'

Lottie explained the details and they worked as quickly as they could, given that they got pricked by the holly every time they touched it. After a few minutes, they stood back to admire their handiwork. Nestled in the snow in giant letters made out of the holly were the words 'MARRY ME?' Lottie held the last piece of holly aloft.

'Where are you going to put that?' asked Joe, appearing wary. Lottie used an uncensored expression to tell him exactly where she'd like to stick it. 'Right,' he said. 'Or maybe on the question mark?'

She did as he suggested. 'Thanks,' she said, picking up the sacks and heading to the pub.

Inside the Bleeding Bear, the Collins family were filling up the small bar area. Emily and Megan took off their coats and joined them by the open fire.

'Oh my, now ain't this quaint? It is quite possibly the cutest bar I've ever been in,' said Megan, looking around appreciatively. The pub had low ceilings, ancient sturdy beams, beautiful wood floors and a roaring fire. Emily had to admit it was a very sweet pub: traditional, warm and welcoming; and now, thanks to the Collins family, it was very noisy too. An excited yap came from somewhere behind all the legs, and Dave's face appeared. He wriggled to get past Scott and made a beeline for Megan.

Megan let out a yelp.

'Oh, no you don't,' said Emily, intercepting Dave before he reached his target. She picked him up and he wriggled excitedly at the attention. Thankfully, he seemed to forget about Megan.

Zach was close behind him. 'Hello Megan. Where's Joe?' he asked.

'Lottie wanted a quiet word with him,' said Emily, and Zach's face registered something that she couldn't quite gauge. 'I'm sure they'll both join us soon.' Emily tried to hang on to Dave, who was squirming more than an eel with an itch.

'Yeah, they will. I guess. I mean I don't know,' said Zach, his eyes darting about warily. What was up with him?

Megan flinched every time Dave moved, which was a lot. 'I'm sorry, but can you keep that dog away from me?'

'I'll take him outside,' said Emily, turning to leave.

'No!' said Zach, almost shouting, making Emily spin back around. Everyone stared. Emily joined in with a glare of her own. She didn't like being yelled at or told what to do.

'Sorry. I mean, I'll take him. It's bitterly cold out there.' Zach took the writhing dog from her arms.

'Thank you,' said Megan, straightening out her blouse as if she'd been under attack.

Zach backed away, opened the pub door a fraction and slipped out. Emily shook her head. He was acting strangely but then he'd been like that, on and off, since Christmas Eve.

'Can I get you a drink?' Emily asked Megan as they reached the bar. Petra greeted them warmly.

'I'll have a Manhattan, please,' said Megan, looking around for somewhere to sit.

Petra pulled a face. 'We don't do cocktails I'm afraid. But we're stocking some new gins.' She proudly waved an arm across her display. Emily was interested for a nanosecond before the unanswered question prodded her conscience. It was a shame, because she liked gin – a lot. She thought about the test in her bag and wondered if she could slip unnoticed to the toilets.

Megan was frowning. 'Just a bourbon then. What do you have?' She was scanning the optics.

'Jim Beam,' said Petra, with a smile. Megan scowled.

'Fine,' said Megan, pulling out a chair and examining the seat thoroughly before sitting down.

'And a lime and soda for me please,' said Emily. She heard Dave's muted bark from outside. She'd need to go and relieve Zach from dog duty shortly.

She was distracted by the sounds of claws on wood. Emily and Megan turned at the same time to see a giant dog bound from behind the bar. It looked to Emily like the one she'd met playing on the green on Christmas Day. The dog was even bigger up close. Emily was sure she'd seen smaller donkeys.

Megan screamed and the dog made straight for her. 'Tiny!' yelled Petra, and the dog stopped abruptly. 'Sit.' And Tiny did as instructed. The problem was he was sitting right next to Megan. His head was at the same height as her shoulder, his tongue lolling out from his foam-edged jowls.

Megan froze. 'Get. It. Away. From. Me,' said Megan, in a fearful whisper that held more than a hint of menace.

Jessie pushed her way through the crowd and took the giant dog by the collar. 'Come on, Tiny. She doesn't like dogs. You can sit with me,' she said, and she led the giant canine away.

'Dogs and children in bars. Surely that's illegal,' said Megan, giving her clothes another smooth over.

'Nope,' said Emily. 'Welcome to England.' And she handed over her drink.

Lottie reached for the pub door just as Zach appeared from inside with Dave in his arms. 'Is it done?' he asked, nudging her back out into the snow.

'Yes, look,' said Lottie, pointing to the green, but as she turned to look over her shoulder she could see they might have a problem. She and Zach stared at the green. Due to a slight undulation in the ground the message she and Joe had laid out wasn't completely visible from the pub. What they had was the bottom third of each letter, making it look like a coded message. 'Bugger,' whispered Lottie under her breath as Joe joined them.

'What's up?' He turned around and answered his own question. 'Ah. Sod it.'

'It's okay,' said Lottie, thinking on her feet. 'You can walk her over there to show her the Christmas tree up close.' No way was she going to rearrange eleventy hundred sprigs of pricking holly.

'Why would I show her the Christmas tree?' asked Zach. 'It's three hundred and sixty-three days until Christmas.'

'Because it's lovely, especially now it has a coating of snow on it.'

Zach was shaking his head. Joe let out a slow breath. 'I'll sort it. You two go inside and I'll move it all a few feet nearer, okay?'

'Great,' said Lottie. She was cold and hungry and in dire need of a large glass of wine. Joe trudged back to the green. 'You coming in?' Lottie asked Zach.

'I can't. Megan's in there and Dave wants to cosy up to her even more than he wants to chase the Duchess.'

His comment made Lottie ponder briefly about the two animals, but that thought disappeared when she opened the pub door and out marched Megan like a woman on a mission.

'Where's Joe?' she demanded. But Megan's gaze landed on him and she strode off across the green. Lottie shrugged and knocked the worst of the snow off her wellies. She was about to step inside when a shriek stopped her.

Lottie twisted to see Megan standing on the edge of the green with her hands on her cheeks. Joe was doing something crossed between jazz hands and the gesture you make when you're trying to flag down a taxi after a few bottles of wine. 'Bugger,' said Lottie, and without thinking she ran to him – he was going to need some help.

'Oh my God. Yes,' squealed Megan. 'Yes. Yes. Yes!' Each word was getting louder and more excited.

'No. No. No,' muttered Joe, his eyes wider than when he got pricked in the nether regions by the holly. But Megan wasn't listening; she was already pulling her phone from her designer bag to take selfies.

Lottie did the only thing she could think of and ran through the message kicking up the holly in all directions. The last thing they needed was Emily to see this on the internet. 'You bitch!' yelled Megan, and she launched herself at Lottie. Lottie dodged out of the way and ran behind Joe. 'What the hell do you think you're doing?' Megan's eyes were demonic with rage.

'I'm trying to save you embarrassment,' said Lottie, making a run for the nearby Christmas tree with Megan in hot pursuit.

'Megan!' shouted Joe. Megan halted and turned to look at him.

'She's right. This proposal – it's not for you.' He hung his head.

'What? You mean you're asking her?' Megan stabbed a finger in Lottie's direction.

'No!' said Lottie and Joe together. Joe's response was a little more vehement than she would have liked to hear but at least they were on the same page.

Megan's head spun between the two of them, like the girl in *The Exorcist* but thankfully without the vomit. They both nodded solemnly.

Megan licked her lips. 'It's not a pro . . .' They both shook their heads in unison. Megan began to cry silent tears and Lottie felt a pang of guilt. That always happened. She always felt like it was all her fault.

She felt for Megan, all the same. 'Why?' Megan was looking imploringly at Joe.

As imminent danger seemed to have passed, Lottie crept from behind the Christmas tree, which was inappropriately twinkling its colourful, jolly lights. 'It was my brother's proposal to his girlfriend. But now,' Lottie surveyed the strewn holly, 'it's nobody's.'

'Eurgh. I hate you, Joey Broomfield!' said Megan, and she shoved him hard in the chest before stalking off.

Lottie looked towards the pub and saw the distress on poor Zach's face. Three proposals scuppered – this was not going well. 'I'm going to . . .' Lottie pointed at Zach and Joe nodded. He looked shell-shocked. She left him standing in the snow.

As Lottie reached the pub, the door opened and Emily popped her head out. 'What's going on?' she asked.

'Nothing,' said Zach, hastily bundling her back inside. 'Absolutely sod all.'

Chapter Thirty-Five

The pub had put on an excellent hot buffet lunch, with something for everyone. Lottie had forgotten to tell Petra that they had one vegan and one fake vegan to cater for, but it hadn't mattered. There were slices of spiced lentil loaf and bean casserole. There was, of course, an abundance of turkey dishes, along with a big pot of pasta and tomato sauce, of which Jessie was on her third helping.

Zach was about as flat as the ribbons of tagliatelle; and who could blame him? His proposal plans had been dashed for a third time. Emily was cuddling up to him. She could obviously sense something was wrong, but she had no idea what.

Lottie put down her spoon after a little bit too much sticky toffee pudding and marvelled at the simple joy of having someone cook her a meal. She had a much greater admiration for how Nana had coped so effortlessly for all those years and she wished she was able to tell her. She steadied her emotions and wiped her mouth on a paper serviette that featured jolly dancing snowmen all the way round its edge.

'I need the loo,' said Emily, leaning forward to catch Lottie's eye.

'I don't think I can move,' said Lottie, thinking how nice it would be to curl up in front of the television for a couple of hours.

'Oh, but it's a bit of a walk back up the hill. Best go to the loo before we set off,' said Emily, giving Lottie a pleading stare. The penny dropped and Lottie sat up straight.

'Yes, good idea. I'd better come with you. I mean go too. For myself,' she said, and she almost tripped over trying to get away from the table.

They walked to the ladies' toilets, checked nobody had followed them and then went into the bigger of the two cubicles together.

Emily let out a slow breath. 'Right.' She pulled the box from her bag.

'Haven't you done it yet?' asked Lottie.

'Not yet.'

'How are you feeling about it all?'

'Not as scared as I was. Kind of excited. Is that weird?'

'No. I can't think of anything more exciting.' She felt a pang of regret. 'Are you going to do it now?' asked Lottie, feeling that she was invading Emily's space somewhat, squeezed in next to the toilet bowl.

'I don't know . . . I mean I want to, but . . . should I wait for Zach?' Emily bit her lip.

'We've been round this roundabout before,' said Lottie.

'I know, I'm sorry. It's just . . .' She stared at the tester. 'What should I do?'

'You should pass me some loo roll please, love,' came Shirley's voice from the other cubicle.

Lottie and Emily giggled. At least that answered the question. They wouldn't be doing a pregnancy test within earshot of Shirley. At least they hadn't said anything obvious enough to set tongues wagging. But they had been foiled again.

They eventually left the pub, all having eaten too much and most having had one too many drinks – apart from Jessie and Emily, who were skipping across the green. It had at last stopped snowing, and Lottie could see patches on the grass where it had started to melt, but given their alcohol intake nobody was driving anywhere tonight.

'Look, holly,' said Jessie, pointing at the scattered sprigs of leaves and berries. Lottie looked at Zach and he thrust one hand deep into his pocket, gripped Dave's lead tightly with the other and rolled his shoulders forwards.

She linked arms with her brother and they followed the group at a safe pace. 'Sorry it all went wrong today,' she said.

'Really not your fault, Lottie. Don't apologise. It's another omen.'

'Don't be daft.'

'It's okay. I don't mean I won't ever propose. I just think that maybe now isn't the right time.'

'Nonsense,' said Lottie. She was heavily invested in her brother's romance now, and even if she couldn't have *her* fairytale ending, she still wanted Emily and Zach to have theirs. 'We just need to come up with an even better idea.' She pressed her lips together and tipped her head skywards. Nothing immediately came to mind.

'Not that easy, is it?' said Zach.

'No, but we will think of something.' She gave his arm a squeeze.

'It's all his fault,' said Zach, indicating Dave, who was trotting along between them obediently.

'Don't blame Dave,' said Lottie, feeling protective.

'I'm joking.' Zach gave a wry smile. 'Don't tell Jessie, but I've liked having him about this Christmas.'

'Me too.'

'I might check out our local dog rescue when we get home. Having a dog of our own might not be so bad.'

'Blimey, Zach. I can't believe you've been converted.'

'It's seeing how Jessie is with him. It must be tough being an only child. When we were kids we had each other.'

'Oi! Are you saying I was the same as a dog?' Lottie couldn't help but laugh.

'If the cap fits . . . But a dog might be nice – Jessie doesn't have a playmate.'

'Or anyone to fight with.' Lottie's memories were a healthy mix of fun and fighting.

'True. It must be lonely for her sometimes.'

'She doesn't have to be an only child forever though.' Lottie had a quick sideways glance at her brother. His expression was unreadable. 'Does she?' she added, emphatically. Lottie waited for Zach to have an epiphany, but his eyes were fixed on Jessie and Emily up ahead, laughing and holding hands, and his mind was miles away. 'Emily would make a great mum,' she ventured.

'She would.'

'And you are a great dad.'

Zach shrugged off the compliment. 'How much flak do you think Joe's taking for the non-proposal?' asked Zach, as they passed Mr Bundy's cottage.

'Poor Joe.' She couldn't help it. She knew most people would have been revelling in Joe's bad karma, but whatever had happened between them she would always care about him. He had been her first love, and the intensity of their relationship had burned a mark on her heart – something indelible, a little like a tattoo. She looked in his cottage window but there was nothing to see; no flying crockery or flailing arms. It was all quiet. Perhaps they were making up, she wondered, and a renewed sadness lay heavy on her.

'You're a good person, Lottie,' said Zach. 'Nana would be proud of what you've done this Christmas.' Lottie shot him a doubtful look. 'Your trouble is you're too hard on yourself. You focus on the stuff that isn't perfect and forget to celebrate all the brilliant little things that are.'

She knew he was right. She watched her mother hanging on to Scott's arm as they walked. She knew why she was the way she was. Constantly striving for her mother's approval, which would most likely never come. It was difficult to focus on the good stuff when the not-so-good things were constantly being pointed out to you. 'I'll make it my New Year's resolution,' she said.

'Good,' said Zach. 'Now, what's for tea? It's not ham sandwiches again is it?' She gave his arm a slap.

'It's the bread you made and the cakes that Jessie made. So if it's no good, it's definitely not my fault.'

Zach gave his sister a one-armed hug.

Everyone abandoned their snowy footwear and many outer layers in the hallway then descended on the drawing room. Lottie left Zach to prepare a fire while she went to put the kettle on for the inevitable round of teas and coffees. As she walked into the kitchen, her eye was drawn to the checked tea towel she had carefully placed over the warm cakes before they had gone out. Though it wasn't so much the tea towel that attracted her attention, but rather the large furry cat who was now curled up asleep on top of it.

'Duchess!' said Lottie, her tone sharp. The cat opened one eye and stretched, pointing her toes and baring her claws as she did so. 'Get off the cakes!' Initially the cat didn't move, eyeing Lottie from her warm bed with disdain, so Lottie gave her ample rump a gentle prod. The Duchess reluctantly got to her feet and, seeming to sense that Lottie was not best pleased, she jumped down and slunk out of the kitchen.

Lottie noted the large, cat-shaped dip in the tea towel and feared the worst. She tentatively lifted the fabric and her suspicions were confirmed. The once-pointy little cakes underneath were now squashed flat, some of them reduced to crumbs.

'Hmm,' said Lottie. 'Trifle for tea then.' She managed to rescue three cakes for Scott, which had been on the outer fringes and missed the full weight of the Duchess, and she put those to one side. The rest went into a large bowl and she covered them with raspberry jelly. She stuck the containers in the freezer and hoped a couple of hours would be enough time for the jelly to set.

Lottie brought drinks into the drawing room, handed them round and flopped down on the sofa. *Back to the Future* was on the telly and everyone was quiet. Jessie and Dave were sitting underneath the Christmas tree having a cuddle.

'Are you okay under there?' asked Lottie.

Jessie's face peeped through the branches. 'I don't think it's working any more now that Christmas is over.'

'What's not working, sweetie?' asked Lottie, cupping her mug with both hands.

'The magic tree,' said Jessie, lifting her head to look up through its branches.

Lottie smiled. 'You're probably right. Maybe next year it will work again.'

Jessie shuffled out from under the tree and curled up on the sofa next to Lottie. She looked furtively around and then beckoned Lottie to lean down to her level. Jessie whispered in her ear, 'I was hoping to get a necklace to match.'

Lottie tried to make sense of the sentence. 'To match what, Jessie?' she asked, keeping her voice low.

'The ring it gave me on Christmas Eve,' said Jessie, tilting her head towards the tree.

Lottie spun around so fast she slopped her tea in her lap. She whispered in Jessie's ear. 'A ring?'

Jessie nodded. 'It's very shiny.' *I bet it is*, thought Lottie.

Zach and Emily were both watching the film, although Zach looked like he was about to nod off. 'Have you still got it, Jess?' asked Lottie, excitement tickling her insides. Jessie nodded. 'Where?'

'Somewhere safe.' Jessie was wearing her most serious expression.

'Okay. Will you show it to me, please? I'd love to see it.'

Jessie seemed to ponder this. 'Okay.'

'And can Daddy see it too?'

'I don't think he'd be interested. He's not a girl,' said Jessie emphatically, as she slid from the sofa and walked to the door with Dave at her heels. Lottie put down her mug, tapped Zach on the arm and indicated with her thumb that he needed to follow them. With exaggerated eye rolls he followed them out of the room and upstairs.

'What's the matter?' asked Zach, with a yawn.

'Jessie might just have solved one of your problems,' said Lottie.

* * *

347

In their bedroom, Jessie went to her camp bed and knelt down whilst Dave had a good sniff about. Jessie put her hand in her pillowcase, had a little rummage around, pulled out her hand and held up a diamond ring. The light caught it just at that moment making it sparkle like a star.

'Bloody he . . . Where did you find that?' asked Zach, attempting to snatch it from Jessie's fingers. Jessie pulled her hand away quickly and the ring pinged out of her grasp and sailed into the air. They all watched it spin, fall, bounce on the carpet and land between Dave's front paws.

'Noooo!' yelled Zach, making a dive for the ring as Dave bent his head towards it.

Zach landed half on the camp bed, sending it toppling over on top of him, but, as it did so, he managed to close his hands around the ring and roll over like a cricketer taking a crucial catch. He grinned up at Lottie and a confused-looking Dave and Jessie. 'I got it,' he said from underneath the camp bed.

'Brilliant,' said Lottie, lowering her voice. 'I have an idea for your proposal – and it might just work.'

Chapter Thirty-Six

A taxi pulled into the snowy driveway and crept up to the house. Lottie saw its headlights from an upstairs window so she was waiting at the front door by the time its doors opened. Dayea stepped out, paid the driver and scurried inside.

'Is everything okay?' asked Lottie, trying to read Dayea's face.

'Yes, yes,' said Dayea. 'My Bernard is getting better.' Lottie was relieved. She shut the door behind Dayea as she stamped her feet to remove the snow. 'I needed my car,' she said, pointing over her shoulder.

'But you'll have a cup of tea first and update us, won't you?' asked Lottie.

Dayea checked her watch. 'I do not have long. I don't want to miss visiting.'

'Of course.'

'Hello,' said an overly jolly Zach as he strode through the hallway brandishing a toolbox. 'I've got a trellis to fix,' he added and Dayea gave him a puzzled look. It wasn't an obvious job to be doing at dusk in December.

'Here,' said Lottie, handing him a large cardboard box. 'You'll need to check them all first.'

'Got it,' he said, taking the box from Lottie and disappearing.

Dayea was frowning after him. 'Don't worry about him,' said Lottie. 'You warm up by the fire and I'll bring you a drink.'

Dayea shook her head. 'Bernard needs some more of his things,' she said. She went upstairs and Lottie went to make yet more drinks.

After a few minutes Dayea joined Lottie in the kitchen and plonked down Bernard's old case.

Lottie nodded at the case. 'Just a few things?' she said, passing Dayea her drink and offering her a biscuit.

'He does not want to come back here. He calls it . . .' She squinted with thought and Lottie wondered what she was about to say. 'Time for new start.'

Lottie was relieved. 'Yes, I think that's very wise.'

'Bernard is worried about Duchess.'

'Oh, she's fine,' said Lottie, glancing around the kitchen. She hadn't seen her since the cake squashing incident, but she expected she was about somewhere. She was touched that in Bernard's current state he was thinking about Nana's cat.

'Bernard worries they'll give her to a cat rescue.'

Lottie involuntarily drew in a deep breath. It hadn't crossed her mind but Bernard was probably right. Neither Daniel or Angie were known for their caring sides. It wasn't just Bernard and Lottie who were about to be made homeless. 'I'll look after her, Dayea. Please tell Bernard not to worry.' Lottie wasn't sure how because she had nowhere to go either. But she wouldn't see the poor cat dumped in a rescue centre. And anyway, Lottie was fond of cats. She admired their egocentricity. She wished she could be just a little bit like the Duchess and occasionally put herself before everyone else. And at least when she was talking to the cat she didn't appear quite as crazy as she would if she was talking entirely to herself.

'Or Duchess could come live with us.' Dayea peeped over her mug.

'Oh,' said Lottie. 'Well I'm sure she'd love that too.'

Dayea beamed. 'I can take her now. Then she be there to welcome Bernard.' It appeared she had thought this through.

'Um.' It all felt too quick to Lottie. 'I'm not sure where she is.' *And I don't want to be completely on my own when everyone departs tomorrow morning*, thought Lottie, feeling a bit selfish. 'How about you get Bernard settled first, then I'll bring her over?'

'If you think that is best.' Dayea looked disappointed. Lottie wasn't entirely sure how two people and a cat in one tiny caravan would fit, anyway.

Lottie mulled over whether to ask the question that was worrying her. Dayea sipped her tea. 'Look, Dayea, I don't mean to be rude, but—'

'But you worry about your uncle. Yes?'

'Great uncle,' corrected Lottie. 'But yes. Nana made a lot of alterations here to help Bernard, like the stair lift,' not that they'd need one of those in the caravan, ' the grab rails and a shower with a seat in it. And I know that all cost a lot of money.' The motorised scooter was the most expensive thing, and Lottie was absolutely sure there was no way that would fit in the caravan.

Dayea stared at her for a moment. She started to chuckle. 'It really is okay, Lottie. Money is not a problem.'

'Nana didn't leave him much, and he only has his state

pension.' Lottie knew Dayea genuinely loved Bernard, but she didn't want her to be under any false illusion about how much money Bernard had.

'I know,' she said. She sipped her tea and continued to study Lottie. 'I trust you, so I will tell you.' Dayea put down her mug, her expression intense. 'My father, he had a hotel business in the Philippines. Lots and lots of hotels. He worked hard, but it did not make him happy. I worked for him for a long time, but when he found out he was dying, he told me to travel. To not marry the company like him. You understand?'

'I think so,' said Lottie, wondering about Dayea's previous life in the corporate world. It seemed at odds with the person she'd grown to know.

'When he died, my sisters and me, we sold the hotels to a big American company and made lots of money. I travelled the world like I promised my father. But I get bored. I found I liked caring for old people. In my country old people are very special. In your country they are not cherished as they should be. I have a number of jobs with the elderly here and I find this is what makes me happy. This is the job I should be doing.'

'So money's not a problem?' She was dying to ask why Dayea was living in a caravan.

'Not at all. I am having my house altered now, making big changes to make it easy for Bernard. That is why I live in the caravan. It's too dusty in the house.'

'The big house is yours?' Dayea nodded.

Lottie couldn't hide her grin. She was reassured her great uncle would have everything he needed, and she was also pleased that her mother had been so wrong about Dayea being a gold-digger. 'I have to say it's a big relief to know you can cope financially.'

'But it's only money. It does not buy you people who care.' Dayea gently patted Lottie's hand.

'Very true.' And yet the pursuit of money was what drove most people; well, certainly most of her family.

'I need to go.' Dayea stood up. 'You like my house?' she asked Lottie.

'I do. It's lovely.' She picked up the heavy case and followed Dayea into the hall. They could hear raised voices coming from the snug and they shrugged their shoulders simultaneously.

'You want to come live with me, Bernard and Duchess?' asked Dayea. Lottie was taken aback.

'That's really sweet of you, Dayea. Thank you. I've got a lot of decisions to make. Please can I think about it?'

'You are welcome, any time,' said Dayea, taking the case from her. 'Bernard says, "Button is the best of the lot".'

'Thank you. Give Bernard my love. I'll visit him tomorrow.'

'And bring Duchess?'

'Um . . . okay,' said Lottie, a little reluctantly. And she waved Dayea off.

Lottie entered the snug and World War Three was in full swing. The tension bubbling between Nicola and Daniel had erupted, volcano-style.

'You don't care about Rhys or you'd never have got involved with that slut.' Aunt Nicola's whole body was shaking.

'It was before he was even b—' Daniel halted when he spotted Lottie hovering in the doorway.

Nicola looked like she was fighting back tears, and Daniel was as cross as she'd ever seen him. They were hurting each other, and it was a hard thing to witness. Truth was, they'd been hurting each other for years. Was this what happened to relationships when the initial excitement faded? Did couples just chip away at each other until all that was left was hurt and resentment, lies and regrets? Or was she just feeling particularly negative today?

They were both staring at Lottie so she couldn't just sneak away. 'I'm sorry to interrupt. I'm looking for the Duchess.' She knew it sounded lame, but it was true; now the cat was going to have a new home, Lottie wanted to spend a bit of time with her before she moved on. She also had a niggling worry that the Duchess wasn't herself; she perhaps needed to get their usual vet to check her over before she went. She really didn't want to have to see Joe.

'No. We're sorry,' said Daniel. 'You shouldn't have to witness this.'

'At least we're communicating,' said Nicola, her expression grim.

'This isn't communicating.' Daniel looked sad. 'I can't keep saying I'm sorry.'

Nicola pulled her eyes from Daniel to address Lottie. 'I haven't seen the cat,' said Nicola, pulling a tissue from her pocket. 'Have you seen Rhys?'

'Erm. Yeah he's in the rockery with the metal detector. He's fired up from finding the coins.'

Daniel's pained expression changed to one of interest. 'In the dark? He must be keen! I've been having a look on eBay and some of those coins are going for quite a bit. We might have a few hundred quid there. But Nicola is guarding them – she won't let me tip them all out of the pot.'

'Because the coins and the pot are delicate. We don't want some sausage-fingered *amateur* damaging ancient history in the hope of making a few quid.'

'Oh, forget it,' said Daniel with a resigned sigh.

'The coins might be an important find,' said Nicola, focusing back on Lottie. 'This could be something credited to Rhys. He could produce a paper on it. It might provide an area of research into Roman life in the Cotswolds. Perhaps it could feed a PhD.'

Daniel looked exasperated. 'How many times, Nicola? Rhys has dropped out of university. There is no more archaeology degree. It's over. Face it. Please, not only for his sake, but for your own.'

Nicola swallowed hard but said nothing.

'Look, about Rhys and uni.' Lottie came into the room fully and shut the door. 'He had mentioned something about working in car sales,' Nicola gasped as if she'd just said Rhys had joined Scott in the porn industry, 'but I thought it was a part-time job he was fitting around his studies. I don't want you thinking I'd encouraged him to drop out or helped him deceive you.'

'I think the deception is hereditary,' said Nicola, her glare resting on Daniel.

'For heaven's sake, Nicola. You don't have to take every opportunity to remind everyone that I cheated – least of all me. Okay. Yes, it happened. It was a mistake. But I have an opportunity to get to know a daughter I didn't know existed, and if you would stop shouting at me for just one second, maybe you could be a part of that? Or maybe this is the thing that finishes us.'

Daniel made to stride past her and Nicola grabbed his arm, halting his progress. Her complexion had faded to deathly pale. 'I love you.'

Nicola's words hung in the air. Daniel turned slowly to look at her.

'I'll look for the cat later,' whispered Lottie, and she quickly exited the room and left them to it.

By the evening, everyone was settled in the drawing room. Angie and Scott were cosied up together, and even Nicola and Daniel appeared to be back on speaking terms. Emily felt like she'd been babysitting Jessie all day. Not that she minded – because she didn't – but when she was trying to grab a few minutes alone with Zach it did make things tricky. Emily loved Jessie. She felt the little girl brought out the best in her. Maybe all children did that, she wasn't sure, but she knew she enjoyed Jessie's company – she had a pure way of looking at things and taking pleasure in the simplest of tasks. It was also a great excuse to act like a child and because of Jessie she had rediscovered her love of board games and custard creams. She'd not spoken to Zach since the walk back from the pub, where he'd been quietly miserable. His moods were unsettling her.

Emily had to admit the whole pregnancy question was also a lot to do with her unsettled state. She had been hoping for an opportunity to take Zach aside so she could explain her predicament and they could do the test together, but he'd been missing for a couple of hours now. Perhaps she needed to find out for herself, she pondered. Otherwise she was building something up that might be nothing. She openly sighed. She was rubbish at making decisions.

Jessie was trying to blow up modelling balloons. Emily knew balloons and children were a hazard, so she didn't want to leave her.

'Angie? I'm just popping to the loo. Can you keep an eye on Jessie please?' she asked.

'Oh, she's fine,' said Angie, without even checking where the child was. Angie was busy playing with Scott's hair.

'But . . .'

'You are such a worrier,' said Angie, appraising Emily from top to toe. 'Children are quite robust. You don't need to mollycoddle them all the time. They learn from getting into scrapes.'

'Like when Zach wanted to slide down the banister and you told him to polish it first and he broke his arm?' said Daniel, with a snort.

'Exactly,' said Angie, returning her attention to Scott. They were grooming each other like oversexed baboons.

'And when Jessie got locked in the cupboard last Christmas? That was you too,' said Nicola.

'How many times?' snapped Angie. 'We were playing escape rooms.'

Emily faltered. She was foiled again. She couldn't leave Jessie with Angie, given her wildly inappropriate parenting style.

'It's okay. I'll play with her,' said Rhys, getting up and moving next to Jessie.

'Perhaps you could do babysitting as your next career move,' said Nicola. 'You don't need a degree for that.'

'Leave it, Nicola,' said Daniel. 'We've been over it a million times. He needs space to make his own mistakes.'

Nicola opened her mouth and seemed to pause before speaking. 'Perhaps you're right.' Daniel patted Nicola's thigh as if congratulating her on her restraint.

Emily turned to Rhys. 'Thank you,' she said.

The door opened and Zach popped his head in. 'Jessie, do you want to give me a hand with something in the garden?' he asked.

'Yeah,' said Jessie, throwing the balloon at Emily and

racing to her father. Zach gave Emily a warm smile before closing the door. Now she had no excuse. She steeled herself, clutched her bag to her and left the room.

At last she was in a toilet on her own. No backing out this time, she told herself. No more excuses, no more changing her mind or convincing herself that it was better to do the test with Zach, no seeking out Lottie as a hand to hold. She needed to take responsibility and do this on her own. She actually felt quite calm. She'd spent most of Christmas Eve in a blind panic. On Christmas Day she'd built herself up to do it and then it had all gone horribly wrong. Throughout Boxing Day she'd gone over so many scenarios her brain was porridge. But today it seemed like the right thing to do. She just needed to do the test properly, and not drop the ruddy thing down the loo.

Emily read the instructions carefully – and then reread them for good measure. It was all very straightforward. In a few minutes she'd know for sure if she was having a baby or not. A wave of something rippled through her – but it was hard to tell whether it was excitement or fear.

'Here we go then,' she whispered encouragingly to herself as she held the tester stick in position and waited. Emily wondered why it was so hard to summon a wee. She'd been drinking juice and water all day, so there was definitely something in there. She closed her eyes and concentrated, and a little trickle escaped.

The deed was done. All she had to do now was wait.

Chapter Thirty-Seven

Lottie was ferrying what she hoped was the last meal she'd be serving this Christmas to the dining room when Emily came downstairs.

'Have you seen the Duchess?' Lottie asked Emily. 'I've not seen her since I shooed her off the cakes, and she always shows up for her dinner. I've just checked and she's not eaten anything today.' Emily shook her head slowly, her face pale and expressionless. Lottie halted. 'What's wrong?'

Emily seemed to be considering her response. She opened her mouth, but quickly closed it again as the kitchen door opened.

'Excellent,' said Zach, rubbing his hands together as he strode into the hallway. 'I'm starving.'

'After what you ate at lunchtime?' said Emily, slapping on a brave face.

'I've been . . . fixing stuff in the garden.'

'Not much point if the place is sold,' said Uncle Daniel, walking past and taking the trifle Lottie was clutching.

'Wash your hands,' said Lottie to Zach.

'You sound like Nana,' he said. 'She was a tyrant too.' He placed a kiss on Emily's cheek and went into the cloakroom.

'What's up?' Lottie asked Emily, but before she could

answer Jessie had popped up in between them. She was bouncing on her heels as if she had springs under her shoes, clearly excited about her secret mission with Zach in the garden.

'Have you seen Dave?' she asked.

'No,' said Lottie. 'Have you seen the Duchess?' Jessie shook her head. 'Then I think we might have a problem.'

'Come on,' said Zach, returning. 'Teatime.' He ushered Jessie into the dining room and the others followed.

'I guess we can look for the animals after tea,' said Lottie, but nobody was really listening.

This was likely their last meal together. Uncle Daniel was due back at work so he was aiming for a very early getaway in the morning, Scott had been talking about booking a taxi to the station for eight o'clock and Zach was planning to leave after breakfast. Lottie would be all alone by mid-morning. She gave herself a talking to. Being alone was a good thing. She had lots to sort out – not least of all her future – and a whole house to pack up. She'd done what she set out to achieve – one last family Christmas together. Now she needed to focus on what *she* needed to do. She'd give herself until New Year's Day to work out a plan, and during that time she'd also make a concerted effort to finish off the tubs of Christmas sweets. Well, it would be rude not to.

Zach helped himself to a large scoop of trifle and pulled her back to the moment. He was looking ridiculously pleased with himself, and she loved him for it. She made a silent pact with herself to see more of her brother in the new year, wherever life was planning on taking her. Zach was who she was closest to in the family, and now she'd made a friend in Emily she needed to make an effort to be more present in their lives.

Jessie was bobbing in her seat with unbridled excitement. She and her father were exchanging winks and
knowing looks like they had some sort of hereditary facial
tic. Jessie was thoroughly enjoying being a part of the
secret. Lottie was a firm believer in things happening for
a reason, and without the earlier failed attempts Jessie
wouldn't have had the opportunity to be involved with
the proposal. It was lovely to see her pleased about the
prospect of Emily joining the family. Lottie really hoped
Emily was going to accept when Zach proposed. Regardless
of whether she was pregnant or not, those two needed to
be together.

Lottie smiled as she looked across at Emily, who was
looking pale and solemn. Unease swept over her and her
face fell. She wanted Emily to look up, but she was staring
intently at her plate. With a heavy heart, Lottie realised
what must have happened. She knew that feeling too well.
There was no baby. She had an overwhelming urge to
scoop Emily up. Lottie had been there herself and she
knew only too well what she was going through. Pain
spiked in her gut – she didn't fancy the trifle any more.
At least, unlike Lottie, Emily wouldn't have to go through
it alone.

Lottie hurriedly cleared the table in the hope of grabbing
a few minutes to console Emily, but Jessie, under her
father's instructions, had already steered her upstairs on
a wild goose chase looking for dice. Lottie put her head
outside – maybe she should warn Zach. It was dark. The
sky was a deep sea blue and a perfect scattering of stars
were already twinkling in celebration.

'Problem!' yelled Zach, running up the garden.
'What?'

'Some of the lights have failed. It currently says "ILL YO MA ME".'

'Bugger.'

'Come on. Think. Quick. I need more lights!' said Zach, panicking wildly.

Lottie tried to think. 'Banister!'

'Already got them.' Zach was waving his arms as if trying to speed up Lottie's brain.

'Christmas tree on the green?'

'Genius!' He dashed across the garden.

'What's going on?' Lottie spun around to see Emily standing in the doorway with a vexed expression. 'Is he leaving?'

'No. No he's not.' Lottie swallowed, she'd never felt so guilty. Emily raised an eyebrow. 'Well, he's leaving the manor.' Emily looked startled. 'Only for like five minutes. He needs to . . .' She'd always thought she was good at thinking on her feet until now. 'He needs to check the roads are okay.'

'But a taxi brought Dayea up earlier, and more has melted since then.' She pointed back inside. 'And Daniel has been giving everyone motorway updates all day.'

'Yes. But the hill can be extra tricky. It gets very icy.' She emphasised the word by sweeping her hands off to one side.

'Are you all right?' asked Emily. Lottie was aware that she was acting like a crackpot. Poor Emily.

'Can I get you a drink of something?' Lottie put her foot on the step and Emily automatically retreated into the kitchen. Lottie followed her.

'I'm okay. Thanks.' Emily didn't look okay.

Lottie remembered her expression earlier. 'Are you sure? Because . . .' Emily started to cry, and Lottie took her hand. She began to speak, but Lottie stopped her. 'It's going to be okay. I promise.' Lottie wrapped her arms around Emily and they cried together.

A few minutes passed before Lottie's phone pinged. She pulled away from Emily, tore off a few sheets of kitchen roll and handed half to her new friend.

'Ta.'

Lottie looked at the text message.

Lights working. Get everyone outside. Z

Lottie looked at Emily, all blotchy eyed and defeated. She texted a reply.

Sorry. Now is not the time.

Within seconds the back door burst open, making them jump. Zach had a touch of the crazy person about him as he scanned the scene. Both women were dabbing their eyes with balled-up kitchen roll. He crouched next to Emily. 'Whatever's wrong?' he asked, his face full of concern.

Emily's lip wobbled. She hiccupped a few more tears. 'I'm pregnant.'

Zach pulled Emily to her feet and hugged her like she was a life buoy and he a drowning man. 'This is the best news ever!' he declared, pulling back from the hug to kiss her. ' . . . isn't it?' he asked. Tears streamed down Emily's face. You could have knocked Lottie over with the tiniest feather. She'd spectacularly misread Emily's emotions. Although she was still concerned about how unhappy Emily was at finding out she was having a baby.

'Are you going to dump me?' asked Emily with a sniff, and Lottie passed her more kitchen roll.

'What? No! Don't be ridiculous! I love you,' said Zach. 'But you've been acting all weird. And I know Jessie was telling the truth when she said you told Joe you didn't want me to be your girlfriend any more.'

'Ah.' Zach pulled his bottom lip through his teeth. 'I'm really sorry about that.'

'Maybe *now* is a good time,' said Lottie, and she went to gather the rest of the family. Reluctantly they assembled in the kitchen.

Jessie ran in and gave Emily a hug. 'It's okay. I promise.' Her cheeks were aglow, and it brought a smile to Emily's tear-stained face.

'Come outside in exactly one minute,' said Zach, kissing Emily's hand and dashing outside with Jessie hot on his heels.

After the required minute, Lottie led Emily outside and down the garden, with the rest of the family traipsing behind. Zach was standing on the patio and hastily ran his fingers through his hair to calm it slightly. It was darker away from the house, but the shape of Jessie bouncing about at the bottom of the garden was just visible.

'Now!' yelled Zach, as he dropped onto one knee in front of Emily.

At the end of the garden the trellis lit up. The words 'WILL YOU MARRY ME?' appeared, a little wobbly but clearly visible in multicoloured fairy lights.

Emily gasped. She turned to Zach. He held up the ring. 'I love you, Emily—'

'I love you too, Emily!' shouted Jessie, from the bottom of the garden.

'Will you make me – us – the happiest people alive and be my wife?'

'Yes,' said Emily through a splutter of tears, and Lottie tore another sheet off the kitchen roll and passed it to her.

After a few seconds the fairy lights began to flash manically like they were on the 'acid house' setting. 'Daddy!' shouted Jessie. 'What did she say?'

'Come here and find out,' called Lottie, tearing off a sheet of kitchen roll for herself.

There were more tears and lots of hugs and kisses of congratulations. Angie was sent to retrieve the champagne that Emily had hidden away at the back of the fridge earlier and everyone went inside to warm up, leaving the newly engaged couple to have a moment on their own.

'It's a shame Dave missed it,' muttered Jessie, as Lottie guided her inside and shut the door.

Chapter Thirty-Eight

'Whoa,' said Emily, letting out a breath. Her head was swimming from all the tears. It felt like a lot was happening all at once. She was overwhelmed by the pregnancy and surprised about the engagement. But above all, she was happy. She looked at the ring on her finger. It was beautiful – just what she would have chosen. 'I wasn't expecting that.'

'And *I* wasn't expecting *that*,' said Zach, pointing at her stomach.

Emily felt herself tense. 'Is that why you asked me to marry you? Did Lottie already tell you?'

'I knew I wanted to marry you months ago, I was just waiting for the perfect moment. And I've known you were pregnant for . . .' he checked his watch, 'nine minutes, and they've been some of the best minutes of my life.' He pulled her into a kiss and she felt the tension disperse. Zach paused and leaned back to look at her. 'Did my sister know before me?'

'I didn't actually tell her, but I think she guessed. She did kind of know that I might be. Sorry.'

'It's okay. How did she know that you might be pregnant?' He was looking puzzled.

Emily's brain rewound back to when she first entered the village stores, and all the failed test attempts since, and it made her chuckle. 'It's a very long story. When did you decide to propose like this?' They both looked at the manically flashing fairy lights at the bottom of the garden.

'That's a long story too.' He kissed her again, this time taking it slow and making all her worries melt away.

Inside, the excitement was palpable. Lottie was hugely relieved that everything was finally out in the open. She hated keeping secrets. They were the rot that kills the soul, Nana had always said.

Champagne flutes were filled, and Lottie had to stop everyone quaffing it before Zach and Emily came back in. Daniel pulled Nicola and Rhys to one side. Lottie had her back to them, and next to her her mother was gushing about an even better proposal she'd read about in a magazine. Lottie tuned out from her mother, something she was well practised at, and tuned in to Daniel.

'I've been thinking about our situation. And before you say anything, Nicola; yes, I created it, and yes, I am sorry. But now I feel I need to do what's best for everyone. Including me. I can't spend the rest of my life feeling guilty and being berated for a mistake I made twenty years ago. So we either need to find a way to move on from this, or . . . not. I don't want to move out, but if you want me to, Nicola, then I will.' Nicola gave a tiny gasp. 'Before you jump to conclusions, if I move out I'll be living on my own. Rhys, you can see me whenever you want to and the same goes for Rebecca . . . if she wants to.'

'And me?' said Nicola. 'What about what I want?'

'It's entirely up to you what you want, Nicola. I'm too tired to argue any more.'

There was a long pause. Lottie realised she was holding her breath.

'I wish it hadn't happened. But I don't want this to be the end of us.'

'I'm not divorcing you, Nicola, unless that's what you want. I'm not saying it's the end. But I *am* saying we need to be kinder to each other, and ourselves.'

Silence followed, and Lottie fought the urge to turn around and see what was happening.

'You're right,' said Nicola.

'Blimey, that's a first,' said Daniel with a snort.

'I think with Rhys at university my hobby has become nagging you. And I'm sorry, Daniel.'

'It's okay.'

'And I think you should make an effort with Rebecca. She's missed out on so much. Including all the big family Christmases.'

'I thought you hated these,' said Rhys.

'I never said that,' said Nicola, her tone light. 'This year, when I thought our little family was crumbling, I finally understood what Rose had been trying to do. She was just keeping everyone together. And that's what I want too . . . including Rebecca.'

'Well done, Mum,' said Rhys. Lottie heard some kissing and backslapping take place.

'Where's Dave?' asked Jessie, appearing from under the kitchen table. 'I've looked everywhere.'

She had a good point. Lottie hadn't seen either of the animals for hours. 'The Duchess is missing too. I think they must be in the house somewhere. Come on, let's you and I go and look for them.' Lottie turned to the others. 'No drinking the fizz until Zach and Emily come in.' She wagged a finger at them all.

Lottie and Jessie started their hunt on the ground floor and searched everywhere thoroughly before moving upstairs. They methodically checked all rooms until the only one left was Nana's. The door was ajar. Lottie hadn't been in there since the morning. She pushed the door further open and crept inside. Jessie clutched her hand. 'I'm scared,' whispered Jessie.

'Why?' asked Lottie, her voice a whisper too.

'What if they've eaten each other?'

Lottie stifled a giggle. 'I think we would have heard that.' Lottie was more worried that they'd run off, or worse still, were seriously ill.

Jessie pointed at the wardrobe. It was open. Lottie knew she hadn't left it like that. They inched closer and Lottie pulled the door open a little more. A low grumble of a growl came from inside the wardrobe. Lottie's fears multiplied; a picture of a rabid Dave loomed large in her mind.

'Dave?' said Jessie.

Lottie stepped in front of Jessie and moved Nana's best coat to one side. At the bottom of the wardrobe, lying on Nana's cashmere cardigan, was the Duchess. Dave was standing guard over her. His tail was wagging, at odds with the murmured growl he was emitting. Lottie peered past the dog to get a look at the Duchess. She couldn't see any blood, which was a good sign, but she knew instinctively something was wrong. The Duchess was panting hard and her body was making strange convulsions like a snake swallowing its prey.

'What's wrong with her?' asked Jessie, peering around the side of Lottie.

'I'm not sure. And I don't know if Dave is going to let us help her. Let me call the vet.' As soon as she'd said the words an icy chill ran through her. Their usual vet was miles away in Stow, he would take too long to get to them.

She didn't want to speak to Joe. But she looked at the Duchess lying there, clearly in distress, and knew she had no option. She dialled his number.

'Lottie?' Was that optimism in his voice?

'Joe. I'm calling you because I need a vet. The Duchess is sick. Can you come?'

'On my way,' he said. She heard another voice in the background. 'Hang on, Lottie.' She suspected that he meant to cover the phone but he didn't do a great job. 'Yes, it's her, and no, I don't know how long I'll be . . . Fine . . . It's Henbourne, it doesn't matter.' She heard a door slam. She longed to know what was going on. Joe's voice interrupted her thoughts. 'Is the cat breathing, Lottie?'

Lottie crouched down. Dave's head followed her. 'She's panting.'

'Does she feel hot?'

'I can't exactly touch her. I don't think Dave will let me.'

'Okay. I'm in the car. Keep her comfortable. I'll be there in two minutes.'

They went downstairs and Jessie joined the others, who were now trying to share Zach's proposal on the internet via Scott's phone. This was proving tricky as there was no WiFi and only a dodgy signal, but it was taking Jessie's mind off the animal crisis.

Lottie was waiting on the steps for Joe. It was bitterly cold. The temperature had dropped again. Lottie hoped there wouldn't be any more snow. She looked up at the stars in the clear sky. She heard the crunch of the Land Rover's wheels on the ice as it turned into the drive. He pulled up right outside and jumped out.

'Hiya,' called Joe as he crunched his way towards the house carrying his veterinary case.

'Hi.' This was beyond awkward.

'I'd forgotten how much fun snow was,' he said, taking off his wellies and hopping around the puddle they'd left.

'Fun?' questioned Lottie, trying to keep her shivering under control by wrapping her arms around herself.

'Yeah. You don't get this in Florida. Where is she?'

'Nana's wardrobe,' said Lottie. Joe took the stairs two at a time.

Lottie hung back, leaning in the bedroom doorway, and let Joe deal with the situation.

'Hey, boy. What's the problem? Is she sick?' Joe asked Dave. The little dog's tail flicked about and then went still. 'I need you to move just a fraction so I can get a good look at her. Okay?' Joe held his fingers in front of Dave and he sniffed them. 'Good boy.' Joe reached his other hand around the dog to touch the Duchess. Dave watched him closely. 'See? I'm not going to hurt her.'

Dave licked his outstretched fingers and Joe gave him a scratch round his ears. 'Lottie, he's fine. Can you come and take him?'

Lottie wasn't sure but she'd try. She was toying with the idea of being an artist of some sort, so she'd need all her fingers. She copied Joe and showed Dave her fingers, but she put forward her left hand just in case things turned nasty. She knelt on the floor and tried to encourage the dog to come to her. Dave was distracted enough to move out of the way and let Joe get to work. Lottie gave Dave some fuss and watched in awe as Joe checked the Duchess over and listened through a stethoscope. Then he inserted a thermometer up the cat's rear end and the cat didn't object at all.

Lottie feared the worst. Sadness pulled her down. She loved the Duchess. She knew it was silly, but it felt like a final piece of Nana was slipping away from her. What would she tell Bernard and Dayea? They were expecting the cat to move in with them tomorrow. She concentrated on cuddling Dave as they both watched intently.

Joe turned around with a silly grin spread across his face. *How can he be smiling?* thought Lottie.

'She's having kittens,' he said.

'So am I!' said Lottie, before what he actually meant registered. 'She's pregnant?'

Joe nodded. 'I can feel at least two kittens – or it could be one mutant one with lots of legs.' The humour was lost on Lottie; she was just hugely relieved that the Duchess wasn't dying. The relief only lasted for a moment before she realised she was going to have more cats to rehome.

'How long has she been like this?' he asked.

Lottie shrugged. 'I don't know.'

'I think she's fine, but we'll sit with her just to be on the safe side.' He sat down and Dave went to him. 'You knew, didn't you, boy?'

'You think?' Lottie didn't credit Dave with that much intelligence.

'Definitely. He's been desperate to get to her ever since he turned up. I bet he could sense what was going on. Animals have senses we can't begin to understand.'

'So the whole chasing thing was because he wanted to protect her?'

'Most likely. You secretly love her, don't you, boy?' Joe scratched Dave's head and the dog's tongue lolled out of the side of his mouth.

Lottie didn't like being this close to Joe. 'Can I get you a coffee?' She got to her feet.

'No, I'm fine. Lottie, about earlier—'

She cut him off. 'I need to update everyone else. Jessie has been really worried.'

He looked sombre. 'Okay.' He turned back to the cat as Dave settled down next to him. Lottie knew they needed to talk, but it wouldn't change anything, so there really was no rush.

Chapter Thirty-Nine

Back downstairs, the kitten news was received with joy and more rounds of champagne. But as much as Lottie wanted to stay away from Joe, she couldn't keep away from the Duchess for too long. She knew the cat was in good hands, but she felt she should be there too as moral support.

'Emily?' Lottie beckoned her to the hallway. Emily was standing wrapped in Zach's arms staring at her engagement ring. She disentangled herself and joined Lottie. 'Sorry to drag you away, but it's a bit awkward upstairs with just me and Joe.'

'You want me to play gooseberry?' Emily gave a cheeky grin.

Lottie tilted her head to one side. 'Not exactly. But it might be nice to have someone to stop me from strangling him with his own stethoscope.'

Emily's grin disappeared. 'Or I could at least be a witness,' she suggested. 'Lead on.'

'Actually,' said Lottie, biting her lip, 'the thing with Melissa.'

'Go on,' said Emily hanging on her every word.

'I really don't want you thinking she was perfect, but

I'm about to tell you something even Zach doesn't know. You see—'

'What don't I know?' asked Zach, stepping out of the kitchen.

Bugger, thought Lottie. There was no going back now. 'Look. I'm really sorry, and I don't want to upset your engagement and everything, but there's a secret I've been keeping about Melissa and it's eating me up.'

'Lottie, it's fine. Just tell me,' said Zach, squeezing her arm and giving her the confidence to open up.

'You know Melissa was a workaholic, right?' began Lottie.

'No,' said Emily, her head swivelling between the two of them.

'Maybe not a workaholic but work was important to her,' said Zach.

'Anyway,' continued Lottie. 'She was offered this massive promotion, but the job was in Austria and . . . well . . .' Emily and Zach were watching her closely. 'She'd accepted the job. So she was going to be living part of the time in Austria. Away from you and Jessie. The day she died, she was going to sign the paperwork. I told her she should tell you,' Lottie pointed at her brother, 'but she was adamant that you'd try and talk her out of it. All the times you said you couldn't understand why she was driving to London when the accident happened. That was why. But I couldn't say because then I'd have to explain about Austria. I'm so sorry.'

'Oh Lottie,' Zach pulled her into a hug. 'You daft thing. I knew about the promotion.'

'What?' Lottie snapped her head back.

'Not when she died, not then. But a few weeks later her boss brought the contents of her desk home.' He swallowed

375

hard. 'She said something about the Austria job then because she assumed I knew.'

'So Melissa put her career before her family?' ventured Emily.

'She did on this one occasion, but that doesn't make her a bad person,' said Zach. 'She was right to think I would have tried to talk her out of it because I would have done. Jess was still a baby and the timing wasn't great. But I would never have stopped her from following her dreams.' He turned to Emily. 'Just like I'll never stop you.' Emily gave him a hug.

Lottie blew her nose. 'I've been fretting over that for five years and you bloody well knew?' She gave him a whack on the arm. 'You could have said.'

'And sound like I was bad mouthing my wife and your best friend? I think not.'

'I guess,' said Lottie. 'Anyway, before I was rudely interrupted, I was just borrowing your fiancée.' Lottie took Emily's hand and pulled her towards the stairs.

Joe turned as they came into the bedroom and gestured for them to be quiet. As they approached, Lottie could see that Dave and the Duchess were no longer the only two animals in the room. Nestled at the Duchess's tummy was a tiny cream kitten and her mum was frantically washing her. Emily's eyes lit up and she gave a strangled sob. 'Sorry. I'm blaming baby hormones,' she said, pulling another piece of kitchen roll from her sleeve like a magician producing a string of bunting.

'Is she all right?' asked Lottie, in a hushed voice so as not to disturb them, forgetting herself and kneeling down at Joe's side.

'She's fine. She's doing a great job.' Dave was sitting next to her looking concerned, and his head darted in Joe's direction as the Duchess let out a yowl. 'And Dave is playing the role of the expectant father brilliantly.'

'He won't harm them, will he?' asked Emily.

'No, he's just alarmed when she cries out. But he's a gentle soul. I'm sure he just wants to help. If she thought he was a danger, she'd have gone for him and she's been very calm.'

The cat started to convulse again and her back leg twitched. She paused from washing her kitten to let out another yowl. Dave stood up and his tail wagged furiously. 'Another one's on the way,' said Joe, stroking Dave.

A few more twitches and yowls later and out popped another kitten. The Duchess immediately set to work breaking into the sac and washing her new arrival. This one had more of a ginger tinge. Lottie was delighted to see it wriggle its way to join the first one – her smile was almost splitting her face. She looked over her shoulder to beckon Emily forward but she was no longer there. She must have snuck back downstairs.

She was alone again with Joe. They stared at each other. His expression was earnest. 'I didn't mean to hurt you, Lottie.'

She straightened her back and replaced her smile with her 'I don't give a crap' face. 'How's Megan? Has she got over the proposal debacle yet?'

Joe checked his watch, which Lottie thought was an odd thing to do. 'Right now, she should be in a taxi on her way to the airport.'

'Oh. And are you going to follow her?' She didn't want to pry, but how else was she going to find out?

'No.' He shook his head. Relief washed over her and she felt instantly guilty.

'Right.' They both watched the Duchess wash her kittens for a moment. 'I'm sorry,' said Lottie, her words sounding deliberate and false. 'About Megan leaving.'

'Why?'

Okay not something she wanted to elaborate on. 'It's not nice when couples split up.'

'We've not split up.' *Oh, for goodness' sake*, thought Lottie. Her emotions weren't just on a rollercoaster; they were doing loop-the-loops.

'Oh. That's good then,' she said, and gave what she hoped was at least a perfunctory smile. But it wasn't good at all. It meant the very glamorous Megan would be back sometime soon. At least by then Lottie would probably have moved on. She needed to get away and leave Joe and Henbourne behind her – that was the answer. At the thought of leaving the manor, more ice plunged into her gut.

'Lottie. Look at me, will you?' His voice was pleading. She slowly lifted her head, looked into his eyes and held on tight to her heart. 'Megan and me. We're not together.'

'Since the non-proposal?'

'Since ages.'

Lottie's mouth opened and closed involuntarily. 'But she said she was your partner.'

Joe's mouth twitched at the edge. 'She was my girlfriend for a while, and she still is . . .' Lottie wasn't sure if it was just her, or whether the pause was as long as the results announcer on a game show, ' . . . my business partner. But that's all.'

'But she said . . . and she thought . . . and I assumed . . .'

Joe smiled warmly at her. 'Megan is struggling to move on. That's why she followed me here. It was only a brief thing, and it was definitely over between us months ago.

Long before I decided to come back to Henbourne.' Joe's eyes were intense and Lottie had to look away. She pushed her hands into her back pockets and felt something there. She'd worn these jeans on Christmas Eve – it was Nana's Christmas card. Nana's words swirled in her mind.

The Duchess had her back leg in the air and she twitched. 'Oh, I think she's having another one,' said Lottie, adjusting her hair clip, hugely grateful to the cat for the distraction.

After kitten numbers three and four arrived in quick succession, Joe checked the Duchess over and advised that she was finished. The Duchess continued to wash them all for another thirty minutes, and they all had a feed before settling down to sleep.

Lottie heard creaking outside the bedroom door as people moved across the landing. 'Hi,' said Scott, poking his head round the door. 'Is it safe to come in?'

'He means is the gruesome bit over?' asked Angie, as a second disembodied head appeared under his.

'Shhh,' said Lottie, but she motioned for them to come in anyway. 'She's had four kittens.'

'I didn't expect they'd be puppies,' said her mother and Lottie stuck her tongue out. Scott gave a conspiratorial smirk and patted Lottie affectionately on the shoulder. He held her mother's hand as they studied the newborns.

'So Daddy was a ginge, then,' said Scott. 'Excellent.'

'They're quite pretty,' said Angie, leaning in to stroke one. Dave stood up and eyed her carefully.

Little footsteps and a large yawn announced Jessie's arrival. She leaned on Lottie's shoulders, her teddy bear flopping in front of Lottie's eyes. 'They're so cute. Can we have one, Daddy? Please?' asked Jessie.

Lottie and Jessie both looked at Zach with pleading eyes.

'I don't know,' said Zach. 'It depends.'

'On what?' asked Jessie, perking up.

'Whether you want a kitten or a dog.'

'A dog, a dog! A DOG!'

'Shhh,' whispered Joe and Lottie together, as Jessie threw herself into her father's arms.

'Thank you, Daddy!'

'We need to find the right dog for us, so it may take a while, but I've seen how you are with Dave and I think it would be nice to have one around.'

Lottie smiled as Emily joined them in a family hug. She gave Emily a congratulatory nod. A friendship had been formed this festive season that Lottie knew would last a lifetime.

'Aw,' said Rhys, peering over everyone's heads.

'We should have one, Nicola,' said Daniel. 'It'll give you a hobby.'

'Oh, great. I've been replaced by a cat,' said Rhys, with a pretend huff.

'Hmm,' said Nicola, having a closer look. 'I don't want a male,' she said.

'Understandable,' said Angie. Lottie gave her a stern look.

'We'll not know for sure for a couple of weeks,' said Joe. 'But I had a quick look when they each arrived and I think we have two males,' he pointed at the pale ginger ones, 'and two females.' He indicated the cream pair.

'Oh, they're just like Duchess. I'd like one of those,' said Nicola.

'Sure,' said Lottie. *One down, three to go*, she thought. If only she was as easy to rehome.

Chapter Forty

Lottie said goodnight to Jessie and eventually managed to shoo everyone else out of Nana's room.

'I'd better go,' said Joe, packing away his equipment.

'When can I move her out of here?'

'Not for a few days if you can help it. She's chosen somewhere she feels safe. If you move her too soon she'll try to move the kittens back, and with the stairs that could be dangerous.'

'Okay. And Joe?'

He whipped his head around quickly. 'Yes?'

'Thanks. You know, for coming up in the snow. Sorry I panicked.'

He looked defeated. 'It's fine. It's what we vets do.'

'Well, thanks. I appreciate it. And—'

'Yes?' He was hanging on her every word.

'Let me have the bill.'

'No need. I was doing it as a friend. I'll see myself out.'

She followed him down to the front door anyway. The silence stretched between them. She needed time to process what he'd told her about Megan. Her thoughts were a jumbled mess.

'Lottie,' he said, and she looked up into his eyes. 'I'm

truly sorry that I've hurt you. I know you'd never do that to me.' Lottie broke eye contact. Her heart started to race.

'We all do stuff we regret.'

'Lottie?' She could tell from his tone that he knew she was hiding something. He just didn't know quite how long she'd been hiding it for. 'Lottie, if we're going to be living in the same village again, I really want us to get on. No expectations of anything else, but above all I value our friendship.' She finally looked up. She could see genuine affection in his eyes.

'Okay. I think we can do that.'

'So no more secrets?'

Lottie felt the colour drain from her face. She couldn't agree to this without breaking his heart.

'Lottie? Do you have a secret?' He held up his thumb for her to push hers against. Their secret sign. She sighed heavily as their thumbs connected. There was no going back now.

Lottie pulled Nana's Christmas card from her back pocket. 'Nana sent the family Christmas cards and they each had advice in them.'

'Ah,' said Joe with a smile.

He listened while she read it. His eyes widened when she reached the line about him:

There is also something I want you to do for me – talk to Joe Broomfield. Life isn't easy and we make the decisions we do with the best of our knowledge and with the best of intentions, but keeping secrets is like a cancer and if you don't sort it out it will eat away at you.

When she'd finished reading, she closed the card. Joe's eyebrows were pulled tight.

'What did Rose want you to talk to me about?' he asked.

'Joe, just after you left, I found out I was pregnant with

your baby.' Her voice cracked and she cleared her throat. 'I didn't know where you were and despite my best efforts I couldn't track you down. Then at four months gone I had a miscarriage.'

Joe let out a tiny gasp and stepped forward to hold her but she held up her palm to stop him. Any show of affection now would reduce her to a blubbering mess, and she needed to finish the story. To get out the secret she'd been keeping for nine long years. 'I stopped looking for you after that. There didn't seem any point. You might have come back for the baby, but it was clear you were never coming back for me.' She lifted her chin and stood strong against the tide of emotion battering her defences. 'I stayed with a friend in Wales for a few weeks to get my head straight and while I was there your dad died. That's why I wasn't at his funeral. I wasn't avoiding you. Nana didn't tell me about your father until I came home. She figured I was dealing with enough.'

'Lottie . . . I had no idea.'

'I know that.' She dredged up a brief half-smile from somewhere. 'Because I kept it a secret. And I am sorry for that. But it's haunted me ever since.'

'Did I cause the miscarriage?'

Lottie shook her head automatically. Then she remembered what he'd said about no more secrets. 'I don't know what caused it, Joe. Nobody does. Maybe it was stress; or maybe it just wasn't meant to be.' She returned the Christmas card to her back pocket. She'd done what Nana had advised, and a great weight had been lifted. As usual Nana was right.

'I don't know what to say,' said Joe.

'It's okay. You'd better go and check Megan caught that flight.'

He drew in a breath. 'Right.' He opened the door to leave and Lottie walked away.

Lottie did feel better for having told Joe, but she wasn't sure anything had actually changed. He knew now why his leaving had had such an impact, but that was nine years ago, and they were different people now. At least she no longer had the weight of it on her shoulders. She straightened her back and headed for the safety of the kitchen. She was going to make everyone ham sandwiches to take home with them, whether they wanted them or not.

The remnants of tea were waiting for her on the kitchen table. The empty trifle dish, a few slices of ham on a platter and a multitude of dirty bowls and plates. They'd not bothered to tidy up. Lottie sighed. Maybe she had been doing all this for selfish reasons. Perhaps it wasn't about bringing the family together; perhaps it was about Lottie needing to belong and to feel needed.

But right now, the kitchen needed tidying up.

Lottie snatched the roll of clingfilm out of the cupboard and in her haste caught her finger on the serrated edge of the box.

'Bugger.' She sucked her throbbing finger. It was the last straw. She sank to the floor, hugged her knees and let the tears flow. She'd been holding them back for far too long.

The back door flew open. Joe walked in and without a word he lifted her into his arms and held her tight while she sobbed. Minutes passed before he put her down on a chair and handed her a tissue. She blew her nose. He pulled a chair up next to her and sat down.

'You're bleeding,' he said, noticing her finger.

'I cut it on the clingfilm,' she said miserably.

'Clingfilm? Only you could do that.'

'I bet I look a sight,' she said, drying her eyes.

'You look . . .' he smiled. 'I can't lie. You look a fright.'

'Cheers. I don't know why I'm so upset.' Lottie blew her nose again. 'I was thinking about Nana and how crap everything is without her. And I know she was just a grandparent and she was a good age and I should be getting over it. But I'm not. I don't know why but I'm not.' Her hands flopped into her lap in defeat.

Joe wore a puzzled expression. 'Lottie, you're upset because you lost your mother.'

Lottie snorted a laugh and was confused by Joe's serious expression. 'My mother is alive and well and right now is most likely snogging the face off an ex-porn star.' *The next time I utter that sentence it's likely I'll be lying on a therapist's couch*, she thought.

Joe looked like he was chewing the inside of his mouth. 'And that is why Angie is not really your mother.' Lottie opened her mouth to speak, but he stopped her with a shake of his head. 'I know that biologically she is, but that's where it ends. Rose took on the role of your mother when you were very young. She's the one stable person you've had in your life. Rose was the one who was always there for you, loved you unconditionally and wanted the best for you. That's what a mother does.' She saw tears well in his eyes. 'I had one of the best, so I know how it feels when you lose them. We've both lost our mothers, Lottie.' He opened his arms for her and she leaned into his hug. So many times she'd wanted nothing more than to be right where she was now.

Lottie let his theory sink in. It did make sense. 'And I guess I treated her like a mother too.' Nana was always the one person she would turn to. The person she shared her hopes, dreams and failings with, knowing she wouldn't be judged. It was a little like the puzzle pieces were dropping into place. She wondered how that had made Angie feel. 'There's always been a rivalry between me and my mother for Nana's affections.'

'Like a sibling?'

'Exactly like a sibling.' This was all a bit of an eye-opener for Lottie. His simple explanation answered so many questions that had troubled her for such a long time.

'Rose was more than a mother to you, Lottie – she was your stability, your rock, your safe place. But you know, you are tougher than you think.'

Lottie sighed and let out an ironic chuckle. 'I'm about to be made homeless, so I'm going to have to get tough pretty quickly.'

Joe leant back. Lottie missed the warmth of him against her, but she knew he had just been being friendly. She stood up to put some distance between them.

'Ah. About you being homeless.' Joe looked sheepish.

'What?' She didn't like the look on his face. 'I'll be fine. I can stay with Dayea and Bernard if I get desperate. I could do worse.'

'What if the new owner of Henbourne Manor wanted you to stay on here?'

She pondered it. It was a nice daydream. 'I'd love that, but it's about as likely as my mother becoming a nun.' She chuckled, but the laughter soon faded. 'The estate agent said a company had bought it, so they'll probably turn it into flats or, worse still, knock it down.' A shiver of dread ran up her spine. If that was the case, she would have to make sure she was a long way away – she just couldn't bear to see it happen.

Joe frowned. 'Nope. That's definitely not happening.'

Lottie's head whipped in Joe's direction. 'You know who's bought it. Don't you?' He nodded but kept his eyes downward. 'Come on, we promised no more secrets.'

He looked up, and as their eyes met, her resolve puddled inside her. She was going to have to get a long way away from Joe Broomfield too. Being this close was going to keep stirring up feelings she wasn't equipped to handle. She pulled a tin from the shelf and busied herself with finding a small plaster for her finger.

'It's me,' said Joe, in a small voice.

'What's you?' She glanced over her shoulder.

'It's my company that's bought the manor. I'm the new owner.'

Lottie was momentarily stunned. She blinked a few times and focused on Joe. His face had broken out into a grin. Lottie felt her jaw drop. 'You?' He nodded. 'I've been worrying myself sick about this place and it was you all along!' She gave him a playful thump.

'Hey!'

'Why didn't you say something?'

'I didn't want it to influence what you did. I still don't.'

'You're not pulling it down are you?' Lottie held her breath.

'No. Definitely not. But it'll get updated. Some new heating for a start.' He gave a shiver.

'Why did you buy it?' Suspicion marauded her happy thoughts.

'I love this place. I always have. And I knew I was ready to come back to Henbourne – what better place to have a veterinary practice than here? I'm thinking of converting the garages and store into consulting rooms and building a theatre at the back for surgery. All in keeping with the original building.'

Lottie's mind was working overtime. 'But surely you didn't know it was for sale until you saw the sign in the garden?' She narrowed her eyes. 'So when you left America you couldn't have known.' She watched him closely as he replied.

'True. But I already had plans for the practice, and I was on the lookout for a suitable property locally. As soon as I saw the For Sale sign that was it, I had to have it.' Joe rummaged in his jacket pocket. 'And I also had one of these.' He pulled out a familiar-looking Christmas card.

'Nana.' Lottie's voice was barely a murmur. Joe offered her the card and she took it. She blinked away tears as she tried to read the familiar handwriting.

Dear Joe,

I hope this finds you in good health and at peace with the past. Lottie is back home at the manor and she's breathed life into the old place and me. Having her here has had me thinking about the decisions we make in a passing moment and then feel we have to live with forever – I do not believe this to be the case. There is little, except for death, that cannot be undone.

You are very much missed by the Collins family. I always considered you one of my brood. I am not a young woman and I find that I am nearing the end of my life's journey somewhat sooner than I expected.

I intend to make this Christmas a special one and we would love you to share it with us. You always have a home here at Henbourne Manor.

Here's to a very happy Christmas, wherever you decide to spend it.

With love,
Rose
X
P.S. Seize every opportunity that comes within reach.
They are often fleeting, so go with your gut.

'Oh, Joe. I have the same postscript on my card.' She turned her tear-laden eyes to face him and found he was welling up too.

'Should we do as she says? Go with our gut?'

'Depends on what it's telling you.' Lottie swallowed. Her pulse was picking up pace.

Joe leaned forward. 'Mine's telling me to do . . . this.' He watched her closely as he placed a delicate kiss on her lips. He slowly retreated. 'What's yours telling you?'

Lottie reached up and pulled his soft lips back to hers. That was all the answer she hoped he needed.

Chapter Forty-One

New Year's Day

Lottie was aware of a shaft of light on her eyelids. She blinked herself awake and stretched. She reached out an arm and, realising she was alone, she scooched herself up onto her elbows and looked around her bedroom. Thing was, it wasn't entirely hers any more. Joe had pretty much moved in. They'd talked non-stop after the family had left, and a lot had healed between them. They'd drawn a line under the past and spent time mapping out their future – or, more accurately, the future of Henbourne Manor. Joe had money from his American ventures, so Lottie had sketched out plans of what they could do. Together they had planned how best to update the building whilst keeping its original features. One new addition was to be an artist's studio for Lottie. She was going to do some website design, too, which would hope-fully fund her passion for painting that was already returning.

The door slowly opened and in trotted Dave, who, on his third attempt, made it onto the bed, wagging his tail furiously in greeting.

'You're awake,' said Joe, following Dave into the room and putting a cup of tea down on her bedside cabinet as he leaned in to kiss her. It was a slow, sultry kiss. 'Happy New Year.'

'Are you coming back to bed?' They'd spent most of New Year's Eve in there, with a short interlude for food, showers and a dog walk.

'No, too busy.'

'On New Year's Day?' She couldn't hide her disappointment. Now they were back together, she wanted to spend as much time with him as possible.

'I've got a shift at the village stores,' he said, with a wink.

'Blimey, you got stitched up there,' she said, reaching for her cuppa.

'I asked Shirley if it was opening today because we needed more fizz for later.'

'Rookie mistake,' said Lottie, shaking her head.

'It's okay. She thinks I'm wonderful because her cat's arthritis is improving. Did you know Mittens was still alive?'

'Yep. She feeds her sherry and peanut butter.' Joe gave her a look that said he didn't know if she was joking or not.

'It feels like I'm settling back into the village already,' he said, and the corners of his lips twitched.

She studied Joe. It still felt like a dream that he was back, and even more so that he was hers. She didn't know what the future held, but she was damn sure she wasn't going to waste a minute of it. 'Come back to bed.' She gave what she hoped was a sexy pout and not the look of a constipated duck.

He sat on the bed, took her tea off her and put it back on the cabinet. 'Actually, I've got a few more minutes before I have to go.' He climbed back into bed. 'And a bit of feedback – that duck face you pull; it does it for me every time.'

Lottie wasn't expecting to have everyone back at the manor house so soon, but she felt it was time to scatter Nana's ashes. It had been delayed because, as usual, the family hadn't been able to agree on what they should do with them. Up until now the manor hadn't seemed like an option – Lottie couldn't have left Nana behind, and the thought of bulldozers marauding over her was unbearable. But now she knew Joe was the new owner of the manor and saw it as his forever home it put a different spin on things. He'd even been the one to suggest that Rose's ashes were scattered there. So that was how they found them-selves all back at Henbourne Manor on a bright but cold New Year's Day.

It was mid-morning and most of the Collins family were sitting around the kitchen table, eating the breakfast Lottie had prepared. Angie was insisting on calling her crushed avocado on toast 'brunch'.

'This is amazing, Lottie. Thank you,' said Scott, tucking in to the same. 'Is that a hint of fresh chilli?'

'Yep. I've been doing a bit of research into vegan recipes since Christmas, so I'm a bit better prepared today.'

Angie rolled her eyes. 'You shouldn't try so hard, Lottie.'

'I disagree,' said Scott. Angie almost toppled over, when she spun around to glare at him. 'I think it's a lovely quality and I really appreciate it. Thank you.' Scott gave a sideways nod as if encouraging Angie to add something.

'She knows I appreciate what she does,' said Angie.

'I don't actually,' said Lottie.

'Oh, well . . .' Angie pulled at the neck of her dress as

if it were suddenly tight. 'I do appreciate what you do. And brunch is lovely . . . thank you.'

Lottie could tell it had taken a lot for her mother to compliment her. They would need to take baby steps to build a relationship without Nana.

'You're welcome,' said Lottie.

Scott gave Lottie a warm smile whilst soothing Angie with a one-armed hug. Lottie liked Scott. He handled her mother well, and from the look of adoration on her mother's face, he did so on a number of levels – many of which she didn't want to dwell on.

'And I found your sparkly pen under the armchair.' She handed it to her mother.

'Fabulous. My life story is coming on well. I've got to the bit where Alejandro seduced me . . .' Lottie turned up the radio.

Joe reached past Lottie and, in passing, kissed her neck gently.

'Oh, hello,' said Zach, noticing the gesture. 'What have we missed?' Emily mouthed *I didn't tell him anything*. 'You knew about this?' He pointed his bacon sandwich at Emily.

'There has been the odd phone call,' said Emily, sipping her orange juice. She and Lottie had been in constant contact since they'd gone home four days ago, so Emily was fully up to speed on developments.

'Is Joe your boyfriend?' asked Jessie, liberally squirting ketchup over her bacon sandwich before Emily took the bottle away.

Zach was on freeze frame, his bacon sandwich on his lips.

Lottie felt her cheeks flush. 'Yes. Yes, he is.'

'Oliver Sadler is my boyfriend,' said Jessie matter-of-factly, as she replaced the top of her sandwich and squashed it down.

'What?' said Zach, completely distracted by Jessie's confession. 'You're too young to have a boyfriend.'

Lottie leaned towards Emily. 'How did it go with your folks yesterday?' Emily had been planning on telling her family about the baby news.

'Good. Actually, really good. Mum is made up about being a grandparent, and my sister was pleased, but not in an "I've won" kind of way. She explained that she doesn't think being a mum is for her and she was worried about letting Mum and Dad down on the grandchildren front. It seems we've both been worrying about impressing them when really they're proud of us both.'

'That's brilliant. I'm really pleased for you,' said Lottie.

They heard voices in the hall and the kitchen was suddenly swamped as Dayea pushed Great Uncle Bernard's wheelchair into view. 'Uncle Bernie,' said Lottie, throwing her arms around him. 'You look so well.'

'I'm being thoroughly spoiled,' he said, with an affectionate look over his shoulder at Dayea, who was smiling broadly behind him.

Nicola and Rhys came into the kitchen. Nicola was wearing the same black outfit she'd worn to the funeral, and Lottie suddenly felt underdressed in her usual jeans and *Star Wars* sweatshirt. Nicola saw her looking. 'Oh, don't mind me. You're fine. I just didn't know what to wear to something like this. And I like your hair. It suits you.' Lottie was surprised by her response but grateful for it. She had dyed her hair pink the day after everyone had left.

Lottie looked past Nicola. There was no sign of Uncle Daniel.

Rhys had his ear buds in, so Lottie tapped him on the

shoulder. 'You okay?' Lottie asked. He winced at her through narrowed eyes.

'Bit of a headache. Big night last night.'

'Bacon sandwich do the trick?' She pointed to the pile she'd just made.

'Sound, thanks.' He grabbed a couple, put his ear buds back in and began to eat.

Dave trotted into the kitchen and curled up in one of two matching wicker baskets with fleecy linings. In the bed next to him lay the Duchess with her recently fed brood. They were all sound asleep, their swollen tummies moving rhythmically as they slept. Dave flopped his head over the edge of their basket and gazed adoringly at them all.

Lottie heard the distant click of the front door and cocked her ear like a spaniel. Uncle Daniel's face peered around the door. 'Happy New Year,' he said. 'I was just on the phone,' he explained.

Lottie noted Nicola's expectant look. 'And how is Rebecca?' Nicola asked.

'She's good. Thanks.' The way Daniel said it you'd have thought Nicola had just given him the winning lottery numbers. It was good to see them being kind to each other, and she admired them for it.

When breakfast (and brunch) had been washed down with coffee, Lottie encouraged everyone outside. They walked solemnly down to the far end of the garden, where Nana's runner beans – and more recently, Zach's fairy light proposal – had once adorned the trellis. Zach and Emily held hands and exchanged loving looks.

Lottie cleared her throat. 'If I've not said already, then thanks for coming. I know it was a bit short notice, but now we know the fate of the manor,' she looked at Joe and he looked down, embarrassed, 'it felt like we'd been waiting too long to do this. And—'

'And we all need closure,' added Angie.

'Er, right,' said Lottie, smiling at her mother's knack of anticipating things incorrectly. She was hoping to learn to be more tolerant and build a better relationship with her now the puzzle pieces of her life had fallen into place. 'Anyway, Nana loved this place. All of it. She loved the villages and the manor. She loved the trees and the gardens and, in particular, she loved pottering about in the vegetable patch.'

'And her runner beans,' prompted Angie.

'Yes, Mum, and especially her runner beans. So here seemed like the right place for her to rest.' The last word caught in her throat; she felt Joe's arm snake around her shoulders and pull her gently to him. 'I thought it might be nice if we all scooped some ashes out and scattered them.' Rhys looked slightly alarmed at the prospect. 'But you don't have to if you don't want to.'

Rhys had already checked the area with his metal detector, so there was no possibility of Nana's ashes being disturbed by treasure hunters. Daniel was holding the urn with Nana's ashes in and Nicola carefully removed the top. Lottie passed her Nana's flour scoop and Nicola dipped it in and liberally scattered a scoop full of ashes into the air. Unfortunately, the breeze took them and a few went in Angie's face.

'Hey! That went in my eye,' said Angie, winking elaborately. 'Scott, check my eye.'

'Sorry,' said Nicola, but she was clearly suppressing a smirk.

'It's fine,' said Scott, after a brief look. 'Blink – you'll be fine.'

'Anyway,' said Nicola. 'All I wanted to say about Rose was that she was a force to be reckoned with and I liked that about her. She made no apology for who she was.'

There were nods of agreement and Nicola passed the scoop to Angie.

'Thanks Mum, for always being there to pick up the pieces. I love you,' said Angie. Blinking furiously, she sprinkled the ashes along the trellis line.

Daniel took the scoop and Scott held the urn for him. 'Bye, Mum. You were the best.'

Rhys quickly got some ashes and let them tumble to the ground. 'Miss you, Nana.'

He filled a scoop and passed it to Bernard, who wriggled forward in his wheelchair. Dayea wrapped her hand around Bernard's and they spread their scoopful together. 'Bye, old girl. We had some laughs,' said Bernard.

'You were a very nice lady,' added Dayea. 'Thank you for finding me my Bernard.'

Zach stepped forward and took the urn, holding it for Jessie. She peered inside and wrinkled her nose.

'I don't think Nana Rose is in there. I think she's a ghost,' said Jessie.

'Okay,' said Emily, crouching down, scooping out a little ash and sprinkling it. 'If her ghost was listening, what would you like to say to her?'

Jessie pouted as she thought. 'I miss your cuddles. And the dolls are *really* scary.'

'Well done, Jessie,' said Zach, tipping a large amount of the ash out into a pile. 'Thanks, Nana, for everything you taught me, and for keeping me on the straight and narrow. Love you,' said Zach. He wiped away a tear and passed the urn to Lottie.

Lottie took a steadying breath and tipped out the

remaining ash. She tried hard not to think about the ash being Nana; it just didn't seem possible. 'We did what you asked, Nana – we had a good family Christmas.' Lottie looked up to nods of agreement. 'It wasn't quite up to your standard, but, hey, you set the bar high. I can't believe it's taken me until now to realise the huge part you played in my life.' She gave a quick glance in Joe's direction. 'I miss you so much. Bye Nana. Thank you for everything.'

'Thanks for inviting me home, Rose.' Joe picked up the urn and wrapped Lottie in a hug.

They all stayed for a few minutes and watched the light breeze spread the ashes around the vegetable garden. Daniel was the first to turn and head inside. Others followed. Lottie saw the Duchess meander over and sit on the edge of the grass and observe them. Lottie smiled to think the cat may, in her own way, be coming to add her own message to Nana. The Duchess got up, stretched, walked over to the ashes and proceeded to dig a hole in them.

'No! Scoot!' said Lottie, shooing a disgruntled-looking Duchess out of the way. 'Cheeky thing,' said Lottie. 'She was going to wee on Nana. After everything she did for her.' That was one message Nana could do without.

Joe appeared with the garden rake and began raking the ashes into the soil. 'Thanks,' said Lottie.

'No problem. You did well. Nice speech.' He put down the rake.

Lottie snuggled into Joe's embrace. 'We went with our gut, Nana,' she said, and as a cloud moved out of the way, a perfect ray of sunshine fell across the garden.

'Come on,' said Joe. 'Before that lot start murdering each other.' He clasped her hand in his and they walked back up to the house together. Lottie felt both melancholy and heartened at the same time.

They could hear the noise increase as they approached. There were raised voices coming from inside. Joe opened the door, but everyone inside was oblivious. Despite Lottie's fears, it wasn't a row going on; it was a singsong, apparently led by Bernard even though singing wasn't a Collins family forte.

Joe shut the door behind them and Lottie leaned back into his arms as they joined in with the Rod Stewart classics Nana had loved. When they reached 'Do Ya Think I'm Sexy' Dave joined in with a heartfelt howl. Jessie copied him until Emily tickled her.

Rhys came to stand next to Lottie. 'Don't tell the rents yet, but I'm going back to uni.'

'Good decision,' said Lottie.

'Yeah. The whole Roman treasure thing got my mind buzzing. My professor is really fired up about it and so am I. I can't ditch archaeology, however good the money at the car dealers is.'

'If you ever need a break from the rents, there's always a room here,' said Joe.

'And you don't have to have the one with the scary dolls,' added Lottie.

'Cheers,' said Rhys, and he and Joe shook hands.

Daniel rattled his car keys and Nicola started to say her goodbyes. 'Thanks Lottie. I'll be back for my kitten in a few weeks.'

'If you're still after a home for one of the kittens, me and your mum would like one,' said Scott.

'Sure,' said Lottie, uneasily. She knew first-hand how nurturing Angie was.

'I promise it'll be well cared for. I'll keep it at my place,' said Scott, in a low tone, while Angie fussed over the kittens.

'Which one, Mum?' asked Lottie.

'I want a boy,' said Angie.

'No surprise there,' said Lottie, and Joe gave her a reproachful look. 'Which ginger one?' she asked, edging up to her.

Angie checked Scott wasn't listening. 'It's quite exciting that Scott thinks we're ready for this sort of commitment,' said Angie.

Lottie had a sharp retort ready, but she bit her tongue instead. Their new relationship needed effort on both sides. 'Yes, Mum. It is. I'm happy for you.'

'I like what you've done with your hair.' Angie tucked a bit of it behind Lottie's ear. 'Happy New Year, Lottie,' said her mother, and she gave her a hug.

At least she was trying. 'And you too.'

'We should do this again,' said Angie.

'Scatter someone's ashes?'

'No – Christmas here at the manor. It was lovely.' Lottie felt a little glow of pride inside; a feeling she was pretty sure her mother had never triggered in her before.

'We should go now too,' said Dayea, wheeling Bernard over Angie's toes.

'Hey, Feeble Knievel!' said Angie. 'These are my new Kurt Geigers!' Scott steered her away because she was literally hopping mad.

'You've not given our kitten away, have you, Button?'

'No,' said Lottie, pleased that Bernard had decided to have one of the litter and let the Duchess stay at the manor with her, Joe and Dave.

'We're going to call her Button,' he said, taking Lottie's hand and giving it a squeeze. Joe appeared at Lottie's side and she tensed.

To her surprise, Bernard straightened his spine and held out his hand to Joe. 'I owe you some thanks, lad.'

'Not at all,' said Joe, shaking Bernard's hand. 'Anyone would have done the same.'

'That's as may be. But thank you all the same. Take good care of our Button. Well, both our Buttons,' he said, with a chuckle.

'I will,' said Joe.

And Lottie knew that he would.

'Auntie Lottie?' said Jessie, and Lottie lifted her into her arms.

'Yes, Jess?'

'What's happening to the last ginger kitten?'

'Ah,' said Lottie, looking at Emily and Zach for cues. 'Why?'

'Because I'm thinking that if I'm getting a dog,' she turned to eye her father, 'like Daddy promised, then it's only fair that my new baby brother or sister has a pet too.' She turned and gave Lottie her best smile.

'Nice try,' said Zach. Jessie's face fell.

Emily stepped forward and stroked Jessie's cheek. 'How about we see how we get on with a dog first.'

'And if you can't find a suitable dog, then the kitten is yours,' said Lottie.

Jessie brightened. 'Can I name him?'

'Sure,' said Lottie. It couldn't be any worse than Dave.

'Thank you, Auntie Lottie,' said Jessie, squeezing her tightly. 'I name this kitten Silas Ramsbottom!' And Dave barked his approval.

Acknowledgements

Firstly a huge thank-you to the Romantic Novelists' Association, which celebrates its 60th anniversary this year. The RNA is a wonderful organisation full of talented writers who are unbelievably supportive of each other. Without the RNA and their New Writers' Scheme I would not have met my first editor or found my tribe.

Huge thanks to my wonderful technical experts for answering my questions:

Dr David Boulton for medical advice.

Faye Tapping RVN BSc for veterinary.

Special thanks to Phillipa Ashley, Jules Wake, Sarah Bennett and Darcie Boleyn for saving my sanity – it's been a tough few months and these wonderful writers have been there every step of the way.

Thanks to my brilliant agent Kate Nash for her ongoing support and my editors Molly Walker-Sharp and Katie Loughnane. Huge shout out for all of Team Avon for pulling out the stops and getting this to print in the middle of a pandemic – you guys rock!

Thanks to my wonderful family for their support but especially for all the very special family Christmases we have shared.

Huge thank-yous to everyone in the blogging community for their continued support and to each and every reader who has bought or borrowed my book. I really do appreciate it. And if you have a moment to leave a review that would mean the world – thank you.

Special mention: Years ago I read a novella titled *Silent Snow, Secret Snow* by Adele Geras and it must have lodged in my mind somewhere. I was well into planning this book when I realised where the concept had come from. Thankfully the lovely Adele was happy for me to go ahead and write my story and I will be forever grateful to her for that.

Regan is holding a winning lottery ticket.

Goodbye to the boyfriend who never had her back, and so long to the job she can't stand!

Except it's all a bit too good to be true . . .

Available in all good bookshops now.

Life's not always a walk in the park . . .

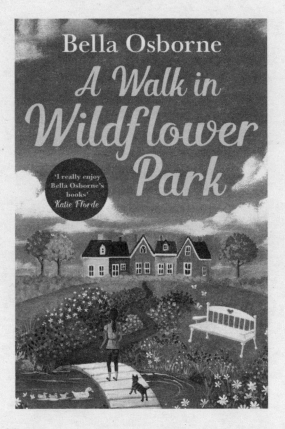

Available in all good bookshops now.

**Join Daisy Wickens as she
returns to Ottercombe Bay . . .**

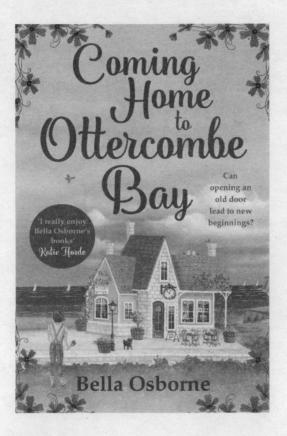

Available in all good bookshops now.

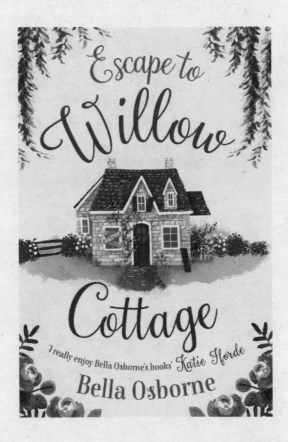

**Tempted to read another heart-warming
romance by Bella Osborne?**

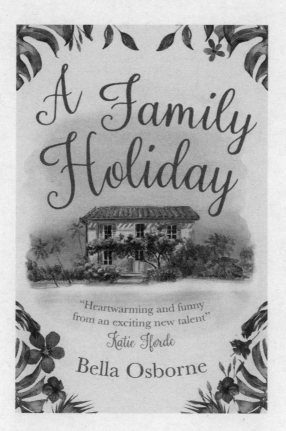

Available in all good bookshops now.